MEAN G

Book 5

The Silence of Being Friendless

Katrina Kahler

Copyright © KC Global Enterprises

All Rights Reserved

Table of Contents

Chapter One- The New Girl

Silence fell upon Remmy and the vampires as they glared over at Sydney. She was sitting next to Charlie and they'd been chatting away for the last five minutes. Remmy stirred her spoon around her barely touched yogurt; all the while her attention remained on Charlie.

There was an aching in her chest, one that wouldn't go away. Before she came to Venice Beach and met him...she didn't think that it was possible to care this much about a boy.

Sydney laughed loudly at something Charlie said and then she flicked her glossy hair behind her back. Remmy sighed and then finally forced herself to look away from them. It should have been her sitting next to Charlie, not Sydney. Worse still, she knew that she only had herself to blame. She'd been the one who'd let Sandy send Charlie a break-up message from her and she'd been the one who'd let jealously infiltrate her mind. Now, she was stuck on a table with the vampires, while the pretty new girl was flirting with the boy who held her heart.

Remmy couldn't stop herself from looking back over at him. Bridget had joined him and Sydney and the three of them looked happy together. She let out another sigh, she felt like she'd been replaced with a shinier, prettier model. Again, she looked away and stared down at her uneaten food.

Sandy finally looked away from Charlie's table.

'I wonder what they're talking about? I hope it's not about you,' she failed to conceal her smirk as she looked at Remmy.

'I don't know,' Remmy shrugged.

She bit her lip and willed back her tears. It seemed that Sandy always seemed to bring out her insecurities. Right now, she needed a hug and reassurance, instead of words that made her head spin.

The bell sounded and Sydney and her new friends walked out of the cafeteria. She watched her walk off, confidence oozed from her pores. She looked so perfect that she half-expected a ball of glitter to surround her.

'Don't worry Remmy,' Rach placed a manicured hand over hers. 'You still have us.'

'Thanks,' she forced a smile.

'Besides, Sydney seems like a bit of a princess and most boys prefer the no-effort-type of girls.'

Sandy and Susie both giggled and Remmy tried her hardest to maintain her smile.

'You and Charlie were never going to work,' Sandy stared at her. 'You need a boy who's more in your league.'

Remmy's jaw dropped open. She tried to reassure herself that Sandy was just being Sandy. Still, her words stung like an angry wasp.

'At least you don't have to sit next to him anymore,' Sandy grinned.

'I feel so sorry for you having to sit next to him,' Susie looked at Sandy.

'I know, right. But I'll sit there...to save Remmy having to do so. I can't believe we got him so wrong,' she gave her best concerned look.

'So wrong,' Rach shook her head.

'Anyway, we'd better get to class or Miss Sutherland will be cross with us,' she rolled her eyes.

'You'd think that having a boyfriend would make her less strict,' Susie said.

'Maybe he broke up with her,' Rach smirked.

'Ha, imagine being dumped by that hideous man? How totally embarrassing,' Sandy said.

'I'm just glad we'll never have that problem. We're all far too pretty for a boy to even look at another girl,' Rach looked at

Remmy. 'Oops, sorry Remmy, I didn't think,' she brought her hand up to her mouth.

'Remmy will find someone else. Someone better suited to her,' Sandy said.

Remmy felt like screaming. It wasn't long ago that she'd had the perfect boyfriend and the perfect best friend, now she was stuck with the vampires. Still, it was better than sitting alone, wasn't it? After that last break, she'd begun to question if sitting by herself wouldn't be better. The problem was that she didn't want to cause more friction with Sandy; she had enough going on without dealing with that too.

Back in class Remmy sat down next to Sydney, who was rummaging through her blue and pink backpack.

'I like your backpack,' Remmy smiled.

Sydney gave a weak smile back before she continued to look through her backpack.

'Erm, did you like it in the cafeteria?'

Sydney put her backpack on the floor and then she straightened her pale pink pencil case.

'Did you enjoy the cafeteria? The lunches aren't so bad and they do great cakes,' she tried again.

Sydney turned her head away from Remmy and rolled her eyes.

Remmy gulped back and sunk down further into her seat. This morning Sydney had been friendly towards her but now she was being rude. What had Charlie and Bridget said to her? Had they told her what a bad friend Remmy was? If so then she wasn't surprised by Sydney's sudden change in attitude towards her.

6

Miss Sutherland entered the room and began to address the class. Remmy stared down at her desk and willed for this day to hurry up. School was no fun without Charlie and Bridget, instead, it had turned into an endurance test. She didn't hear a word Miss Sutherland said, as she was too busy thinking about Charlie, Bridget and how the new girl didn't like her.

For the rest of the day, Sydney hung around with Bridget and Charlie, while Remmy was stuck listening to the vampires gossiping about people. By the time the final bell sounded, she was so relieved that she quickly pushed back her chair and jumped to her feet. This caused her pencil to roll onto the floor and moaning under her breath she bent down to pick it up.

'Bye Remmy,' Sydney gave her a weak smile and a feeble wave.

'Bye.'

She clutched her pencil as she watched her walk over to Charlie and Bridget and leave the classroom with them.

Remmy walked out of school alone and got into the passenger seat of Grandma Noreen's car. She noticed how she had a bright gold and silver scarf tied around her neck and she wore black-framed sunglasses, which were far too large for her narrow face.

'Hi,' Remmy smiled.

'About time,' she huffed. 'You do realize that I'm having dinner with June in a few hours time and I'm yet to get ready?'

'Sorry,' Remmy blushed.

'It's okay, no harm done,' she sighed.

The rest of the journey was filled with the Beetles songs blaring out of the stereo and Grandma Noreen bobbing her head along to the beat as she hummed. Remmy slumped down into the seat and replayed her day.

By the time Grandma Noreen dropped her off in the driveway and then promptly drove off, all she could think about was Charlie and Bridget spending time with Sydney.

With her mom and Marcus at work and Sandy with the vampires...she had the house to herself. Normally she'd embrace this rare occasion but instead, she grabbed a glass of orange juice and a bag of chips and then trudged her way to her bedroom. She closed the curtains so that the gloominess of the room reflected her mood and then she fell down onto her bed and lay there staring up at her ceiling.

She imagined Charlie and Bridget sitting in Pop's diner with the pretty new girl. Charlie would have at least two milkshakes and then he'd probably drink some of Bridget's. Would Sydney laugh at this? Would she get on with her former friends better than she had?

Remmy wasn't being bullied anymore yet she felt more alone than ever. She'd lost her friends and it had been all her own doing.

Eventually, she forced herself to sit up, she grabbed her laptop from her bedside table and she turned it on and then logged onto FB. She typed in Sydney's name and a smiling picture of her standing in Times Square came up. She sent her a friend request and then waited for her to accept it.

After a few minutes had passed she reloaded the page. Sydney now had thirty-five mutual friends with her, which meant that she'd recently added kids from school. Still, she hadn't accepted Remmy's friend request. Remmy told herself that maybe Sydney was busy and that she'd accept

8

her request as soon as she saw it.

Five more minutes passed and still Sydney hadn't accepted her friend request. Worse still, they now had forty-seven mutual friends so she knew that she had seen her request, she'd just chosen to ignore it.

Remmy typed a message to Sydney and then quickly sent it before she had a chance to talk herself out of it:

<Hi Sydney, it was really nice to meet you today. Would you like to go to the Boardwalk and get ice cream?

Time passed, the message was marked as read. A further fifteen-minutes passed and there was still no reply. Remmy angrily logged out of FB and then slammed down her laptop lid. Tears began to trickle down her cheeks, which she brushed onto the back of her hand. She was just being friendly but she'd been rejected, which hurt like crazy.

'Amelia, what should I do?' she said out loud.

She longed for Amelia to be here right now, as she always knew what to say and how to make her feel better.

'I know, she would tell me to stop being silly and so sensitive. So what if Sydney is ignoring me, she's not my friend anyway,' she stood up and paced her room. 'I should do something to cheer myself up.'

Remmy changed into a pair of leggings and a loose comfy t-shirt.

'Thanks, Amelia,' she smiled.

Remmy left the house and got a bus to the beach. Running was the one thing that cleared her mind and cheered her up so it made sense to go and do that.

It was a sunny afternoon so the boardwalk was pretty popular. She walked past a group of teenagers eating ice creams and stopped by the wall. She put her water bottle down on it and then began to do some warm-up exercises. She heard laughter coming from the teenagers so she looked at them, a boy with floppy brown hair had smeared ice cream onto a pretty girl's face and she was scowling at him as she tried to wipe it onto him. Remmy smiled but this soon turned into a frown. She didn't have any friends to laugh and joke about with anymore, instead, she was on her own.

She grabbed her water bottle and then began to run. Instantly her mind began to clear and the world didn't seem so bad. The beach blurred past her, as did other runners and stationary people. She heard wheels coming up behind her, followed by familiar laughter. Her heart instantly fluttered but she forced herself to continue running.

Charlie and Sydney whizzed past her on their skateboards, her hand was entwined in his. He briefly looked at Remmy before he looked away, his main focus on Sydney. They were closely followed by Bridget who was on her rollerblades. Her cheeks were red and she was gasping for breath yet she hurried past Remmy and zoomed after her friends.

Remmy slowed down and watched as her old friends became smudged blurs in the distance. She came to a stop and then plonked herself down onto the wall.

Was Charlie holding Sydney's hand because he liked her or was he just making sure she didn't fall over? Did he want her to be his girlfriend? Was he happy that he wasn't going out with Remmy anymore?

She tried to shake away these thoughts but they remained as vivid as neon signs inside of her head.

This new girl had only been here a day but she'd already managed to steal her life. Remmy felt like she didn't even exist to them anymore. She'd worked so hard to fit into Venice Beach but now she was the loser sitting by herself and the shiny new girl was holding hands with her boyfriend.

Before she could stop herself, large, hot tears trickled down her face and dampened her cheeks. Everything was a massive mess and she didn't know how to sort it out. She'd apologized to Charlie and Bridget but they hadn't forgiven her. They both thought that she was a horrible person and she was beginning to think that maybe they were right.

A hand gripped her shoulder and her first thought was that it was Amelia.

'Are you okay?' a male voice said.

Could it be Charlie? She quickly wiped her eyes on the back of her arm and then turned around. It wasn't Charlie, instead, it was a boy with messy black hair...Mike.

Seeing him made Remmy feel even worse. She had been mean to him in class in an attempt to impress Sandy and her vampires, yet here he was asking how she was. She couldn't stop herself and her tears flowed without restraint. Without saying anything he grabbed her arm and led her across the boardwalk and over to a bench that was situated below a palm tree.

She sat down on it and tried to wipe away her tears, only they were soon replaced by fresh ones. She made sure that her head was turned away from him, she felt embarrassed. Her old friends didn't care about her, instead, the only person who was being nice to her was a boy who she'd humiliated in front of the entire class.

Mike riffled through his worn looking khaki backpack and pulled out a tissue.

'Here,' he held it out to her. 'It's clean.'

'Thanks,' she gave him a half-smile as she took it from him.

She dabbed her eyes with it and then blew her nose. The tears had finally stopped, she just hoped that her cheeks and eyes weren't red and puffy.

'Here,' he passed her a bottle of water. 'Drink some and pour the rest over your eyes, it will stop them from swelling up.'

She blushed as she took the water and poured it over her eyes. She was pretty sure that her eyes were already swollen and that he was just being nice. She must have looked a complete mess, yet he wasn't laughing at her. If Sandy was here she probably would have laughed and then told her that cool kids don't cry in public.

She gulped back some air before she took a few sips of

water. She hesitated before she poured the rest of the water over her face. Some went in her eye and she furiously blinked. Mike smiled to himself but he didn't laugh.

'I'm sorry,' she croaked.

'It's okay to be upset sometimes,' he replied.

'No, I mean for how I was with you that time in class. I should never have been so mean.'

'It doesn't matter,' he shrugged.

'Yes, it does. It wasn't me, I mean, I'm never usually like that to anyone.'

'I'm used to it,' he shrugged again.

This made her feel even guiltier. She rested the bottle on her lap and blew her nose again.

'Thank you for the tissue and the water,' she smiled.

'It's nothing,' he shrugged again.

'No, it was really kind of you. You didn't have to do that, especially after I was so mean to you,' she sniffed.

'It's fine. Anyway, what's wrong?'

'Everyone hates me,' she blurted out.

Mike laughed and then smiled at her.

'That's nonsense. You seem pretty popular to me, everyone seems to like and respect you. Why do you think you were voted the class rep?'

'Maybe,' she muttered. 'But that was then, now, well, now, not so much.'

'They voted for you because they like you. They wouldn't be crazy enough to vote for you if they didn't think that you're a pretty great person.'

He began to laugh again and it seemed infectious, soon Remmy found herself laughing too. She wasn't even sure what she was laughing at but it felt good to be doing that instead of crying. Okay, so her life wasn't great right now but Mike had a point, she'd been voted class rep, that meant that the other kids liked her, didn't it?

'You're pretty and you're smart. I don't get why someone like you would think that people hated you?'

Remmy looked at the boy in front of her and for the first time, she saw beyond his messy exterior. He was kind and caring and he didn't hate her. Maybe that meant that the others didn't hate her either, maybe they just needed time to forgive her.

'Thanks, Mike and I promise I'll never be mean to you ever again.'

'I'll hold you to that,' he grinned.

He'd made her feel so much better that she found herself flinging her arms around him. He looked like a startled rabbit but after a brief pause, he hugged her back.

'Thank you,' she mumbled into his t-shirt.

They pulled apart and she looked up and saw Charlie standing in front of her, with Bridget and Sydney behind him.

'Well, it didn't take you long,' Charlie scowled. 'Let's get out of here,' he gestured for the girls to follow him.'

Remmy stared at him open-mouthed and watched on as

they all skated away from her. He hadn't even given her a chance to explain, not that it mattered. He'd moved on, he'd flaunted Sydney in front of her and made her feel terrible. Finally, someone had been nice to her and Charlie had come along and made her feel bad again. Yes, she'd messed up, she knew this...but Mike had seen the good in her so why couldn't Charlie? Did he really think that little of her? Had he ever even known her at all?

'Ignore him, he's an idiot,' Mike said.

Remmy nodded her head and forced a smile.

Still, she found herself staring at Charlie and she continued to do this even after he was no longer in sight.

Chapter Two- The Silence of being Friendless

As Remmy entered the classroom she found herself searching for Charlie. On seeing that he hadn't arrived yet she let out a disappointed sigh and slumped down into her seat. She took her pencil case out of her backpack and rearranged her pens on her desk.

She saw a swish of glossy hair as Sydney sat down next to her. An awkward silence seemed to surround them and she deliberated whether to be the one to break it or not. Seeing as Sydney seemed to be going for the ignoring treatment, she decided to say nothing.

Time seemed to tick by extra slowly and the silence was becoming too much for Remmy.

'So,' she croaked, 'how are you finding Venice Beach?'

Sydney gave a brief pause before she smiled at her.

'It's great, thank you. I wasn't sure if I'd like it here because it's so different to New York but I love it. I've already made the best two friends ever. Things are great.'

'Oh, that's great,' Remmy forced a smile

'I know, right? I'm so glad my parents moved me here. I just know that I'm going to be super happy here.'

Remmy didn't reply, instead, she tried her best to compose herself. She didn't want to look flustered in front of her. She wondered if Sydney knew that her new friends used to be hers or if she was oblivious to this? She'd turned up like a whirlwind and had stolen her life and now she was gloating to her about it.

Charlie and Bridget walked into the classroom and they both waved in Remmy's direction. She instantly waved back, a smile on her face. Then she noticed that Sydney was waving back at them too. Charlie was laughing and Bridget was rolling her eyes, so she quickly looked away from them and pretended to swot at a fly.

'I'm such a loser,' she thought to herself.

Of course, Charlie and Bridget hadn't been waving at her. They hated her. They'd been waving at her prettier, shinier replacement.

Miss Sutherland entered the room but Remmy couldn't concentrate. A dozen thoughts were soaring through her head like paper airplanes. By the time morning break arrived, Remmy felt extra anxious and alone. She sat at a table by herself and chewed on her muesli bar, the sound of her chewing was heightened at the otherwise silent table.

She looked over at Sandy and her vampires chatting away to each other. She knew that she could have sat with them but she didn't want to sit there and listen to them gossiping about people.

She looked over at Charlie's table and saw him laughing at something Bridget had said. Sydney was sitting in Remmy's old seat, smiling away.

Remmy sighed to herself before she stared down at her table. The rest of the room was loud...yet in her corner it seemed silent.

'The silence of being friendless,' she said under her breath.

She looked around the room for Mike but then remembered that he had detention for arguing with Miss Sutherland

18

about homework; again. It felt like everyone was looking at her. Were they calling her a loser loner? Did they think she was pathetic? Did they think that she deserved to be by herself?

It was the longest twenty minutes of her life. For once she was actually relieved when the end of break bell sounded. She rushed out of the room before anyone else had a chance to and was the first one to take her seat back in the classroom.

She couldn't concentrate in class again. She had no idea what Miss Sutherland was going on about, all she could think about was how being lonely sucked. She missed the simplicity of Sweet Lips. She missed her Monday meetings with Amelia and most of all she missed having Charlie and Bridget as her friends.

She decided that she couldn't carry on like this and that she needed to be brave. At lunchtime, she was going to go up to Charlie and Bridget's table and apologize. They might not like it but surely they wouldn't be rude to her? Her hands began to shake at the prospect of doing this and an unsettling feeling formed in her stomach. She couldn't go on like this...she couldn't be friendless and miserable forever.

She felt a tap on her shoulder and zoned back into the room. Sydney was the one tapping her; she looked from her to Miss Sutherland who was glaring at her. Everyone in the room was now staring at her. Worse still, she had no idea what question Miss Sutherland had just asked her.

'Outer space to Remmy. Come in Remmy,' Miss Sutherland said.

Remmy felt her cheeks reddening. She didn't know if her teacher was trying to be funny or sarcastic. Either way, it caused some of the other kids to laugh, which made her feel even more uncomfortable.

'Seventy-four,' Sydney whispered to her.

'Urm, seventy-four,' she called out.

'Remmy, are you okay?' Miss Sutherland raised an eyebrow.

'Miss, I don't feel very well. Please, can I go to the bathroom?'

'Very well,' she gave a nod. 'Would you like to take a friend with you?'

'It's okay, thank you, I wouldn't want to bother anyone.'

She definitely didn't want to announce to her teacher that she didn't have any friends.

'I'll go with Remmy,' Sydney said.

Remmy gave her a weak smile. She thought that she had only volunteered to go with her so that she could get out of class. They walked in silence along the hallway and Sydney held the door open for her as they walked into the girls' bathroom.

She walked over to the basins, poured water into her cupped hands and then splashed it onto her face. As she looked up at the long rectangular mirror that spanned the length of the basins a sickening feeling formed in her gut. There was a message written in marker pen on the mirror: *Remmy No Friends*.

Sydney followed her gaze and looked at the message.

'Oh!'

'Yeah,' Remmy covered her face with her hands.

'Are there any other Remmy's in this school?' she asked.

'No,' she shook her head. 'I am the only loser.'

Sydney rushed into one of the cubicles and returned with a handful of toilet paper. She wet it under the tap then scrubbed at the message. The ink smudged across the mirror but it wouldn't go away completely.

'At least you can't make out the words anymore,' Sydney said reassuringly.

'It could have been there all day. Loads of girls could have seen it,' Remmy sighed.

She slumped down onto the floor and leaned her back against the wall. She looked over at the smudged ink and wondered how many girls had laughed at the message? Sydney sat down next to her, which surprised Remmy. She was wearing an expensive looking pleated skirt, yet she hadn't hesitated in sitting down next to her on the floor.

'Whoever wrote that message is really mean,' she rubbed Remmy's arm. 'It'll be okay, no one would have taken any notice of it.'

Remmy nodded her head. She knew that Sydney was trying to be nice but she didn't believe her words. Of course, the other girls would have taken notice of the message. No wonder she'd felt like everyone had been laughing at her at lunchtime.

'Do you have any idea who would have done this?'

Remmy chewed on the side of her lip. She knew exactly who would have been mean enough to write that message.

'Yes,' she sighed out. 'Sandy, Rach, and Susie.'

'But isn't Sandy your step-sister?' Sydney raised an eyebrow.

'Yes, but she wasn't very nice to me when I first arrived here. She and her friends used to bully me. They shoved me into that cubicle,' she pointed over at it. 'And wrote mean things on my face and arms with a permanent marker.'

'How horrible!' she gasped.

'They've been nice to me recently though. I thought that their bullying had stopped but, I don't know...' she sighed.

Sydney leaned over and squeezed her into a hug.

'Don't worry about those mean girls, Remmy,' she smiled as she loosened her grip on her. 'Now, let's go back to class and show them that they can't bring you down.'

'Okay,' she nodded.

Sydney stood up, brushed down her skirt and then held her hand out to Remmy. She took it and was helped up to her feet.

'Don't let the bullies grind you down,' Sydney patted her shoulder.

'Thanks,' she forced a smile.

'No problem. I just don't get why girls have to be so cruel.'

'Yeah,' she looked down at the floor.

'Rinse your face, stand up straight and look the bullies straight in the eye as you walk past them.'

Remmy stared in the mirror at her swollen eyes. She splashed water on her face and looked at Sydney. She was so confident and pretty but she was being nice to Remmy. Maybe she wasn't trying to steal her life after-all?

'Here,' Sydney pulled a candy pink lip-gloss out of her pocket. 'This will give your lips a subtle sparkle, it also tastes of cherry.'

'Thanks,' Remmy took it from her.

She didn't normally wear lip-gloss but she didn't want to be rude to Sydney so she applied a thin layer to her lips and then puckered them.

'You're ready to go,' Sydney took the lip-gloss back.

When they stepped outside of the bathroom Sydney linked her arm through Remmy's and marched her up the hallway.

'Stick with me and you'll be just fine,' Sydney smiled. 'You should totally join me and my friends for lunch.'

'Yes, that'd be great,' Remmy said eagerly.

There was no way that she was going to turn down an invitation for lunch with her old friends, even if Sydney didn't realize the history between them.

As they neared the classroom Remmy began to panic at the thought of seeing all of her classmates. Would they know that she'd been crying? Would they know that she'd seen the message? Would Sandy and her vampires be smug knowing that they'd upset her?

She looked at confident beautiful Sydney; she was being so nice to her so maybe the other kids would too? They stopped in front of the classroom door and Sydney unlinked their arms.

'You can do this,' she smiled, as she gripped her arms.

Remmy stood up straight and forced a smile.

'I can do this,' she said to herself, as she followed Sydney into the classroom.

The room fell silent and everyone stared at her. She purposely looked away from Sandy but made sure to maintain her smile as she walked over to her seat.

'Are you feeling better Remmy?' Miss Sutherland asked.

'Yes, thank you, Miss,' she said as confidently as she could.

'Good,' she replied.

Remmy looked at Sydney and she gave her a reassuring smile back, which instantly made her feel better. She looked over at the back of Charlie's head and hoped that with Sydney's support that lunchtime wouldn't be a complete disaster. Still, the nerves rose up in her stomach like a flower in spring. Lunchtime was her last chance to put things right with Charlie and Bridget and end her friend drought. She just hoped that they could tell how truly sorry she was for upsetting them and that this time they'd forgive her.

Chapter Three- Awkward

The lunch bell rang and Remmy's stomach flipped. She knew what she had to do but that didn't mean that she wasn't afraid of how it would go. She longed to have her old friends back but she was worried that they would never forgive her. If Sandy ever gave her a list to follow again...she would rip it up without hesitation. By trying to spare Sandy's feelings she'd hurt Charlie and Bridget.

'Are you coming?' Sydney encouraged her as she stood next to her desk.

The doubt had crept into Remmy's mind and she began to panic.

'I um, I need to go to the library to do um, to research something.'

'Nonsense. Research sounds ridiculously boring and therefore it can wait. You need to be around other kids after what Sandy and her friends did to you today...nice kids. Also, I'm going to get you a cupcake to cheer you up.'

Remmy gave a nod before she pushed back her chair and stood up.

'Great,' Sydney yanked on her arm. 'Let's go.'

The closer they got to the cafeteria the more anxious Remmy began to feel. She was beginning to think that she should have refused Sydney's offer of sitting with her at lunch. Maybe staying as *Remmy No Friends* would have been easier.

'You don't need to worry Remmy, Sandy wouldn't dare upset you with me around,' Sydney flickered her hair behind her back.

'Thanks,' she muttered.

She was still pulling on her arm as she led her into the cafeteria and over to the table where Charlie and Bridget were sitting.

'We'll leave our bags with them and then we'll go and get our lunch.'

Remmy looked down at the floor as she neared their table but she could still feel their glares on her.

'Hey guys,' Sydney said cheerfully.

Remmy stood to the side of Sydney, her mouth dry and her heart thudding.

Bridget couldn't meet her eyes, the hurt visible on her face. This made Remmy feel even worse and she gave a dry gulp before she forced herself to look at Charlie.

'Please go away, we don't want you here,' he snapped at her.

Remmy gave a weak nod before she turned around and began to walk away. Sydney grabbed her arm and stopped her.

'You're not going anywhere,' she pulled her forward. 'I don't know what is going on with you two but this girl has had a rough day and she's in some serious need of friends. She was badly bullied by that horrible Sandy today so she needs people to be nice to her.'

Bridget looked up at Remmy with teary eyes.

'Remmy did have some really great friends but she burned them so badly that they feel hurt and used and they don't really want to be her friend anymore.'

'Oh, who were they?' Sydney asked.

Charlie looked at Sydney, he suspected that she already knew the answer to her question but regardless of this he still answered her.

'Remmy burned Bridget and me…badly.'

'Oh well, we all make mistakes. I'm sure Remmy didn't mean to upset you both. Why don't you guys all have a fresh start?' she suggested.

Charlie sniggered and Bridget glared down at the table. Sydney stood there with a smile on her pretty face but even she seemed overwhelmed by the situation. Remmy knew that she couldn't expect Sydney to fix this for her; she needed to be the one to do it.

'I know I was a total jerk and if you can forgive me I promise I'll never be one again,' Remmy croaked.

'Yeah right, we've heard that before,' Bridget murmured.

'I am really sorry. I know I messed up and I understand why you're both still mad at me but you're the best friends that I've ever had and I miss you both like crazy. I know that I totally don't deserve your friendship, I get that,' she gulped back a breath of air.

'I'll leave you to it,' Remmy looked away from them and gave Sydney a half-wave before she began to walk off.

'Wait!' Charlie shouted.

Remmy turned around and looked at him. Was he going to say something else to make her feel like the world's worst friend?

'Sit down, Remmy,' he sighed. 'You can have one more

chance, so don't blow it.'

'Really?' she looked at him with hopeful eyes.

'Yes,' he grinned.

'Thank you, thank you so much,' Remmy eagerly sat down next to Bridget.

'I've missed you,' Bridget looked at her with teary eyes.

'I've missed you too,' she smiled at her.

Bridget leaned forwards and wrapped her arms around

Remmy. They kept on hugging, neither of them wanting to be the one to pull away first.

'Let's never fall out again,' Bridget looked up at her.

'I'm making sure of that,' Remmy smiled. 'There's no way I'm losing you both again. No chance.'

'I've missed you too,' Charlie choked up.

He coughed to clear his throat and tried to discreetly wipe his eyes with his sleeve.

'Thanks, Charlie and thank you both for giving me a second chance,' she beamed. 'And thank you Sydney for helping me out before and helping me to get my friends back.'

'No problem. I'm glad you've cheered up, the puffy eye look is so not your thing,' she grinned.

'I won't mess up ever again. I'm going to be the best friend to you all and never ever risk losing you. I'll be the best friend that I can possibly be.'

'We know,' Bridget smiled.

'It's good to have you back,' Charlie grinned.

'I'm so happy,' Bridget beamed. 'My friends are the best and we're all back together.'

'Maybe I should be a peace-maker when I leave school?' Sydney chuckled.

The others all laughed as they looked at her.

'I think you should,' Charlie said.

'Yeah, I totally should.'

'Thanks, Sydney. This day started off as a shocker...but now it's turned into one of the best days ever.'

'I'm glad everyone's friends and all, but I need cheese fries,' she yanked on Remmy's arm.

'Now, cheese fries sound like a great idea,' she smiled.

As Remmy was led over to the food line she couldn't help but glance back at Charlie and Bridget. They were her friends again and this fact caused a large smile to firmly fix on her face.

Chapter Four- Confrontation

The rest of the school day had been great. Remmy had her old friends back and she didn't feel like *'Remmy No Friends'* anymore. Her mood changed when she arrived home and realized that she would soon have to face Sandy. She had done some pretty mean things to her since she'd arrived in Venice Beach but Remmy had hoped that this had stopped. Now she feared that it never would. She didn't want to spend the rest of her life being tormented by Sandy and her vampires.

Sandy was out with her friends, which meant that Remmy had time to mull things over. Soon her worry turned into anger, how dare Sandy write that message on the bathroom mirror. So much for being her friend, it seemed that some people aren't capable of changing.

She tried to work on her homework but all she could think about was how mean Sandy was. This thought was still at the forefront of her mind as she walked downstairs. As she neared the kitchen she heard Sandy laughing. She stood in the doorway with her arms folded as she watched her mom, Marcus and Sandy all standing around a mixing bowl. To any other onlooker...they would have looked like the perfect family.

'Sweetie, come and help us. I'm making cookies,' her mom held up the batter covered wooden spoon.

Sandy was standing next to Janice, she had speckles of batter on her face but she still managed to look perfect.

'I'm not doing anything with her,' Remmy glared at Sandy.

'W-what?' Sandy gave her a confused look.

'You know exactly what you did today at school. It's all been an act, hasn't it? You were just pretending to be my friend but really you still wanted to make my life a misery.'

'No. Look Remmy, I don't know what's upset you but-'

'It was you who wrote that message about me on the bathroom mirror. Did you and your friends have a good laugh about me? You may have found it funny but I didn't!'

Remmy was red with anger and to make it worse, Sandy was looking at her with that princess-perfect look of hers. She longed to pour the bowl of batter over her head.

'I didn't write anything. It wasn't me!' she shouted.

'Yes, it was, I know it was! Who else would it be?'

'I don't know and I don't care! It's not my problem if you've upset someone, so don't go blaming me.'

'Girls,' Marcus said sternly. 'What is all this about?'

'She knows what,' Remmy huffed.

'I don't have a clue what she's on about. All I've done is try to make it up to her by being nice. I've let her hang around with me and my friends, I've hung out with her and I've helped her make new friends. I shouldn't have bothered if this is all the thanks I get.'

'Help me,' Remmy snorted. 'All you've done is make my life worse. And you know exactly what you did today. I know it was you!' she screamed. 'Why can't you just admit how much of a horrible person you really are?'

'At least I'm not ugly and boring,' Sandy shouted back.

'Sandy, go to your room right now!' Marcus shouted.

'But I haven't done anything wrong!'

'Sandy, room, NOW!'

'With pleasure!' Sandy stormed across the room and shoved past Remmy. 'I hate you all!'

She ran up the stairs and slammed her bedroom door with such force that the sound echoed through the rest of the house.

'Sweetie, what is going on?' Janice walked over to Remmy.

'Remmy, did you have to scream at Sandy?' Marcus scowled at her.

'Well, I'm sure your daughter deserved it,' Janice snapped back.

'Right, I see,' he strode across the room.

'Marcus, where are you going?'

'To see my wayward daughter,' he said sarcastically.

'Fine, you do that,' she huffed.

'I will.'

Silent tears streamed down Remmy's cheeks. Janice pulled her into a hug and she buried her head in her mom's cardigan. Her mom smelt of cookie batter and lavender perfume...scents that she took comfort in.

Eventually, they pulled apart and Janice led her over to the breakfast bar. Remmy sat down and Janice poured a glass of orange juice and then passed it to her.

'Thanks,' she gave a weak smile.

'Sweetheart, what's been going on?' she looked at her with concerned eyes.

'It's Sandy, being friends with her has caused me even more

trouble than being enemies with her. I nearly lost everyone because I followed her stupid list and then today she wrote *Remmy No Friends* on the bathroom mirror. Loads of the girls in school would have seen it and it was obviously about me as I'm the only Remmy at school,' she gave a solemn sigh.

'List…what list?'

Remmy took a sip of her drink. She wasn't thirsty but she wanted to stall time. Why had she mentioned the list? Now she'd have to explain it to her mom.

'Sandy gave me a list of things I had to do to become cool. I didn't even want to be cool but I was so worried about upsetting her that I followed her stupid list.'

'What was on it?' her mom raised an eyebrow.

'That I had to hang around with the cool kids and I had to be the one to break-up with Charlie first. I didn't want to upset Bridget and I didn't want to lose Charlie but I lost them both because I followed Sandy's list.'

'Remmy, we all make mistakes,' her mom put her arm around her. 'I am surprised that you would take on advice that you didn't believe in…but I imagine that Sandy can be very persuasive. Life's full of lessons and it sounds like you learned one the hard way.'

'I guess,' she sighed. 'Charlie and Bridget are talking to me again but I still feel awful that I hurt them so much. I've made my own list to follow, one with rules that I believe in.'

'I see, what rules are these?'

'Be nice to everyone as you never know what someone is going through. Not to gossip or to listen to gossip. To dress how I want to. To own up to my mistakes and um…not let my own jealousy ruin my relationships.'

35

'Remmy, that sounds like a wise list to follow.'

'Thanks, mom.'

'Also, embrace the fact that no one else in your school has your name. You're unique, which is exactly why your father and I choose it. Well, saying that, he suggested we call you Ethel after this grandmother,' she chuckled.

'I guess Remmy's not so bad,' she gave a brief smile.

'I always thought it was a rather pretty name, so I think it's rather fitting for my beautiful daughter.' She kissed the top of Remmy's head and then ruffled her hair.

Remmy sighed and gave a glum look.

'Do you want to talk about it? Sometimes it helps to unload your feelings.'

'It's Sandy. She's turned on me again and I don't want to have to deal with that. I've tried so hard to be nice to her but she is so mean to me. Now I don't know if she's only being nice so that it's easier for her to be mean.'

'It'll be okay, leave it to your mom to sort out.'

'I don't want to cause any problems between you and Marcus.'

'Nonsense, we'll be fine. Besides, it's you I'm worried about. You're my baby girl and I just want you to be happy.'

'I am happy,' Remmy forced a smile.

'I do hope so,' her mom hugged her. 'I worry about you and if moving you here was a good idea.'

'It was mom,' she emphasized her smile. 'I just need to always stick up for what I believe in, although I'd been failing at this badly.'

'Yes, you do. But I know that you can do it, I'm very proud of you.'

'Thanks, mom.'

'Right, these cookies won't bake themselves. Are you going to help me?'

'Of course, mom.'

Remmy stepped down from her chair and followed her mom over to the bowl of batter. She was stirring it when she heard someone cough in the doorway. She and her mom both turned to see Marcus standing there, his face expressionless.

'Janice, can I please have a word with you?'

She gave him a nod and then Remmy a reassuring smile before she walked over to him. Remmy stopped stirring the mixture and watched them leave the room. She knew from the sound of their footsteps that they'd gone into the television room. Curiosity took over and she left the spoon in the mixture and crept across the kitchen floor.

She leaned against the wall by the door to the television room and tried to control her erratic breathing. It wasn't long before she heard raised voices coming from within the room.

'My daughter is NOT a liar. It's your daughter who has been the bully in the past so it stands to reason that she would do it again,' Janice snapped.

'Cassandra has apologized and befriended Remmy. She's been trying really hard to make amends so I know that she wouldn't jeopardize that,' he shouted back.

'Because she's never lied before, has she?' Janice said sarcastically.

'That is unfair. You can't hold her past mistakes against her. She says that she's telling the truth and I believe her. Remmy knew that by saying this you would take her side, she's clearly in need of attention.'

'How dare you say such a spiteful thing when you're the one with the attention-seeking child!'

I can't reason with you when you're like this. I'm taking my attention-seeking daughter and I'm taking her out for dinner.'

'Maybe that's for the best!' she shouted back.

'Fine then, I will!'

Remmy heard footsteps so she quickly darted up the hallway and back into the kitchen. She peered out of the room and saw Marcus storm up the stairs. She stood out of sight behind the door as he came back down with Sandy and they both left the house.

Knowing that the house was Sandy and Marcus free, Remmy went into the television room and found her mom slouched on the couch, her head in her hands.

'Mom, are you okay?' Remmy asked.

'Yes darling,' she sniffed, as she looked up at her.

Remmy walked over to her and sat down next to her.

'I'm sorry, I didn't mean for you to argue with Marcus.'

'Oh Remmy, it's not your fault,' she sniffed again. 'Besides, we were only bickering. We will soon sort it out.'

'I shouldn't have said anything,' she was on the verge of crying.

'No Remmy, don't say that,' she grabbed her arm. 'You must always tell me if something's upset you. Always.'

Remmy nodded her head, even though she didn't believe that she'd stick to this. She felt terrible that she'd caused another argument between her mom and Marcus and she never wanted to cause another one.

'I'm sure this will all blow over soon. Why don't we finish making those cookies and then we can give Sandy and Marcus some on their return?'

'Okay mom,' Remmy forced a smile.

'It will all sort itself out, I can't be angry with Marcus for long,' she gave Remmy a reassuring smile. 'Now, let's go and make cookies.'

'That sounds great.'

'It sure does.'

Janice stood up and rubbed the creases out of her cotton skirt. Although she tried to hide her distress beneath a smile, her deflated posture and constant sniffing told otherwise.

Remmy knew that their problems couldn't be solved with cookies but she was prepared to go along with the façade that they would. She just wanted her mom to be happy and right now her somber mom was anything but.

Chapter Five- Turmoil

Saturday morning arrived but the gloomy atmosphere continued. It didn't match the clear skies and the beaming sun. Remmy decided that she was going to escape early, as she didn't want any confrontation with Sandy. So, she woke up early, changed into her running gear and then left her mom a note on the breakfast bar saying that she had gone to the beach.

The previous night had been a difficult one for Remmy. Her mom had tried to make conversation as they ate dinner but Marcus's absence had clearly upset her. He hadn't returned until later on in the evening, by which point both Remmy and her mom had gone to bed. They had left a plateful of cookies on the table as a goodwill gesture and Remmy had noticed that morning that a couple of them had been taken. She had also noticed that Marcus was asleep on the couch, a fact that made her feel even more dreadful. She didn't want to ruin her mom's happiness; she just wanted Sandy to stop tormenting her.

It was still early when her bus pulled up alongside the boardwalk. The beach was currently quiet, so she made the most of the uncrowded pathway and began to run. Instantly she began to feel better as the world blurred past her. By the time she had finished running the beach had become busier. Families and groups of teenagers had claimed their spots on it.

She wasn't ready to go home yet and deal with the atmosphere so she found a fairly quiet spot on the beach and shook out her towel. She knelt on it and squirted sunscreen lotion into her hand and then rubbed it on her arm.

'Hey, girlfriend. The sunscreen's a good idea, it's roasting today.'

Remmy turned her head and saw Amelia standing there. She was wearing oversized sunglasses. She looked beautiful.

'Hi Amelia,' Remmy smiled.

'What's up?' she knelt down on the edge of Remmy's towel.

'Well, this week's been super eventful. Charlie and Bridget have finally forgiven me, with the help of the new girl, Sydney.'

'That's great news, I knew they couldn't stay mad at you for long,' she smiled.

'I was beginning to think that they would.'

'Nah, you're an awesome girl. Yes, you made a mistake but you realized that you messed up and apologized. Admitting that you're wrong can be hard sometimes and waiting for people to forgive you can be even harder.'

'Thanks, but I messed up badly. I was stupid! I can't believe I followed Sandy's rule list,' she sighed.

'We all do foolish things sometimes but that doesn't make you any less amazing. So, what has this week taught you?'

'Um,' she ran her fingers through the sand. 'To always be myself and to do what I believe is best. And if something doesn't feel right, then it probably isn't. Also, I don't want to be one of the cool kids.'

'Remmy, you are one of the cool kids,' she chuckled. 'You're kind, funny and smart. If people don't want to be your friend then that's their problem.'

'Thanks, Amelia. I'm so over trying to be cool, besides trying to be like Sandy hasn't stopped her from being mean to me.'

'Oh! What happened?'

Amelia sat down on the towel and hugged her legs.

'She wrote *Remmy No Friends* on the bathroom mirror. I told mom about it and now mom and Marcus are mad at each other. He slept on the couch last night.'

'Oh, that sucks. What are you going to do?'

'I'm not sure,' she sighed. 'I need to somehow settle things down at home but I don't know how I'm going to do this. I don't want to be anywhere near Sandy, she's so mean. I never know if she's being sincere or plotting her next evil plan. She totally has Marcus fooled that she didn't write the message, he just won't believe that Princess Sandy is capable of anything that cruel.'

'Remmy, are you sure it was Sandy who wrote the message?' she enquired.

'I didn't see her do it but it can't have been anyone else.'

'Okay,' Amelia nodded. 'But you don't have any proof so maybe Sandy is innocent, which would explain why she was so angry at being accused.'

Remmy thought about this. Sandy had been adamant that she was innocent but then she had lied about bullying her before. She was an excellent actress and Remmy was well aware of just how mean she could be. She decided that she had to be guilty; it was classic 'vampire' behavior.

'Nah, I think that she did it. She will never admit it though, which sucks.'

'Well, if you're sure. Anyway, enough Sandy talk, let's go for a swim,' she smiled.

'That sounds like a great idea,' Remmy replied.

'Good,' she stood up. 'I'll race you there,' she began to run off across the beach.

'Hey, that's so not fair,' Remmy laughed.

She quickly rushed after her, weaving her way around the other people who were on the beach. Even though Remmy was quick, the obstacles of people delayed her. By the time she reached the ocean Amelia had taken off her sundress and was already dipping her feet in the water.

'Come on slow coach,' she chuckled, as she waved Remmy over.

Remmy grinned back at her. She had to admit that it felt

good to have Amelia around to take her mind off her problems at home. Sandy and the vampires weren't here and neither were her mom and Marcus. It was just her, her friend and the ocean...and right now there was nowhere she'd rather be.

'Come on Remmy,' Amelia broke her out of her thoughts.

'I'm coming,' she shouted back.

She quickly took her vest top and shorts off to reveal her black bikini (she'd learned from her white bikini mistake) and she placed them down next to Amelia's sundress. She looked out at her pretty friend, she was in a dark pink bikini and the water was now up to her knees. She looked like a

Venice Beach girl but as Remmy made her way over to her, she didn't feel ugly or self-conscious next to her. Amelia had taught her that she was fine being the way she was.

***

Remmy's day at the beach had been loads of fun but like all good things, it had to end at some point. Now, she was back home and trying her best to avoid Sandy, who was currently sunbathing by the pool. She'd managed to sneak unnoticed into the kitchen to get some potato chips, but she wasn't so lucky when she left the safety of her room to go and get a drink.

She poured herself some soda and was taking a sip of it when she heard footsteps behind her.

'Oh, you're back!'

Remmy reluctantly turned to face Sandy who was standing there with her hair tied into pigtails and her hand on her hip. She was wearing a multi-colored polka-dot bikini and glittery white sunglasses which were placed on top of her head.

'Yeah,' she dribbled soda down her chin and quickly wiped it onto the back of her hand.

Sandy sniggered as she moved her hand from her hip up to one of her pigtails and fiddled with it.

'Good,' Sandy smiled. 'I want to sort things out with us. I didn't write that message, I wouldn't.'

Remmy couldn't help but snort on hearing this. She knew first hand that Sandy was fully capable of doing something so mean.

'Honestly, I didn't,' she looked directly at her. 'Anyway,

please can we still be friends?'

Remmy looked back at her pretty, sun-kissed step-sister. She had the Venice Beach look, just like Amelia did, yet Sandy was a bully and Amelia was one of the kindest people she'd ever met. She thought about what Amelia would say and came to the conclusion that she had two choices. She could either remain angry and resentful towards Sandy or she could move on and forgive her.

'Okay, let's move on,' she looked her in the eyes. 'But don't ask me to sit with your friends again.'

'Okay,' Sandy gave a sickeningly sweet smile.

'And if you find out that your friends were responsible for the message then you need to tell them that being a bully isn't cool.'

'I totally agree.'

She walked over to Remmy and wrapped her arms around her, which caused Remmy to instantly stiffen. She gave her an awkward hug back and hoped that Sandy hadn't noticed how uncomfortable she was.

Sandy pulled out of the hug and beamed at her.

'I'm so glad we're friends again. Are you coming out to the pool?'

'Um, no thanks. I really want to get my project finished,' Remmy replied.

'Okay, I'll see you later then.' Sandy gave her a wave before she headed back outside.

Remmy didn't want to be anywhere near Sandy but she also didn't want to be her enemy.

Chapter Six- The Gift of Giving

It was dinnertime and the four of them were sitting around the dining table. Janice had cooked roast beef with plenty of side dishes. It looked and smelled amazing but this wasn't enough to dispel the awkward atmosphere that hung over the table.

Remmy was trying to avoid seeing Sandy smile at her, so she didn't have to smile back. So, she stared down at her plate as she cut into a piece of beef. Worse still, Janice and Marcus still hadn't sorted things out. They kept on glaring at each other as they continued to give each other the silent treatment.

'Girls, did you have a nice day?' Janice broke the silence.

'Yes thanks, I sunbathed for most of it and now my tan is looking great,' Sandy held out a bronzed arm.

'You are looking very tanned. I hope you put plenty of sun lotion on?'

'I did.'

'Of course she did, my daughter is not stupid enough to forget such a thing,' Marcus commented.

'I never implied such a thing,' Janice flustered.

'Sure sounded like you did,' he muttered under his breath.

Remmy became extra self-conscious of her slightly reddened arms and face. She'd applied plenty of sun lotion but her pale skin burnt so easily that it was now blotchy red.

'Remmy, what did you do today?' Janice looked away from Marcus.

'Um, well,' she placed her knife down on her plate so that she could put one of her red arms behind her back. 'I went running along the boardwalk and then I hung out at the beach.'

'Did you apply enough sun lotion because it doesn't look like you did?' Marcus said snidely.

'Marcus, you are well aware that my daughter and I have far

paler skin than you and your daughter do. We burn easier. I suggest you think about your next comment very carefully or you may find yourself with the remainder of the gravy on your head.'

'You are unreasonable, stubborn and a tyrant,' he put down his cutlery and scraped back his chair. 'I have work to do,' he stormed out of the room.

Silence prevailed and both Remmy and Sandy looked down at their dinner in a bid to avoid eye contact with Janice. The only sound that could be heard was that of cutlery scraping against plates. Remmy cut her potato in half and then popped it into her mouth. She purposely chewed it as slowly as she could so that she had an excuse to not talk.

This was excruciating, and worst of all she blamed herself for it. Maybe she shouldn't have confronted Sandy about the message? Maybe she should have just kept quiet?

'Who wants chocolate layered pudding for dessert?' Janice gave an exaggerated smile. 'Now that there's only three of us...we'll all get a bigger portion.'

'Great,' Remmy forced a smile.

'Um, thanks for dinner Janice but I'm just going to go to my room,' Sandy scraped back her chair.

'Oh, okay. If you're sure?'

Sandy gave a nod of her head before she tottered off across the room.

Remmy didn't want dessert; instead, she wanted to evaporate out of here. Her mom stood up and began to clear up the plates so she quickly began to help her.

'Thank you, Remmy.'

They loaded the plates and cutlery into the dishwasher and then Remmy sat back down at the table. It seemed so empty without Sandy and Marcus there. She found this odd, as back in Sweet Lips she was so used to it being just her and her mom. Then again, back then the smell of their dinners had filled the entirety of their small house.

She wondered what her friends back in Sweet Lips would be up to now? She wondered who was now living in her house and calling her bedroom their own? Had they covered up her height markings in the living room? Had they filled in the hole in the wall that her dad had made when trying to nail in a picture? Sweet Lips wasn't her home anymore...it hadn't truly been since they'd lost dad. Going back there wouldn't have changed this; it wouldn't have brought him back.

Her mom was happy here. Her mom loved Marcus.

'Would you like some toffee sauce with your dessert?' her mom interrupted her thoughts.

'Urm, yes thanks.'

Yes, I'll have some too.'

Janice walked over to the table carrying two plates with huge pieces of chocolate-layered pudding on them. She placed one down in front of Remmy and the other on her placemat.

'Thank you,' Remmy smiled.

They both had ridiculously huge portions. Remmy knew that she would never have been able to eat all that, she wasn't even that hungry, she just didn't want to offend her mom.

'I wanted to use it all up, so that means more for us,' Janice commented.

'Great.'

Janice put a spoonful of dessert into her mouth and chewed on it.

'Who am I kidding,' she sighed. 'I'm not even hungry.'

She pushed it away from her.

'I'm a foolish idiot,' her eyes teared up.

'No, you're not,' Remmy looked at her. 'You're the best mom in the world and you make the best dessert.'

'Then why did no one want it?' she sniffed. 'It's not even about the dessert, I know that. It's me they don't want! And I don't blame them. I am a silly old fool.'

Remmy didn't see her mom as old. Grandma Noreen was old with her wrinkled skin but her mom was anything but.

'You're not old and you're not a fool.'

'Then I'm silly, a silly non-old idiot,' she chuckled through her sobs.

Remmy walked over to her mom, leaned over her and wrapped her arms around her shoulders.

'I love you mom, more than the sun.'

'I love you too sweetie, more than a tortoise.'

'I love you more than the beach.'

I love you more than a mountain.'

'I love you more than a hippo.'

'I don't know what I'd do without you, you're my baby girl and I love you so much,' she rubbed her hand.

'I don't know what I'd do without you either mom.'

'I think it's about time I sorted things out with Marcus.'

'That sounds like a good idea.' Remmy let go of her mom.

Janice stood up, sniffed and rubbed her eyes with the back of her arm. She rubbed the creases out of her skirt and then leaned across the table and grabbed her plate.

'Do you think he'll notice that I took a bite out of it?' she grinned.

'Maybe, just say you were tasting it,' Remmy laughed.

'Good idea,' she smiled.

Remmy watched her mom walk out of the room, she hoped that if the dessert didn't sort things out with Marcus then her mom's clear love and devotion towards him would.

She stared down at her own dessert and decided that her mom had the right idea. Remmy didn't like Sandy all that much but she did have to live with her. She didn't ever want to go back to how it used to be. They didn't have to be the best of friends but being some sort of friends was better than being enemies.

She got another plate out of the cupboard and an extra spoon and transferred half of her dessert into it, then she added some whipped cream, strawberries and some more toffee sauce.

She checked that the hallway was free of her mom and Marcus before she walked up the stairs with both plates. Then she carefully balanced one of the plates on her arm as she knocked on Sandy's bedroom door.

'Yeah?' Sandy shouted.

Remmy pushed open the door and then took the plate off her arm. Sandy was stretched out on her bed looking at her laptop and swinging her legs out behind her.

'Oh, hi,' she muttered.

'Hi, Sandy. I brought a peace offering,' she held out the plate.

'It smells and looks so good,' Sandy said, as she sat up.

Remmy passed Sandy a plate and then lingered next to her.

'Sit down,' Sandy patted the space next to her.

'Thanks,' Remmy perched down on the edge of the bed.

'Are Janice and dad still arguing?' she asked.

'Mom's gone to make it up with him.'

'I hope it works.'

'Me too,' she took a bite out of her dessert. 'Woah, this is *so* good.'

Sandy smiled back before she put a spoonful of her dessert into her mouth.

'We're okay now, aren't we?' Sandy asked.

'Yeah, we're okay,' Remmy smiled.

Remmy didn't trust Sandy and she doubted that she ever would...but their feud was tearing Janice and Marcus apart. She needed her mom to be happy and if that meant being nice to Sandy then she'd just have to get on with it. Besides, Sandy's mean message had resulted in her making up with Charlie and Bridget and making a new friend in Sydney. She would always be wary of Sandy but acting friendly towards her was far better than being angry at her.

She was a kind person, she was a Hufflepuff and she was determined to stay this way forever. She just hoped that her mom and Marcus had sorted everything out too. They may have been an unconventional family but they were still a family. Surely having an unconventional family was better than not having one at all? Even if hers included an evil step-sister.

***

Miss Sutherland stood in front of the class with an excited

look on her face. Remmy wondered what she was about to say and hoped that it was something exciting and not a trip to the park or something equally as lame.

'I have an amazing announcement to make,' she grinned, as she addressed the class. 'I have to say that as school trips go, I'm very excited about this one and I have a feeling you'll all be as thrilled. This is a once in a lifetime opportunity and we're all so lucky to have been given this chance.'

'Miss, will you just tell us what it is?' Mike shouted out.

'Yes Mike,' she blushed. 'I am pleased to announce that as part of the ocean unit that we are studying, we will be spending the night at the aquarium.'

There were whoops and cheers from the class.

'Who has been there before?' she asked.

The majority of the kids put their hands up.

'Who has stayed the night there before?'

No one put their hand up.

'This is so exciting. We will get to sleep in one of the tunnels with fish swimming above us.'

'What if the glass breaks and a shark falls on us?' Colin shouted out.

This received laughter from the class.

'Colin, I doubt very much that is going to happen,' Miss Sutherland tried to hold back a chuckle.

'If it does, I hope it falls on Sandy's head,' he grinned.

'I hope it bites your arm off,' Sandy replied.

'There will be no glass breaking or shark bites. What there will be is an amazing experience, one that we can all cherish forever.'

Remmy and Sydney exchanged excited looks with each other. They never did anything like this back in Sweet Lips, the only school trip they had was wildlife spotting down by the creek.

'There is a slight problem though,' Miss Sutherland remarked. 'As you can imagine this is a highly popular trip and there are very few dates that the aquarium allows for this experience. This has only become available because a cancellation came up...for this weekend. I hope everyone can make it, all you'll need is a pillow, a sleeping bag, and thirty dollars.'

Mike's head hit his desk with a bang! Everyone turned to look at him.

'Mike, are you okay?' Miss Sutherland rushed over to him.

'Yeah,' he muttered. 'It's just I know there's no way my dad will give me that much money for a trip.'

'Oh! Well, you never know. At least take the form home and see,' she tried to remain positive.

'There's no point,' he sighed. 'I know what he's going to say.'

Miss Sutherland got Sophie to hand the forms out to everyone. They chatted excitedly to each other about what fish they might see and how cool sleeping at the aquarium would be.

Remmy tried to listen to Sydney go on about the enormous aquarium she visited in New York but she couldn't stop thinking about Mike. It was so unfair that he was going to be the only kid in class that wouldn't be going. There had to be something she could do to help him.

She zoned out as she thought about this. Suddenly an idea came into her head, she still had some birthday money left, and she decided that she would give it to Mike to pay for the trip. It would make up for her being mean to him and be a thank you for how kind he was to her that day at the boardwalk.

She decided that this was a great idea but she had to be smart about it. Mike was a proud boy, so there was no way that he'd accept the money from her if she tried to give it to him. She needed to come up with a way to pay for his place on the trip without him knowing that it was her.

'I hope they have Sand Tiger Sharks, but I imagine they don't have them here,' Sydney said.

'Yeah, sounds great,' Remmy replied.

'What sounds great? Are you even listening to me?' she raised an eyebrow.

'Sorry,' Remmy blushed. 'I'm just so excited about the trip I can't think properly.'

'I know, me too. In New York they also have an aquatheater where they put on shows with the seals but I doubt they even have seals here,' she remarked. 'I don't expect this aquarium to be as good but I guess it'll still be cool to sleep in a tunnel there.'

'Yeah, it will,' Remmy thoughtfully replied.

Remmy volunteered to clean off the whiteboard so she could have a word to her teacher after school. When all the children had left, she told Miss Sullivan of her plan to pay for Mike. Miss Sullivan smiled and her eyes became teary.

'That's one of the nicest things anyone could do, Remmy. And I'll keep it a secret,' she promised.

Chapter Seven- Feeling Great

As Remmy arrived, she quietly sneaked an envelope onto her teacher's desk. Miss Sullivan gave her a slight nod.

Remmy had placed her permission form on her desk and she noticed that most of the other kids had too. She took a quick glance behind her and noticed a gloomy-looking Mike. She smiled at him and he gave her a weak one back.

'I'm going to walk around the class and collect all of your permission forms,' Miss Sutherland said.

There were a few rustles from the few kids who hadn't already placed them down on their desks. The teacher walked around collecting them and then she stopped in front of Mike. He was hunched over and he couldn't meet her eyes.

'Where's your form Mike?' she asked.

'I told you, I'm not going,' he sighed. 'It's just a stupid sleepover anyway and not worth thirty bucks.'

She gave a nod of her head and then she walked past him.

The morning class went by and soon the first break arrived. All of the other kids hurried out of the room apart from Mike, who looked downwards as he trudged across the wooden floor.

'Mike, please can I have a word with you?' she beckoned him over.

She shut the classroom door and then walked over to Mike who was now standing by her desk.

'I wanted to talk to you about the aquarium trip.'

'I told you, I can't go. It doesn't matter, it sounds like a lame trip anyway,' he shrugged.

'That's a shame,' she gave a slight smile. 'Because the aquarium has told me that they are offering one free place on the trip and I've chosen to give it to you.'

'Huh?' he looked at her. 'Are you being serious?'

'Yes Mike, I wouldn't joke about this. So, what do you say?'

'But I don't have my form signed.'

'Here,' she took a new form off her desk and passed it to him. 'Get your dad to sign it tonight and then bring it in tomorrow.'

'I will,' he took it from her. 'Thank you.'

'No problem Mike, now, go and enjoy your break.'

'I will,' he grinned.

He was still grinning as he walked into the cafeteria. Remmy spotted him and found herself smiling. Making someone else's day made her feel amazing and it was definitely the best way to spend her birthday money. She thought about how horrible it would be to be the only kid in the entire class who wouldn't be able to go on a trip. Thankfully, this no longer applied to Mike, a fact that made her beaming smile even wider.

Charlie gave her a questioning look. 'Why are you smiling?' he asked.

'Because I'm so happy to be back in the group.'

'It's good to have you back,' he smiled back at her.

Chapter Eight- The Sleepover

It was 6 pm at the aquarium and the foyer was full of kids. Remmy stood with Janice and Marcus whilst Sandy gave them a wave as she hurried over to her friends.

'Have a great time Remmy,' Janice hugged her.

'Thanks, mom.'

She gave them both a wave and a smile before she walked over to Charlie and Bridget.

'Hi Remmy,' Bridget smiled, as she clutched onto her sleeping bag. 'I'm so excited.'

'Hi Remmy,' Charlie grinned at her.

'Hey,' she blushed back.

'I could barely sleep last night,' Bridget jumped on the spot. 'I just want to get in there right now.'

'Calm down,' Charlie chuckled.

'Yes, Mr. No Fun,' she giggled back.

Sydney walked into the foyer wearing a pink striped blouse and a pair of skinny jeans. A glamorous woman who looked like an older version of Sydney followed her in, wearing high heels and clutching an expensive looking handbag. A handsome man dressed in a dark grey suit followed them, he was clutching a metallic sleeping bag, two pillows and a large overnight bag.

'Hi guys,' Sydney hurried over to them.

'Hi,' they all smiled at her.

'Bye darling,' the glamorous looking woman kissed her on the cheek which left a red lipstick mark.

'Mom,' Sydney rolled her eyes, as she wiped at her cheek with her hand.

The man placed the bag and the sleeping bag on the floor by her feet. He was just about to place the pillows down on top of the sleeping bag when Sydney grabbed them off him.

'Don't place them on the floor, it's dirty and I've got to rest my head on them,' she huffed.

'Sorry Syd,' he looked flustered.

'Come on, our reservation is waiting,' Sydney's mom tugged on his arm.

'Bye darling,' she waved to her.

'Have a great time,' he said before he was dragged across the foyer.

'This place looks okay,' she looked around her. 'Charlie, can you hold these for me?' She gave him a sweet smile as she held out her pillows.

'Um, sure,' he readjusted his sleeping bag under his arm so he could take them off her.

'Thanks.'

She picked up her sleeping bag, shook it out and then held it against her chest.

'Have you got enough stuff?' Bridget looked down at Sydney's large overnight bag.

'I know, right? But it's just for one night, so I cut back on what to bring.'

Bridget tried to disguise her smirk beneath her hand.

Remmy looked around her, the foyer was packed with kids but it looked like all of the parents had left. She glanced over at Sandy, who was standing with Rach and Susie and hoped that there wouldn't be any trouble from them tonight. This trip was an amazing experience and she didn't want it ruined by the vampires.

The foyer was noisy and crowded, as kids chatted to each other about sharks and the tunnel.

'Can everyone be quiet please?' Miss Sutherland said far too quietly.

Half of the kids didn't hear her and the ones that did, ignored her.

'Silence please,' she tried again.

Once again, her request was ignored.

'QUIET PLEASE,' a voice echoed across the foyer.

All of the kids fell silent and they looked over at the middle-aged man standing next to Miss Sutherland.

'Thank you,' Miss Sutherland blushed to the man. 'Hello everyone, I'm very pleased to see you all here. I know that you're all excited but please remember your manners. There will be detention for anyone who misbehaves. Now, I'll pass you over to our guide for the night,' she gestured to a man.

'Hello everyone, I am Mr. Bernstein but you can call me Mr. B,' his voice filled the room.

'I know nearly all there is to know about the sea life here at the aquarium, especially sharks. So, I will try my best to answer your questions,' he scratched his head.

'For now, please can you all follow me and I'll take you to the tunnel, which is where you'll all be sleeping tonight.'

They all quickly grabbed their belongings and rushed after Mr. B and Miss Sutherland. They knew that the nearer to the front of the line they were, the better the sleeping spot they would be able to grab. Remmy got elbowed in the arm by a boy and knocked out of the way by a girl's rucksack. Charlie grabbed her hand and saved her from falling over, she smiled at him and he smiled back.

She was about to spend the night surrounded by her friends, sleeping beneath sharks, and the boy she liked was holding her hand; life was good. She peered down the line and saw Mike, he was standing near the back by himself.

'Can you save me two sleeping bag spaces?' she asked Charlie, as she let go of his hand.

'Sure,' he raised an eyebrow.

She squeezed her way back past the other kids and then stopped when she got to Mike. He had his hands in the pockets of his black hoodie and he was staring at his feet.

'Hi Mike,' she smiled at him.

'Oh, hi Remmy,' he looked at her.

'It's so squashed up there, I got elbowed and shoved. It's much better back here.'

'Yeah, it is,' he muttered.

'Mike, I'm sorry again for being mean to you that time.'

'It's fine Remmy, we're cool.'

'Thanks.'

'No problem,' he gave a slight smile.

They shimmied along the corridor, which was surrounded by brightly colored fish.

'Woah,' Mike took a step back as an enormous fish swan past.

'Watch it,' the girl stood behind him moaned.

'Sorry,' he muttered back to her.

'I've never seen fish like this before. I've only seen the ones that were caught in the creek back in my old town. Oh, and I had a goldfish once.'

'I'm glad I'm not the only one who hasn't been here before, it seems that everyone else has.'

'Sydney hasn't either. Although she has been to an aquarium in New York.'

'I've always wanted to come here,' he sighed.

'You're here now,' she smiled.

'Yeah, I am,' he smiled back.

When they reached the tunnel, all the kids raced to claim a good spot. Remmy looked over at her friends and then she looked back at Mike.

'So, I was wondering if you wanted to hang out with me and my friends?'

He paused briefly and Remmy was worried that he was going to turn her down.

'Yeah, I'd like that,' he gave her a shy smile. 'Thank you.'

Her friends were in a great spot at the far side of the tunnel and when Bridget saw them, she waved them over.

'Hi guys,' Remmy smiled. 'Good spot.'

'I know right. I charged for it,' Bridget grinned.

'She sure did, I've never seen her move so fast,' Charlie smirked.

'Hey,' she play-hit his arm.

Mike was standing just behind Remmy; he was staring down at his sleeping bag.

'Mike's going to be joining us.'

'Cool, hi Mike,' Bridget smiled at him.

'I saved you both a spot,' Charlie gave them an awkward smile.

It suddenly dawned on Remmy that Charlie might think that she'd invited Mike to join them because she was interested in him. After all, he had seen them together at the boardwalk.

'Thanks,' Remmy placed her sleeping bag down next to him and Mike put his by hers.

Sydney hadn't said anything to Mike, instead, she tried her best not to look at him. Remmy decided that this was just because she didn't know him, surely there wouldn't be another reason why Sydney was ignoring him, would there?

'Right kids,' Mr. B shouted, and they all fell silent and looked over at him. 'We are going to go to the meeting point so please leave all your sleeping gear here.'

'I hope my things will be okay here,' Sydney whispered.

'Yeah, your stuff will be fine,' Charlie replied.

'It had better be,' she caught Mike's eye before she looked away from him.

All of the kids left their sleeping bags and overnight bags in the tunnel and followed Mr. B and Miss Sutherland into a room with long benches in it. It had several huge fish tanks fixed into the walls, all of them full of smaller fish that shimmered as they swan.

'Right kids, are there any questions before we start the tour?' Mr. B asked.

'Can't we look around by ourselves?' Colin shouted out, which caused Miss Sutherland to glare at him.

'I'm afraid not,' Mr. B replied.

This received groans from some of the kids that were here to have fun and didn't have any interest in learning.

Then they all followed Mr. B around the aquarium. He stopped in every room and told them facts about the sea-life there.

Remmy found Mr. B interesting and she liked the way he got excited every time he spotted a specific type of fish or shark that he liked.

They were all squashed on the moving walkway through the tunnel listening to Mr. B talk about sharks when a horrible smell wafted down the line.

Kids giggled and pretended to retch as it reached them. When the smell got to Mr. B he tightened up his face.

'Let's go and see the turtles.'

'Good idea Mr. B,' Sydney called out.

He quickly led the group around the corner and then began to talk about the turtles.

'Sandy did the fart, pass it along,' a boy in front of Remmy whispered to her.

Remmy didn't want to spread the rumor so she just ignored it. Other kids passed the rumor along the line and soon most of the kids had heard it. Remmy wondered who had started the rumor? It was mean but surely no one would believe it, would they? There was no proof that it was Sandy.

'Turtles have a hard shell that protects them like a shield, this is called a carapace.'

'Mr. B, where are the toilets?' Sydney called out. 'Sandy, do you want to join me?' she shouted up the line.

Laughter erupted between the kids, including Bridget who was laughing so hard that her face had turned red.

'I don't need to go,' Sandy looked puzzled.

Her comment caused more laughter. Remmy bit down on her lip to stop herself from laughing. Sandy blushed as she quickly glanced down at her shoes.

'Let's have a break, then anyone who needs to use the bathrooms can,' Miss Sutherland shouted. 'Everyone should meet back in the tunnel in thirty minutes.'

There was a hectic surge for the bathrooms and soon there was a long line outside of them. Remmy found herself near the back of the line standing next to Sandy.

'What's all the laughing about?' Sandy asked her.

'Nothing,' she gave Sandy a strained smile.

'Remmy, I know you know. Tell me?'

'It's cool here, isn't it?' Remmy tried to change the subject.

Sandy folded her arms and glared at her.

'Can you please just tell me?'

'Okay,' Remmy sighed. 'Someone started a rumor that you were the one who did the smelly fart.'

Sandy gave a horrified look and her face reddened.

'B-but I didn't do it,' she blurted out. 'Who started the rumor?'

'I don't know,' Remmy gave her an awkward look. 'I wouldn't worry about it, people know that rumors are usually made-up.'

'Yeah, I guess,' she muttered.

Sandy noticed that some of the other kids were looking over at her. They were laughing and pointing at her! Sandy wanted the floor to engulf her, she wasn't used to having rumors spread about her and she didn't like it.

Remmy didn't know what else to say to Sandy so she just smiled at her. She didn't think that the rumor about Sandy was very nice but she also didn't think that it was very serious. Sandy had never hesitated in spreading mean rumors about other people and at least this one was sort of funny. Still, she thought it was a mean thing to do and found herself wondering again...who had started it.

The girls' bathroom queue seemed slow moving, so by the time Sandy got out of there most of the other kids were back in the tunnel sitting on their sleeping bags. She tried to ignore the sniggers aimed at her as she walked over to her friends.

'You've been ages,' Rach said.

'Yeah, the queue was long,' she sighed.

'I don't want to go back with Mr. Boring B, I want to stay here and watch the fish swim by,' Susie stared through the glass.

'I know, right? Mr. Boring is totally trying to ruin this trip with his lame facts, don't you think so Sandy?'

Sandy was looking down at her sleeping bag. Someone had poured yogurt all over it.

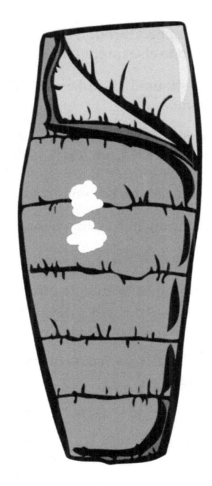

'Sandy, don't you think that Mr. B is lame?' Rach asked.

'Yeah, I guess,' she rooted through her bag and took out a tissue. 'Did either of you see who spilled yogurt on my sleeping bag?'

'No,' Rach shook her head.

'No, sorry Sandy,' Susie shrugged.

'Great!'

'We can help you get rid of it though, I think I packed some face wipes,' Rach searched through her bag. 'Oh, it looks like I forgot them. Someone else might have some, I could ask?'

'No!' Sandy almost shouted. 'It's okay, this tissue's working fine,' she forced a smile.

The tissue had dissolved in her hand and she now had yogurt and mushed up tissue on her. She didn't want the other kids to know about this though, she was getting teased enough without them calling her yogurt girl.

'Here,' Susie tried wiping at it with a tissue.

'Thanks,' Sandy muttered.

The yogurt was now smudged across more of her sleeping bag. It smelt bad now...so she knew that it would stink through the night.

'I'm going to go and wash my hands quickly,' she hurried off before they could reply.

'Sandy, do you need the toilet again?' Sydney shouted out.

This caused more laughter from some of the kids. Sandy just huffed and quickened her pace. Tonight was supposed to be fun, but currently, it was anything but. She wanted to cover whoever had spread that mean rumor in stinky yogurt and see how they liked it.

When she walked back into the tunnel Miss Sutherland tapped her watch as she looked at her.

'Sandy, you're late.'

'Sorry Miss,' she muttered.

'Maybe she should just stay in the toilets,' Colin shouted.

Most of the kids laughed and Sandy felt her face redden.

'Who wants to see some sharks?' Mr. B asked.

There were excited cheers and Mike gave a wide grin.

'Come on then,' he waved them all forwards. 'The sharks are waiting for us.'

Mike rushed to the front of the line and eagerly followed Mr. B. Remmy smiled at this, she liked seeing Mike so happy.

'Money well spent,' she thought to herself.

'Hi Remmy,' Charlie sidled up to her. 'I've never seen Mike move so fast,' he chuckled.

'Yeah, he really likes sharks.'

'So, how long have you two, you know?' he flustered out.

'Mike and I are just friends. He was kind to me, even after I was mean to him. He's a good person.'

'Ah, okay,' Charlie couldn't hide his smile.

Remmy smiled back; did this mean that he still liked her? She hoped so because she still liked Charlie like crazy.

'The shark tank is really cool,' he said.

'I've never seen a shark before,' she couldn't hide the nervousness from her voice.

'Don't worry, I'll look after you,' he said sweetly.

'Thanks, Charlie.'

As they neared the shark tank room Remmy began to feel anxious. She didn't want the other kids to know that she was worried but she didn't know what to expect. Charlie reached over and grabbed her hand and smiled at her. She instantly felt herself relax and mouthed the word 'thanks' as she smiled at him.

They shuffled along the line and entered the shark tank room. It was as wide as it was high and the water glistened and rippled as the sharks zoomed past. Remmy stared open-mouthed and watched as a spear-shaped tail whizzed past her. She saw Mike with his hands pressed to the glass; he was gawping at a huge shark with a hammer-shaped head.

Charlie was looking at a massive shark, it was at least double the size of the others and she didn't want to get any closer to it. She pressed Charlie's hand, thanked him again and then squeezed her way past the other kids and then she stopped by Mike.

'Hi,' she smiled at him.

'Hey,' he quickly glanced at her before he looked back at the shark.

'It's amazing, isn't it?'

She noticed how the shark's eyes were on each side of its head. They reminded her of the googly eyes found on some stuffed toys and she realized that she didn't feel afraid anymore.

'Yeah, it's impressive.'

'It's a Hammerhead shark. I have a poster of one on my bedroom wall, I never thought that I'd ever get to see one for real.'

'Now you have,' she smiled.

'Yeah, now I have,' he grinned.

Remmy felt good. Seeing Mike happy confirmed that using her birthday money for him to come on the trip was the right thing to do. The Hammerhead shark swan off and Mike immediately followed it. She stayed where she was and smiled.

As she peered through the glass at the sharks...an awful smell wafted past her.

It was far worse than the smell from before and she put her hand over her nose. The other kids moaned in disgust and gagged as the smell reached them and even Mr. B quickly placed both his hands over his nose and mouth.

Miss Sutherland tried to hold her breath as she walked over to Sandy. She reluctantly took a breath of air in and then coughed out.

'Do you need to go the toilet again?' she quietly asked her.

'It wasn't me,' Sandy protested. 'Why are you accusing me? It wasn't me the first time either.'

Miss Sutherland gave a nod of her head. The smell became too much for her so she placed her hand up to her nose and pinched her nostrils tightly.

'Follow me, let's go into the next room,' she shouted.

All of the kids rushed out of there, apart from Mike who reluctantly peered back at the hammerhead shark. The awful smell hadn't deterred him from being close to his favorite shark.

Sandy trudged into the next room and folded her arms. Most of the kids were laughing and looking at her. She could feel herself growing in anger, so she lingered near the back of the room and tried to feign interest in a tank of seahorses that was fixed to the wall.

'Sandy stinks,' Sophie said to Melody, as she waved her hand in front of her face.

'She should come with a warning sign, her farts are hazardous,' Colin sniggered.

'Stop it guys,' Sydney grinned. 'She can't help it.'

This was met with roaring laughter, it echoed off the walls and rang through Sandy's ears.

'Shut up!' she shouted. 'Stop saying I did it, it wasn't me!'

'I think everyone's overexcited. You all need to remember that we are Mr. B's guests and therefore we need to be on our best behavior. I think we should all go back to the tunnel, grab our toothbrushes and brush our teeth and then settle down for bed,' Miss Sutherland said.

'That's an excellent idea,' Mr. B smiled. 'Once you are in your sleeping bags you can all watch the fish swan past you. It's very relaxing.'

The kids chatted amongst themselves as they followed Mr. B and Miss Sutherland back to the tunnel. Sandy trudged behind Rach and Susie with her arms folded. Her friends sensed her bad mood so they didn't dare talk to her, instead they made comments about how funny the clownfish looked.

'Having a good laugh, are you?' Sandy snapped at them.

'I was just telling Rach that the fish looked funny,' Susie said.

'Likely story,' Sandy huffed.

'It's true,' Rach added. '*Finding Nemo* is sooo overrated. My little cousin watches it on repeat! But I think clown fish looks beautiful and they are so funny the way they chase each other around the coral.'

'Whatever,' Sandy grunted.

'Sandy, are you okay?' Rach asked her.

'I'm fine,' she snapped. 'Why wouldn't I be?'

'No reason,' she exchanged a look with Susie.

'What was that look for?'

'Nothing Sandy. We're just worried about you, that's all.'

'Sorry,' she shook her head. 'Maybe I'm just tired.'

'That's okay,' Rach smiled. 'I'm tired too, I didn't sleep very well last night because I was sooo excited.'

'Me neither,' Susie added.

'Same,' Sandy sighed.

She had been looking forward to this trip all week but it wasn't turning out how she thought it would. It was supposed to be an amazing experience but right now she longed for it to end.

Remmy sat down on top of her sleeping bag and watched the fish swim past her. Bridget and Mike were talking about sharks and Sydney was in the restroom. Charlie was sitting on his sleeping bag and he kept on smiling at her.

'I'm glad I'm here with you,' Charlie said.

'I'm glad I'm here with you too.' Remmy's heartbeat began to race.

'Although Miss Sutherland is living in cloudland if she thinks anyone's going to be sleeping anytime soon,' he grinned.

Remmy looked around the tunnel. It was full of kids excitedly talking and their voices echoed through the tunnel.

'I think you're right,' she smiled.

She wanted to remain in that moment with Charlie for as long as she could but she looked over at Sandy and noticed how glum she looked. She deliberated on what she should do.

'Charlie, I won't be long,' she grabbed her toothbrush and toothpaste and then stood up.

'Okay, Remmy,' he smiled at her.

She walked over to Sandy. She didn't notice her coming as she was looking down at her phone.

'Hi Sandy,' she said.

'Oh, hi,' she grunted.

'Are you okay?'

'Not really,' she continued to look at her phone. 'I'm really mad that someone started that rumor. Even my own friends don't want to be around me now.'

'I'm sure that's not true,' she looked around and spotted

Rach and Susie further along the tunnel. They were talking to Sophie and Melody.

'Yeah,' Sandy rolled her eyes.

'It's cool here though, isn't it? I mean, all the fish and everything?'

'I guess,' she shrugged.

'Sleeping here's going to be so cool.'

Sandy sighed and then threw her phone down onto her yogurt stained sleeping bag.

'I'm going to brush my teeth; do you want to come with me?' she smiled.

'I suppose so,' she muttered.

'Great.'

Sandy riffled through her rucksack and pulled out her sparkly pink toiletries bag. They both walked alongside each other in silence. As they walked into the bathroom two girls walked out. When they saw Sandy they began to giggle. Sandy felt the anger grow inside her but she didn't confront the girls.

'It will soon blow over,' Remmy said.

Sandy grunted and then quickly walked away from her. When Remmy caught up with her she saw her standing open-mouthed...staring at one of the toilet cubicle doors. Written on it in a black marker was a message.

'Did you do this?' Sandy glared at her.

'No, of course not!' Remmy looked hurt. 'I would never do something like that.'

'Well, who then?'

'I don't know,' she shook her head before she shoved her toothbrush and toothpaste into her jacket pocket and then rushed into the cubicle and grabbed some toilet paper.

She dampened it and then began to scrub at the message.

'That won't work,' Sandy sighed.

Sandy took a flannel out of her toiletry bag, wet it and then joined Remmy in trying to rub away the message. It barely smudged and the toilet paper in Remmy's hand was disintegrating and sticking to her fingers.

'It's no use,' Sandy shouted before she threw her flannel onto the floor.

'Calm down, we'll get rid of the message,' Remmy said.

'No, I won't calm down. Someone's written this about me,' she pointed at the message. 'It's okay for you. How would you like it if someone did something like this to you?'

Remmy put her hands on her hips and raised an eyebrow.

'I do know what it feels like Sandy,' she said as calmly as she could.

Sandy picked up the flannel off the floor and went back to scrubbing at the message. Remmy sighed before she gathered more toilet paper from the cubicle and helped Sandy scrub at the message.

It took them twenty-minutes and Remmy now had a red hand from all the rubbing, but the marker was now faded enough to be illegible. All the girls who had walked into the bathroom in that time took one look at Sandy's angry expression and knew better than to say anything to her.

When they'd finished, Sandy looked at the cubicle door,

sighed and then stormed out of the bathrooms without giving Remmy as much as a thank you. This annoyed Remmy, she'd spent ages helping Sandy get rid of the message, even after she'd accused her of writing it, so some appreciation would have been nice. Still, she understood how Sandy was feeling. Having mean messages written about you wasn't much fun.

She brushed her teeth and then left the bathroom. She returned to her friends, relieved that she wasn't stuck in the bathroom with a moody Sandy anymore.

'The wanderer returns,' Bridget giggled. 'We thought you were lost.'

'Sorry, I got distracted,' she blushed.

'I was about to send the girls to look for you,' Charlie grinned.

'No way was I moving, I'm comfortable,' Sydney said.

Her pillows were plumped up behind her head, she had a pink eye-mask rested on top of her head and she was zipped up in her sleeping bag.

Remmy glanced over at Sandy, she was curled up in her sleeping bag and her head was turned away from her friends. She felt bad for her, this trip should have been an amazing experience for her but it hadn't turned out that way.

'Remmy, are you okay?' Mike asked.

'Yes, thanks Mike,' she looked away from Sandy. 'Are you having a good time?'

'The best,' he grinned.

'I can't wait till midnight,' Bridget said.

'Why?' Charlie asked.

'Midnight is feast time, of course. I brought supplies,' she opened up her backpack to reveal a load of potato chips and chocolate.

'I just brushed my teeth,' Remmy said.

'So,' she shrugged.

'I'll have the chips but chocolate at midnight is super bad for the metabolism,' Sydney said.

'I'll eat the chocolate,' Charlie replied.

'Me too,' Mike grinned.

'I'm not going to turn down chocolate,' Remmy giggled.

'Eek,' Bridget clapped her hands together. 'This is the best sleepover ever!'

They continued to chat quietly to each other, then when midnight arrived Bridget discreetly passed her food out between them. The others fell asleep before Remmy did, so she watched the fish swim past her. She found herself looking over at Sandy and wondering whom it was that was bullying her.

Chapter Nine- Not a Happy Girl

The next morning the kids gathered up their belongings and made their way to the aquarium foyer. Remmy hugged her pillow as she listened to her friends talk.

'That was the coolest sleepover ever,' Bridget said.

'Yep, it totally was,' Sydney smiled. 'Even though this aquarium isn't as big as the one in New York, I had a great time.'

'It was the best time, with the best friends,' Remmy yawned.

'Remmy, I think you need an early night,' Bridget chuckled.

'I think you're right,' she chuckled.

'You should have brought earplugs with you,' Sydney said.

'I didn't want to sleep, I wanted to keep on watching the fish swim past me.'

'You should buy a fish tank,' Mike suggested.

'That'd be cool.'

'I don't think you'd be able to keep a shark in it,' Charlie grinned.

'Shame, that would be awesome.'

'Bye guys,' Bridget said, as she spotted her mom in the foyer. 'See you tomorrow,' she gave them a wave as she hurried across the foyer.

Janice and Marcus showed up so Remmy said bye to her friends and walked over to her mom and stepdad.

'Did you have a good time sweetie?' her mom smiled.

'Yes thanks, the best.'

'That's good,' Marcus said, as he took her pillow and sleeping bag from her.

Sandy trudged over to them, shoved her sleeping bag at her dad and then marched out of the foyer.

Janice shot Marcus a look and he shrugged.

'She's probably just tired,' he said.

Remmy gave her friends a wave and then followed her mom and Marcus out of the aquarium foyer. She felt sad that the night was over as she'd had an amazing time that she'd never forget. She was so relieved that she had her friends back, as this trip would have been horrible if she hadn't been able to hang out with them.

She passed her bag to Marcus and he placed it into the trunk of the car, then she got into the back next to a glum-looking Sandy.

'Who wants to stop off at Pop's for breakfast?' Janice asked.

'That sounds great,' Remmy smiled.

Sandy grunted and then buried her head in her arms.

'So, did you girls have a great time?' Janice asked.

'Yes, it was amazing. There were so many different types of fish and we got to sleep in the tunnel right by the glass. It was so relaxing.'

'It sounds lovely.'

'I'll take you there sometime,' Marcus said.

'I'd like that,' she smiled.

'So, tell me more about the aquarium, did you see any sharks?'

'Yes, they had ten different types. They were cool, weren't they Sandy?' Remmy asked. Sandy didn't reply.

'I remember going on a school trip when I was your age and we dared each other to stay awake all night. I was a zombie for days afterward,' Marcus chuckled.

'I think you're both in need of an early night.'

'I'm not tired,' Sandy grunted, without looking up.

Marcus and Janice exchanged looks. They thought that Sandy was only saying that because she was tired and didn't want to admit that she had stayed up for most of the night.

'Did you have a good date night?' Remmy asked.

'Yes, thank you. We went to this lovely restaurant and I tried lobster for the first time, it was terrifying and exciting at the same time,' Janice laughed.

'Although you did nearly take the man on the next table's eye out because you couldn't work the lobster cracker,' Marcus smirked.

'Marcus, we agreed not to mention that again,' she blushed and gave a soft giggle.

'I think you did a great job darling,' he smiled at her. 'We should have another date night soon.'

'I'd like that,' she smiled back.

Remmy was glad that her mom and Marcus had enjoyed their night. Her mom certainly seemed happy, which made her happy too. She hoped that this was it and that they wouldn't argue again.

'The food was delicious, I still feel full,' Marcus said.

'It was but I still have room left for pancakes.'

'If our tired girls can stay awake long enough to eat them,' he chuckled.

'I'm not tired,' Sandy mumbled. 'In fact, sleeping was the best part of the trip.'

'Sandy, are you okay?' Janice asked.

'No,' she muttered. 'No, I'm not.'

'I'm sure pancakes will cheer you up. Or a milkshake, it's not too early for a milkshake, is it?' she looked at Marcus.

'I'm not hungry!' she shouted. 'I just want to home!'

'Pumpkin, what happened?' he asked.

'Why don't you ask her?' Sandy scowled at Remmy.

'Maybe we should just go home, I can make pancakes there,' Janice quietly said to Marcus.

'Maybe that's for the best darling.'

For the rest of the drive home, there was silence. Sandy kept her head buried in her arms, Remmy stared out of the window and Janice and Marcus exchanged a worried glance at the prospect of yet more drama.

As soon as they pulled up on the driveway, Sandy got out of the car, slammed the door behind her and stormed off into the house.

'Remmy, what's going on?' Janice asked.

Remmy didn't want to answer because she knew that this would cause more tension. She couldn't lie to her mom and Marcus though; they deserved to hear the truth.

'Well, erm, someone is bullying Sandy by doing mean things to her. I don't know who it is though, they wrote a mean message on the cubicle door but we didn't see who did it.'

Marcus rushed off into the house but Janice stayed behind.

'Sweetie, thank you for telling us. We'll get the bags later, why don't you go and wait in the kitchen and I'll be in there shortly to make pancakes.'

Remmy nodded and then watched her mom hurry off after Marcus.

She didn't go into the kitchen, as she didn't feel hungry anymore. Instead, she went up to her bedroom and sat on her bed. Last night had been one of the best nights of her life but instead of reliving how great it was, she was stuck in yet another drama caused by Sandy.

She could hear sobbing coming from Sandy's room which soon turned into yelling. She looked up when she heard her name being said but she couldn't make out the rest of the conversation. Surely, Sandy wasn't blaming her, was she? Remmy had tried to help her scrub the message off the cubicle and she'd been nice to her.

Deciding that it was out of her control she turned her laptop on and scrolled through her FB newsfeed. It was full of pictures from the aquarium and she found herself reminiscing about how great it had been. She liked a selfie of Colin posing by a shark and she liked another picture of a group of colorful fish. She paused when she got to the next picture, it was a close up of the message on the cubicle door:

DANGER!
DO NOT ENTER
ONLY FOR o
SMELLY BUM SANDY

It had been posted by a girl with curly chestnut hair. She didn't recognize her and she wasn't FB friends with her, she could only see the post because several of FB friends had laughed at it and liked it. She thought that these were probably the kids who had been picked on by Sandy in the past. Then someone new liked the picture; it was Mike. She couldn't blame him; after-all Sandy and the vampires had been horrible to him.

She clicked on the curly haired girl's profile. She only had the one picture and she was only friends with kids from school, so it was clearly a fake profile. This made Remmy feel sick, she wasn't Sandy's biggest fan but she knew how horrible it was having mean things posted about you by fake profiles. She was also afraid that Sandy would think that she had done this in an attempt to gain revenge.

There was a knock on Remmy's door and she quickly shut

the lid of her laptop.

'Come in,' she said.

Janice peered her head around the door.

'Remmy, please can you come into Sandy's room so we can have a chat.'

Remmy gave a nod before she got up and walked over to her mom. She had butterflies flapping in her stomach as she followed her into Sandy's room. She tried to reassure herself that she hadn't done anything wrong but the uneasy feeling remained in her stomach.

Sandy was sitting on the edge of her bed; her eyes were swollen from crying and her arms were folded. Marcus was next to her; he had his arm around her shoulders and a distressed look on his face.

Both Janice and Remmy lingered in the middle of the room. Marcus glared at Remmy but Sandy stared at her feet.

'Sandy has told us what happened, do you know anymore about it?' her mom asked.

'No,' she shook her head. 'Only that someone spread a rumor about her and then wrote that mean message on the cubicle door.'

'But you don't know who did it?'

'No,' she shook her head again.

'Phffft,' Marcus said under his breath.

'I didn't do it!' Remmy protested. 'I would never do something like that.'

'Sweetie, are you sure you don't know who it was?' her

mom asked again.

'No, I don't know,' she sighed.

She felt like her mom was accusing her and that hurt. How could her mom think that she could be a bully?

'Can I go now?' she muttered.

'Sweetie, we just want to know what happened. If you did this then you need to be honest about it,' her mom gave her a pleading look.

'I didn't do it!' she shouted. I would never do such a horrible thing, I'm not mean like Sandy.'

'See, I told you it was her,' Marcus snapped.

'It wasn't me!' Remmy shouted again.

'Can you blame her, she was bullied by your daughter for months,' Janice retaliated.

'I didn't do it!' Remmy shouted before she stormed out of the room.

She slammed her bedroom door shut and slumped down onto her bed. Hot tears began to stream down her cheeks, she tried wiping them away but they were soon replaced by fresh ones. Sandy and Marcus thinking that she was capable of bullying wasn't as hurtful as her mom believing this.

She sat there sobbing until her sadness developed into anger. She was mad with Sandy for blaming her and she was mad at her mom for believing Sandy over her. She lifted the lid on her laptop, stared at the photo of the cubicle door and then she clicked on the like button. She closed her laptop lid, lay down on her bed and stared up at her ceiling. As her anger began to mellow down...the guilt set in. Liking that photo was the wrong thing to do, it was mean and hurtful and she knew that she shouldn't have done it.

She grabbed her laptop and went onto FB, hoping that she'd be able to unlike the comment before Sandy saw it. She chewed on the side of her lip as she stared at the comment that had been written below the picture, it was from Sandy.

You're all mean, I hate you all! And it wasn't me, it was Remmy!!!

Remmy unliked the photo and then quickly wrote a private message to Sandy.

>I'm sorry for liking the picture, I was mad but I shouldn't have done that. It wasn't me who wrote that message on the cubicle door, I would never do something like that. I hope you're okay?

She picked at her nails as she stared at her laptop screen. She didn't expect Sandy to reply to her, but still she found herself unable to look away. Her laptop dinged and she felt her heart thud as she stared at her messages, a message from Bridget popped up.

>Hey BFF, do you want to meet up for a shake?

>YES! Can we meet at the mall right now, please?

>See you at the fountain in fifteen minutes :)

She instantly felt better, leaving the atmosphere of the house for a bit and seeing her best friend was just what she needed. She had a quick shower, changed into a loose top and some black leggings and tied her hair into a ponytail. Her mom and Marcus were in their bedroom with the door shut, so she left a note on the kitchen table telling them where she was going.

She arrived at the mall to find Bridget already waiting for

her by the fountain. When she saw Remmy she beamed as she ran over to her.

'How are you feeling? Are you tired? I'm not, I'm still buzzing, last night was amazing, wasn't it?' Bridget rambled out.

'Yep, it was,' she forced a smile.

The aquarium trip had been amazing but all Remmy could think about was the Sandy drama.

'No school trip will ever top that.'

'Nah, it won't,' she sighed.

'Remmy, are you okay?' Bridget stared at her.

'Sorry, it's just Sandy causing problems again. She's told my mom and Marcus that I wrote that mean message on the cubicle door.'

'Surely they know that you'd never do something like that? Sandy knows it too, she's probably just upset.'

'My mom seems to think it was me,' she felt her eyes welling up and quickly wiped her tears with the back of her sleeve. 'Even though I'm the one who helped Sandy scrub the message away. My hand's still red,' she held out her reddened palm.

'Remmy, you're not a bully, Sandy is. She's bullied so many kids at school so it's about time someone was mean to her. Maybe now she'll realize how much it hurts to be picked on and will think twice before she does it again,' she snorted. 'Although that's doubtful.'

'You're probably right,' she gave a thoughtful sigh.

'It's a definite,' she grinned. 'Now, come on. We have

98

shopping to do,' she yanked on her arm.

Remmy felt better about things now, Bridget made a lot of sense. Sandy was a bully and now she was being bullied...but it had nothing to do with Remmy. She was kind to her, even after everything Sandy and her friends had put her through. She had nothing to feel guilty about, and hopefully her home situation would have calmed down.

Bridget took her into a music shop that had opened last week. It had old concert posters stuck to the walls and the ceiling, and some eighties' song that Remmy had never heard before was blaring out. The shop was full of retro vinyls, which Bridget thought was great because she liked to listen to old songs on her mom's record player. They both got involved in searching through the stacks of records and reading the back of ones that caught their eye. Remmy was enjoying herself so much that she'd actually forgotten about Sandy for a bit.

Suddenly two hands covered their eyes from behind them.

'Guess who?' a girl's voice said.

Remmy froze on the spot, she didn't know who it was but she felt uncomfortable.

'Sydney, I know it's you,' Bridget grinned.

'You got me,' Sydney giggled, as she moved her hands away.

Bridget turned around and greeted Sydney with a hug. Remmy smiled at Sydney and then gave her an awkward wave. She didn't know her well enough to feel comfortable hugging her in a shop but she didn't want to appear rude.

'Wasn't the school trip awesome?' Sydney gave a sly smirk.

'Yes, it was amazing,' Bridget grinned.

'It was so funny what happened to Sandy. She's is such a horrible person, she totally got what she deserved,' she grinned.

'Yeah, totally. It's about time she knew what it felt like to be bullied,' Bridget replied.

'She thinks she can treat people however she wants but then expects everyone to be nice to her. She needs to realize that she's not the number one girl in our class.'

'Well, whoever wrote that message sure showed her up. They should get a medal.'

Remmy remained quiet. She wasn't comfortable talking about Sandy like this so she decided it was better not to say anything. She found herself zoning out as she thought about how happy Sydney seemed at Sandy's expense. Could Sydney have written the mean message about Sandy? Remmy shook her head, Sydney had been so kind to her over the *Remmy No Friends* incident. She'd never do something so mean, would she?

'Earth to Remmy, earth to Remmy. Come in Remmy,' Bridget waved her arms in front of her.

'Oh, um, sorry,' she muttered.

'It's okay,' Bridget chuckled.

'Where were you?' Sydney gave her a questioning look.

'Sorry, I zoned out. I guess I'm just tired,' she shrugged.

'I don't feel too bad, I slept okay,' Sydney replied.

'I wanted to stay up all night and watch the fish swim past but I was too tired.'

'I know what we need. Sugar!' Sydney smiled. 'Why are you in here anyway, this shop kinda sucks?' she stuck up her nose as she peered around the shop.

'No reason,' Bridget blushed, as she quickly placed the vinyl she was holding back on the rack.

'You came in here,' Remmy looked at Sydney.

'Only because I saw you both through the window,' she remarked. 'Anyway, let's go and get donuts; my treat.'

'Thanks, Sydney,' Bridget grinned.

'Thanks,' Remmy smiled.

Sydney linked her arms through Remmy and Bridget's and led them out of the shop. Remmy glanced at a glossy-haired Sydney, sure, she was super confident and a bit outspoken but she was also really nice. She decided that it couldn't be her bullying Sandy and that it must have been someone else.

Chapter Ten- Trouble is in the Air!

Remmy had spent the rest of the weekend trying to avoid Sandy, which wasn't as difficult as she thought it'd be, as Sandy barely left her bedroom. She'd also tried to avoid her mom but she seemed to appear like a shadow around each corner of the house and give what Remmy thought were suspicious looks.

Monday morning arrived and brought with it a grumpy Sandy. She trudged her way into the kitchen and slumped down next to Remmy at the breakfast bar without so much as looking at her. Remmy thought about saying something to her but decided that it was better to stay quiet. Last time she'd tried to be nice to Sandy it had resulted in her getting the blame; she didn't want to be accused again or receive a rude comment.

Janice wasn't there as she'd gone to work early, which made Remmy feel both relieved and uncomfortable. She loved her mom but it hurt her a lot to think that her mom thought she was a bully. She didn't want her accusing glare on her but at the same time, she didn't want her to be so ashamed of her daughter that she left for work early. Remmy sighed as she stared down into her bowl of soggy cereal.

'Girls, are you ready?' Marcus said from the doorway.

Remmy got down from her chair, grabbed her backpack and then hurried over to him, while Sandy slowly got down from her chair and then trudged her way across the room.

A Katy Perry song was on the car radio and even Marcus was humming along to it. Normally this would amuse Sandy and Remmy but it didn't today. Remmy sat in the back seat and stared out of the window and Sandy sat in the front with her arms folded and a frown on her face.

'Pumpkin, if anyone gives you trouble today then let me know,' Marcus smiled at her.

'Yeah, I will,' she grunted.

'They probably would have forgotten about it by now.'

'Yeah,' she snickered.

'You're worth more than those horrible bullies,' he commented.

Remmy sank down further into her seat; she knew that his snide comment was aimed at her. The car journey seemed never-ending! Marcus finally pulled up at school, Remmy shouted 'thanks' as she hurried out of the car. She rushed over to Bridget, who was waving at her from the school steps.

'Hi Remmy, are you okay?' she smiled at her.

'I am now,' she muttered.

'Okay,' Bridget gave her a skeptical look.

'I'm just happy to be here.'

'Even if we have double math?' she groaned.

'Yes, because I get to be with my friends.'

'Yeah, I suppose we are worth the double math,' she grinned.

Sandy elbowed Remmy in the arm as she barged past her. Rach and Susie scowled at them as they hurried after her.

'Did you smell something?' Bridget said loudly to Remmy.

Remmy gave an awkward look and then stared down at her feet.

'Come on, she deserves it,' Bridget said.

Remmy understood why Bridget didn't like Sandy but her

comments were making her feel uncomfortable. Bridget was normally so happy and friendly but her dislike toward Sandy and her vampires had morphed her into someone different, someone that Remmy didn't recognize. Maybe Bridget had been the one who wrote the mean message about Sandy? She tried to shake this thought away but it wouldn't budge. Could kind-hearted, caring Bridget really have been capable of doing that?

'Anyway, we'd better go to class. Can't be late for our favorite subject,' Bridget grinned before she grabbed Remmy's arm and pulled her along.

The more Remmy thought about it, the more she decided that there was no way that it could have been Bridget. As much as she didn't like Sandy, she wouldn't have done something like that. She wasn't just a good person...she was the best person.

When they got to class, Miss Sutherland was already sitting at her desk, so they smiled at each other before they hurried over to their seats. Remmy whispered 'hi' to Sydney as she sat down next to her. She smiled back at her before she continued to line up the contents of her pencil case.

As Miss Sutherland began to ramble on about percentages...Remmy found herself staring at the back of Sandy's head. Sandy was spiteful, cruel and malicious and she had made it pretty clear that she had preferred her life before Janice and Remmy had moved in. Could she have written the message herself to turn Marcus and Janice against Remmy? She tried to shake the thought out of her head. Sure, Sandy was manipulative but there's no way that she'd want other kids laughing at her, as being popular was important to her. No, it couldn't have been Sandy. So, who was it?

105

The bell for the first break rang and Remmy stood up and waited by her desk for Sydney to finish what she was writing. She looked around the classroom and noticed that Sandy and her vampires had cornered Melody and were talking to her.

'Math on a Monday morning should be banned,' Sydney said, as she put down her pen.

Remmy didn't hear her; her focus was on the vampires. They had left Melody now and were walking away from her.

'Remmy, did you hear a word I said?' Sydney glared at her.

'Sorry, I think I must still be tired from the trip.'

She watched as a flustered looking Melody dug around in her backpack.

'I made sure I had my beauty sleep,' she flicked out her hair.

'I'll be back in a minute, I just need to ask Melody something.'

Remmy hurried over to Melody and stood in front of her. She was too busy looking through her backpack to notice her.

'Hi Melody,' she said.

Melody looked up with a start but relaxed when she saw that it was Remmy.

'Oh, hi,' she gave a weak smile.

'Um, I was just wondering what Sandy, Rach, and Susie were saying to you?' she probed.

'They asked me if I know who's responsible for the FB post,' she looked concerned. 'I told them that it wasn't me.'

'Thanks, Melody,' Remmy smiled at her.

Melody gave a nod of her head in Remmy's direction before she scurried out of the room. Sydney was waiting by the classroom door with her arms folded.

'If all of the raisin muffins have gone, I'm blaming you,' she raised an eyebrow.

'Sorry,' she muttered.

'Come on,' Sydney pulled on her arm.

They walked into the cafeteria to see that Sandy and her vampires were standing close to the table that Charlie and Bridget were sitting at.

'What do *they* want?' Sydney remarked.

They walked over to the table and Sydney gently pushed Rach out of the way so that she could sit down next to Charlie. Remmy tried to avoid eye contact with Sandy, as she sat down next to Bridget.

'Can you guys smell that,' Sydney wafted her hand in front of her face.

'Yep, smells real bad to me,' Bridget giggled.

Remmy noticed that Charlie was grinning too. It seemed that everyone found what had happened to Sandy funny, except for her.

Mike walked over to them, a carton of apple juice in his hand. Before he could get to the table Sandy and her friends stepped out in front of him, blocking his path.

'Move,' he grunted.

'Make me,' Sandy folded her arms and glared at him.

'Whatever,' he tried to walk past her but she quickly stepped back so that she was blocking him again.

Rach and Susie both sniggered, as they moved closer to Sandy.

'We know it was you,' Sandy scowled at him.

'As if I'd go in the girl's toilets,' he snorted.

'Well, then you know who did it, and you're going to tell us?' Rach snarled.

'I don't know who did it but whoever it was gets a thumbs up from me,' he gave a thumbs up.

'You're a loser Mike and no one likes you,' Sandy remarked.

'No one wrote a mean comment about me, they wrote it about you. Have you asked yourself why that is?' he said taking a sip of his apple juice. 'It's because you're a horrible person. All of you,' he looked at Rach and then at Susie.

'Says the freak who has no friends!' Sandy shouted.

'Actually, he does have friends,' Remmy waved him over.

Mike stepped around them and walked over to Remmy.

'Thanks,' he said, as he placed his lunch on the table and then sat down next to her.

'No problem,' she smiled. 'Ignore Sandy, she's been a grouch ever since she got back from the aquarium.'

'Those girls are ridiculous,' Sydney said.

'I know,' he sighed.

Remmy peered across the room and saw that the vampires were now harassing Colin.

'They are just silly little girls who think they are far more important than everyone else,' Sydney said.

'I used to think that they were okay but not anymore. They are bullies,' Charlie said.

'They're pathetic,' Sydney remarked. 'They are painful, stuck-up little witches who like to rule over everyone. I think it's time they learned they're not so special.'

'Totally,' Bridget grinned.

Remmy found the uncomfortable feeling returning to her. She didn't agree with the way that the vampires were behaving but she didn't like the mean things her friends were saying about them. They knew how hard she'd tried to settle the situation; even after all of the cruel things the vampires had done to her. She believed that Charlie and Bridget would never do anything to unsettle the situation. Mike didn't like the vampires but he kept to himself, besides, the message was in the girls' bathroom. That left Sydney, the trouble had started when she'd arrived here and she clearly didn't like the vampires. Could it have been her?

'Look out,' Bridget looked across the room.

They all followed her gaze and saw Sandy and her friends marching over to them.

'Here comes trouble,' Sydney smirked.

They stopped in front of the table and glared at everyone.

'All of the cowards in class say that it wasn't them, so which one of you lot was it? Own up now and we'll consider not beating you up too badly,' Sandy said snidely.

'Easy on Sandy, that's not a nice way to talk to people,' Charlie said.

'Sorry Charlie,' she fluttered her eyelashes at him.' I know that it wasn't you; you're so lovely and kind. I just don't trust the people you hang around with. I mean, why are you hanging around with them? You're damaging your reputation; you should hang around with us instead.'

Charlie stared at them open-mouthed.

Sydney scraped back her chair and stepped in front of the vampires.

'You might think that you're special but you're not. You're boring, ugly, nasty little girls and we want you to go away, NOW!'

Mike stood up and looked at the vampires.

'Yeah, go away. No one wants you here.'

'Who are you to talk? No one likes you,' Rach snorted.

Remmy stood up too and moved next to Mike.

'Sandy, I feel sorry for you. Believe me, I know what it's like to be bullied and it sucks. But I have to say that I really like Mike, he's a good friend.'

Sandy, Rach, and Susie all burst out laughing.

Charlie jumped to his feet and glared at them.

'That's it, we are sick of you horrible girls and my friends and I have had enough.'

They immediately stopped laughing and stared at him in shock.

'Fine, you lot stink anyway,' Sandy huffed before she gestured for her friends to follow her.

'No Sandy, you're the one who stinks,' Sydney called out, as she pinched her nostrils.

Sandy scowled back at her, before the three of them stormed off across the cafeteria.

All five kids smiled as they high-fived each other.

'The fab-five will never let the vampires be mean to us again,' Bridget called out.

'Too right!' Charlie said.

Remmy continued to smile, she was happy that she was part of this cool friendship group. Still, as she peered across the room and watched Sandy's golden hair disappear out of the room, she wondered if this would be the end of it.

***

Find out what happens next in

Mean Girls – Book 5: The Secret Bully

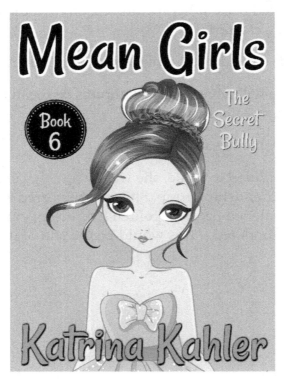

Thank you for reading Mean Girls Book 5!

We hope you loved it.

If you could please leave us a review,

it would be greatly appreciated.

Thank you!!!

Katrina xx

Made in the USA
Middletown, DE
03 February 2021

The OUTLAW STILL

Clayton Lindemuth

Hardgrave Enterprises
SAINT CHARLES, MISSOURI

THE OUTLAW STINKY JOE

Baer Creighton 4

CLAYTON LINDEMUTH
HARDGRAVE ENTERPRISES
SAINT CHARLES, MISSOURI

ALSO BY CLAYTON LINDEMUTH

TREAD

SOLOMON BULL

COLD QUIET COUNTRY

SOMETIMES BONE

NOTHING SAVE THE BONES INSIDE HER

MY BROTHER'S DESTROYER

THE MUNDANE WORK OF VENGEANCE

PRETTY LIKE AN UGLY GIRL

STRONG AT THE BROKEN PLACES

For Faith, Layla, and Wallace.

Rescued Pit Bull puppies

AND

THE BEST DOGS IN THE WORLD.

The last enemy to be destroyed is death.

— 1 Corinthians 15:26

Chapter 1

Stinky Joe wandered a channel of pavement cut through rows of trailers at the Mountain View Mobile Home and RV Resort. Should he find a few scraps to nourish him, beyond the park waited a small hill. Farther still, a lair where he spent the last few nights, curled and shaking.

He was three days hungry. His stomach had constricted to a ball, and his eyesight grew sharp. The long winter had passed but not without its toll. His coat stretched over his ribs. Below his eyes, the flesh was hollow, making their darkness sharp.

Other dogs had more hair. Over the frozen months, Joe rarely encountered them. When he did, they showed interest. Some were aggressive, and while his strength was high, he made abrupt ends to their confusion. More recently his fortitude waned, and he'd been careful to avoid them. Easy because, as winter matured, the other dogs also weakened.

Joe roamed at night, appraising terrain by scent and sound

before arriving.

Weakness dictated wariness. He would flee a well-fed housecat. But so far he'd only encountered one beast worthy of real fear.

The perplexing animal. Most times ruthless. Sometimes kind.

Like a conscious dream, he remembered curling in a man's sleeping bag, the scent of cheese mingling with the man's cabbage farts. The man laughed and grumbled.

The thought passed.

While he studied the hill ahead, a sound issued from a human living space, a trailer, to his front right. Joe darted behind a parked truck. Peered around the tire.

A door opened. Shapes were motionless under the streetlight glow. An ample woman extended a shadow, finally bursting free to become a separate form.

"Heeeere, doggie-dog."

The woman was not new to him. Each week she deposited a plastic bag in the snow that, disemboweled, revealed nourishing goodies. Breads. Bones. All manner of fermented and soured meats and treats.

He'd discovered her by scent, many weeks before. There'd been flurries that night, with wind. Hunger called him to root out each odor and eat whatever promised sustenance.

"Heeeere, doggie-dog. Mama's got tasty treats for you. Little shithead. Yes, you little shithead. Heeeere, doggie-dog."

Joe lurked.

She pitched left, right, and with each waddling step dragged a bag across the ground. His memory returned to the week before, the flesh and bones that burned hot though they were almost frozen. His mouth watered, and his hunger outweighed his fear.

Joe skulked forward from behind the truck tire. His body

tingled with dread; his stomach gnawed with desire. One foot ahead of the other.

"There you are."

The woman's tone was pleasant. She stopped walking. Released the bag from her hand and retreated.

"I've been waiting for you, you miserable wretch. Yeah, come on. Mama's got something yummy for you. Come get it, doggie-dog."

He waited.

The woman was soon behind the corner of the trailer, again hidden. The door closed gently—not like last time.

Her tone. Her manner. Her slow, careful walk. The quiet closing of the door. All sounded alarm.

But his intestines pulled themselves in knots, and the odor from the bag summoned.

Somewhere deep within his insentient existence bloomed a comprehension. Without food, he would soon no longer exist.

Joe stepped forward against his fear.

Chapter 2

Shirley Lyle smiled at the dog—one of the fighting breeds, a mastiff or pit bull or something. Wide frame. Blocky head.

"C'mere you little prick. Pricky pricky. C'mon. Mama's got something real good for you. Over here ... Mmm?"

Careful as she backed out of the trailer, Shirley pushed the door with her butt. In her hands, she balanced a steaming stainless steel bowl of beef broth, containing a surprise for the dog.

The little starving beast had shredded her garbage three weeks running. She had to go outside in the snow and gather cardboard and plastic—the only thing the he didn't eat. If she wanted refuse strewn across the lot, she could have done it herself. Clyde, trailer court slum-master, was ruthless about trash. So she put on her clothes, hat, coat and gloves. Tried to figure out how to get on all fours without the benefit of carpet friction.

Shirley Lyle weighed in a hundred pounds north of a big

girl.

The whole affair was ridiculous. Half bent over, she fell against an ice bank. After the big storm in February, a snow plow had shoved a six foot bank next to her car. Now it had melted to a foot, but was solid ice. Years of work had given her sensitive breasts. Slipping, her first thought was terror as she anticipated them smashing against ice.

At all costs, prevent damage to the mammage.

She flailed with her left arm, bruised her thigh and tweaked her shoulder.

Shirley landed on her rear end, and because of her luxurious body composition, no bones shattered. Instead, she bruised her upper buttock and lower back—exactly where Clyde slapped her while collecting rent.

There were plenty of other people who put out trash. Why had the dog singled her out for torment?

"C'mere, sweetie. Mama Lyle's gonna knock you out. C'mere, sugarbums. You'll love this, I promise."

Shirley looked at the half rotted steps. The stoop would do. Partly bending at the knees, partly at the back, she lowered the metal bowl to the deck and backed into the trailer. Closed the screen. The door.

And waited for the thud.

Shirley Lyle hailed from Florida. Born with acres of fair skin, after a year at community college, she moved to Seattle. It wasn't like she was leaving the family windfall behind. Her mother collected her dead father's Social Security and half his pension.

To pay rent and utilities, Shirley bussed tables, then waited them. For spending cash, she hooked on the side. She gave a discount to one of her steadies because she liked his cockney accent. He'd called her *me own sweet brass babe.*

When she bore her only child, not knowing brass babe meant prostitute, she'd named her son Brass. She was twenty one.

Over the next thirty hardscrabble years she raised him on love, rice, and beans. When her knees gave out she quit waitressing and got on Social Security Disability. Whoring had never been her ambition. She'd worked regular tax-paying jobs, but being both a flirt, and easy, she developed skills. She'd asked herself, why work for low wages using low skills, when she could exploit her other talents, and make better money?

Her hooking income remained steady, even after the injury. There were plenty of ways to conclude a man's arousal that didn't stress the knees too much.

She had regular clients but never a regular man. Brass grew up with an unclouded perspective on human sexuality. At puberty, he was ready to explore it. During his teens he considered himself bi. In his twenties, gay. Then he met a woman in San Francisco. He brought her home for Thanksgiving. When Mama Lyle stared, he explained, "She screwed me straight."

They could talk like that.

Brass was her pride and joy. One day soon, he'd be a U.S. Congressman. When he was young, she had been unable to provide all the toys and nonsense he craved. But she'd provided precarious finances, giving root to his success. He wanted better, and had her to thank.

Brass set his sights and started working. When he had something in mind he couldn't live without, he'd have it in short order. He could focus. He didn't so much overcome obstacles as fail to see them.

As a teen he'd read in some magazine at the laundromat that public speaking was fundamental to success. The article outlined a process for gaining experience. Join a Toastmasters group, then volunteer to give speeches at Rotary clubs.

"More power to you," she'd said. "I was you, I couldn't

do it. They'd laugh because I'm fat."

"You're fat, they're stupid. So what?"

Now, age fifty-five, she lived in a Flagstaff, Arizona mobile home park. Brass rented an apartment in Phoenix with his wife Claire and daughter Vanessa. He'd completed his master's in Human Services, and like everything else in his life, as soon as he conquered one goal, he set another. The U.S. Congress.

Shirley sat on the sofa. Brass's 8x10 high school graduation picture hung on the wall behind the television. He'd know what to do with the dog.

Shirley looked at the clock.

Funny the dog hadn't dropped to the deck yet. Shirley listened. Being mere skin and bones—perhaps it didn't have the weight to make a thud.

The situation should never have come to this. Flagstaff had a dog catcher. Animal control. She'd called, and the man promised to come out.

He came out.

But it was three in the afternoon, Monday. Not Tuesday night when she put out her garbage.

"What good does that do? You didn't want to work at night."

He looked at her. Up and down.

Shirley swallowed. "I'm a taxpayer," she said.

He smiled, dimples cracking his face. Judging her.

Brass would have beat the man silly.

Actually, Brass was a charmer. His name sounded like trouble, but he was all smooth talk and magnetism. It wasn't wrong for a mother to admire her son's handsomeness.

She eyed his photo. Wondered if she loved him so much because he was the only good thing to come out of her life.

Still no thump outside?

Shirley climbed up the side of the sofa. Careful to avoid walking on her heels and giving the dog warning, she returned to the door and twisted the knob. Eased it open.

Peered.

The stoop was empty.

The silver mixing bowl, licked clean.

No dog.

"You little turd."

She stepped out.

"Ah!"

The dog lay motionless on the driveway next to the bag of trash.

"Gotya."

She went back inside. From her bedroom she grabbed an unused leather belt and returned to the door.

She thought.

Anything else?

No.

She advanced to the porch and shivered. She'd only stay outside a couple minutes. And the trailer was hot. Shirley climbed down the steps. Shoved the dog with her foot.

Still as the dead.

She worked her way to her bruised knees and settled her weight on the side of her left thigh. Fed the belt through the metal loop and slipped the noose over the animal's head. Cinched it.

Keeping the other end of the sixty-inch leather strap in hand, she backed a few inches and began the process of climbing herself back erect.

She dragged the dog. At the steps, she found if she lifted straight up, then forward, his head cleared each eight-inch obstacle. With its head on the porch and its body draped like a slinky, the dog slid aboard when she tugged.

"You hurt my shoulder again, you die for sure."

Shirley dragged him inside the trailer. Back the hallway, past an unused bedroom on the opposite side of the home from her master suite. Another door down, the bathroom. She yanked him on the tile and navigated her body to the floor. Easy, with the toilet for support. She removed the leather strap from the animal's neck.

The dog's slitted eyes showed whites.

A moment later she was standing.

"What the hell am I doing?"

The dog must be crawling with fleas and ticks. Ebola. Who knew? It wore no collar, so it was likely wild from birth. It smelled horrible.

She should have used rat poison in the beef broth instead of her prescription Temazepam. Then left him with the other trash. But now he was inside. She leaned against the door jamb and thought through the same details as last time, several days before.

The idea came to her earlier in the shower: she needn't kill the little wretch, only kidnap him.

Dognap.

No more picking up the garbage.

Of course, Clyde hated dogs. Didn't permit them in the mobile home resort. Especially not inside one of his trailers. He'd been clear. One time she was paying rent with the back door. Clyde looked out the window and saw a neighbor leading a dog into his trailer. Clyde raged. Couldn't close his mouth long enough to finish. He had to stop and take a Viagra.

So she'd bathe the beast, even though it was feral. To conceal the dog stink, she'd coat him in baby powder. He'd be happier, smelling perfumed and clean.

But she couldn't allow him in her home for days on end, unclean. The bath had to be first.

Second.

First, sedation. She'd given him enough Temazepam to render a rabid wolf comatose for half a day. She thought.

Shirley stepped over the dog and, at the tub, set the plug. She twisted the hot and cold water faucets. Three quarters for the hot, one for the cold. Fifteen years in the same single-wide, you know things.

"All right, douchebag. Don't wake up."

She stooped. Dug below his shoulders. Heaved.

The dog was much lighter than she'd imagined he would be. She felt bones beneath his flesh. Hoisting him over the tub wall, she eased him to the inch-deep warm water.

Shirley glanced around. No towel. What soap to use? Shampoo? And how to rinse him? She needed a cup.

"Fuh-huh-crap!"

She looked at the faucet, on full blast. The depth of the water. The dog's nose, inches away.

She'd only be a minute or two in the kitchen.

Chapter 3

Clyde Munsinger stood in the trailer court office. He turned off the light, ready to leave for the evening. Tonight he collected rent from Ulyana.

He looked out the window to the road and, at the corner of his field of vision, beheld a shadowy form.

With distance and darkness broken only by an occasional street lamp, Clyde couldn't tell which direction the animal walked. He waited for the image to resolve.

Ah.

Away.

Right after he'd bought the trailer resort, law enforcement cited him for firing his .357 within city limits.

No pets.

He'd advised the tatted up white boy before he signed the

papers. No pets. No way. Not allowed. Human animals did enough damage to his property. But the skinny headbanger thought he could sneak in a shit-zoo and keep it hidden.

Clyde discovered a cigarillo-sized turd next to a juniper, adjacent the man's Toyota RAV4. He drew the obvious conclusion. The Toyota wasn't the culprit.

Clyde knocked on the door, and the dog erupted. The punk spouted nonsense about inheriting the dog from his dead mother. The rights of man. The US Constitution. The situation escalated. Gunfire into a cupboard. Shattered plastic ware.

Tenant evicted. Misdemeanor fine.

The gunshot underlined the message three times. *No dogs at the Mountain View Mobile Home and RV Resort.*

Now, seeing a canine swagger up the middle the street of his resort, Clyde clenched and unclenched his jaw. Worked it side to side, his molars shifting with the pressure.

He sat on the corner of his desk, where the line of sight through the side window allowed him to follow the beast's progress. Extracted a can of Copenhagen from his back pocket and circled the disc with thumb and middle finger. He snapped his wrist. His index finger thumped the lid and packed the tobacco. Clyde filled his lip—the left side. The right was raw.

Clyde worked up a good spit and let it hang a second over the Coke bottle before cutting it off. The first moment of tobacco changes things. He waited for it, but he'd been chewing nonstop all day. Instead of the nicotine rush, he felt queasy in the belly and a little dizzy. A joint would be more to his liking. But that would have to wait until after collecting rent.

With his tongue he dislodged part of his chew and spit it in the bottle. Now he had loose grains in his mouth.

Damn dog.

Given the animal's size, maybe it was a coyote. But not

likely.

Nah, this animal had the swagger of a rabble rouser, not the skinny quick stride of the coyote.

Clyde watched.

He'd bought the trailer resort with his father's life insurance money while his brother Harold served time. Their father changed his beneficiary the week before he died, believing if Harold inherited, the state would come back on him for it.

"You make sure your brother gets his half."

Clyde had nodded, but he didn't affirm the point before the conversation passed. How did that put him on the hook? Screw Harold. Clyde needed seed money and a quarter mil would stake him a lot farther than a buck twenty-five.

The resort?

The idea came to him watching porn. On his favorite series, a guy made his rounds collecting rent. The foxy renter didn't have cash and forgot her underwear that morning. Clyde liked how they had a little setup, a little story to make it believable. Not like the old stuff, the girl bailing hay naked, that kind of thing.

You wouldn't expect a porn producer to think too hard on the business strategy. The concept worked for a skin flick, but to do it right, you didn't want to rent a house. You'd only have one tenant. Only having one girl presented a host of problems. There's a week a month you don't want to go near her. Then, how many times can a man have one girl, and enjoy it? There had to be an upper threshold, before boredom would make him find a rotted knothole and poke it instead. Last, with a single house and a single girl, what happened when her situation changed? God forbid, what if she got a job and had cash for the rent?

To do it right you need a stable. A lot of potential babes— who didn't know each other, so their cycles wouldn't match—each with her own attributes. What did they used to say? Why go out to dinner when you can have steak at home?

Because a hamburger's nice, every now and again.

Chicken, pork, fish. All of it.

And you want girls forever bordering insolvency.

Hopeless. Mired in it.

It added up to one thing. The porn shows always had the super-hot babes living in swanky quarters. But the business model demanded a trailer park.

Clyde lived in Phoenix when his father died. Hating the heat, he took a trip up 17 to go hiking in the mountains. Lightning struck when he picked up a real estate magazine and saw an ad. Met the owner, a seventy-nine year old woman named Betsy Peck, who wanted done with the headaches. He reviewed her books. Applied his bachelor's in business to the numbers.

He deciphered how she fixed them. She didn't care to hide her lawlessness. Sloppy. Or didn't know better.

"What's your partner think about you selling the park?"

Betsy beheld him. Like he glowed or something. Like, in her mind, it would take an Einstein to figure out her laundering, when it only took a glance.

"You're supposed to keep a separate set of books for the auditor," he said.

She smiled.

No one audited her.

He'd have to be nuts to buy a trailer park and inherit an unseen laundering partner. Only one kind of money needed laundered.

Dirty.

Crime money passed through criminal hands, which were also known to carry guns.

But Clyde had seen evil at work up close, long before. So close he grew accustomed to its ways.

And confident in his.

As he stood with her in the office, he envisioned the trailer park under new management. It would be a resort. Tourists came to Flagstaff. He'd tap that market. Open up a few pads for RVs. Hire someone to plant some shrubs. Women found security in shrubs.

The place needed a new name. New signs. Rent high enough to cover the mortgage plus desired profit, allowing for five or six girls a month to substitute ass for paper.

And as for the silent partner who didn't know the old lady was selling?

Clyde would be thrilled to meet him.

Some days, Clyde felt unstoppable. He saw himself making the man a partner on terms beneficial, or dealing with him some other way. Maybe like Harold. Or one of the others, rotting in the bottom of a mine shaft.

He negotiated terms with Betsy Peck. In mere months under his leadership, the Mountain View Trailer and RV Resort was an unmitigated success. From conception to cleanup, it delivered cash flow and sex flow... what else could a man want?

The other aspect, his interface with the criminal element, had been less successful. He would resolve it tonight. But first, Clyde needed a woman.

This was a steak night. One of his tenants was a Ukrainian stripper down at the Pink Lady. Ulyana. She had money but preferred to keep it for other things, like groceries. She couldn't hardly drop a boob next to the cash register and expect to walk out with a bag of frozen dinners.

Not every time.

Ulyana. Beautiful. Except her hips stayed wide a little too high up her mid-section, and one breast was heavier than the other. Otherwise, top shelf. She wanted one poke per rent due; he insisted on five. She met him half way. One poke, fully naked.

But then Clyde saw the dog.

Why did the sight of a single dog drive him to rage?

Synapses and muscle response. At thirty-eight years, Clyde Munsinger had seen things most never would. He'd been up close with terror. Intimate, the psyche doctor said. "You've been intimate with unimaginable trauma."

Clyde thought the doctor was a pandering asshat, but he had the prescription pad. Scrips didn't write themselves.

Clyde's older brother Harold—Worm, his friends called him, because he ate them—tricked him when Clyde was six years old. Harold was ten.

The family penned a German shepherd inside a chain link cube the size of a baby's crib. Their father had earned a promotion from manager of one thing to manager of another. No pay increase—but the company paid for transportation out of Boise. Of course Phoenix was in the desert. Everyone knew that. But Boise never was hot enough to allow a reasonable man to imagine the stalking death heat of Phoenix.

Growing up in Clan Munsinger, dogs didn't merit the traditional Western title of Man's Best Friend. The Munsingers held them in more of a Middle Eastern esteem: mangy nuisances. Less worthwhile than a woman, or a child.

The Munsingers grew up tearing wings off flies and sticking firecrackers in frogs asses. They arrived in Phoenix in March. Temperatures were wonderful. The logical place for the dog crate was in the corner of the back yard next to the cinder block dividing wall.

By August, the dog nearly died of heat stroke every day— but it was actually kind of fun to watch.

Clyde's father was into Nazis but didn't have the stones to name the dog Hitler, so he named him Rommel instead. Under a withering sun and daily stone throwing abuse, Rommel learned a short temper. You could take a bowl of ground liver to him, and the dog would growl.

One day Rommel baked next to the concrete block wall, pressed into a sliver of noon shade. Harold unhooked the door, grabbed Clyde by the shoulder and shoved him inside.

Harold latched the door and left his brother. Later Harold told the police he had his headphones on, and didn't hear his brother scream.

The psyche doctor said that day rewired the neural pathways in Clyde's brain. Every time after, when he saw a dog, it was like a wagon wheel cutting the groove a little deeper. Age thirty-eight, the rut was so deep, there was no way to tread near it without falling in.

Clyde said to hell with that psychobabble nonsense. Write the scrip. He'd work it through his own way.

Chapter 4

Clyde Munsinger beat the trailer door with the side of his fist. He heard her inside, sounds that ought to be gasped into his ear. Instead she chewed on some other dude's neck and hair.

Clyde didn't own Ulyana. Didn't think of her that way. He believed in the proverb there were fornicating women and marrying women. Clyde had never encountered the latter. But she existed like gravity, regardless of his discovery. He'd locate her one day, like an apple falling on his head.

The door was ajar. Why would she do that? An invitation? No way he was down for the gay stuff. He held the handle and kicked the bottom of the door. The report sounded like a single rap on a snare drum. He drove his toe to the corner again.

The prick she was with had been so eager he didn't close the door. That had to be it.

Clyde's chest grew tight. He squared his shoulders. Inhaled deep. Used both hands to press on his sternum, but the anxiety didn't release.

Clyde punched the aluminum siding.

Until he met the marrying kind, Ulyana sat near an apex of carnal desirability. He didn't own her, felt no attachment to her. In addition to her hips staying wide too far up the torso, her left breast was a smidgen bigger than the right. Sometimes in the throes of passion, he grabbed both and meditated on how much he preferred the smaller one. Mildly disconcerting from a masculinity standpoint. But Ulyana had a dancer's derriere and legs, and her face glowed pretty when she looked elsewhere. Put her in a magazine or video, she was a seven or eight, tops. But against the other six girls in his stable—no comparison.

He examined his knuckles. The aluminum had ripped the skin and left a white smudge.

His anxiety resulted from his awareness of his superiority to the people around him. Befitting a man of his worth, Clyde liked to know which girl he'd have, and when. Food, clothing, shelter were nice. Procuring each on a foreknown, reliable schedule undergirded the advancement of human civilization. But on a personal score, asserting power over the acquisition of sex was next on the list. Clyde's system beat the traditional, one man, one woman, lifetime misery agreement.

The need to couple caused most men to succumb to marriage. Clyde solved the problem while increasing his authority, freedom, and diversity of satisfaction. Being able to go to the trailer and get laid as easily as to the refrigerator for a beer ... the arrangement was a hallmark of genius and a pillar in Clyde's self-esteem. Clyde carved a notch an inch or two above other men.

All that glory, stymied by a stripper dancing on a different pole.

Inside the trailer, the grunting continued. Male and female voices intertwined with the same sweaty lust as surely their limbs and tongues.

The deal was several months old.

Routine.

And Ukrainians were smart. She didn't forget rent day.

"This won't stand, Ulyana!"

He kicked the door again—while holding the knob. He pulled a 9mm from a butt holster, then wondered how to proceed. His impulse was to beat the base of the pistol against the door, making a louder, more abrupt knock than possible with his hand. But he'd paid five hundred, and didn't want to mar the grip. And who knew if rapping a pistol that way might make it discharge? Clyde shoved it back in the holster.

He thought. Now that she was already with some other guy, why enforce his claim? Clyde Munsinger, second batter in the box?

He turned from the door, contemplated his harem.

Michelle: decent rack, but wicked halitosis. On purpose.

Amy: pretty nice, but don't go near her while high. The mole on her face starts to look like a bug, crawling around.

Margarita: black dude special. Trunk space like a Lincoln Continental.

Nicole: ass hair.

Shirley: fifty-something, four hundred pound prostitute with bad knees.

Shirley.

The woman knew her art. But the age mismatch and her size advantage always left him feeling a little unnerved. Like sometimes when he had her bent over and growling the act seemed like prodding a mama bear with a short stick.

The least desirable girls granted the easiest access, which is what you'd expect in a capitalist society. But a problem attended that loose availability. What with the bad breath, moles, ass hair and staggering obesity... even a half-enjoyable performance required ramp-up time. Ten years ago Clyde could grow wood if he sat wrong. Now a stiffy took coaxing. Hard living did that.

And with his empire about to take a leap forward later in the night, maybe he shouldn't bother with a lower-shelf girl.

But there was the insult to consider.

In a sense, if Clyde didn't claim rent from somebody, he took whatever life handed him, like every other punk. Someday he'd be a couch potato feeding on government slop.

Not his style.

His fortunes were beginning to come together in a big way. He stood atop a mountain of achievement, and the altitude made him crave even thinner air.

This was his night.

Clyde rolled his fingers and clenched, held the knob and beat the white aluminum door.

"It's my night, Ulyana. My night."

He stopped, glanced across the street to a tenant getting out of her car, eyeing his direction. Always paid on time, kept quiet. He waved, turned back to the door. Held short of rapping.

"This is gonna change the deal. You—"

The door opened.

Ulyana, naked, a wad of cash in her outstretched hand.

"Screw off, yes?"

"Uh."

She turned and he saw the left breast a little lower than the right, clear in the bold purple light of the street lamp. Heavier, and with a hickey beside the areola.

Clyde counted money, and Ulyana slammed the door. Inside, a man loosed a throaty bellow.

Later.

Ulyana and her new stud would get something. Later.

Clyde exhaled hard. Rubbed his groin. Snorted in surprise, finding himself ready.

He stepped from the landing and headed deeper into the resort.

Chapter 5

The faucet blasted. As the water level increased, the comatose dog became buoyant and slid deeper into the tub. On the sloped end away from the drain, his nose bubbled the water.

Shirley stood with hands resting on hips, a water glass in her right hand. The animal looked horrible. How could a short-haired dog appear so bedraggled and unkempt? His ribs showed and his legs were like chicken baked too long, meat pulled clean from the joints.

She watched the water roaring out the faucet. Two minutes, there'd be five inches in the bathtub. Count to a hundred while holding the dog's head under, and the miserable experiment would end. It would be a mercy to him. For her, the outcome would be the same. No more picking up shredded ice cream boxes from the pavement. She'd slip him inside a trash bag, right in the tub. No mess. In a couple of days, she wouldn't even remember she was a murderer.

"You poor little asshole."

She held the water glass in front of her. A symbol of betrayal. Beyond, her face in the mirror.

"Dog killer."

She turned tubward.

Shirley worked to her knees and lifted the dog's muzzle. With her spare hand she turned off the hot water, then the cold. Grabbed her Vidal Sassoon, always open, and squirted pearly slime up his side. Keeping one hand under his head, she kneaded the shampoo into his coat. Splashed water to move the foam to his back, chest, neck, legs.

"Clean your weenie last," Shirley said.

She rubbed, and though the season was winter, paid attention to every small bump. No tick would escape her. Turned out they were all scabs.

The dog was a scrapper.

She found a nick on its hind quarters, not fully mended. Another on his back, toward the neck. Grooves that seemed incompatible with animal teeth. Wounds that never healed.

She rinsed his unsubmerged half and rolled him on his back, legs up, dead dog, and then to his other side. Repeated with the Vidal Sassoon, this time including his weenie, testicles, and hiney hole.

Her affection grew.

Last, she pulled her wash cloth from the rack and held it under water. She wiped his muzzle, between his eyes, and back to his ears.

With her thumb she stroked the thin fur below his eye, the hollow cheek where nothing cushioned between her finger pad and bone.

Shirley thought of Florida. Her father dead at fifty. A giant while alive, the cancer had eaten him away to nothing. In the casket, he looked like a distant skinny cousin, maybe, not the man.

She coughed loose a chunk of phlegm stuck in her throat.

Pounding at the door. She glanced around. Still holding

the dog's head, twisted.

"Cheese and rice!"

That would be Clyde. No one else knocked like they owned the world. Except this wasn't rent night. This was the stripper's night.

She reached for the plug. The dog's head thumped. She unplugged the drain. Planted her hand on its rump and pushed the dog until his head was above the water. Splashed him to clear some suds.

Pounding at the door.

"Double Fudge!"

She stood. The dog slid back into the water.

As owner of every trailer in the resort, Clyde had keys. He let himself in plenty of times. A month ago she woke to his stiffy against her nightgown. Any second he might twist open the lock, find the animal, and Shirley Lyle would be out like strewn garbage.

She turned. Stuck her head in the hallway.

"I'm coming! Can't a woman crap in peace?"

She sprayed the toilet with Poo Pouri.

Turned on the fan, closed the bathroom door.

Navigated to the erupting outside door and opened it. "Damn, Clyde. Stop your pounding."

He grinned at her. "Lookit this." He pulled aside his untucked flannel shirt revealing what appeared to be a cucumber—one of those skinny English cucumbers—in his pants. "Don't make a Munsinger wait."

He unbuttoned his shirt from the top.

"Get that little thing in here. I need to wake up early tomorrow, and I'm coming down with a cold or something. Strep maybe. And I found a new wart this morning."

"Yeah, Shirley, but you got to pay the bills. Can't leave the bills unpaid."

"Screwing you ain't a bill. It's screwing. For rent. Come inside, if you're going to. I'm not heating Flagstaff."

Clyde nodded. "What's this?"

"That's a mixing bowl. Pick it up. Be a sweetie."

"Why's a mixing bowl on your porch?"

"I dunno. But I need one that size."

He turned sideways and rubbed his tool on her fold as he entered the trailer.

"What's that smell?"

"I had chicken livers for dinner."

"What?"

"Yeah. They're healthy. I saw a diet guru on TV."

He looked across the living room area, studied the sofa, inert television, the kitchen.

"Say, you want to commence the copulation, or what? I said I don't have all night."

Clyde nodded. Held her eyes while his head moved. He looked a little unhinged.

"You got another man in here?"

"So what if I did?"

Clyde stepped toward the bedroom. Stopped.

"He here now?"

"Would you just pull out your willy? Come on. I told you I got a cold coming on, and I need my sleep. Plus I took a bunch of vitamin C and zinc. I need to keep the backside puckered—you understand me? I'm about to crap bean soup. But if you want rent, let's start before I need to run down the hall again."

Clyde opened his right hand wide, then closed his fingers. He said, loud enough to be heard throughout, "You got a man in that room, I'll beat his ass dumb. I ain't into three ways. Not with a dude."

"Tell you what. You stay here and pull your pud. I'm going to the bedroom."

Shirley rubbed past him. She let the bedroom door jamb dislodge her left breast from its normal stance, and squeeze it to a bubble as she passed through. She paused, boob about to pop. Shirley parted her mouth, pouted her lower lip. Bit it. Rolled her eyes.

Dragged that boob slow, the way a mama bird might pretend a broken wing to lure a wolf from the chicks.

Clyde followed.

Chapter 6

Clyde Munsinger scratched his thigh, scrunched a pillow, and sat upright in Shirley Lyle's bed. His gaze fell on his pants on the floor, and the faded circle worn into the back pocket. He could use a rub—nicotine after sex was as good as after a meal. But that required he climb out of bed and fetch his can. After the workout Shirley gave him, he needed a few minutes for his vertebrae to settle back into alignment.

Plus he had nowhere to spit.

He took her pretty rough while they were doggy, but not like she wanted. "You even hard?" she said. She dropped him on the mattress and rode him cowgirl. Until you've played the bronc with a four hundred pound hooker, you haven't been ridden cowgirl. Clyde hadn't known whether to brace for doom or marvel at the spectacle. After twenty seconds, he remembered a story on HuffPo about a girl who smothered her boyfriend. She had a heart attack and fell forward on him. Both of them dead, like that.

If Clyde could climb from under her, he would ensure he never wound up below her again. Then, instead of riding upright on the dally wrap, she put her hands on his shoulders. Bent her elbows and closed in. Claustrophobic, having that much woman above him—like the news story.

But afterward, the silly precariousness of the adventure took away his anxiety. He scored the fornication event a win.

Shirley spread out on her back next to him, a flooded lake of rose-colored flesh. Her stomach lifted and fell. She rolled her left leg partly outward, foot sideways on the bed.

Needle tracks? Or varicose veins?

And behold: he'd taken out a milestone without even realizing: he was poking a woman with gray pubic hair.

Time to move on. Clyde closed his eyes and thought to the night ahead. He was about to meet Lester Toungate and advance his business interests a decade in the space of a night. On that score, he had a small problem to solve.

"I got a job for you. A favor."

"Oh. Great."

"Listen."

He rolled from bed, kept his legs aboard but walked out with his hands to his pants. Fished out a thumb drive. "I want you to keep this. A couple days, at most."

"What's on it?"

"Some numbers. If I don't come back, I want you to mail this to the FBI."

"What trouble are you in?"

"I'm taking a precaution. I need you to do that. Right?"

"Whatever."

He handed the USB memory stick to her. The drive fell between them on the bed.

"You got a towel? I'm gonna grab a shower."

Shirley jumped. Planted fists on hips.

"Not here."

"I have someplace to be in an hour."

"So walk two hundred feet and use your own bathroom."
He studied her.

Shirley stood naked, shoulders broad, chest thrust strong and proud. "I don't know what you tell yourself about us, but the sex—that's the full agreement. Nothing more."

"What?"

"You don't say what I do and don't do. Where I go. Who I see. And you damn sure don't go through my things. You ain't the boss of me."

Clyde pulled the bed sheet over his unit. "I'm in a hurry."

"You look like a hurry."

"Woman—"

"Don't you *woman* me. Climb your sorry ass up outta my bed! Go on!"

She leaned in, and that claustrophobic feeling overcame him. The tightness was back, constricting deep, like a vise squeezing his heart and lungs. He glanced at his pistol in his butt holster, right there in the seat of his pants, on the floor.

"You grab that thing you better pull the trigger. Or I'll tear you limb from limb."

"What the hell? I said I want a shower."

"And I said not here, and you acted like I didn't say a thing, like all I am is a snatch and two handles. Now leave my house! Go on."

She moved for his gun.

Clyde threw back the sheet and twisted his legs to the floor.

This was exactly why his system was superior. How many men slept on the couch because their women were batshit nuts? They didn't explain. Didn't apologize. Oh, you're a woman? I understand. I'll remove myself while the hormones eat you from the inside.

"I'm going. Easy, now."

He jumped into his jeans. Shirt on and tucked, he slid out the 9mm and checked the safety. Tucked the holster, held by its tacky surface, between his lower back and denim. Grabbed his coat.

She backed as he approached the door.

Funny—he thought she'd have put herself between him and the bathroom. In the kitchen he turned. She was at the bedroom door.

"I'm going to take a leak."

"No!" She stomped toward him. "Get the hell outta here!"

He backed, nodding.

But inward a new dimension of chaos overcame him. He stepped toward the door in a daze. Pieces of the evening assembled. Not in answers, but questions:

The stray dog?

The mixing bowl?

Ulyana with another man, on Clyde's night?

And Shirley calling forth her inner grizzly—with a queer guy in the bathroom?

The world was large and Clyde small. Its workings mysterious and his comprehension tiny. The threat looming, his confidence zero.

His brain sputtered.

Except he sensed danger the way sometimes you notice an evil spirit in the room. Not Shirley—but the force animated her and gave her assurance.

"You remember about that thumb drive. I'll be back tomorrow or the next day. Keep it safe."

At the door, Clyde checked the surroundings outside, before stepping into them.

"I know what's going on," he said.

She squinted.

He closed the door and eased out the 9mm while still on the stoop. Thumbed off the safety. The door clicked as Shirley twisted the lock. He thought of the scene in every western movie, where pedestrians scuttle off the sidewalks, expecting gunplay.

Clyde stepped down, stood beside the trailer—his trailer—and listened. Inside, Shirley pounded back and forth, walking on her heels.

The stray dog.

The mixing bowl.

Ulyana poking another man, on Clyde's night.

Shirley, launching a preemptive war over him wanting to clean off the stink of sex.

Looking toward the road, he about-faced and strolled the length of the mobile home. Senses acute, each step slow. Ear cocked. Eyes narrow. Heart pounding ... and tight. He circled Shirley's trailer. At the tow hitch, he lit a joint of synthetic weed, called spice. Cigarette tobacco, with a layer of laboratory-made cannabinoids sprayed on the leaves. Most users reported the same high as from pot, but a few exceptional people became violent. Depressed. Suicidal.

But not Clyde. It made him feel more himself—and gave him a happier edge.

He finished his joint. Looked at the stars, made dim by security lights.

Something weird was going on, and you don't tangle with a guy like Lester Toungate without knowing all the angles. He could go back inside and beat it out of Shirley.

Yeah, why not beat Shirley?

Chapter 7

Paul Toungate walked to Ulyana's bathroom, wetted a washcloth he found hanging beside the sink, and cleaned his sex-fouled nethers. You'd think for a young girl shaved bare, the odor would have been more antiseptic.

He gave her rent money and listened as she told Clyde Munsinger to screw off. When she returned to him, he finished and resumed his post at the window.

Lester insisted he not poke her at all. His father: four hundred years old and still sticking his nose in other people's business. Paul tooled her once, early, on the sofa, watching through the glass toward the mobile home park's office. When Clyde arrived, beat on the door, and pulled his pistol, Paul lifted his from the lamp table. Ready to end the show right there.

Why Lester messed around with Clyde made no sense. His father had a weird tolerance for him. Like a cat playing with a mouse, and the mouse gets a good lick in. The cat laughs and keeps torturing him because the mouse isn't the enemy. Boredom is. Being old did that to a man. To Lester. So world-weary he tolerated enemies for their entertainment value.

Leave a fool like Clyde Munsinger grasping for opportunity for too long, the situation gets hard to control. From Paul's surveillance, he understood Clyde's game. He thought it best to finish it.

But Lester didn't agree.

His half-brother L.J. had something to do with Lester's behavior.

L.J.

He used his initials, and nobody knew his name. El Jay— like that rap star.

Lester was losing his marbles.

Ever since the wiry little prick showed up looking for work, Lester seemed smitten. Paul asked, "What's your interest in the kid? We don't hire people off the street—and you bring him in without so much as asking me?"

"Asking you? Whose business do you think you run?"

"Well, excuse me. I'm your only son running the show for twenty years. Maybe at this point I got a little clout?"

Senile prick. Lester had to have things his way.

El Jay started off selling Ziplock bags of weed to varsity-jackets cruising the block after school. A couple years later he ran the tree cutting company. Year or two after that, Lester made him his personal assistant. Would he follow the old man to the nursing home and wipe his ass there?

Time to have a judge declare Lester incompetent and park him somewhere he couldn't do any more harm. Well, he had a plan for that.

He and El Jay, working together for the greater good. Then he'd finish that too.

Paul left the wash cloth in the sink. He'd scrubbed himself, and the white cloth looked wiry with pubic hair. He turned away.

In the back of his head, the voice.

That's a shitty thing to do. You're an asshole.

Since Paul was young and his mother died, and he and Lester lived by themselves, the words in the back of his head popped up like a conscience. As a kid it spoke to him every day, every hour.

"You suck."

As he aged, it interrupted him less. When he took over the pavement company, and after bruising a few egos, brought the business into line. He hadn't heard the voice so much then.

But that was twenty years past. After moving to the real enterprise, the true source of family wealth, the voice came back. Didn't matter where he was. He could be driving his new Harley—every year a new Harley. He could be getting blown for the price of paying a beer wench overtime. He could be setting up a hundred thousand dollar wire to an offshore account. Back of his mind was the little voice with big amplification.

You're a shithead.

Suppose I am.

He left the washcloth in the sink.

Chapter 8

Mind surging on a dark, edgy glee, Clyde Munsinger extracted his keys and found the one matching Shirley Lyle's door. He inserted it, then pulled his 9mm from his holster. He looked at the safety—off—which didn't matter because there was never a shell in the chamber.

Easy, he twisted the key. Pushed. Not a sound.

Shirley's voice wafted slow, silky.

"There, baby. Lick that up. Ohhh, yeah. You never tasted anything so good in your sick little life ..."

Synthetic cannabinoids hopped ... Blood pressure ... eyes hot ... Clyde crashed through the door.

"You got some kinda nerve. I said I wasn't queer. Who you got—"

He slammed the front door and it bounced back open.

Cacophony in the bathroom. Yelps and scratches. A thud in the tub.

He stomped ten feet, swung up his pistol arm as he faced

the closed bathroom door.

"Go away, Clyde! This ain't what you—"

She'd tricked him into sloppy seconds. As queer as it gets.

He lifted his foot. This was his trailer anyway. Reared back and kicked forward, boot landing flat on the door. The jamb shattered at the latch bolt. The door punched inward, bounced off Shirley.

Pistol up, Clyde stared into the bathroom. A feral-eyed dog glared from the bathtub, half covered in a blue beach towel, the rest of him soaked, gaunt, yet beefy at the shoulder and blocky in the head. Below the dog on the faucet side sat a bowl with a few drops of milk and beside that, an empty plastic plate. Under the bowls, mud and hair that hadn't drained with the water.

Shirley sat on the commode. In a bath robe. Closed up front. Calves planted like oaks on the shag carpet.

His mind flashed to the stray dog wandering his park.

The mixing bowl.

This didn't have anything to do with Ulyana. Couldn't— unless they'd let the dog loose and forced Shirley to participate in the subterfuge.

Clyde pointed the 9mm at her. At the mutt. Back at Shirley.

"You know the policy."

He swung the pistol back to the dog. Squeezed the trigger. Nothing.

"Damn."

He held the gun sideways while he studied the button on the slide.

"No!"

"What?"

"Don't point that at me!"

"Huh? Oh." Clyde thumbed the safety and pointed the muzzle back toward the dog. "Say goodbye, asshole."

Nothing.

"Shit!" He racked the pistol.

Shirley breathed hard, almost asthmatic. "You got a—?"

Claws on plastic—he looked. The dog was midair, towel flapping like a cape.

Shining teeth.

The dog's position changed faster than Clyde's brain could triangulate. He absorbed the impact. Felt wetness, breath sweet like heavy cream and ham gravy. The back side of his hand smashed against the splintered jamb. Wood stuck in him and the pistol dropped. The tube flashed. The blast deafened. The mirror shattered but the sound entered his consciousness unregistered, part of the unfolding chaos of teeth and fury.

Clyde's face ripped—he knew without feeling the skin tear. The dog collided, thrashed, and Clyde fell backward into the hall. The beast rode him down. As he thought he should push, the dog leaped to the trailer door, spun around and bolted outside.

"Ahhhhh!"

Shirley screamed.

Clyde brought his hand to his face, pulled it away bloody.

"Ahhhhh!"

He dropped his head against the hallway wall. Slumped his back into the corner, exhaled like to let the fear out. But it was in him deep.

What just happened?

Lester Toungate?

Blood rolled into his shirt collar. Clyde pressed along his neck on both sides where the carotid hid under the jaw. The flesh seemed sound. Slippery, though.

The pistol was in there with the hyperventilating, crazy woman. And the wild dog was outside, with the door hanging open. Clyde rolled to his side, righted himself.

Shirley sat snot-lipped with her hands at her cheeks, black mascara streaming. Chest wheezing.

His 9mm lay on the floor. A starburst split the mirror into segments, with the missing shards in a jagged pile in the basin. Glass dust glittered.

"It's over," he said.

Clyde swiped a white towel from the rack and wiped the blood from his hands. His pulse thudded in his face, and blood dripped to the carpet. He stooped. Recovered his pistol. At the sink he removed the magazine, ejected the bullet from the chamber into the glass shards in the basin. He tried to shove the round back in but it slipped in his hand. He put the shell in his pocket and slapped home the magazine. Returned the automatic to his butt holster.

He caught his reflection in the mirror, fractured into a dozen splinters. Pieces of crazed eyeballs stared back at him. He shifted to an unmarred section on the other side.

A gash split his right cheek from below the eye to his jaw. A war wound. His flesh gaped, already turning outward, swelling from deep in the cut. Inside his mouth he pressed with his tongue and found the wall intact.

It looked like it should hurt.

"You need a doctor," Shirley said. Her breathing had slowed.

He couldn't no-show his meeting with Lester Toungate in an hour and a half. That'd be like abdicating. But his wound needed dressing.

Since moving in, he had yet to fill his bathroom cabinet with the necessaries. No hydrogen peroxide, nothing.

He turned to Shirley. "Medical stuff."

"What?"

"You got peroxide? Bandages?"

"In the cabinet." Shirley nodded to the door beside Clyde. He opened it.

"Let me see that. You need a hospital. That looks awful."

She rose with inspecting eyes. He pushed her back, and she sat again.

He grabbed gauze, peroxide, antibacterial ointment, and tape.

"I'm going to deal with you about that dog. You won't like it."

Chapter 9

Back at his house, Clyde Munsinger placed his 9mm on top of the toilet tank, pointed away from the shower. He finished another synthetic joint and, holding the last quarter inch between tweezers, dropped the roach into the commode.

He left the bathroom door open. After entering the tub, he twisted the shower head inward and kept the curtain bunched at the wall. He lowered his head under the jets and the cascading water burned the gash in his face. Woke him. Coffee would be good. The pain was good.

He wasn't spooked. Just prudent.

Some kind of hex was going on. Beyond coincidence. He sensed synchronicity working against him. But that's what made great men great. You take a fellow like George Patton. Clyde was a magnificent bastard like George Patton. He read his book in college. Patton would stand on the battlefield and observe the terrain from a thousand years ago—because he was there—and intuit how to win today. He had an extra sense of things and did what he had to do. Would a little dog bite rattle George Patton?

No.

Hell no.

Clyde dried his body, patted around his cheek. Squeezed a half-tube of ointment on his finger and filled the gash, top to bottom.

He wiped his hand clean on his towel and contemplated the gauze and tape.

This wound was an opportunity. You see guys with fresh white gauze, they look like GIs back from war, skulking around recuperating. Valorous, yeah. Battle ready, no.

But a guy with gaping flesh and wild eyes? Doing damage satisfies a need.

Lester Toungate would be clueless.

Clyde pulled on fresh underwear. Stopped. The synthetic cannabis had him smoothed out. He fetched his tin of Copenhagen and put a small wad in his lip. Finished dressing.

When he bought the trailer park from Betsy Peck, he already knew she'd been washing money for a silent partner. One glance at the books, and the dollars paid for services rendered, cued him to the deception.

The key was that the same businesses kept showing up. Toungate businesses.

Toungate had a tree removal service. The number of times the trailer park had trees removed, Clyde expected to look out the window and find denuded land, windswept and eroded. But trees were everywhere.

Toungate had a pavement treatment business. Betsy paid three hundred thousand dollars, over two years, to treat her pavement. But the roads in the park were one step above dirt and gravel.

Toungate had an appliance repair shop. What trailer court needed a hundred thousand dollars of oven repair, per year?

He opened the books, and the guts fell right out. There were more instances, but the obvious ones painted a clear enough picture.

Clyde reviewed the numbers. Despite the money laundering partner, the property retained tremendous investment potential. His back-of-the-envelope calculations would give him a capitalization rate of nineteen percent. If he could validate Betsy's verbal assurances on revenues and costs, he would make bank. On a two million dollar deal, with half financed, that put him ahead $190,000 per year. Not bad pay to manage a trailer park.

If the numbers held.

He drove home with notes. Did research. Then thought of a question he wanted to ask Betsy Peck in person, to watch her eyes when she answered. Instead, he phoned her.

"Why don't you sell the property to Toungate?"

The phone was silent.

"Hello?"

"Because I won't."

"What's that mean?"

"None of your damn business. Plain enough?"

"Well, if you expect to sell the property, especially encumbered by ... a relationship ... you'll need to answer some questions."

"How about I say, he's a son of a bitch, and if I could shoot him, I would? That good enough?"

"Did you two always have a bad rapport?"

"We're not talking about this over the phone."

"I'll come back up. You understand. I need more facts."

"Fine. Whatever."

The next day he drove back to Flagstaff and brought Betsy a cardboard cup of coffee from Starbucks. She nodded toward the counter. She never tasted the coffee.

"I need you to tell me how you and Toungate work together. Money laundering is a crime."

She looked at the wall. Seemed older than seventy-nine.

"You understand," Clyde said. "Right? I can't sink my inheritance into this place, plus another million in loans, without understanding the deals you've made. Not me. No investor. In fact, no legitimate investor will buy this place. They'll find the flaws in your bookkeeping faster than I did. That only leaves the idiots—and there aren't many with two million bucks lying around—or someone like me. A little flexible. Maybe."

"I was stupid to think I could get out of this mess."

"Well if you want out, why not sell to Toungate? He'd be happy to buy. In business they call the move vertical integration."

She huffed.

He did a trick he learned on television. He put his hand on hers. Raised his brows and partly frowned. "What's the real story, Betsy?"

You can trust me.

She pressed her eyes with her other hand, and tears irrigated her cheeks. She blinked. Eased her hand from under his.

"My boy used to run with his boy. Toungate's boy. Hellion stuff. Then Toungate brought his boy into the operation. Drugs. And all that evil nasty stuff. Then he hired my son. And my son didn't last as long as his."

"What happened?"

"He was stuck in the neck. Shanked."

"What?"

"And face. In prison."

"Toungate was responsible?"

She shrugged. "My boy was going to MIT. Had smarts. But Lester Toungate showed him the easy money."

"Well, if you hated him, why did you launder money for

him?"

"Because when my son was working for him, he told me if I wanted to keep Joey safe, I better do what he said. He gave me the money. I paid him for the services. Wrote it off my taxes. It was great for taxes."

"So to be clear. Lester Toungate—none of the Toungates—have any ownership interest in the property?"

"No. This is an LLC. All mine."

"I can work with that. But I need to study the property's numbers in detail. I need to make copies of this." He nodded at the paper spread on the desk, her ledger, receipts. "I need to analyze the cash flow and find if it'll support the financing I'll need. Is that good?"

She agreed. He took the paper to a Kinkos, Made a full duplicate.

Then, when he saw her a week later: "So here's the deal, Betsy. You're going to sell this place to me for five hundred thousand."

Her eyes ghosted over. Her mouth opened.

"You'll take half a million for two reasons. First, no financing company in the world is going to lend money based off your books. They're corrupt, top to bottom. You're supposed to keep fake ledgers. But you'd need to go back and fudge numbers for years, to create the records they'd ask for. You can't do it. Not you. I don't think I could."

"And let's say I could ..." She wiggled a pencil between thumb and forefinger. "What's the other reason?"

"You let me make copies."

"So?"

"Let's say I turn them over to the FBI. Or— the Secret Service actually handles money fraud. Or is it the Treasury? They have a top secret group too. I met a girl in Phoenix, works for them. Rachel. Anyway, one of those agencies would be interested. I should have looked that up before coming back with my offer, I admit. But who I give the evidence to doesn't matter."

"What matters?"

"Looking in my eyes, you see damn well I'll show them what you've done."

She looked in his eyes.

She placed her pencil on the desk. Her chin drifted lower until her hair hung at the sides of her face. "Okay."

Victory. Over a seventy-nine year old woman, he was hardly going to take a lap around the trailer court. But besting her felt good. Real good.

A sign of what was to come.

Clyde would use the same technique on Lester Toungate, and who knew what empire he'd steal for a story.

Dressed, his wet hair combed straight back, cheek gaping and shiny with ointment, Clyde studied his 9mm. He removed the magazine and locked the slide. Replaced the bloody shell from his pocket in the magazine and examined his empty gun. Turned it over in his hand, registered the weight of it.

The joint did a good job of easing the constricted feeling—but it was fading.

Unlike Betsy Peck, Lester Toungate wasn't a seventy-nine year old woman.

If he was in his seventies, they were a damn hard seventy years.

After Clyde bought the mobile home resort, he waited and, four days after moving in, Lester showed up to have a conversation. They stood awkward, like a boy and girl who liked flirting, but not each other. Their words were code, with neither sure what the other meant.

Clyde thought an old timer in the drug business, by this late stage of the game, would favor blunt speech and action. But Lester Toungate appeared more intent on communicating with his rocky eyes than his fumbling words.

Finally Clyde said, "Look, I bought the place knowing what Betsy was doing, and I expected to take her place. By my numbers, she's been moving about seven hundred a year for you. I plan to do some renovating, and I can clean a hell of a lot more than seven hundred. Is that what you want?"

Lester had said nothing. studied the floor with narrow eyes and a brow that seemed plowed for seed. He left, and Clyde wondered at his ease of motion. Some old guys build barns, run marathons—right up to the day they don't. Lester was such a man.

Clyde didn't see him again for three weeks.

He had a spare magazine somewhere, but the odds of needing it were small. Clyde thumbed the slide release and the pistol jumped in his hand. He pulled the trigger to dry fire it, but the trigger wouldn't move. He thought a moment before he realized it wouldn't release without the magazine in it.

He loaded the 9 and placed it in his butt holster. Glanced at his watch. Stepped to the bathroom to drain his bladder, and stopped in front of the mirror.

"You are some con artist."

Chapter 10

Joe bolted from the trailer court with strength restored. Milk fat and beef broth in his belly combined with blood on his snout roused a furious hunger. The force had slumbered while his body had been dying. But now, stomach enzymes dissolved fats and shipped calories to his cells. His vast unsatedness stirred. He desired more blood. More fat. Provoked by a hope of survival, appetite roared with life-saving bellicosity.

He would use his new energy to find more before the winter resumed and death again advanced.

Joe stopped and turned his head backward to the place he'd escaped. The female and the man with the pistol. Such devices were not foreign to him. The man who farted cabbage carried one. Though he never pointed it toward him, Joe knew the danger. The gun blasted fire and exploded with noise. The percussion deafened him, and tickled his whiskers. And every animal around the fight ring died.

He saw it again during the vast weeks confined to the vehicle, while trees gave way to plain, and plain to mountain. It was an instrument of death. When the man at the trailer brought it out and pointed, Joe had responded.

At the edge of the court, he looked into the woods and instead aimed his nose into a gust. The air carried the intoxicating odor of charred meat. Burned soybeans and other human intoxicants. Bread and sugar. The olfactory ensemble dizzied him. A car passed. Blasted its horn. Joe leaped to the cover roadside trees, and loped toward the smell.

After a few hundred yards, he wriggled under a large clump of beargrass. Across the road, a fast food restaurant lured people with neon signs. He closed his eyes. The overpowering goodness of the aroma washed through him.

Joe opened his eyes. A car drove out of the parking lot. As headlights splashed over him, Joe detected motion behind their glare. The car entered the street, and a skinny man marched away from the restaurant, carrying a sizable black bag. He recalled the giant woman at the trailer court—her bag had ice cream and fish sticks, among other miracles. Joe's stomach tickled. His legs tightened. He studied the surrounding terrain.

The man walked deeper in the parking lot, away from Joe, toward a square structure. Three sides were solid blocks but the front was chain link.

Joe backed from under the beargrass and angled across the road. At the edge of the pavement, he wove between the trunks of cottonwood and aspen. The man dragged open the gate far enough to squeeze through, and chucked his cargo to the top of the dumpster. The bag rolled off. The man again tossed it, and again it fell. Now he leaned against the block wall, his body hidden, and lit a cigarette. The glow illuminated metal on his lip and nose.

Crouched behind a boulder, Joe watched. The scent of smoke arrived, mingled with meat and bread and ketchup.

Humans were gods of intoxication. Even fresh blood from a wriggling rabbit couldn't come close to the narcotic attraction of human food.

Another car entered the parking lot and, after pausing a short while, rolled around the side. The man tossed his cigarette and stepped on it. He returned to the building.

Joe stalked forward. The man had left the gate ajar.

Joe grabbed the plastic with his teeth and backed toward the aperture. In the wood, he'd shred the bag and devour its contents. But the puncture released an intoxicating, meaty perfume.

Joe became rash.

Fish. Hamburger. Oils and proteins and sugars. He jerked and the plastic tore. He rooted through the debris, pawed boxes that fell open with the barest pressure. He gagged down their contents, burger after burger. Sometimes paper. All still warm and delicious. His mind swam in the high. It was like when he discovered the stinky man in the cave, who'd left a bag of burgers beside his wood-rotting contraption.

A memory from a different life. From a different dog.

The gate crashed closed.

Joe spun, thumped his rear against the dumpster.

The man stood on the other side of the link fence with another black bag in hand. He reached and a latch fell in place. The man put his face close to the mesh.

"You a pit? C'mere, you."

Joe stared. His heart thudded. He shrank backward into the gap between dumpster and cement block wall.

The man pulled a lighted instrument from his pocket and a moment later said, "Hey, yeah. It's me. You still lookin' pit bulls?"

Joe growled, almost inaudible.

"'Cause I got one trapped. He was in the trash. Hardee's. Yeah he's big—for a pit. White. Mostly. I don't know. No collar—listen, I don't have time to hang and convince you.

Want him or not?"

The man closed and pocketed the device. Left.

Joe pressed his nose to the tiny gap between cement block wall and wire gate. Pushed forward, but though it gave a little, the ultimate resistance was firm.

He wriggled, turned the other direction. He circled the dumpster and, at the back, stepped through cold water. Returned to the front. He sat. Pawed at the fence.

Joe ate another cheeseburger, this time nosing aside the bun.

Metal grated on blacktop. Joe looked. The man walked from a car with the trunk lid open and light on. He dragged a chain on the pavement. His stride carried purpose. His head set level.

Joe shrank from the fence.

"All right. You go easy, I go easy. But you make this hard, I'll beat you to death. You got it?"

The man looped the chain and wrapped the ends around his hand for a solid grip. He opened the gate. Held his arm high and back.

Joe retreated.

"C'mere."

Joe hunkered. Growled.

The man raised his arm and hurled downward. Behind him, the chain swung out, up and around, and with unseen speed the heavy links smashed into Joe's shoulder and lowered head. The impact moved through him. His hide stung but the pain inside was intolerable.

As the man dragged back the chain and readied his arm for another swing, Joe clawed forward and leaped. His paws reached the man first, but he relaxed, allowing his teeth to deliver the brunt of his weight. As the man shrieked and fell backward, the gate yielded and Joe rode him to the pavement. He slashed at his attacker's neck, felt the spurt of blood that signaled victory. The man's shrieks became garbled.

Joe bounded across the lot and swerved to miss a pair of lights rushing toward him. At the ditch across the road, he jumped over the bank and darted into tree cover.

Chapter 11

Lester and his son Paul Toungate waited beside Lester's truck. Headlights approached. Lester said, "Now."

Paul eased around the bed, ducked.

They met on Road 2310, after the right turn from 231, a short scoot past Rogers Lake. Both roads had been closed for winter and were now reopened. The area attracted eagles, pronghorn, mule deer, and black bear. Wading birds and the famous leopard frog.

Lester Toungate appreciated wildlife, but he chose the location because the ground was soft. Sometimes it mattered. This time, maybe not.

He leaned against the open tailgate of his Ram truck. The headlights hit him. Lester lowered his head until his hat brim shielded his eyes. With the glare on him, his breath turned white in the evening cold. Dust rolled in, and the approaching vehicle stopped. The light came on inside the cab, and the engine still ran. Clyde stepped around the front. Lester waved him closer.

"Come, sit with me a minute so we can figure this quarrel out."

Clyde approached with his back to his headlights and his face hidden in shadows. Lester knew what would be there, if he could make his features. A cocksure kid—like any other—tore up by cowardice. Few parents inoculated their children against sentimentality. Lester was a flat paint man—a rarity—a man never burdened by empathy for another. He was aware—more than most—of the trouble he made. But his understanding of causality, decision making, and personal responsibility informed his views. He long ago concluded, if the ramifications of other people's actions against him were his duty to solve, the reverse must also be true.

The consequences of his actions were rightly other people's problems.

It wasn't polite to meddle in other people's troubles.

Lester's gift of indifference arose from deep introspection. He'd learned when he was young that he alone was responsible for what he felt and how he behaved. He was separate from the world. They weren't fluid, a cause outside him, flowing into and automatically triggering a response in him.

For Lester, the cause came against him like a wave against a rock. He studied a force, projected it, and if he liked the destination, joined. If not, he turned it away. No one herded Lester into action. If his indifference pissed them off, they could go to hell.

Or adopt his way of thinking.

No one surprised Lester by turning out evil. Lester was ahead of them, expecting it. His opening stance was unsentimental. He refused to embrace the complacency of "civilization," where everyone cooperates and everyone prospers. No one put a gun to his head. If they did, they'd find Lester already had a bullet speeding at their belly.

Lester knew Clyde inside out from the moment he met him, once he'd acquired the trailer park.

Clyde leaned on the tailgate. "Cold out," he said.

Lester looked at him, now that his face was in the light. "Dog chew your face but good."

"You can tell it's a dog?"

"I'll give you one thing," Lester said. "Balls. Way you moved on Betsy. And I guess I'll give you one more thing. You look for opportunity."

Clyde smiled like Hannibal crossing the Alps on elephants. Or drugs.

"But you're about the biggest fool I've run across in a lotta years."

"Old man," Clyde said, "You may be a king around here, but you're in the same predicament as Betsy. The world's moved on. You're fighting the last war."

"You my enemy?"

"Dunno. Maybe."

"Oh?"

"Lester—I have all Betsy's books. I'm the one with the numbers, and it isn't like the old days when you could just kill the numbers guy and hire another. You take me out, your whole show gets razed to the ground and you and your son die in prison."

"Better than a mud hole."

"What?"

"Never mind."

"All my books are digital," Clyde said. "That means they're stored electronically."

Clyde pulled his hand from his jacket and unfurled his fingers.

"This is a thumb drive. After I bought the place, I took photos. Every page, of fifteen years' worth of ledgers. Every entry Betsy ever wrote—a hundred grand for you to remove a tree—is in those books. I highlighted each place I suspect she was washing your money. I went through two packs of highlighters. Even the queer colors. What she was doing was obvious. Someone should have bought her a course on bookkeeping."

Lester waited. "You finished?"

"Not quite. Capone went away for tax evasion. My guess, near as I can from the books, is you've run three million, four hundred fifty three thousand, and change, through Betsy."

Lester looked at the gash in Clyde's face. Ran scenarios in his mind. Should the disfigurement alter his plans?

Nope.

"And don't understand me wrong," Clyde said. "I want us to have a real good relationship too. But the power dynamic is different this time. Betsy didn't fairly value her worth."

"As you value yours."

Clyde nodded. Exhaled a white cloud. "Not so much that. You're a smart man. You know I wouldn't come out like this without a failsafe. I gave the evidence to a bunch of other people. I don't return to work tomorrow, they give it to the US Postal Service. Two days later, the Federal Bureau of Investigation."

Lester said, "You shoulda smoked more dope."

"What?"

"Yeah. You'd been more paranoid. Might have thought through your process a little better. Your odds."

Lester glanced beyond Clyde.

Clyde turned.

Paul emerged from the dark into the headlight glare. He wore blue latex on his hands and had orange plugs in his ears. Lester saw the gloves, but doubted Clyde did. The sparkle of a gun barrel commanded the entire focus of a coward at heart.

Clyde jumped.

"Don't," Lester said. "We're going to put you back inside your truck and send you home. That's all."

Paul tromped in close. Grabbed Clyde's collar at the back

of his neck and shoved him forward, steadied him.

Lester extracted a .357 with an eight inch tube from a cowboy holster hung from his belt and tied to his leg. Pointed the barrel at Clyde's back. He lifted Clyde's jacket and Paul removed his 9mm.

With Clyde's jacket still held high in the back, Lester said, "What is that?"

"What, my holster?"

Lester pulled it from Clyde's pants and chucked it to the tailgate. "Turn him around."

Paul shoved Clyde's shoulder. All three faced Lester's truck.

"Step aside, Clyde. You're blocking the light. Okay good. Here's what's going to happen. Pay attention."

Paul placed his pistol in his holster and removed the magazine from Clyde's 9mm. He pulled the slide a quarter inch, held the chamber to the headlights.

"You didn't have one in the pipe?"

Paul snorted.

"I guess I just have more respect for a firearm—"

Lester wiped his nose. "All right. Paul?"

Paul thumbed the shells from Clyde's magazine to the tailgate and stopped with the last in place. He pocketed the ammunition. Slipped the magazine back into the 9mm and chambered its only round.

"Right now, you're making some calculations in your head. Or you oughtta be. Let's go."

Lester waved his pistol toward Clyde's truck.

"So this is how the evening will proceed. You'll climb inside the cab of your F-150. Turn on some country music. No, you'll put on the Christian station. Which one is that, Paul?"

"Damn if I remember."

"Twist the knob to the top end. One oh something. We'll help you find it. And, when you're satisfied you're right with the one who made you, you're going to stick this barrel where your chin meets your neck. Then you're going pull the trigger."

Clyde stopped. "No! What? Why? I got the evidence. You'll go down. I got it spread all over the place. I got thumb drives here and there. The minute I don't show up, they're going to the FBI and police. You won't last a day. You can't!"

"Clyde, listen to me. You're going about this all wrong. You're making the same argument as a minute ago, like I didn't hear it the first time. You're misinterpreting the situation. See? I know all that."

"Well ... This is crazy—what should I say?"

"I can't stop myself from giving advice. You'd think I'd a quit by now."

"What? What advice?"

"You come out here to make the same play on me as you did on Betsy. Right?"

"Well—"

"So when you attack, and I don't seem to mind, at that point you need to re-evaluate."

"I don't—"

"Perdition! It ain't worth it. Paul, let's just be done."

Paul holstered his weapon and grabbed Clyde from behind, arms circling his upper body. He heaved and walked him toward the front of Clyde's truck. Lester scooted past and opened the cab door. Clyde bucked and Paul shoved. Clyde lifted his legs and braced against the threshold. Both men growled and cussed.

"All right," Lester said. "Paul, ease up. Let him go. Now Clyde, be still a minute. I'm going to explain my thinking in more detail than I ever done. You got to go back, to understand what I'm going to say. I began after Viet Nam. I wasn't there. I said that wrong. I started in nineteen seventy-five, regardless of Viet Nam. I only mention the war 'cause I run with a fella was there.

"Anyhow, the drug business had a pull on me from an early age, but I didn't quit the nine-to-five world until my forties. Now I'm eighty-three. Since my start in nineteen seventy-five, I've killed twenty-two men. You'll be twenty-three. In all that time, all twenty-two, I assumed it would work best if I didn't give a man a choice in the manner of his death. Most people don't like to muse on it, so to keep it simple, I surprised them. A quick one to the head. But with you, once I decided you needed to go, I decided to test an idea, been festerin'. I'm not gonna live forever, and I want an answer."

Lester smiled. Looked at the dirt. Back to Clyde. "Most people never realize the biggest gift life gives them. The ability to make decisions. Most people don't decide anything. They do things, then look at themselves and wonder why. Like you. There's stuff you want—my stuff—and you come up with a plan and set about it. But you never make a decision. You slide right through the whole process. You comprehend what I'm saying?"

Clyde gawked.

"I see you're not getting my meaning. Making a decision means you sit and ponder something. You look at each way a thing might turn out. What goes into each being more or less likely. Which outcomes you can live with. Which you can't. After noodlin' all that, you map out all the different ways the possibilities can manifest. So you'll recognize which one you're dealing with, and the right course will be evident. Am I making sense?"

"Sorta."

"You didn't do any of that. I know you didn't, or else you'd have picked up on how Paul's been poking your stripper girl. Though I told him he'd get a disease. You'd have seen him keeping tabs on you. You'd have found the camera inside your office, connected to my computer. You'd have noticed some of that. And when the dog chewed on your face, you'd have pulled back just a hair, to reevaluate."

Clyde buckled at the knees.

"Now you're getting it. I knew about your thumb drive. And you only made one. And you left it with the fat girl."

"Oh, Christ have mercy."

"That's the right way to look at it. His mercy is guaranteed, and is all that matters. Mine ain't, and it doesn't matter anyway. Stand, boy. Step in that cab."

Paul stooped and lifted Clyde. Shoved him to the truck seat. Lifted his legs for him and spun him. Paul stepped away and Lester closed in, .357 at Clyde's ribs.

"So I'm going to give you a gift like none other. Your whole life's been a mistake. It's writ on your face. You've taken actions of consequence, but never made a *decision* of consequence. Well, tonight you get to make the most consequential choice of your life."

Clyde leaned his head against the seat. Closed his eyes. Opened them. "What choice is that?"

Paul crossed around the vehicle to the other side.

Lester jabbed Clyde's ribs with his gun barrel. "First off, kill the engine. Turn the key to accessory."

Clyde did.

"Now reach over there and unlock the door."

Clyde did.

Paul entered on the passenger side.

"Now here's your decision. When I tell him, Paul's gonna hand you that nine of yours. You saw it only has one shell. You know the math ain't good on you killing both Paul and me with one shot, when we're on opposite sides of the truck. When you think it through, you might get one of us. But then you get shot, and since we know you don't have any more bullets, we shoot to maim. Whichever of us is alive, we'll do some god-awful desecrations to your body, in retribution. You'll choke on your own dick, for sure. And if you go that route, it means you ain't embraced the power of choosing your death. You'll endure all manner of humiliations before you succumb. You understand? Nod your head."

Clyde blinked. Nodded. Tears fell.

"Okay. Now, the next choice. You can put the gun up under your chin, against the neck. When you fire, it'll remove the part of your brain that does all the heavy lifting, terms of keeping your body alive. Your eyes'll look bad, but your face'll be intact. If that matters to you. But it'll be over in less than a heartbeat. You understand? This is the easiest, fastest, least painful way. Nod your head."

Clyde nodded.

"Your last choice is the one I don't expect you to take. You'll put the gun at your chest, a little left of the sternum, and shoot yourself in the heart."

"Why don't you expect that?"

"You'll live a while. Fifteen or twenty seconds, 'fore the lights go out. And that one? You'll feel that one."

"What would you choose?"

"You're stalling, but I'll give you one stall. If it was me, I'd choose the third option. I'm eighty-three. I've thought on mortality more 'n you. I think it'd be kinda nice to anticipate it coming. Not to have it sneak up like it does on most people, but to watch it roll in, dark clouds and all. That's the way I'd go. Given my druthers."

"And if I don't decide?"

"Well, part of my plan is that if you kill yourself, there won't be any questions. Suicide solves easy—but only if you pull the trigger. You need the residue on your hands, and the blood spatter can't have no holes where someone was beside you. I watch TV too. The only way suicide flies is if it's suicide. So if that's the route you want, I'll trust you. But if you fight me on this, and make us do it for you, we'll need to do some of the desecration I mentioned. On account no one wants to dig a hole."

"I could dig the hole."

Lester shook his head. "I said I'd give you one stall. You're out."

Clyde wiped tears from his face. "Give me the gun. Now, while I have the nerve."

"Hold on. Paul, turn the radio on. One oh six or something."

Paul pressed the dial. Twisted it. The preacher spoke.

"Climb out the cab, Paul. Give him his gun."

Paul backed out. Flipped the safe off and, by the barrel, handed the 9mm to Clyde.

Chapter 12

The antibiotic wasn't working. Clyde Munsinger's cheek burned hot inside, where bacteria from the dog's teeth smoldered, reproduced, slew white blood cells. The infection blazed, even if his synthetic marijuana blunted the pain.

Lester didn't register the war wound. His demeanor remained unchanged.

Clyde's brain jumped to the moment.

Lester's son Paul flipped Clyde's 9mm in his hand and passed the grip to him. Almost inviting treachery. Surely, the old man anticipated his next move. He seemed always two steps ahead.

But Clyde had a surprise for him—if he could figure out how to reach it.

He sniffled. For show.

"That, uh, that isn't the Christian station I prefer. When I listen. You mind?"

Lester blinked watery eyes. Shook his head like Clyde's will to live evidenced a shameful condition. He held his pistol level at Clyde's hip. The front end bounced a quarter inch. Clyde took that as his signal. He eased for the knob with his left hand, across his chest. Paul now pointed a shooter at him too, through the open passenger door.

Clyde considered his next actions, like Lester said he should.

He foresaw pulling the trigger and hitting Paul in the ribs. The bullet would take him down and kill him quick. Or Lester lied, and the gun wasn't loaded. Then Lester would fire and hit Clyde.

Reach for the passenger door, yank the handle?

Lester shoots me.

Turn on the engine and stomp the gas?

Lester and Paul both shoot me.

Or neither ... if I warn them about the crossfire.

Lester would say, Paul, stand down. I'll cap him.

Fire at Paul? Lester kills me while I'm turned the other way. Shoot Lester and go for the door? Paul takes me out.

Clyde moved the radio frequency higher, and the station went fuzzy. He focused on lessening the static—easier to solve the small problem than the big one—and realized leaving the small problem unresolved might keep him alive longer.

Up the dial, noise. He needed a moment to thrust his hand below the seat—just a second before the old man fired.

Would Lester give him a split moment?

Did Lester say more pot would help? Not a helpful observation, if he wouldn't let Clyde smoke another joint. He needed a better distraction than the radio.

No—he needed the spare .45 under the seat, either without Lester or Paul knowing, or so fast neither had time to react.

If he shot the old man first, he couldn't turn on the engine and pull forward faster than Paul could shoot him. But—

Clyde understood.

He couldn't game it. He had to take action. Hope for havoc. And, as he turned the knob, the Christian radio station dialed in. Like the Lord cared for his troubles, during the chaos.

Knock, knock, knock and the Lord Almighty will answer.

Hell yeah. Clyde had the Lord with him.

Clyde placed the 9mm under his jaw, with his right hand. Screwed his eyeballs to Lester, beheld the old man's raised brows and open mouth. Not today. In this town, I'm Hitler. Rommel. Clyde threw his pistol arm right and, as it snapped fully extended, fired at Paul. The blast deafened him. He kicked with his left foot and missed Lester but caught the door. He withdrew and blasted another leg at Lester. Light flashed from Lester's tube before Clyde knocked him back.

His right hand dropped the 9 on the seat and moved toward the steering column, the ignition, and turned the key. Old man fired another blast of orange and his bullets didn't go anywhere. Funny. Didn't hit the glass or anything. Clyde jerked the wheel and stomped the gas. He had another gun under the seat, but in the moment, it made more sense to escape rather than shoot it out.

The truck roared and the rear tires spat gravel and dirt. Inside, Clyde comprehended with clarity. All the adrenaline and raw intellect juicing along at full throttle. Come on, loud as it gets. Jesus right there with him. He won a gun fight.

The gunplay went down different from what he wanted. Time to fix that later. The old man dead was safer than alive, anyway. And other drug pushers would step into his shoes. They'd need their money washed. Clyde would reach out when the time suited him. Meantime he earned a cool two hundred a year to run a trailer court and get blowjobs from ugly girls.

His lungs ached. The dirt road was smooth a second ago, but now rocks made the truck vibrate. The engine revved like stuck in first. His tires spun. Hadn't moved five feet. Light flashed outside both doors. Explosions. Thunks like a sledge on thick metal. *Just turn to the Lord and repent of sin. All it means is turn away from your ugly, murderous, sinful-in-the-eyes-of-God past. You too can have everlasting life. All it takes is to admit you're nothing close to holy, and if you're going to have any future at all, it's through the loving grace of the one who made you.*

Clyde hit the radio. Peace. He needed to ease off the gas to allow the treads to grab. But outside there were three more flashes and bangs. Somewhere beyond his chest, his heart pounded like a drum; if he reached out his hands would sense the percussion through the air. The truck fishtailed. Sprayed rocks.

That bounce a second ago... the right rear wheel chucked Paul out the back.

Up ahead, he'd kill the lights, circle back and shoot that old bastard Lester while he cried over his dead boy. Christian station playing, cranked up volume, windows down, give the old man time to find peace. Fitting, after the courtesy he showed Clyde.

Another courtesy: maybe shoot him in the heart and let him realize death spread its wings and dropped its ass for a landing.

But not let him do it, so he didn't have the choice. Cold. That would impress him. And having the Lord there on the radio. Good stuff.

Wait ... Why not smoke more pot now?

Nah. In a bit. Copenhagen now. One hand on the wheel, he fished his can with the other. Snapped a pack and twisted off the lid. Filled his lip. All with one hand and without spilling a grain.

Clyde released a long exhalation as the nicotine hit his

already-THC-infused veins.

Ahead was dark cut by yellow light. He switched the high beams. Exhaled hard. Eyeballs glowed at him. Pronghorn maybe. Be a hell of thing to kill one with his truck. Hell of a thing. After all this. Cool like sticking three girls in one night. Hell of a thing.

Clyde coughed.

Whooeee.

Spat.

Something in his stomach didn't agree. And his butt was warm like he loosed his bladder.

If he had—he didn't but if he had—it wouldn't mean he was a pussy. He'd been in a gunfight.

Whooee.

That was blood.

Clyde slowed.

His guts didn't feel good at all, and now that the cab was closed it smelled like someone set off a firecracker in an outhouse.

Clyde reached for the dome light. Missed. Hit it.

Blood all over his lap, belly. Hands.

He was a half mile away, and the old man couldn't be on him yet. Clyde pulled over. As the truck rolled, he felt along his left side, under the arm. Put his finger in a hole, and spat blood.

Coughed.

His lungs constricted, but not like before, when it was the anxiety. Now he couldn't fill them. He wondered if the air was going out his side, from the bullet punctures. Who was he kidding? He found two more wounds, each high in the rib cage. Thinking made it real. His heart shook, and pain sucked his chest, drawing open his mouth and curving in his shoulders. Like a black hole just popped into his heart and sucked everything up. It pulled outer space into his head, blackness and stars swooping in over headlights, over that pronghorn.

Lester would arrive any minute.

Clyde grabbed the wheel. Reached below the seat but couldn't get his arm far enough, and the pain took over his thinking. The void from space blinded him, and in a mere moment he slipped into it like a serene bath, out of his clothes, through the metal of the truck cab.

Right into the cool black nothing.

Chapter 13

Arriving at a stream, Joe stopped. He listened to the land behind him. Satisfied, he lapped water into his belly, where a half dozen unmasticated Hardees burgers rested like so may pounds of lead. His stomach expanded to accommodate the water. He gagged, but the distress passed without his vomiting.

Joe nosed through the low-hanging branches of a nearby evergreen, sniffed around the trunk. After digging a bed in the fallen needles and curling there, Joe looked to the forest beyond the knoll. His line of sight through the wooded slope allowed him to watch the neon food place. His eyelids closed half way.

A man walked from the restaurant to where the other lay, ran back, then returned with many others. A large vehicle with flashing lights arrived, followed by smaller ones.

Unease spread through Joe.

He licked the sides of his mouth, removing the last of the man's blood.

The people at the restaurant moved his body, and Joe closed his eyes.

He remembered.

When he was tiny and new, three children played with him. They tossed a stuffed animal, and he ran after it and pounced. They shouted at him, and confused him, until one time he carried the toy back to them. They rubbed his belly and ears. The oldest child scratched his bum, and that gave the most pleasure. They threw and he fetched. Sometimes he would tire of the sport before they.

The children fed him intoxicating scraps from the table— all the choicest cuts of fat—while keeping the mere meat for themselves.

They invited him on the sofa and snuggled, so long as the angry man wasn't nearby.

One day the angry man patted his head, like regular play. Joe gnawed his hand and growled. The man smacked him. Joe flopped across the wood floor and slid into the wall so hard he couldn't breathe. The man shouted, and when Joe could move again he ran to the bathroom and cowered between the toilet and the wall.

He never nipped at a human after that, no matter what they did. Never bared fang at the young buck who electrocuted him one day, and threw him in a crate in the back of a truck.

He hated the beatings the humans gave—but somehow he hated their harsh words more. When he was a pup.

Joe thought of the other man. The one that defied his ability to comprehend. The one who destroyed everything near him—except never had a harsh word or raised a hand to Joe. They were a two-dog pack for a while.

He thought of his voice, very often using the same angry words as the other men—but when the cabbage fart man uttered them, their tone conveyed mildness and fun.

The man disappeared into a mountain.

Joe had watched for his return, but soon winter demanded he seek survival elsewhere. He wandered east, following human scents to Flagstaff. From history he knew he could always find places to hide and things to eat near people.

The trick was avoiding them.

The eventual product of interaction with human beings was pain. Whether harmful to him by their nature, or by accident, the majority of humans caused trouble.

Except the cabbage fart man.

Joe opened his eyes, uncurled his body, and flopped to the other side. Re-curled.

In doing so, for the first time in months, his blood flowed with vigor. His muscles twitched with power. The mass of Hardees calories had passed through his stomach. Most remained in his lower gut, but he'd converted some into life force. Exuberance.

Cold from the ground and his thin coat, Joe stretched until his body warmed and loosened.

He looked below to the neon food place, and the revolving lights were still there. Joe remembered the man with the chain, and tearing open his throat. He recalled the other man in the trailer that smelled of ham grease and human sex. Surely one or both of these attacks would bring the retributive hand of man.

But no man was near.

Joe emerged from the limb cover. He tromped toward the dome of the knoll, sniffing, listening, seeking someplace more permanent to curl up and sleep.

From far off, he heard the *yipyipyip* of coyote.

Joe loped toward the call.

Chapter 14

Lester Toungate dusted the ass of his pants while he looked at the lump fifteen feet away, to his right. Clyde had gotten off one shot. That aligned with the plan.

But the bullet didn't take off the back of his head.

Turned out Clyde loathed himself, and would rather be killed than take his life right and honorable himself. So much for that experiment.

The lump to Lester's right, fifteen feet into the dark, troubled him.

He liked to think that after so many years of deliberate living, nothing caught him by surprise. Or if it did, he could adjust. Now this. Something he should have anticipated and prepared for.

The moon would be full tonight, when it climbed full

above the trees. His eyes adjusted in the starlight.

Paul, on the dirt.

A decision floated between them.

Lester's ass hurt—the bone. Not as much meat as years past. He swung his hips back and forth while he allowed the previous moments to wash through him. The shootout, the roaring engine, the thump of a tire chucking a man five feet.

Before he walked to Paul, shouldn't he think on the last sixty years of having his son on the planet with him? While, so far as he understood, Paul lived?

Forty years Paul had worked with him. Twenty, running operations. Grooming to take things over, Paul said too often.

Lester didn't take any money from the business. He had enough. Paul made day to day decisions and took home the pay. Paul needed the lifestyle. The women. Driving a Range Rover one day and Porsche the next. Paul wanted the accouterments.

For Lester, satisfaction resulted from building something. The dollars, when they came in, weren't important because they bought things. They signaled he was on top. No one met him in the coliseum without shedding blood. Few learned Lester Toungate's full history. But those who did made sure to communicate their goosebumps in his presence.

Not Paul. Lester spoiled him and blamed himself for the way his first son turned out. Partly. But beyond a certain point, age five or six, Paul was Paul. Can't scapegoat others your whole life.

He wanted the cherry red Mustang—deserved it—before he had a paper route. It took Lester a decade to graduate him out of the pavement treatment business into the other enterprises. The boy seemed oblivious to responsibility.

If Paul was laying dead over there, Lester should try to see him in an unadorned light. Fluorescent, clean. Not some wintry soft candle glow, hiding his boy's faults. If he was going to lose his first son, he ought to have a bright light expose what he was losing.

Since Paul had been making most of the major decisions the last decade, business was down.

Relationships don't stay in place forever. In the drug world, nothing is static. Because a man was trustworthy yesterday doesn't guarantee he is today. Or because a route was safe last week, doesn't mean no harm will come this week. And a seller who provides a good product one month, doesn't prevent him from adding a pound of Borax the next.

Relationships were fluid, every day forging, testing, breaking, welding back together. It took a man of insurmountable will to keep them afloat. Some business ties needed defended, some destroyed. Only a professional understood which, and only the most energetic builder would bring the stamina the empire required. Otherwise, things sour. You slip up and trust people, and they rob you. Kill you. And since you've only been visiting the arena, instead of spending nights, your allies desert you. Resources dry. You wander streets like a tourist, remembering how things looked long ago.

You never feel the point of the blade slip between your ribs.

If you're an entitled prima donna, things sour with haste.

So ... If Paul was dead, like it looked he was, things would change.

Some.

Might be good to muse on those changes before stepping over there.

Lester would reassert some old relationships. Take a few road trips. He'd promote somebody to the associate role. Funny—he'd been Paul's sidekick. From that angle, Paul laying dead over there could almost look like a coup.

As if Lester had intended his son to get shot.

That's how it looked, from that angle.

The new apprentice, of course, was Lester Junior.

At some point Paul learned about him. You can't keep a half-brother from learning about a half-brother forever.

"Dad?"

Lester looked at the sky. Down the road, to where Clyde's truck had stopped, headlights askance, the truck run into a ditch.

"Dad?"

Clyde shot Paul, then ran over him. And Paul lived.

Lester withdrew his .357 and, remembering the shots already fired at Clyde, holstered it. Instead he withdrew a snub .38 from his jacket's inner pocket and pulled the trigger five times.

At his truck he pressed the latch. Opened the door. "Hey Lucky, get out the vehicle. Take a leak, wouldya? C'mon. Take a leak."

A German shepherd climbed down, hesitant to leap into the dark.

"I feel you, old dog."

The shepherd half-jumped, half-climbed down the seat. He trotted to Paul's corpse and sniffed. Satisfied, he walked a few feet to the grass at the plain, and lifted his leg.

Chapter 15

Dream.

I'm hard as the nether millstone, and those dream titties in my face are real as apples and just as tasty. She rides like I'll buck her if she doesn't break me quick.

"Ruth—what?"

I'm on the edge. No such thing as closer. I got part of her rear end in each hand—Ruth's been eating salad. Going to the gym.

And she smells better.

Start rousing out ...

She bounces off my ugly, and I pull her hips back square. Stick ugly back home. We froth and splat. I notice the bed under me, sheets made of flannel—not like the sleeping bag, and not like the hotel with Ruth.

See the glow of those tiny LED lights they placed all through the bunker, since there's no natural light. They never turn off.

I smell her scent and those dried chilis she's been throwing in everything, and it ain't Ruth I got my meat in.

Wake.

Open my eyes.

It's one of the girls.

"What the—?"

"Ay papi—"

"Tat?"

"Mi amor—"

"TAT?"

"Nadie me lo das como tu—"

"Nah. Ahh What! Nawh!"

"Voy a venir!"

She works her hips like an oil rig, up and down, up and down, up and down. Each time she hits home her fingernails dig in my skin a little deeper. I want to throw her but all my squirming makes the situation worse.

"Baby, oh, *si*, there, there, there—"

"Tat, this ain't—that ain't—"

She clamps her hand on my face, then pulls it away and drop her chest so my cheeks are awash in boobs.

"That ain't fair!"

I got to decide.

She doesn't weigh a buck twenty, and I could pitch her to the hallway.

If.

Ain't had liquor in five months, and all these dried veggies and meat's restored me to prime. I got a dick like a dagger and this girl's got an animal need—and thinking on it that long was long enough. I got no control. Muscles do what they're supposed to. She shakes and I do too. After a couple seconds of almighty glorious torture, she peels off and drops beside me, one leg up over, sweaty chest stuck on my arm and long hair in my face.

Eyes wide open, now.

"Shoulda maybe asked."

She burrows her head close to mine, and if I slap her silly, she'll say I didn't have to go along.

"You better do something about that."

"What?"

"Go do what girls do. Go to the bathroom. Whatever. So you don't end up preggers."

"I won't get pregnant."

"Says every girl ever knocked up."

Lungs get back to normal and sleep comes on me hard, but all these months I been fighting to ensure this didn't happen. I've seen Tat warm to me. How she sits on the plastic sofa with the television on, and after a show or two she's right up next to me. How she grabs my arm when the bad guy pops up with a gun—like Tathiana somehow learned to fear a man with a gun.

Watched the news a month after holing in the mountain. Learned somebody cut a piece of leg from the Mrs. Graves.

Had to be Tat.

So I got this cannibal like to snuggle.

She's eighteen. Perfect and legal—because legality is important. But she a girl and I'm fifty something.

Holed up and alone, not knowing if she'll ever get out of the concrete house ...

Nah.

Those FBI people don't search the woods any more. Luke Graves put devices all over, and they never found one. They stepped on some of his man traps, but nobody got messed up like I did with the punji stakes. Graves put as many cameras out there as bombs. All wired to the television so you can flip through. Go from the nightly news to the live camera, press a button, shazam. So I watch FBI boys day in and out for two weeks. Thought sure they'd dig us out. Brought in some special hush-hush unit. They was on the news with it. Said they're sure I was here somewhere, most likely in a cave. And they'd ferret me out if it took ten years.

Now they hardly come back to do the maintenance on their gizmos. I studied their cameras with ours. Mapped them on a topo map, the routes they walk, where they stop. Fourteen grease pencil X's, and I drew a route to whisk me out of Dodge without waking the sheriff.

Then the local news lady did a special report. Inform the citizens what their masters were doing to protect them from the nutjob from North Cackalackee. Said they deployed infrared and heat sensing cameras.

I come up with a plan for that, too.

Two months later, they return for another report. The hottie FBI gal that was always yammering about Baer Creighton being ten on the list... The bigshots assigned her back to the Salt Lake, where she came from. Hired a new spokes-jackass, and the gist of his nonsense is Baer Creighton probably isn't in Flagstaff. So they're waiting for new leads. You got information, please call.

Truth is I can bust out the second I want.

But what for? It's bad here, girls gibbering, cooking and cleaning and learning true American history when I teach them. But out there I'd have snow and—well damn anyway, these girls ain't so bad I want to leave, so much as complain.

Until I wake with Tat bopping squiddles.

Sometimes I dwell on all my evil. Try and count the men. See their death faces. If I can't do it awake, I can with the dreams—the corpses in trees.

Shudder at what torment I'm due from the Almighty.

"This ain't right. You're a pretty gal, and if the situation was different it'd be different. But things is rarely what they ain't. And if I was a better man I'd not let you ride me like that. So. How about you go back to bed. This can't happen again."

I stand. Wonder how she got my shorts off.

"Where my shorts?"

She stands beside the bed. Stoops, stands, and hurls them at me.

The LED lights show her face. Cheeks soft and brown but streaked in tears.

"Aw, hell, Tat. You're pretty."

She shakes her head. Confounded. Leaves the room and slams the door. Good. Now she woke Marisol.

"Ahhh piss. Grow up."

Pull on my shorts. Pants and shirt. Grab a jacket—this concrete cave's always a little too chilly and damp for right living. Go to the main room and sit. Could make coffee, but what for? Like I want to be awake?

There's a show comes on the television late at night. Hard to sleep, knowing Stinky Joe's out there alone, and I left him. We're responsible to look after ourselves. World's pretty hard-set on that rule. So Joe ran off when I was laid low by the man trap, and it's his fault. Animal made a choice.

But when the lonely gets to us, instead of being responsible for ourselves we pair up and make a pact. Stinky Joe taking off kind of stings. Fred never left. Maybe we were better matched.

A show comes on the television late at night when I'd rather watch TV than cut my veins, so I turn it on and flip. But soon as the picture comes in, I switch the sound to nothing. Watch the man in his robe with the purple stripe, the way he grabs the lectern and stares dead in the camera. Sharp eyes and bold.

I behold the Almighty's man on earth, and for all his square shoulder certainty, I can see the red in his eyes right through the God damn screen.

Chapter 16

From the dark ahead arrived the *yipyipyip* of coyote.

Joe paused. Cocked his ear.

Coyotes were small. Joe was not large, but as their measure, the animals were mostly fur. He outweighed them but knew from his limited experience in the fight circle that weight only meant so much. Animals had wiles, did unpredictable things. A small dog with surprise and wit could flip you.

Wild animals had greater wiles.

These cousins worked together, as dogs who find one another agreeable sometimes join to pursue common interests. But Joe also observed them alone, ears high, stalking a rabbit or rodent with no one to share.

As with humans, in groups they were more prone to belligerence.

So far, Joe had contented himself to watch from a distance, and avoid their odor where he found it. The forest was large, and his journey eastward toward the mecca of human scent, Flagstaff, had many approaches.

But tonight, twice attacked by man and having nonetheless feasted on rich human food, Joe opened toward adventure.

Abundance.

Would he find common purpose with the coyote?

One, in particular, emitted an inviting fragrance. Female and young and frolicking fun. After filling his belly and napping, he yearned for company. Sniffing. Commiserating. Playing.

But there was also danger.

The unknown.

This *yipyipyip* came from a small pack. Joe caught their scent as the breeze shifted, and when he imagined them, they were not surprised to see him. The wind kept no secrets.

He could go elsewhere, but before when he'd found his first comfortable and safe hideaway, deep in the warm earth, it stank of coyote. This pack had several new ones among their number.

They had a den.

Joe tromped. A mile from the neon food place and its flashing strobes, he wound between trees. Followed gullies until the scent of coyote thickened. He tingled. Sniffed the base of a tree. The territory marking was pungent and recent.

Yipyipyip!

They advanced.

Joe stood, nose high. He looked into the darkness. A ghost veered and bolted toward him like lightning.

They chose attack.

He braced, ready to feint at the last second and throw the animal.

Low in his register Joe growled. His muscles trembled. But before the first arrived, another, unseen and unheard, exploded upon him from the rear. Teeth sunk into his haunch, deep in the muscle but above the tendon. Joe whirled to face the stealth attacker and the one from the front flew at him in a silent arcing leap. While he was half spun to meet his rearward assailant, the other collided into him, ripped into his shoulder. Joe flopped to his back, and they closed. One at his leg and the other his throat.

But Joe was strong, and his viciousness matched their savagery. On his back, he bounced and cast his jaws at the frontal attacker—a male—who withdrew and lunged again at another angle. The second attacker—female—bit again, this time higher on the Joe's thigh. She slashed outward, tearing apart muscle.

Joe snipped and missed.

He snarled.

They yipped.

Joe kicked. His rear legs shoved away the female and propelled him within closer reach of the male's underside. Again Joe lunged—from his back—and this time caught a full hold on the male coyote's throat.

The female slashed his back legs, but as Joe wriggled and shimmied her teeth failed to penetrate.

Joe clamped his fangs, but the coyote's fur was thick. He ratcheted deeper, tiny short release-pulses that settled the other's neck farther into the vice.

But the female at his legs slashed again, and something tore that sent panic through him. Joe released the male just as he tasted blood.

Joe flipped to his feet and shuttled back five steps. His rear leg faltered. There was no backing out of this fight. No springing the fence and running. As with the man in the trailer and the other at the concrete wall, fleeing could not save him. His wiles would not postpone death.

Only butchery, the nexus where his willingness to destroy life met his waning capacity, offered hope.

He eased backward. Each step brought his male and

female attackers closer in his perspective. He addressed them both with the same low-headed stare and growl.

Beyond these two glowed the eyes of another coyote, almost full sized, but patient. She was a helper, still learning the ropes, waiting to join battle when needed.

Beside her gleamed the eyes of three more pups.

One licked its jowl.

Chapter 17

Lester Toungate called Lucky into the cab and climbed beside him. He reloaded his .357, and put a handful of shells from the box in his left pocket. Then drove deeper into the intermittent scrub trees, following a path that meandered to Rogers Lake.

Though he stored a point nosed shovel in the bed of the truck he didn't feel like digging a hole deep enough for two bodies. Certainly not deep enough for Clyde's truck. A hundred yards from road 2310, hidden from all but airplane, he killed the engine. Rubbed behind Lucky's ears, then along the dog's jaw. Lester looked at his hand.

The old dog had been coughing blood. But not now.

He reached past Lucky and unrolled the window to the bottom. Dog could get out if he wanted.

Lester was all about letting others make decisions.

From the back of the king cab under the seat, he grabbed a signal flare and from the other side, so the two would never mingle, a can of WD-40.

Lester locked the truck. Circled back to the open window. "I'll be a while. It's bedtime."

Lucky whined. Lester walked.

Lester approached Clyde Munsinger's truck from behind, .357 in his right hand. He carried the flare in his pocket and the WD-40 in his left. The air was chilly, but only seemed colder than usual because Lester hadn't been out at midnight all winter. He had other people for that.

Most of that.

Clyde's engine ran, and though Lester had first thought the boy wrecked into a ditch, he'd parked on the side of the road.

Lester paused. Clyde wasn't necessarily dead, or so mortally wounded he lost control of the vehicle.

Easy and slow, he raised his pistol as he neared the passenger door. The headlights' glow only made the dark interior all the more impenetrable. Attuned to any sound, he eased his hand to the door. A voice came to him from far off, like it was only in his mind. Lester canted his head.

He'd been listening for the voice for forty years. Craving it. Provoking it. But nothing.

Maybe killing Paul did the trick. What was more biblical than a father killing a son?

"That you?"

Nothing. Lester aimed his head skyward.

"I said is that you?"

Lester waited. Remembered the radio.

He pulled the door handle with his WD-40 hand and studied the scene. The boy was dead, bled out all over everything, body slumped to the driver's door. His eyes probed the cab roof. Lester drew the door open all the way.

The radio was still on.

Anyone who turns to the Lord can be saved by the Lord. It doesn't matter what you do! You can't do anything! Remember the thief on the cross next...

Lester threw the passenger floor mat to the ground outside, and grabbed the dead boy by the hair. Slipped. Drug him by his shirt collar over the seat and pushed him into the footwell. Exactly where a tragic waste of DNA like Clyde Munsinger ought to take his final ride.

He slammed the door, heard the crunch of bone. Opened it and shoved Clyde's hand back inside.

Lester picked up the floor mat from the dirt. Circled. At the driver side, he opened the door.

All he did was let his soul cry out—Lord! I'm not holy. I need you to be holy for me. I need you to carry the load I can't carry.

Blood pooled on the driver side mat. Lester flipped it upside down and placed it on the seat. Then put the mat from the passenger side on the seatback.

Friend, if you're that thief on the cross, Jesus Christ has a message for you. I said friend, if you're that prostitute standing bare toed in the dirt, Jesus Christ has a message—

Lester hit the knob.

He grabbed the wheel and pulled himself into the cab. Checked his mirrors. Looked ahead, back, and engaged the truck's transmission. Three point turned and drove.

A minute later, he eased alongside Paul's corpse. He again three-pointed to align his son with the passenger door.

Outside he opened the door and with the light from the vehicle observed his dead son.

Lester removed his jacket and placed it on the bed rail. Stooped and snaked his arms under Paul's armpits, then interlocked hands at his chest. He lifted with his legs until standing. His muscles strained. Pressure built in his head. He backed to the truck, twisted, and heaved. Paul slumped, but

Lester fell forward with him and his upper half landed on the truck seat. Lester shifted to his legs—smelled his son's evacuated bowels—and jerked the rest of him on top of Clyde.

Lester kicked some dirt over the blood on the road, but figured hell, the most anybody would think is an animal got hit by a car and wandered off. Or a poacher loaded a pronghorn there. Wasn't worth the effort.

Back inside the truck, he shifted to drive. As he cut the wheel the headlights crossed a set of eyes staring bold from the scrub. He parked a minute. Rolled down the window.

"You wanna get in the truck?"

The eyes blinked.

Lester exited. Opened the tailgate and Lucky bounded. His back legs missed and Lester scrambled to him. Lifted. He closed the gate and Lucky stationed himself forward, where the wind would be less.

Lester rubbed his dog's ears. "You're gonna be working all night and then some. Up to you."

He drove.

It got a little hairy closer to Flagstaff, up 231 and weaving his way onto 40. But the bodies were low and the dark pervasive. Even with the full moon rising, none of the rare vehicles knew they were passing a truck with a killer and two corpses.

That was something fun to muse about: what people didn't know. Like when he touched a lady cashier's hand at the grocery store, to get his card back. She gave a tingle, like a spark of soul going from him to her, or the other way around. Probably the other way around. She didn't know how many throats those hands had throttled. How many triggers they'd pulled. The things she didn't know. Maybe he took a little of her too, just with the touch.

Onto Interstate 40 toward Williams. That was a spooky place lately. Suits everywhere for months, looking for the man from North Carolina. Kind of exciting to haul two bodies right through the thick of them. After Williams, Lester exited on 89 toward Prescott, again feeling that butt-scrunching tickle of fear while driving through town with corpses in the truck.

The delight of being around dead people—didn't matter if he killed them or someone else—never grew old. He'd gotten over being an outlaw from man's laws long ago. That was a thrill back when stealing cookies made him quake.

Something happened in his forties. Before, he'd fret about offending the rules of man, as if they meant something. After forty, Lester knew the kind of men who became legislators, and quality of their minds. Their souls. Made it hard to care about breaking their laws.

Nowadays, Lester's only outlaw thrill came from violating the laws of God. The so-called God. Violating the universal rules everyone thought came from a supreme law giver.

Making dead men was a thrill. The pastor said God owned everything, and Lester thought of killing men like breaking into a rich man's house and smashing the jewels.

Of course, the thing God loved more than his animals and people was his rules. So killing Paul, his son—that had to break a dozen rules. Like boiling a goat in the milk of its mother, Old Testament stuff, sure to provoke divine rage.

Killing his son felt satisfyingly provocative.

The feeling ... how would he describe it? Looking at the black sky, listening for a voice that never came down from above, so much he doubted it existed—yet everything in him said it did, or should—ah, hell, what nonsense you think, driving two hours with corpses.

He knew what he was doing: jabbing a stick at the Creator, trying to provoke him out of his cage.

That's why killing men—and women—was such a thrill.

All these years and no response.

He pretended where he needed to pretend. Smiled and

volunteered at church. He lived as ostentatious a lie as was possible, taunting a lightning strike five times a day, minimum. Blasphemed, murdered, and still ...

No voice.

Should have brought coffee.

At Prescott he headed out on 10. Turned here and there, cut across the plain. Ninety degree turn into the woods, out of the woods. When the road was near impassible, he turned left to a doubletrack. The path was a couple of ruts over a rocky meadow with trees vying to make it forest. For a mile neither won nor lost.

The circuitous route led to the center of the eleven mile loop called Sycamore Rim Trail. Then crossed the thin-wooded plain to Sycamore Canyon. Road intersected trail about fifteen feet from the edge. Trees climbed the canyon. From the air, the green rendered its depth invisible. But the drop at the edge made a man feel small. The cliff opened to a massive expanse of open air and, a couple hundred feet below, the forested canyon floor. Backpackers loved this section of the trail, where they camped beside the cliff.

Lester slowed on the approach, watched for anything reflective, such as a tent or gear, at the campsite off to the right.

He pulled the truck to the edge, engaged park, and turned off the headlights.

Opened the door and mused for a moment.

Sycamore Canyon was a superb place to hide dead men, in Lester's schooled estimation. People didn't go to the bottom. Well—guides sometimes led elk hunters down, where the story went, herds had never seen anything but the canyon floor. But regular folks had no idea how to get there. While it was possible someone would stumble along and find a truck run over the cliff, the chance was remote. With the bottom-land covered in trees, spotting the vehicle from above seemed unlikely.

Back in the day, he'd have spent the night shoveling earth in the middle of the woods, holes three feet deep. But the nice thing about age—he didn't get his drawers in a scrunch over every perceived risk. With age came discernment. He knew which risks were real—such as Clyde's threat to expose him—and were less so—the random passer by discovering bodies at the bottom of a canyon no one ever went to.

It was good being old and wise. Or rather, if he had to be old, best to be grateful for what the age purchased.

Still, by force of habit, Lester thought it out:

Let's say, worse case, someone finds the bodies at the bottom. If one of the dead men's IDs survives the flames, will it matter? Anything connect him to them? Except one being his son?

Yep. Everything. They'd learn the truck belonged to Clyde, and if they investigated deep enough, they'd find Lester and Paul's ties to the mobile home park.

Best to destroy the IDs separate. Slow them down. Hell, at his age, slowing the law down for a month might be enough to live his last days in peace.

Nah. Hell. Deep down Lester knew he'd never die. And that's why given the choice, he'd never put the gun to his chest and pull the trigger. No man was big enough to kill him; God seemed hell bent on not giving a damn. If he didn't do it himself, it would never happen.

You don't think those things out. You know them.

The thought nagged: he should dispose of Paul someplace different from Clyde. So law enforcement couldn't tie the two together, if they were ever found.

Lester shook his head, exasperated with himself. "Yeah, well, that's why I'm putting them at the bottom of the canyon. So they're not found."

Lester exited, crossed behind the truck, opened the passenger door. Fished wallets out of soiled drawers, then called Lucky out of the truck bed. The dog sniffed along the rim, oblivious to the hundred-plus foot sheer drop.

"Post!"

The dog walked ten feet and sat at attention, facing outward to the dark.

"Good dog."

Lucky whined.

On the open tailgate, Lester made a pile of drivers licenses and credit cards. He folded and pocketed the cash. He lit the flare and held the blinding red flame to plastic. The cards melted but failed to ignite quickly. He rested the flare on the metal, flame to plastic, and went to the cab.

Inside, he sprayed WD-40 on the bodies until the can was empty.

Lucky growled.

Lester halted. Eased out of the truck and let his hand fall easy to his hip, while he searched the dark beyond the dog. The flare cast a red-tinged glow into the trees. Two forms approached. Hidden behind the truck, Lester pulled his .357.

As the men entered the area lit by the flare, they slowed. One wore a black holster, small, such as for a short-barrel automatic. The other appeared unarmed.

"Whatcha doon, mister?"

The armed one. Intoxicated.

Lester stood full height. Hand on the butt of his revolver, ready to yank, he stepped to the side. He stopped with his right arm exposed but his lower half blocked by the truck's bed.

"I got a couple bodies in the truck. Gonna run them over the cliff here, so nobody finds em. Say, it's awful cold for backpacking. What are you boys doing out here?"

"Ain't too cold. Damn. You say you got bodies in there?"

"Yeah. Wanna see?"

"Nah. You punking us? Why you drive right up to the cliff?"

"Why you up this late? Where'd you park?"

"Nah, man. We packed in."

"I bet."

"We came from up thataways."

The other spoke. "We'll leave you be, mister. C'mon, Steve."

"I wanna see the bodies."

"Fellas," Lester said, "I need to know where you parked."

"At the trailhead. Why? We'll let you go about your business."

"So you camped up there a bit?"

Lucky growled.

"Beyond the trees." The armed man waved. Lost his balance. The other grabbed his arm.

"Who's with you?"

"Oh, wow. A bunch of us," the unarmed man said. "We've got another dozen men up there."

"Okay, good. Well, you head back that way, and we'll forget we run into one another."

Lucky's growled turned to a high pitched whine. The men stepped backward, still facing Lester.

Lester turned, aligned his right arm so the upward swing tracked the sober man. He jerked his pistol and fired twice on the way up.

From the distance arrived a clipped female shriek.

The sober man fell, and the other, leaning on him, stumbled. Lester strode to him, fired one into his head, and kept walking.

Chapter 18

Joe studied his adversaries. His throat rumbled quiet, almost for encouragement. He'd backed a few steps and now stood in a small clearing of mostly level ground. To his right, a line of boulders joined a seam that became a wall a hundred yards away. Behind him, open space, affording more room to maneuver.

The male and female coyote approached.

Trees combined with the blackness of deep night to form the fight ring's border. Starlight penetrated the center, but the full moon had not yet overcome the valley walls.

Spectators ringed the outside; Joe made the forms of the young female and three pups under her charge. She hadn't advanced with Joe's retreat, as had the others.

The male wheezed.

The female stopped.

The male growled, his voice lower than Joe had ever heard from a coyote. But it warbled into a cough, then throat-clearing. His breath came husky. He resumed with the female beside him, ears flat to her head and teeth pale and shiny.

She would attack.

Joe reared—not high, but inches.

The she-coyote dashed in. Joe turned into her; met her swooping face with a snarl. She slashed but her fangs glanced his shoulder. He caught the fur of her neck, but closed his jaw on nothing.

She leaped away, out to the darkness.

The female helper with the pups yipped her excitement.

The male growled low, again threatening to advance.

Joe had fallen for the trick before. He tuned his ears to the sporadic rustle of leaves. There, there, there. He turned as she bounded around the perimeter, appearing like a phantom in flashes between trees, there, then blackness. The male snarled.

If he attacked the male, she would launch herself at him. As he turned to keep her in front, at some point the male would sense advantage.

Joe's hind leg weakened as he turned. The tendon between hock and thigh had been partly severed by the female's last attack. Now as Joe turned, the side to side motion exposed his infirmity. He could move. His agility didn't seem hampered. His attitude surged with end-of-life fear combined with adrenal optimism. But his injured leg couldn't propel him. It could barely support him.

The female circled.

Finding himself facing the male, Joe stalked close. The male held his ground.

Leaves rustles behind ...

She charged.

Joe rushed past the male coyote, turned. The female missed but homed in for another assault.

Joe turned, reared, and while the coyote lifted herself to meet his strike, Joe dove below her. He caught her front leg in his jaw, rolled, and snapped her forearm.

She flopped with him; cried out. Joe returned to his feet.

The male rushed, but stopped short, coughing. Joe darted into the gap and drove with his shoulder. With the male coyote thrown, Joe again jawed his throat. Pinning him with his superior weight, Joe opened his jaws, closed them hard. The wind pipe collapsed and the coyote gagged. He shredded Joe's belly with frantic paws.

Joe flopped to the other side of the male while the female, yelping and hobbled, attacked his haunches. Remaining on top of the male and his jaws tightening with all his force, Joe spun, revolving the male coyote with him.

Incapable of swift motion, the female followed Joe's rear as he twisted. The male's lungs heaved. Joe tasted blood, but not the jugular spurt.

Favoring her broken ankle, the female leaped. Joe turned again, and this time the male coyote's leg caught hold of a root.

Joe's torque ripped open the male coyote's throat.

Joe spat out hair and meat.

Blood flowed free from the male's neck, and he flopped to his feet and fell. Tried to bark but garbled his churrup. Each wheeze grew shorter.

Joe faced the female.

She held her injured paw above the ground.

Joe inhaled the cold air. They stared at one another, but neither moved for advantage. The female lowered her left leg, but with the barest pressure, whimpered. She held it aloft.

She growled, starting off low, rolling through her register into a high pitched bark. The tenor reminded him of the man in the bathroom. The warbling signaled weakness. A primal request for mercy. Not to escape death, but to make it quick.

Joe attacked. Again he came in high. Joe spread his forearms, this time instead of dashing at her leg, he boxed her between his arms and rolled her. While she struggled to regain her feet, Joe found the female's throat, and he squeezed with reinvigorated power.

He jerked mightily and blood released from her neck. The flow pulsed salty in his mouth and dripped out the sides. The female quaked, issued a sucking sound.

He was intoxicated by it, his body filled with frenzy. He growled. Heaved. Turned, and with his jaws clamped, sought to regain the helper coyote and three pups in his sight.

When she struggled no more, Joe released. With her exhalation came a whimper.

The male had stopped moving. Only the barest breath, audible from the many obstructions in his throat, evidenced he was still alive.

Joe sat. Though his hind had felt weakened, during his singular focus he felt no pain.

Now he turned to the helper coyote guarding the pups. Joe watched how she observed him in return. Her loyalty pledged to the winner.

Joe stepped closer. She was young, barely more than a pup. She inched into the circle, then catching sight of something behind Joe, pivoted.

She leaped away.

A pup mewed.

Above the two coyotes' death scent Joe smelled another ... and understood why the helper coyote bolted and the pup cried its weak warning.

Mountain lion.

Joe spun.

It had crept to the edge of the circle and waited for the fight to end.

Joe beheld its disguised size. The lion faced him with head low and shoulders bundled, taking the shape of a large dog. But Joe had seen one of these animals ride down a deer, chewing its head until the deer's brains were crushed and sliced in skull bone. These cats were huge; their paws swung like clawed mallets, but they preferred to attack from behind.

Joe stepped backward.

He growled a warning that faltered in his throat. From behind him came the stupid yip of one of the pups.

The helper was long gone.

Joe again retreated.

The lion halted its approach at the body of the male coyote. It sniffed.

Joe backed farther.

The lion closed quick and swiped with its paw, catching Joe on his chest and rolling him.

Joe sprung to his feet and leaped away, his injured hind leg useless. Pain came from his sliced open chest. Joe scuttled a dozen yards and glanced back. The lion had not followed. Joe stopped.

The cougar stood above a coyote pup and lifted it in its jaws. The cat crushed each pup, then raised its massive head toward Joe and sniffed. Stepped back to the dead she-coyote, gripped her in its teeth, and dragged her into blackness.

Joe watched a long moment. His pulse slowed as emergency faded to cold reality. The cat had shredded his chest muscles. The coyote had partly severed his left rear tendon. But Joe was victor.

He lived.

Joe walked away with what ability remained.

Chapter 19

As he left the area illuminated reddish-white by the flare, Lester slowed. Lucky sniffed a few feet ahead, and the distance between them grew. Lester ran his free hand through his hair.

Should've brought coffee.

Only once before had unexpected witnesses followed those they had seen.

He should have expected the possibility. Even this early in the season, some college idiots might camp in the cold.

As he walked, Lester considered. Assuming the guys had brought a couple girls with them—which he'd verify soon enough—and other people weren't camping nearby, allowing them to live might pose little threat. They'd hide all night in terror. The moon was out, but barely broke through the tree cover. They wouldn't have seen his face well enough to identify him.

But say he let them live, and he drove the truck over the

cliff, and later joined up with El Jay for a ride home ...

Soon enough, whoever he left alive would tell police a story. They would point to the canyon. A detective would saunter up to the edge and look down. Spot four wheels and an undercarriage. They'd find a way to the bottom. Leaving witnesses made Paul and Clyde's discovery certain.

Lester arrived at a campfire with reddish coals and a single blue flame. They'd pitched the tents too close. Inspired, Lester considered: kill the girls, drag the boys up here, put them all in the bags, and set each tent on fire.

But that wouldn't explain the bullet hole in the boy's head, and it'd be pretty tough getting rid of the blood on the trail. And he couldn't assume there'd be time for rain to wash the dirt clean any time soon.

"Go away! We've got a gun!"

Lester halted. "Lucky, c'mere."

The dog came back to Lester.

"Well, you have a situation to deal with. I can see what I'm shooting at, while you can't. If you want us to hash this out so you end up alive, you better come out the tent. Otherwise I'll fill it with holes.

"I'll shoot back!"

"Yeah, but I'm behind a rock. I'll give you a minute to think. Then I expect you to come out the tent so we can talk. Maybe there's something you ladies can do for me that'll make things better on your end. Give you a little bargaining power, if you understand me?"

From inside the tent came mumbled voices. Two girls, maybe three.

"You talking about sex?"

"Girls, girls. I'm an old fella mindin' my business until your boys minded it too. I want some sort of remuneration for my troubles. I'm flexible, like you. Just want to be made whole. Be reasonable."

Lester smiled at the cat and mouse. This was the fun part,

the outwitting part. He could shoot up the tent easy enough. But the back and forth, well that was sweet.

Regular people wanted to believe in regular things. Couldn't fathom the irregular. The girls listened to their men die, but they wanted to trust in a good world. A calm voice and the promise of clear reasoning would entice their return to stupidity. Every woman considers trading sex for their lives a hundred times, regardless of whether any bad guys make the offer.

"Girls, no man wants to hurt a lady. God give you holes and made men to fill them. That's what we both want, you and me. So let's see if we can't find a compromise."

That was another word. *Compromise.* Kids loved that word.

World falling apart, all the compromise.

"Just want a little *tolerance*," Lester said, grinning.

The moon cut through the tree cover, but the fire's blue flame was near useless.

"Try to be... *open minded.*"

The tent zipper jerked six inches. Again. A delicate hand thrust a pistol into a shaft of moonbeam. The zipper moved a third time. She was clumsy with fear. Not nearly as sporting an interaction as Lester had hoped.

"You was in the sleeping bag?"

Her clothes seemed thick on her, baggy like sweats. She held her arm at a ninety degree angle. Though Lester saw the pistol, he couldn't now discern its dimensions.

The girl moved aside as the next came out.

Side by side, they looked the same. Baggy. Each holding a gun on him.

Peculiar.

Why would two girls looking at the man who murdered their lovers not shoot him?

They didn't understand the functionality of their firearms, and that, in the cosmic sense, was a shame.

"What kind of deal did you want?" the first said.

"And how can we trust you to let us go?" said the second.

"None, and I won't." Lester fired from the hip, one for each. Stepped closer and put another into each girl's skull.

At the beginning, the exchange was pregnant with fun. But the stupidity of two girls holding guns they didn't comprehend how to save themselves with kind of turned Lester's stomach. He almost wanted to leave their bodies, guns in hand, as a lesson. But Lester's job wasn't to teach the world shit.

"Any more of you in there? Come on out. You can add to the *diversity*."

He moved to the tent, pushed aside the flap with the tip of his barrel. Too dark. "You inside, pretty?"

He listened.

Lester knelt. Felt along the bottom and found a flashlight. Turned it on, saw sleeping bags, back packs, jeans and boots. Lester withdrew from the tent and shined the light to the other. Useless.

"Best come out."

From the intelligence he'd so far witnessed, that ought to do the trick. But no sound issued and he pulled the zipper, led with the light and peered inside. The backpacks were bigger. This must have been the boys' tent.

Boys in one tent and girls in the other. Lester shook his head.

He dragged the closest pack outside. The flap on top was open, the contents recently rifled—such as to find a packed gun. Lester rooted through the clothes and gear and found what he wanted: a plastic bag with packets of instant coffee. He searched out a canteen, dumped in three packs and shook. Drank the caffeine elixir cold.

He shined the light to the girls. They'd fallen apart from each other, each crumpled a different sideways. Minus the hole and blood, each face pretty.

His life could have ended, Lester realized. All the taunting he'd done, God could have dropped him into fire and brimstone right there. And almost taunting him back, God chose not to. Just so Lester wouldn't find clarity. A rotten thing to do. Lester cut the flashlight to the first girl's hand, and knelt.

He lowered his head. It couldn't be ...

The safety was off.

He took the automatic from her hand. Pulled the slide a half inch and tilted it to the light.

Yep, one in the chamber.

All she had to do was pull the trigger.

Lester shook his head. Stared at the girl a long while, wondering how she'd framed it in her mind. Had she preferred rape, over killing a killer?

Couldn't be. Impossible to wrap the brain around it.

Lester righted himself. Looked away, to the expanse of black nothing over canyon's edge. A perfect place to look while pondering imponderables.

Preparation allowed him to avoid random danger. Sometimes, however, sound strategies had gaps. One girl out of two might *want* to pull a trigger. Thinking with superstition instead of logic, he could infer God preferred his survival.

But the existence of happenstance ridiculous curiosities, such as two girls dying with life-saving pistols in hand, only proved God didn't exist. For in no one's book was Lester virtuous and the world wicked. Some of the craziest of killers, Lester read, considered their actions noble. Usually the ones who murdered prostitutes. But Lester was not so deluded. If good and evil existed, Lester understood which uniform he wore.

If it existed.

Most likely, evil was a brand imposed on others by the folks who had the power, to keep it from the ones who didn't.

From that light, Lester's work was virtuous.

Coffee—even instant coffee—did the mind good.

But now he had a problem.

He couldn't add the kids to the body pile in the truck and send it over the cliff. Someone surely knew the kids were packing Sycamore Rim Trail. The search party would stumble on the blood. An observer from an airplane could see the windshield reflected through the trees.

This whole thing went from simple to compound disaster.

Better take it slow and think things out.

If he hadn't shot each man in the heart, setting up the murder/suicide would have been easy. But folks rarely— Lester knew it for a fact—shot themselves in the chest, and then the head. Plus, neither girl had a .357, and the striations wouldn't match if they did, and he didn't want to leave his .357, as he was fond of it.

No choice but gather the bodies and move them someplace else, unassociated with any of the victims. Give himself more time to think.

Lester looked at his watch. Still only 1:30. Plenty of night left to handle things.

His plan was to call El Jay for a ride from the forest road at dawn. Now he'd leave El Jay out of it.

For now. There were things to consider on that front as well.

Lester found a stump and rested the flashlight with the beam on the camp. He pulled pegs, collapsed each tent, rolled a girl on it, and dragged them each to the truck. There he stood them like he did Paul, except the cab had no room for more corpses. So he placed them in the bed, to ride with Lucky. He shoved the tents into their backpacks, along with sleeping bags and everything else lying around, in the bed as well. So long as not viewed from above while under a street lamp, it would do.

The engine had been running. Lester worked himself to the seat and let his back settle in, let the vertebrae loosen, while his mind calculated the angles. He rolled down the windows to let the smell of WD-40 dissipate.

The real problem was the proximity of the bodies to each other, and to the truck. Paul and Clyde together without identification were just bodies. But the truck's registration would lead to Clyde. Paul was in Clyde's outer orbit, and once they identified him, Lester would be within their circle of inquiry. And the kids, they associated with each other, but not Paul or Clyde. None of the kids could illuminate the identities of Paul or Clyde. It seemed the only trouble was the truck.

So why the hell was he ready to haul six corpses back to Flagstaff, when all he had to do was separate the bodies from the truck?

Lack of adequate caffeine. Brain can't think without adequate caffeine. He drank more from the canteen.

Lester stepped out. Placed the still-burning flare two feet from the rim edge. He turned the truck, backed in so the extended tailgate was over the cliff. He shoved each corpse over, listened for the impact, then pitched the backpacks after them. Next he pulled forward, loaded Paul and Clyde in the back of the truck, and again backed the tailgate over the abyss. Easier to pitch them, with the added clearance.

He dumped Clyde, then Paul, invited Lucky up front. Pulled forward twenty yards, and swept the ground with a branch to remove any tire imprints.

Chapter 20

A few dozen yards from the site of the showdown, Joe detected the scent of the young female that had left the coyote pups to their destruction. The way she bounded high, graceful like a pronghorn, suggested vitality. Joe's biology urged him to find common purpose with her.

His rear leg sent a twitchy pain signal akin to a tingle—a caution. He distributed his weight to his other limbs. The change in his gate emphasized the discomfort of having his chest ribboned by the lion's claws.

Blood had coagulated and the gashes, though deep, barely seeped. But his right front was as ineffective as his left rear. As he walked, the injured limbs moved at the same time. They stayed planted at the same time. He was weak regardless of whether the legs provided thrust or stability. He attempted to trot, but tumbled.

Resuming his footing, motion resulted from will, not strength.

Joe arrived at a stream and lowered his head to the water, parched but reluctant to limit his senses. Who knew what invisible attack might be drawing close?

He sniffed the air. No mountain lion—unless it had circled him, and remained downwind.

Joe lapped cold water. He'd had so many mouthfuls of hair and blood, the water rolled cool down his throat, washed his mouth clean, and invigorated him.

Again putting his nose to the breeze, Joe waited for scents to accumulate. He'd prefer the wind to come from ahead.

Weakened by the fights and attack, biology urged Joe to locate the young female coyote who abandoned the others. In not attacking him, perhaps she had chosen him.

Joe drove onward, each step tightening his muscles and sharpening the pain of using them. Every few feet he smelled the ground, following the she-coyote's steps. Finally he stopped at a crag that stood half the height of the nearby trees. The rocks formed a wall as far as night permitted him to see. It seemed built of boulders, some small and some the size of houses. Between them, overhangs and caverns provided winter shelter for animals over many centuries. The territory burst with their scents. Porcupine. Skunk. Mountain lion.

And coyote.

Joe followed her along the base of the crag. He turned inward at a crevice, nosed inside and lowered his shoulders. Squeezed to make them fit. The rock abraded his cuts; his rear leg throbbed with the pressure of trying to thrust him through the hole.

From inside—very near—she growled.

Joe halted. Her scent was strong—but the lair presented her smell in mixed form, jumbled with the others he'd vanquished, and the pups. Inside must be large, but the opening tiny.

Her growl increased intensity.

Joe wriggled back, but the rock held him. He pushed with

his front paws and shook his rear but barely moved. The pressure from the walls was great, as if they closed tighter to trap him. Unknowing what beast stalked from behind, and unable to lift a paw or jockey his shoulders and head to fend off an attack, Joe snarled. He wriggled off his backside and heaved with both rear legs. The pain in the left, where the tendon was half torn, shot a bolt of panic through him. Near frantic, he raised his back high, planted his feet and dropped downward. The motion stretched his shoulders, and he popped free.

Joe fell back, landed sitting. He spun, anticipating attack by a mountain lion or some other speedy beast.

None came.

From inside the crevice the she-coyote growled again, this time her voiced turned higher in pitch.

Plaintive.

Joe continued along the face of the crag, stopping to investigate likely rest areas. A hundred yards beyond the she-coyote's lair, he stopped at a cavern with an opening large enough for a bear. There were no recent animals there.

He sniffed to learn the history. The dry leaves and rock walls were a maze of ancient smells. Mountain lion. Bear. Coyote. Dog. Man. And a dozen small beasts he couldn't place, most likely ones that had already tasted delicious to some other predator.

Compared to the hole he'd nearly trapped himself in, this lair was huge. The large opening would permit entry to any attacker, no matter the size. Joe sniffed along the base of the wall and, at the back, found where ground had been stacked high. Some digger had enlarged a passage. Joe lowered himself and followed an old scent into the hole. After a foot, he could turn around.

The temperature was much warmer than outside, and the air, while fresh, was still. The outer cave blocked most light, and inside the back room, dark was near total.

Curled, Joe attempted to lick the slash on his left rear leg, then gave up and licked what he could reach of his chest. At last, he lowered his head to his paws.

From outside arrived a long howl—the wind.

His wounds ached. His eyes sometimes opened and sometimes closed, until at last he trusted he was hidden from a world that attacked at every turn.

Chapter 21

Wake on the couch. Cover's hard like the quarter inch of rubber they made dodge balls with. Television on all night. Crick in my neck. Feet cold. Old Baer. No dog.

But I got an eighteen-year-old girl so desperate for love she'd poke a grizzly Baer.

And I have so many dead bodies accusing me, the stink clawed its way through two feet of concrete.

"JOE!"

Fall off the couch.

"Where's the remote?"

Volume's off—morning news on the screen. Crime scene lights a-flashing. They cut to a grainy black and white from some surveillance camera, and freeze the shot.

"Where the fu—"

Grab the remote. Hit the volume. That's Stinky Joe if ever I saw him.

... gruesome scene was discovered by Trevor Smith, of

Flagstaff, night manager at the Hardees restaurant located on Richmond Drive. Viewer discretion is advised.

They show blood on pavement. Cut back to the police car strobes. Uniform walking about, thumbs in his belt loops, but serious writ on his face.

The tape will show—okay, here's the tape. This is the victim before being attacked, apparently after discovering the pit bulldog trapped in the pen surrounding the restaurant's garbage dumpster. He'd dragging a chain, which he planned to use to secure the dog, to help the animal to safety.

"He tell you that?"

Ah! Woman got the red eyes.

I look close. Man has the chain doubled and the end wrapped on his hand, ready to swing.

That man beat Joe.

The killer pit bulldog—and the killing—was caught on video.

"No such thing as a pit bulldog!"

The animal about to come on the screen is a pit bulldog, the breed known for its destructive jaws and violent nature. Although the full attack was recorded by the restaurant's security cameras, out of respect for the victim, we're only showing the aftermath, as the killer trots away, perhaps to hunt another.

I'm so close to the television there's little dots. Back away. They show the police car. Yellow tape. A couple uniforms.

Hardees on Richmond, she said.

Richmond.

Run to my room. Pull on boots. Grab the map book. Shows Arizona, got a section for the towns. Find Richmond on the street list and the grid square for J-23. Okeydokey. Street right at the edge of civilization, got the wood on the other side. Back a ways, a draw—and what I seen of Flagstaff, that'll be where the rocks are. If Joe lived all winter, he's familiar with the caves and fissures. Somewhere in those rocks—I guarantee—that'll be where I find Joe.

Either that or shot dead.

I had wheels, it'd be forty-five minutes to Flag. But even if there are vehicles at the Graves place, I can't get one.

Best I can do is hijack a car on the interstate. Except I got no gun. Left Smith on the ground at Graves' when I was liquored up and Tat gave me the orange hair drugs.

Tat has a gun—a Sig Sauer ole Cinder gave her. But she loves on that gun like most girls love on kittens. No such thing as borrowing it. Have to knock her cold to steal it.

And all the guns and ammo Graves bought to withstand Armageddon are still at the house. Lazy bastard never hauled anything up here save dehydrated food, and I suspect that was part of the construction deal, like the Flintstone furniture.

Figure thirty, forty mile to Hardees. One-two days' hard march.

Got the escape plan already figured. Just needed the reason.

I find a ride, so much the better.

"What's that?"

"Uh, morning, Tat. That's a map."

"Because of last night?"

She's cool. Shoulder on wall. Hip out, arm hangs graceful. I was twenty, I'd be begging another poke.

"Huh?"

"You want to leave because of last night?"

"No. No. Hell no. Stinky Joe. They had him on the television. They'll hunt him down. Kill him."

She studies me.

All of a sudden my mess is itchy.

"I got to save my dog, is all. Plus—time to move on, Tat. I—uh, wish you the best."

Got nothing here so packing is easy—I'll leave with what I'm wearing. Got a buck knife one of the Graves boys gave me. A coat. Boots. Ready to trot.

"They will find you."

"Yeah."

"You will go to prison."

"No."

"You need help."

"Need aluminum foil."

I step past her. She grabs my hand. Stares, haunted. Girl has demons. She connects long and hard like our brains are wired, and she's trying to shoot love across the lines, but has so much despair, it just comes off lonesome. I squeeze her elbow." You're stronger than you think."

"We—"

Shake my head. Pull free. "Accident, is all. You and me. And I have to save Joe."

"Baer?"

"I was young or you was old, we'd scrog sixteen hours a day. Lordy, I promise. But it's the moral. I can't poke a kid."

"You didn't like the sex?"

"Nah. You kidding? If I was in charge—"

"Who the hell is in charge? Of what?"

"Your English is coming along fine."

She got me. I dunno. Who put it in my head that screwing young girls is wrong?

"You're a tight ass man."

"You mean hung up?"

"I mean a prude."

"Yeah, that. Well—"

At winter's start, we stocked a closet in the kitchen with one of everything stored in the warehouse they dug on the side. I grab a box of foil and roll out eight foot strips until I hit cardboard tube. Stretch them on the floor and fold the seams over like Ma used to make a tent for turkey. Press the seams flat with a rolling pin, three folds over. In fifteen minutes of cussing, I manufacture a single sheet of silver, seven feet tall and eight wide. I fold the ends several times over, make a quarter inch solid so nothing will tear, then fold the whole sheet twice.

Grab a pocket of dried meat and a couple bites for the belly.

Tat hasn't moved.

"That won't work."

"Okay."

"You are stupid man."

"Yes."

When I was a boy, I didn't understand myself. I got not a shot in hell grokking a girl.

Marisol joins her at the kitchen entry.

"What is he doing?"

"He is leaving."

Marisol shrugs. Comes in the kitchen and fills a cup with water. What the hell is it with girls walking around in panties?

I squeeze past. Got to save Joe. Can't save everybody. Especially since most people I meet end up dead or wanted. These girls have a safe place, and their smarts have done them fine.

"You ladies will get on just fine."

Push open the main door. A foil dunce cap covers my whole body, except a scrunched up oval at the eyeballs—looks like a tin asshole—so I don't bust my leg walking blind. The wound in my calf from the punji stake seeps now and then. I press out the nastiness every couple of days. The drip smells like sewage, but in all, the wound doesn't hurt much, and I'm stronger every hour. Barely favor the leg.

Five months inside. Ain't comfy breathing cold, natural air. Feel like a thousand eyeballs study me. I swing the door closed so if the FBI comes on me quick, they won't grab the girls too.

I take a minute to figure the lay. Look about the slope, how the trail feeds down a steep drop-off and joins a hundred year old logging road.

Full grown man wearing foil head to toe.

Way I figure things, safest route out of here's straight up the hill behind me. They placed cameras down the front, all about the Graves house and lawn. The quarter mile driveway to the road and most of the hill. I head straight up the dome, I'll pass through a hundred yards they pay attention to. According to my map.

I had to guess some locations for the X's where the FBI boys located their surveillance. I watched the federal police through Graves' cameras, but some of the fields of view have no recognizable point of reference. Not without knowing the name of every tree on the property, like an owner might. But a fella walks off one camera view and ten seconds later into another, the second's close to the first. So my life rests on guess work.

And maybe they have satellites too.

Satisfied nobody watches, I follow the bend around the hill, until I spot a deer path goes straight up the dome.

Muse on Tat, now that I left her. She's a good girl. Hard girl, but good. Sometimes you can't reach the itch between the shoulder blades. I have a thought like that. Tat. Can't scrape out the thought.

How she felt, on me.

The thinking is there, but I can't think it.

How would life be, if I stayed and enjoyed her regular?

Or come back with Stinky Joe—sneak back inside the mountain home? Old men hole up with pretty young gals all the time.

Not like I asked for the situation. I went looking for Joe and had to choose between prison with the girls or prison with the boys.

She dropped in my lap, so to speak.

Man walks into a gallery of fine art, he's supposed to say, *groovy*. A man ought to appreciate beauty. And if he doesn't embrace a pretty girl when he has the chance, that's an insult to the one who made her.

Plenty reasonable.

God made that fine ass woman.

Right. Hell. Every waking minute I live insults the Almighty. All I do is hate and kill.

And fornicate.

Though I kill more than I couple.

It's a hard slog straight up hill. Don't see FBI cameras. Good—as my path is supposed to avoid them. But I don't see much at all, save the narrow cut in front of me. Wearing foil all over. Crinkles when I walk. If they use the heat-sniffing cameras, or the infrared, or the satellites or helicopters or whatever, maybe this tin suit will hide my body heat. Maybe they'll spot my face and think I'm an overweight squirrel. That levitates.

Once I make a mile, I'll fold up the foil and if anybody crosses paths, I'm just a feller in the woods. Fact is, it's probably worse being seen in the foil than out.

Eventually, I'll blend in with every other fool in the woods looking for Joe.

Except I'm the only one who wants him to live.

Should have waited on nightfall. But who knows what trouble Joe will find by then?

I've done evil. Killed men for watching dog fights. Killed lawmen thinking they were on the right side—though they were wrong. And someday the Almighty above is set on burning my soul for eternity. I got real suffering coming. There's no getting right with God. Not with him.

But if I can rescue Stinky Joe, maybe I'll get right with me.

Chapter 22

Lucky barked. He'd been snoring on the sofa for hours. Lester opened his eyes. Fuzzy clogged his brain. Needed coffee. Why was he awake?

The back door rattled. Someone pounding.

Lucky barked.

"Shut up. All right."

Lester grabbed his .357, swung the leg rest down and climbed out of the lazy-boy. At the door, he glanced at the monitor showing the feed from the patio. Bold sunlight—the angle said early morning. Brain felt like two hours' sleep.

He nodded at Lucky. Unlocked and opened the door.

El Jay said, "I was up half the night. You said you'd call."

"Yeah. Well, I didn't."

Lester backed from the door, and El Jay followed him inside. "We got to talk. We had a load pinched. Two nights ago. And I can't raise Paul anywhere."

Lester headed straight to the kitchen and turned on the

front burner of the stovetop. Prepared a percolator so the coffee'd come out like tar. Set it to boil.

"Pinched?"

"Miguel and Lopez."

"I told you about Lopez."

El Jay flickered a grin, went flat-mouthed. "I don't think they were involved."

"Why?"

"They're dead."

"How you know?"

"I went to the drop. They were still in the car. Shot."

"Who were they meeting?"

"Paul set it up."

Lester shook his head. "Still coulda been involved. Just everything turned against them."

El Jay pulled a chair. Sat. Nodded at the percolator. "Make enough to share?"

Lester opened the coffee bag and spooned a mouthful of grounds. Chewed and washed it with tap water. "There'll be enough."

"So we gotta find out who hit Miguel and Lopez," El Jay said.

"One hit does not a pattern make."

"What's that mean?"

"We don't necessarily need to find out anything."

"So we do nothing?"

"We wait. Tell everyone to keep their eyes open. If they rob us again, we have a problem. But unless you have some detective skills I haven't heard about, we hold off."

"What will a second hit tell us the first didn't?"

"That it wasn't random. Look, I been doing this a lotta years. A couple guys getting robbed once, it's collateral damage. Every business deals with slippage. We're like Sears and Roebuck. You tolerate some, because no CEO has the time to stamp out all human mischief downstream. You only solve the problems that matter—and you only make a move when you have clarity. Besides. I'm working an angle."

"Well, if you call losing five keys slippage, maybe it's time we talk about the next stage of your golden years."

"Grab that coffee 'fore it burns."

"You let people steal from you, even a penny, they start making bigger plans."

Like you?

Lester half smiled.

El Jay fetched mugs from the cabinet and filled them with coffee.

"You been watching too many movies. Crooks are crooks. You don't kill them to keep them in line. You gotta be smarter than that."

"Costing you money."

"Listen. I'm going to teach you something. Lesson applies to every dimension of your life. You and me, we open a cheeseburger joint. We make loads of money and you say, we can do better. You say, Lester, I studied the books. We make a hundred percent markup on the fountain soda, but we lose five percent on the cheeseburgers. Right? You tracking?"

"I'm tracking."

"So what do you do?" Lester blew across the top of his coffee mug. Sipped.

"I don't understand."

"Do you stop selling cheeseburgers?"

"Yeah. No."

"Why not?"

"No one would come to a cheeseburger joint without cheeseburgers."

"So the markup on the cheeseburger doesn't matter, by itself. It matters to the whole."

"What?"

"See, you're looking at the thing. You want revenge. You want to stamp out the guy who stole. Whatever. What you need to be looking at is the whole. How you lose money on the cheeseburger so you can make a hundred fold on the fountain soda. You got to think through how a decision will affect the entire operation. I have some cheeseburgers on the grill you don't even know about. Trust me. Do more thinking and less talking for a while."

El Jay drank coffee. "You mind?" He reached for his smokes.

"Of course I mind."

"What do we do about Paul? He ever not turn up? Not answer his phone?"

"What you need him for?"

"I wanted to tell him about the hit."

"Anh. No. Paul's usually punctual."

"Well, maybe—"

Lester studied El Jay. "Paul's taken care of himself a long while. He'll turn up. Meanwhile we got a job. Finish that."

El Jay stared long and hard at him. He gave a short nod as his lip curled upward.

Lester gulped his remaining coffee. El Jay knew. Whatever.

Lester sniffed his arm pit. One of the agreeable things about early spring.

Good to go.

Lester looked up at the sign and snickered. Mountain View Mobile Home and RV Resort.

"Which one belongs to the fat girl? I don't recall."

El Jay's mouth withheld a smile. Barely.

"Yeah," Lester said. "You think senility jokes are funny. You won't when I take a bat to your head and put you in the home."

El Jay pointed. "She lives down there. Turn left and—see

the light blue?"

Lester parked next to a Ford Festiva. "You don't need to say anything unless I ask you to say something."

"Uh. Whatever you say."

They exited. Lester beat the door. Waited. Beat it again. He listened and heard stomping.

The door opened as Lester raised his fist for another go. A women filled the entry, pretty, of sorts, at least in her practiced smile. Her hair glistened and her hand was shiny.

"I don't know you," she said. "So how do I know you?"

"What's that on your hand?"

She held her palm at him. "Olive oil. I was treating my hair." She ran her fingers through greasy locks.

"You got oil on your clothes. All over."

"You startled me."

Lester stepped to enter. The woman was still.

"Fine. He pulled his .357, shoved his boot forward as she slammed the door. He strode inside.

"I didn't do anything!" the woman hoofed away, and the trailer shook.

"Oh, quit your nonsense." He holstered his gun. "Little common decency."

The woman peered from the corner where kitchenette turned into hallway.

Lester looked around. An uncapped jug of olive oil sat on the counter.

"You put that in your hair in the kitchen?"

"I don't store food in the bathroom."

He nodded, slow. "What's your name?"

"Shirley."

"Okay. That fella named Clyde. Your new landlord. He gave you something for me. One of those computer memory jobs."

"I don't know what you're—"

"Look, I'll kill you. Understand? I'm old. I got a gun.

You're an obstacle, not a woman. We won't dance two steps before I send the band home. Now where's the memory stick?"

"He said to mail it to the FBI if he didn't come back."

"But you didn't do that."

She shook her head.

"You still got it."

Another shake. "I didn't want it to begin with."

Lester rested his hand on his gun. El Jay stepped out to the side. "So where's the USB drive?" El Jay said.

Lester glanced at him.

"I got rid of it."

"Where?" El Jay said.

"Ain't telling. 'Less you pay me what Clyde offered."

"What's that?"

"Ten grand."

Lester snorted. Raised his hand at El Jay.

"He didn't tell me what's on the memory stick," Shirley said. "But Clyde—"

"First you don't want it at all, now it's a lottery ticket," El Jay said. He reached to his back and pulled a Glock.

Lester debated what to address. El Jay's muddled line of questioning or his use of an ass holster. Things were cropping up everywhere. Interesting.

Lester looked at the floor. Let the man-child lead. If the situation blew up, he'd maybe learn from the consequences.

"Where's the drive?" El Jay said. He pointed the automatic at Shirley's face and marched to her in three steps. Pressed the barrel against her temple, pinned her to the wall.

"This ain't fair!"

Shirley squeezed tears from her eyes.

Lester gave a slight headshake, and El Jay pulled back the pistol. Lowered his gun arm to his side.

"Miss, I don't mean any disrespect." Lester glanced at the sink. The cloudy window above. "Ten grand is a large sum to you. You're a hooker, right? Ten grand is a lot of cock. But I'm more liable to tie you up and burn this place down on you, as pay you any money. See, I don't need the computer memory thing, so much as need it destroyed. The straightest line is the simplest. You hear me?"

"The memory stick is on the dog."

"Tell me."

"You see Clyde last night? Half his face chewed off? That dog. It has a collar with one of those barrel things, like the Saint Bernards in the Andes mountains."

"You mean Alps."

"Those ones."

"Where you get a collar like that?"

"He wore it when I found him. Empty. He was wandering up the street, and I fed him some broth. Gave him a bath. Clyde came in like to raise hell, and the mongrel went a little nuts on him. Took off and I ain't seen him since."

Lester looked at his feet. Glanced up and saw El Jay searching his face. Good. The boy was waiting on a cue.

"You should go back and look for yourself. Clyde's blood is still on the wall. The floor. He shot my mirror."

Lester gestured. El Jay walked back the hall. Returned. Nodded.

"No," Lester said, as much to El Jay as Shirley.

"No?" Shirley said.

"You're telling me you think that thing's worth ten grand, and you put in on a dog's collar?"

"I didn't think so then."

"You just wanted someone else's money," El Jay said.

"Don't interrupt me, boy."

Shirley stared.

"What he said," Lester said. "Trying to cash in."

She nodded.

"So here's what we're going to do. I don't believe you. I think you got that thing hid. So we're gonna turn this place inside out."

"Mister—it's on the dog!"

"Before we start, I'll maybe spare us some work and check one place." Lester strode to her, and while Shirley's jaw dropped three inches, he inserted his right hand into her sweatpants, wove through the pubes, and hooked two fingers deep as he could. Twisted his wrist until his forearm cramped.

"Kick your leg out a little."

Lester kicked her foot with his boot. Probed. Withdrew his hand.

"You goat," she said.

He stepped to her sink. "You got dish soap or something. Never mind." He spotted a purple bottle behind an empty two liter of Pepsi. "El Jay, Find the USB stick. Inside out. Upside down. Find it."

Lester washed his hands and dried them on a dish towel.

"Mister! It's on the dog."

El Jay squeezed past her to get to the bedroom. In a moment, Lester heard drawers landing on the floor.

"Don't dump stuff! Search, El Jay."

Shirley shook her head. Cried. Adjusted her sweat pants. Strutted by Lester like she found her pride, and sat on the sofa. Taking out his .357, he took a spot beside her.

"What kind of dog? Describe him."

"White. Blocky in the head. Like the ones they fight all the time."

"A pit bull?"

"Yeah, maybe. I don't like dogs so much."

"Was he all white? All over?"

"Mostly. Got some brown too. Tiny bit on the muzzle. And his butt."

"What was you doing with the dog? You said he was stray."

"I wanted to save him. He looked half dead."

"You got anything that smells like him? You said you

give him a bath?"

"Yeah."

"You dry him off with a towel?"

"Uh-huh, I got it back there."

"You gonna charge me ten grand?"

Lester smiled.

Shirley bit her lip. Rolled her eyes. "You can't go around feeling up women any time you want. This ain't nineteen twenty."

"No, we're agreed on that. But you have something that belongs to me. Oh, we'll be friendly and civilized. To a point. And then we'll do what we have to do. Don't lose sight of that."

He nodded, smiled. Waited.

She blinked back.

"Good." He chinned at the photo on the wall. "Who's that?"

She searched his stare.

"That's your son," he said. "Why'd you name him Brass."

"I always liked the sound."

Lester planted hands on knees, tried to sit upright. The sofa wouldn't allow it. He stood, sat on a wood chair at the kitchen table. "How about you make us some coffee."

"You got a lotta gall."

"Secret to my success." He flicked the barrel of his .357.

Shirley made coffee.

An hour later, Shirley's dresser was emptied on the floor. Mattresses flipped. Jewelry box dumped. Bathroom cabinets scattered. Closet thrown. Boxes shaken bare. Kitchen pots and pans cast to the floor. Shelves unloaded. Refrigerator strewn. Sofa cushions unzipped and the pads tossed. VHS videos thrown from their cases. Everything that had a place was someplace else.

Tears dripped from Shirley's face. "I'm telling you, it's on the dog."

Lester studied her running mascara.

El Jay stood gritting his teeth by the door, sweat beaded on his forehead. His eyes moved from Lester to Shirley and back. Lester always had good peripheral vision. While deciphering Shirley's face he saw El Jay again pull his Glock.

El Jay strode to Shirley and jabbed her right breast. "WHERE IS THE THUMB DRIVE?"

Lester closed his eyes. El Jay might be his son, but he surely didn't inherit the knack. He'd been raised on mob movies and thought raw violence made people talk. Hadn't yet learned the nuances—deep fear only makes people sputtering idiots, incapable of saying the words that would save them. Just like those two girls, unable to use the guns in their hands. Lester was trying to teach El Jay the finer points, but the boy was headstrong and had a mutinous streak. Refused to learn—except by the fruits of his own disasters.

This time, Lester didn't have the luxury.

El Jay shoved his gun back into his ass holster and a moment later whipped a butterfly knife back and forth.

"I'm gonna cut you," he said.

"Enough," Lester said.

"You ready to bleed, bitch?" El Jay grabbed Shirley by the hair. Stuck the point below her eye. "Don't worry. You can still be a whore with a scarred face."

Lester stood.

He placed his hand on El Jay's neck, from behind, and squeezed. El Jay stiffened. With his other hand, Lester drew his .357 and readied the nose at his son's torso. "I like your gumption. I won't fault you. But I said enough."

El Jay pulled away the knife.

Shirley released her breath.

Lester stepped back. Shoved El Jay's neck.

"Go back to the laundry basket. Get the blue towel she used on the dog."

Head down and nostrils flaring, El Jay strode back the hallway.

"Now Shirley, I'm going to find that pit bull. And you need to know something. If I don't also find a collar with a barrel, and that memory stick inside, I'm going to destroy you and everything you own. That doesn't mean I'm going to wreck your finances. I'll turn you, this place, to ash. Am I understood?"

She stared without expression.

"I'm telling you this now, so you can make the best decision possible. Not to scare you."

Shirley's head moved up, down. Slow.

El Jay returned with a towel in hand.

"Is that the one you used on the dog?"

She nodded, short, fast.

El Jay pulled a shiny tin from his front pocket. Tucked a business card between her bra and skin.

Lester looked at him.

"If the mutt comes back," El Jay said.

Lester connected eyes with Shirley. "Thank you for the coffee, and your hospitality."

Chapter 23

Unreal. Pip Squeak El Jay had to dump the kitchen cabinets.

Wearing flip flops, Shirley stepped on the linoleum, careful to avoid broken glass. She stooped. Her rectum pinched. She cinched the outer ring, steadied herself, and lifted a bottle of Two Fingers tequila from the floor. It had landed on its neck—she'd watched while El Jay dropped it from the upper cabinet. Something to be said in favor of her trailer's shoddy 1970's construction: some glass bounced.

Not all. Most of her drink-ware was shattered; the bastard hadn't been as ruthless in sending her plastic dinnerware to the floor. Careful to avoid loose shards, she swiped a heavy-bottomed snifter.

The object in her back end again shifted. She'd deal with it shortly, but first: fortification. She needed to steady out her breathing.

Take the rage from boil to simmer. Before she did something stupid.

Shirley twisted off the cap, rinsed the snifter of any stray glass and toweled it dry to protect the integrity of the high grade tequila.

Staring at her utterly wrecked trailer, she knew from history—screw that—*herstory*, she had three choices.

Laugh.

Cry.

Get mad as hell.

Not crazy buzzsaw mad, going off unhinged. But crafty and skilled. Patient and merciless.

Woman mad.

She poured and gulped four shots of Two Fingers tequila. Enough to get started. Enough to hold steady her fury while she handled a piece of back-door business.

She stepped over clumps of pillow stuffing. Over DVDs and VHS tapes spilled from their boxes. Over the remote batteries. He'd removed the batteries from the remote, like she'd been crafty enough to hide a USB memory stick inside a AA battery compartment.

Where was Lester getting his help?

The hallway was clear but the bathroom ...

Woo. Whoa. Tequila just swung a baseball bat at her head.

She grabbed the jamb. Closed her eyes and let her brain enjoy the swim.

Rectum!

She shoved open the bathroom door. Gagged.

The Listerine bottle had held but the black plastic cap had broken. The air stank of yellow Listerine, the old kind that smelled like the stuff you'd use to clean the walls in a nursing home.

She bent at her back to lift the bottle and again almost squirted.

The rectum has an inner ring and outer ring, she recalled. Hers were strong. After all these years, inviolate. Invincible.

Mighty sphincter.

The rings would hold.

Shirley placed the Listerine bottle mouth-down in the sink and kicked aside the towels from the base of the toilet. Hooked her thumbs under sweats and undies and scrunched them both down her thighs. Dropped to the seat and blasted out a painful load that began with a sandwich baggie—she'd been in a hurry and hadn't thought of using a condom—secured with a rubber band, creating a large flower of sharp-edged double zip-lock plastic, and was followed by a movement typical of a woman who consumed four thousand calories per day.

The smell displaced the Listerine and Shirley relaxed against the commode tank. Leaned her head way back, closed her eyes, so the light was like two distant suns on her eyelids, tossed in a sea of tequila.

Her neck hurt. She righted her head. Opened her eyes. She'd played it right so far.

She'd seen Lester swing into her lot beside her Ford Festiva, and from the first moment knew his mission. She'd raced to the bedroom, grabbed the thumb drive, and by the time the first knock sounded on her door, had a baggie in hand and a jug of olive oil on the counter. She rubber-banded the sandwich bag, slathered it in oil, bent like to touch her toes, and shoved it deep. Pounding erupted at the door, and she walked to it while pulling up her sweats and wiping her oily hand in her hair.

She stood at the door, exhaled big. Collected her mind, fluffed her prodigious rack and got into role. Just another hooker ready for business. She'd pulled open the door.

The baggie floated at the top of the bowl, but so did her defecate. She thought of grabbing tongs from the kitchen, but the tequila argued she could just as easily wash her hand as tongs. She reached in the bowl and fetched out the plastic. Twisted to the sink, saw her fractured self in the mirror Clyde had broken, and placed the plastic-shrouded USB memory stick under a stream of running water.

With most of the defecate removed from her hands and the baggie, she smelled them. Nope. She took off the rubber band, dropped the USB stick to the sink top, tossed the baggie in the trash and soaped her hands again. The tequila was helping. Improving clarity, righteousness. She'd taken bull crap sixteen ways to Tuesday. Suck this. Let me put it here. There. More of that. Less of that. Watch the teeth. Teeth!

They pulled her tits. Tugged her ears. Her ears.

But she'd been the strong one. She paid the bills. Clothed and fed her son. Raised him right, so one day he'd rule the United States, if he could just get his ass in state congress.

Always taking men's crap. Playing by their rules. The meek shall inherit. All so some octogenarian asshole and his retarded sidekick could tear apart every single thing she owned.

Shirley grabbed the USB memory stick and strode down the hall like thunder through a hollow. Pit stop in the kitchen, amid the glass. She stopped, turned, with her eyes drank in the destruction of her home. Took it in like fuel ... and added another double of tequila to the fire.

Back to the bedroom. She pulled an old IBM Thinkpad her son Brass had second-handed to her, fired it up. Went to the kitchen to convert her double shot into a margarita, proper, and returned before Microsoft Windows could scare up a start screen.

Finally, yes I'd like to log on.

She typed *SLYLE*.

Then, *PASSFCKNWORD*.

No-go.

MICROSOFTSUX.

No-go.

SLYLE58-402!

Hot damn.

Shirley mixed another margarita.

Came back to a waiting Microsoft Windows 2000 desktop. She stuck in the thumb drive. Searched and located the folder. Opened it and looked at a dozen more, marked with years. 2009, back to 1993.

She double clicked 2008 and found twelve photo files. Clicked again, and then expanded the image to cover the full screen.

Numbers.

Too many numbers.

A page from a ledger?

On the top: January, 2008, written in a female hand.

Clyde Munsinger had taken photos of a ledger. And these were ... important?

She zoomed in and studied the top and bottom. Nothing indicated ownership. Then she looked at the individual entries. One, highlighted in yellow, drew her eye.

Tequila brought it into and out of focus. More tequila! She sipped. Margarita needed salt. She closed her eyes. Opened them.

Whoooey.

Screw men.

Haha.

She did screw men. That's how she knew men.

Shirley leaned back on the bed. Found her pillow in just the perfect spot, and lay back her head. The room twisted and her stomach queased, just enough to warn against finishing the margarita. The room accelerated into a full spin, and she opened her eyes.

The data! She had to protect it.

Shirley looked at the yellow highlighted line again, focused, and the letters resolved:

1-JAN-08, Wash/Dry Machines, #204, $13,092.98

Oh. Clyde was interested in laundry.

Shirley closed her eyes. Rallied them back open. She X-ed

out the image. Then, as sentience blurred into blackout, dragged the main folder from the thumb drive onto her desk top.

She pushed aside the laptop. Dropped the lid. Eased down her eyelids and slept.

Chapter 24

Lester Toungate drove back to his house with El Jay in the passenger seat. Lester wondered at him. How a man in his thirties could be so prone to the glee of angry excess. When Lester thought El Jay had cooled off, he said, "You took a severe step backward, today."

"How's that?"

"My estimation."

Lester parked outside the garage since the pencil-necked geek Clyde Munsinger's truck was still inside, with blood all over. He'd thought of asking El Jay to clean the mess. But after his son's cockamamie stupidity with Shirley Lyle, Lester wondered if he'd made a mistake bringing him in.

His son.

Sons.

He'd thought hard about Paul. Made a decision. But you're never certain whether you're feeding yourself facts or opinions.

Paul's entitlement mentality combined with his incompetence were too dangerous to tolerate. Fact? Or not? If Paul ever decided to harm his father—such as Lester suspected he'd done by murdering his own drug carriers two nights before—or by turning state's evidence on the old man, bidding to go legitimate—Paul held enough secrets to bury him.

Why was killing Paul any different than Clyde? Sentiment?

El Jay was in the same situation.

Blood was blood, and Paul being his son counted for something.

Paul had better opportunities than all the mongrels he grew up with. A better shot at making something for himself. A kinder, more protected world to grow up in. No one touched Lester Toungate's son. Paul gathered his strength without everyday life knocking the snot out of him. Other kids, circumstances beat them down early and held them down long.

Paul's blood relationship with Lester had bought him everything. Except one thing.

Lester's sentimentality.

No, eliminating Paul was fair.

Now El Jay seemed poisoned by the same water. Too willing to freelance. Not only that. His disobedience in front of an enemy gave him away.

Shirley Lyle wasn't likely to exploit a wedge in their thinking, but principles mattered. That was the problem with youth. Too prone to indulge their fancies.

So said every old person who ever existed.

Lester turned off the engine.

"Stay a minute."

El Jay gazed straight ahead.

"You got anything to say for yourself?"

"You weren't getting any answers."

"Is that what you still think?"

"I dunno. Maybe. Like I said."

Lester looked at the steering column. Kid had all the backbone in the world, when he was beating on a four hundred pound hooker. Now with an old man, I dunno, maybe, like I said.

Lester put on his CEO hat. Sometimes he'd rather shove it up someone's ass. But he always reminded himself: you don't want what you have a right to.

You want what you want.

A monkey could lash out in the name of justice. But getting what he wanted required making peace and deploying some strategic manipulation. Preferring to satisfy the call for vengeance by destroying a man's entire life, instead of his nose.

"I like that you think for yourself. Your generation has a shortage of independent thinking. I appreciate you ain't a pussy. I do. Hell, you run a pavement company. But you won't be ready to take over the real show until you learn you're always better off keeping your mouth shut. Let someone else bear the brunt of being wrong. And violence... think of it like a knife blade made of paper. Yeah, they beat cardboard with a hammer. Soak and dry the pulp. Hone it. Comes out sharp as a razor. But cut a tomato and it's dull as a dick. Violence cuts, but loses its edge quick. So use brutality to cause harm, not change minds. I'm rambling. Need coffee. But that's my criticism for the day. Now, don't go off and sulk. I got a job for you. Huge, huge important."

"Yeah?"

"Uh-huh. I got a truck in the garage, bloody from six people."

"Six?"

"I want you to load that Harley of mine. The Sportster. Start the engine and make sure the battery's charged. Use the nylon straps and anchor all four corners in the bed. Grab three jerry cans of gas. Tie them down too. Pack yourself some long underwear and gloves. You'll be cold on the ride home, north of Bumblebee. Go down to Phoenix, take the 101 west, all the way down to 10. Shoot half way to California. You follow?"

"Yeah."

"You'll be six hours getting where you're going."

El Jay nodded.

"Go into the desert so far, you don't see a human being for an hour or two. After the road ends, drive the desert. I'm saying, go way the hell out. Then unload the truck, dump the gas in and out. Soak the bed, the upholstery, everything. You'll see. Those bodies left blood everywhere."

"So I'll be driving a truck dripping blood from six murder victims through Phoenix."

"Not through Phoenix. Off to the side. The 101."

El Jay looked out the side window, head turned away.

"You want the corner office, you start in the mail room."

El Jay turned to him. "I could go to jail. Forever."

"That's what being a crook means."

"I thought everything you said before was to push risk out to other people. So you're never caught with your hand on the evidence."

"What do you think I'm doing?"

"Making your son take the risk."

"And if you ain't up to it, go run a pavement company."

El Jay put his head against the backrest. Turned to Lester.

"Okay. I'll do it. But afterward ... You have to bring me in. I'm sick of being on the outside. I need to know your contacts. They need to be mine too, not just yours. Because—"

"I won't be around forever."

"Right."

"Fine. You deal with the truck—which by the way—the blood came from a couple fellas who would've taken the family business away altogether. You handle the truck and I'll find that dog. Then I bring you in. All the way."

"All the way?"

Lester offered his hand.

El Jay shook it.

"All the way," Lester said.

Chapter 25

Should have took a squat before leaving the mountain bunker, but I wanted gone. Now I got a load backed up so far I have to swallow every three steps. Sheer good fortune I spot a long dead log, still has some bark. In the middle, a Y sits level. If I ever see a crapper so fine in the woods again, I'll camp beside it.

This foil suit—I doubt they got the heat sensors more than a couple hundred yards, after all this time. And it's tore up anyhow. I tug, and it falls like it would have anyway. Crinkle it tight and drop the ball in my pocket. Ain't so noisy to move, now.

Guts are pushing hard.

Climb over this branch and duck under that. Shed my britches and plant cheek to wood. They say dropping a good loaf is better than sex—least when you're old.

Mebbe yesterday I'd a thought so. Truth is, I only been with—lemme count—three women, my whole life. Ruth young, Ruth old, and Tat too young. But each was markedly superior to taking a squat.

Should have grabbed some leaves or moss.

Well, damn.

Plumb my pockets and find nothing.

That load didn't pinch clean—I can sense it. Close my eyes, and it's this mood again. Sudden like, the mind goes dark and prickly. Just the way life'll treat a fella.

"FREEZE!"

Shake my head. Law? Out here? Already? What the holy hell did I do? Head down, eyes closed, I sit like if I don't see him he won't see me. It won't work. Just I'm not ready for this.

The killing to come.

"You're under arrest."

"Ahhh, piss off."

I look up. Turn my noggin to study him straight on. He has his gun on my body so I'd take a bullet in the shoulder. Wears the navy blue jacket. Shiny shoes, out here in the leaves and dirt. Spot a black tie at the V of his neck. Glasses. Marks on his face like Gorbachev, but low where he can't cover it with a hat.

Just ducky.

"What are you doing?"

"You said freeze."

"I mean, what are you doing in that tree?"

"Look, my drawers are down."

"Oh. Well, finish up. You're under arrest for murder."

"Murder? Nah—Sedition, more accurate. Say, you got any paper? Or maybe fetch me a handful a leaves? Grab them close off the ground, so they're damp and not so prickly."

"I said you're under arrest. Climb out of that fallen timber, sir."

What kinda law enforcement accosts a man with his drawers at his knees? Man has no respect—wants to take full advantage because he got the drop. I ain't saying all lawmen are lying thieving force mongering thugs, but I just come out the mountain, ain't seen sunlight close to five months, no liquor to salve the mind, living with teen girls, eating dried food and steeped in the evil called television, I confess my mood is low, and I'm quick to judge.

"Well, I heard you. But I got to wipe things clean, right? And since you're the one in a hurry, that makes the problem yours as much as mine."

"I'm an FBI agent. I'm placing you under arrest."

"I understand. Logic has no sway on the federal police. Still got to wipe. Shoot if you want."

Nah. Not true. Don't shoot if you want. Stinky Joe's out there. Responsibility sits like a boulder on each of my shoulders. Poor dog. And me sitting up in the mountain, wicked as a priest.

I ease forward, try to keep my cheeks apart. No good. "Just so you can follow the action, I'm about to bend easy at the waist and fetch some leaves."

"Hurry up."

"Nah, this'll proceed at my pace, not yours."

I stand straight, and he looks at my pecker.

"I'm tired of the nonsense. Put that gun down. I'm standing here with pants at my knees. You got the gall to get tough on me? Who do you think you are?"

"I'm with the Federal Bureau—"

"That gangster jive is no good on me."

Bend and grab some leaves. Do my careful best not to spread death and destruction over my backside. Another handful of the damp oak wipes, a good couple slaps up and down, knock the dirt off my skin. That'll do until I can sit in the crick. Pull up my drawers. Glower at the lawman. One thing is sure, Baer Creighton has a dog to save and nothing else worth fighting for.

"Since you look the jittery type, let's get a plan together

for me to come out between these branches without you killing me."

"Just come out. I won't fire unless you attempt to escape."

"Fine as water. Ducky."

I grab the limb above and swing below, slow as not to give alarm. These police state cops seem to recruit from the kids everybody picked on. Got something to prove. I stumble on a branch and catch myself.

Not shot yet. Whooeee. Living big.

"So what you want? Put that down. You don't need it. What you want with me?"

"You're under arrest for murder."

"Well, none of what I did was murder. Exactly. And besides, you got no authority. Your company credentials ain't valid."

I walk like I'll keep going, provoke some red or juice to tell me what he's thinking. His eyes skitter. He's a modern pussified man. That's the one to fear. Take a regular man who works with metal or wood, gets oil under his nails. He's no better a truth teller than any other man, but at least he doesn't scare quick and need to shoot a man before he turns into the big bad wolf. These wusses were raised to know they're worthless, so where a normal man has confidence, they fill it with violence.

They get to crazy, fast.

This little shit's one of them.

"Freeze. You are under arrest. If you do not comply, I will shoot you!"

I stop.

"Okay, McNulty. Your name McNulty?"

"What? No. What the—? Place your hands in the air."

"You look like a McNulty."

I got Stinky Joe out there with all of Flagstaff's finest wanting to run a bullet through him. Cowering low under some brute's hand. I spent the winter warm while Joe was off in the drifts, cold and hungry. And I didn't do anything about it until I got the moral crisis riding me cowgirl. Meantime, Stinky Joe's getting beat with a chain. I'm worth no more'n a lump of whale shit. That's as low as a feller can get.

Guess I got to crazy faster.

"You shoot me, for real?"

He holds the square nosed gun steady, no jiggle. No juice. No red. Just a puss with total clarity. Wants to kill a man.

Me.

"I say, you shoot me? Now, I keep walking, you figure to pull the trigger?"

"You are under arrest. Lay down on the ground. Arms spread."

"I'm unarmed. I'm a citizen. Looking for a dog—"

"You are under arrest! Lay down on the ground! Spread your arms!"

"Aright, aright! Easy, brother."

Lift my arms, but I want to watch the end of this story. I'm so tired of it. It's a bare-knuckle life, is all. No matter how a feller chooses to live it. After a bit it's hard to give a damn about yourself or any other.

Got my hands high. Keep walking.

He strides toward me—closes fast. Lifts the gun from center mass to head shot—what I want. Easier to shift the head than the heart.

That's always the truth.

I think on Stinky Joe, how he came to me at the cave like I was messiah to the puppydog. Slobbering and dancing.

Man got a duty.

But this fella thinks he upholds the law-and-order side of things. Thinks he's on the side of the righteous.

Man made a mistake.

Size things up, look to where he's weak and I'm strong. I cut right. Jump in close so his gun ain't so comfy to point, and drop arm to hip. Come back up with a deer knife held for slash work, blade at the bottom, and zip that cutter up his right armpit.

His eyeballs pertineer dance out his head. Yeah, I got the artery. Should have thought on that before you decided to bring force on a citizen who didn't buy your bullshit.

He holds the pistol in his left hand and that arm still works fine. I swing my blade back down and plant it where his neck turns to shoulder. Leave the knife and take his gun in both hands. He wrestles hard for one second then he's a rabbit in the wolf's mouth. Limp.

Pry the pistol free, and he reaches slow with his left hand toward the right side of his throat. That won't work. I wallop him good, next his ear, and he falls over.

He makes the death sounds, the blood gargle-cough. Does the shaky. Eyeballs bulge like I stuck a compressor hose in his mouth. Guilt flashes through me but damn, none of this would have happened if one man hadn't tried to push his will on another. Oh, they pretend they got the right because the bunch of them say so, but who has any right to violence, except the victim of it? They're just carrying through in the name of Joe Stipe, on the perverted word of every other asshole with a badge, the whole law and order cartel that doesn't live up to the law and sure as almighty hell don't keep the order.

They started this mess.

Like it's noble for the innocent man to just give himself up while these dipshits sort it out? I got but one life. Sacrifice your own.

To hell with all these FBI types.

His gun's a Glock. I pull the slide. 40 Smith and Wesson. That'll do. Tuck it in my backside and, truth told, I never liked a gun in the ass.

FBI man ain't all the way dead but I don't want to just stand here, so I kneel and jerk my knife out his neck. Wipe it on his coat, clean the corner of the thumb guard.

He connects eyes on mine. "Murderer."

"You don't even know why you tried to arrest me! Just took the word of the chain of command. You're lazy and he's corrupt."

I cinch his belt, free the pin and yank. He rolls. Feed leather through loops and grab my new holster. Got a spare magazine in the back. Good thinking.

"I use to ignore people like you. You lie all the time— well, credit where due, you said you'd kill me—but you people lie all the time. You take what you want. Never wait a damn minute to bust in walls, burn people down. The badge makes it justice. Well, you and yours can burn. All I care. Bunch a no-count thugs. I had my fill o' your type. Go to hell, y'all."

Spit flies off my mouth. I look at him. Prick's dead.

Ain't like the lesson woulda took.

Before I stand tall again, I look about the land. All this commotion's bound to bring in the next lawman. But I'm the only one here.

Piss me off. Don't care if I never meet another human again. Just Lord above, help me save my dog. I'll do anything you say. I got the evil same as any man and worse than some. Most. I talk righteous, though I ain't. So I don't deserve anything but darkness. So help me free my dog, and I'll walk here to Idaho just to find some space. Live in the wood until you've had enough of me down here, want me to muss up hell. Since that's where you'll be sending me.

Christ, I lost my mind.

Amen.

Well, better take his cash. Pull his wallet from his butt pocket. Grab three twenties and some ones. Stuff the billfold back where it was.

Take off my belt—courtesy Luke Graves—remove the sheath, and thread it back with the Glock on my right hip and buck knife on my left. No more gun in my crack.

Nobody ahead or behind.

Give the dead feller a long look. Try to muster respect, find virtue in him. But he's nothing but a fool following orders of another, sucking up to the demon on top.

I comprehend it like divine revelation: You don't have to be evil to do evil. It's all by proxy, when a dumbass thinks he doing good.

Me?

Me too.

Time to find Stinky Joe. I set off at a walk, but I got some juice in the veins after the knife work and I haven't had booze in so long my body feels like a brand new machine.

Hang in there. When the situation's so bad you think all's lost, hang in there, Stinky Joe.

Chapter 26

Shirley Lyle groaned into consciousness. Eyes closed, she became aware of light and pain that seemed to have been deep within her brain for hours.

Something else ...

She'd heard the door.

She rolled. The motion increased her blood pressure, and the ball of pain in her frontal lobe exploded into eye-rattling torture.

Rotten tequila. One more manmade wrecking ball to the human experience. Screw men, and screw tequila.

Shirley's feet hit the floor.

The door ...

Someone was inside her trailer. Hadn't said anything, but the smell was different, maybe. Or the air pressure, the breeze. Something had roused her, because the best route through this kind of hangover was comatose.

Careful as possible, she tipped on her toes for two steps

then, unable to continue, made sure she didn't land hard on her heels. She slunk around clothes and books on the floor. Noticed her laptop on the bed and threw a blanket on top . She grabbed a mini baseball bat, akin to a night stick, from between her dresser and the wall. Slipped the leather loop over her wrist and clenched the handle.

Unless this intruder was here to put all her belongings away and buy some glasses, she'd beat him to death.

She dragged the mini bat against the faux-walnut paneling the length of the hallway.

"I'll beat you to death, mothe—"

"Ma?"

"Brass?"

"Ma? What happened here?"

"I thought you were with the bigshots this week. In Phoenix."

"What happened?"

"I know, right?"

She came around the corner. Stopped before stepping on glass.

"You got a broom?" he said. "I'll clean this."

"In the closet. By the bathroom." Shirley winced from another spike in blood pressure.

Brass froze at the edge of the living room.

"Go ahead. I don't watch them anyhow."

He tromped over her VHS tapes and DVDs.

"No one uses VHS anymore," Brass said.

He entered the hallway. Shirley looked at the sink. The faucet. Her tongue felt like a slab of venison with deer hair still stuck to the fatty lining.

"Ma—who died back here?"

"I'm sorry. I did that last night. Thought I flushed."

"No, the blood all over the wall."

"Oh. Well. That's a totally separate story."

"Separate from what?"

"All my stuff on the floor."

He arrived to the kitchen with a broom and dustpan. Shirley leaned into the kitchen and dragged a chair by the aluminum top to the hallway. Sat, and cradled her head in her hands, elbows on knees. Pressed her temples. The pressure helped, then quit helping.

"Love, gimme a glass of water."

Brass stopped brooming. Looked around.

"Plastic cups are in the cabinet."

He found one with Mickey Mouse waving his finger like to say, *don't be a dumbass*. Filled and rested the cup on the counter. He swept a path to Shirley. Returned with Mickey Mouse and water, twisted so she'd see the finger.

"You trying to make a point?"

"No. I always thought Mickey looked like—you know with his index finger in the air—like he was saying, now don't you worry. Everything's gonna be all right."

"Oh, baby. My head. Do you have to talk so loud?"

"I'll hush. So what happened?"

"Grab me some aspirin. Cabinet in the bathroom."

"How many?"

"Six."

"Ma, your liver."

"My head hurts. Not my liver."

Brass returned to the bathroom. Came back with a bottle of generic aspirin. She opened the bottle and downed a small handful. Brass resumed sweeping.

"You remember that new landlord of mine?"

"You mentioned him."

"Well, that's his blood back here."

"And the mirror?"

"That was his bullet."

"Where's he now? Stuffed under the trailer?"

"I wish. No, I didn't say that. He's just a dumb moron."

"That's redundant."

"He's that dumb."

"Why'd he bleed out on your wall? What'd you do?"

"I didn't do anything. A dog did."

"Dog."

"Yeah. He—it—kept ripping into my trash. Three times. Each week in a row, he ripped open each bag I put out. Spread garbage everywhere. I had to walk ten miles to clean everything up. Give me more water. Here."

She passed him Mickey. Kept talking while Brass moved to the sink.

"So I set out some broth. Added some sleepy stuff, and when he zonked out, I brought him into the tub. Thought to drown him. But I spent my life in the love business. I don't have any experience killing dogs. Or anything. So I filled the tub and I thought, here's this desperate animal, people just hate him all the time. Look past him. Jeer at him, if they look at all. Cuss him and throw shit at him, and I thought, if I kill an animal like this, then I can't expect good out of anybody. It ain't Christian."

"Neither are you."

"Who says?"

"Uh."

"I don't proclaim it. But I don't proclaim being a whore either."

Her voice broke. Her lips cast into a clown frown and water spilled from her eyes. She wiped them with her palms.

"I didn't mean anything."

"Well, leaving out the spiritual matters, my landlord hates dogs. I think a dog ate one of his balls as a kid or something. No kidding. He's all scarred and lopsided. But he comes in waving his gun, and that's when the dog jumps up to kill him right back. Just like that. Ripped open his face and bolted out the door."

Brass had been standing close by. He passed a fresh cup of water to her.

"And all that blood is from his face?"

"Uh-huh."

Shirley finished the water in a single pull.

"And after the dog attacked him, he did all this?" Brass waved at the damage to her home.

"No. After that, he left. He gave me a thumb drive and then left."

Shirley related how Clyde had instructed her regarding the drive. How she'd preserved it when Lester Toungate and El Jay came for it. How they'd tore her place apart, threatened her life, and how she'd barely escaped.

"You blamed the dog?"

"What should I have done?"

"Give him the drive."

"That wouldn't have been right. Clyde trusted it to me."

"Ma, you've been around long enough to realize you need to give before you receive. Meaning, Clyde was ready to screw you over to save himself. Use you. And you don't owe him anything."

"Yeah, well, at least he asked. Lester come in here and did the damage. Disrespect like nothing I've ever seen. And I've had a couple beatings, let me tell you. But that's different. A man beats you, it's cause of how little he is and how big you are. In his mind, right? Like he's loopy in the head. But Lester, he treated me like a bug. Like he'd as soon step on me as not. Destroy everything I own. Pull my wings off and burn me under a magnifying glass. Not because he's little and I'm big, but because I'm nothing at all, and in his mind, he's God."

"Well, you need to lose the thumb drive. Either give it to him so he leaves you alone, or throw it away somewhere."

"Nah. Mm-mm. Hell no. I'm going to ruin him. I'm going to toss his life like he tossed my house."

Brass pulled a chair beside his mother. Sat. Took her hands in his. "I know you're upset. But you don't want to pick a fight with Lester Toungate. He's the baddest news in Flagstaff. There's people afraid of him in Phoenix. Hell, Tucson. He's been pure evil a lot of years, and he's gotten away with it because he's good at it."

"Look what he did to me!"

"Not to you. To your house." Brass shook his head. "I have the day off. I'll clean it. You go back and rest. You're blowing tequila. You got to feel like death."

"I thought you were looking for an issue to run on. Well how about that? You'll be the man who takes down Lester Toungate. If he's got people scared all over the state, you'd ride that straight to higher office."

"I'd take any office. But I want to arrive alive. Go to bed. I'll clean this up."

Chapter 27

Lester Toungate packed an overnight backpack with coffee, socks, a sleeping bag, tarp, and food. Of the three Remington .30-06s he owned, he grabbed his favorite, with the dinged-up stock kept at a dull, linseed oil glow. He loaded the rifle and threw the rest of the ammo box in the pack. Put it in his Dodge Ram. Brought the blue towel that held the renegade dog's scent, and called Lucky.

Time to settle this mess.

El Jay had pissed around two hours loading the Harley onto Clyde's F-150. If ever a man didn't want a job...

Now Lester needed to figure out what to do about El Jay when he came back. Part of him thought, you only got one son left ... kind of limits your options. And the other part of him said, I'd rather have no son, and the man who takes over the show be from some other blood. Make him a Russian. Whatever. Let Darwin solve it.

I didn't get here by birthright.

Like I'll ever die.

Finally El Jay drove off, slow, as if afraid he hadn't tied down the Sportster right. But the bike didn't jostle on the driveway. El Jay was gone.

By then, Lester was throwing his bag in the truck. He turned to Lucky.

"Let's go find a white pit bull." Lester opened the passenger door, and the dog leaped. He failed to attain the seat and fell part way out. Lester hoisted him. Lucky yelped with the pressure at his mid-section.

Lester ran his finger along the dog's jowl.

Blood.

Again.

"You hang tough. We got one more job."

Lester drove to the Mountain View Mobile Home and RV Resort and parked at the main office, but around the side, where the truck would be less visible.

Stepping to the passenger side for Lucky, Lester glanced at the trailer park office.

If any man exhibited confidence beyond his means, it was Clyde Munsinger. The way he took the place over without having a deal in place. He had balls like they used to say, made of lead, gave him a swagger when he walked. Though Clyde just had guts. He walked like a fairy.

So what were the odds he left the USB drive in his office?

Probably not. Shirley had said she put it on a dog. She didn't deny he gave it to her. But it would be a hell of a thing not to bust in the door and take a gander, when he had the opportunity. Lester had told Clyde he had a camera installed, but in truth, it didn't see much, and the video quality was grainy. If not for Paul watching Clyde go to Shirley's place, he wouldn't have had a lead.

It would only take a minute.

Lester stood at the door. Checked to see who watched. Kicked it in.

He stepped inside the office. Didn't touch anything except with the soles of his boots. The television was on. He glanced things over. Allowed his gaze to drift back to the screen. A news lady posed before a wire fence in front of trash. A night scene, with a fast food joint behind.

A white pit bull killed a man at the dumpster last night.

Lester stepped back outside. Stared at the sky.

Back at the Ram, Lester scratched Lucky's ears, roughhoused his face a little to elevate the dog's exuberance. Then allowed Lucky to sniff the blue towel.

At almost eleven years of age, Lucky had lived a full life. Old man. Old dog. Perfect match.

Lester had spent the last two years thinking Lucky was hands-down the best person he knew.

He parked near the restaurant he'd seen on the news, not a quarter mile from the trailer park. Helped Lucky out, and let him sniff the blue towel again.

Lester grabbed his pack from the bed of the truck and slung his raggedy .30-06 on his shoulder. Lucky trotted off.

Lester watched the dog's gait. He followed, and swinging his arm noticed blood on his sleeve, from Lucky's jaw.

After a bit Lester checked the distance. They'd climbed a small hill, by Flagstaff standards, but both Lester and Lucky desired a moment of rest at the top. Lucky hadn't been excited about the search, but he'd been persistent. He kept his nose to the ground a long while, a couple of times stopping to raise his snout into the breeze. Sometimes he was a tracker, sometimes, he did area-search, seeking a short cut by zeroing in on the wind-borne trail.

Dark clouds had wandered across the sky and with them the air temperature dropped, a sudden change like stepping into a room without a heat vent. Lester studied the direction of the clouds and, without formulating a clear thought, felt apprehension in his belly. He recalled looking at a sky like that, and shortly later being buried in snow. That was the deal in Flagstaff. Any storm, any time of year, might produce snow. April was nothing special.

"You ready?"

Lester waited for Lucky, almost expecting the dog to answer. Instead, Lucky whined. At least he didn't cough more blood.

"Maybe you need a reminder, what you're looking for."

He produced the blue towel and let Lucky bury his nose in it.

"Track," Lester said.

Lucky moved out.

Most dogs in the winter, Lester surmised, found a den. The elements, the cold ... A pit bull didn't have a heavy enough coat to survive, unless he had shelter. With the scent leading to the woods and not some old shed or garage, he figured the dog had holed up in a cave, a crevice, even a hollow tree. And that meant, since the dog spent most of his time at a single location, eventually the wind borne scent would be stronger than the one on the ground. Probably within a mile of the starting point, they'd find the dog's shelter.

Shoot him and claim the prize.

Chapter 28

Shirley woke from fitful sleep, late in the afternoon. Her head didn't pound like before. Now the pain was like a cancer, small, black and tentacled, reaching through her mind and coloring her mood. She could force herself to stop thinking about the agony, but not to stop suffering it. She needed more aspirin. More water.

More tequila. Less men.

She rolled, and when her feet found the floor the blood pressure spike was small, barely painful at all. Maybe a couple cups of coffee would do the trick.

Shirley found her flip flops, and realized the contents of her dresser were no longer scattered on the floor.

She smiled, picturing Brass when he was young. They didn't have money for toys and one day he discovered how powerful bra elastic had to be to float a couple thirty pounders. He turned a chair upside down, tied off each end on a leg, and—one corner in each massive cup—used the bra to slingshot sofa pillows across the trailer.

She stood in the hallway, looking across to the far end of the living room. Saw Brass there, couldn't have been seven—maybe ten—years old, launching pillows.

Of course, he didn't recognize exactly what a bra was for, and years later when she needed to give him guff about something, she gave him guff about that, and his embarrassment made her marvel at her parenting skills, how she raised a soft boy in a hard world.

He put away all her undies and bras, all without waking her. That was what a man was supposed to be.

Shirley looked to where she left the laptop and thumb drive before napping, on top of the dresser.

The thumb drive was gone.

Brass had likely taken it, and from his stance earlier in the day, wanting nothing to do with taking on the evil empire of Lester Toungate, he probably wanted to mail it to him.

"Brass, what'd you go and do?"

The only bad thing about raising a tender boy—he was a wimp. She could love him like a mother should and still discern his faults. Wasn't that the definition of motherly love?

She paused. In the recess of her mind, somewhere in the blackout drunk memory pit, she sensed not all her tools of vengeance were lost.

Maybe ...

Hadn't she worried about the laptop falling and breaking the thumb drive?

Hadn't she ...

Shirley opened the laptop, waited. The screen came up. Went down.

Battery dead.

She blasted out a lungful of huff and plugged in the laptop.

Made coffee to give the charge a head start. Turned on the computer, got in her robe and showered—Brass had cleaned the entire place before leaving—and when she returned, the computer was ready.

Ah! She was a genius! Even pass-out drunk, she had the foresight to save a copy. She located the file on the desktop and double clicked. Opened the next file folder, and the first image. Like she remembered, a ledger.

Numbers.

Line after line, fancy script, nonsense. In a way, numbers were the downfall of humankind.

She needed a number person to tell her what they meant.

Shirley found her cordless phone in the living room. Back at the computer, she searched for Lorell Higgins, CPA. She dialed.

"I need Lorell."

"Who's calling, please?" The receptionist's tone was cool.

"Mizz Lyle."

"Just a moment." Crap music played across the connection. Then a soft click.

"Uh—this is Lorell."

"I need you to look at some numbers and tell me what they mean."

"Uh—Shirley?"

"Who else still says Mizz?"

"What kind of numbers?"

"In a ledger. A business ledger. Something is funky about them, but I can't read a ledger. Ergo, get your ass over here."

"I—uh. This is uh, not copacetic. I—"

"I'll let you lick my toes."

"Now, Mizz Lyle—"

"Throw in a foot job."

"When?"

"Right now."

Some men, tits. Others, ass. But, as Shirley learned through the years, an oft-under-counted contingent preferred feet. Add the freaks who were into ankles, the fraction was big enough an efficiency-minded business woman wanted an offering suitable to match demand.

Her first foot job, ages and eons ago, was ugly. Rubbing a shaft with both feet didn't come easy like walking, where your feet do what they were built to do, and you pay attention to other things. With a foot job, you had to twist the ankles and make the legs go up and down. Joints had to be flexible. Agile.

Well, some folks painted with their feet. Played violin. Shirley set her mind to mastering the foot job.

Not having a line of sight to her feet was a disadvantage. She learned how to position a mirror, and interpret the signals in reverse.

She practiced.

On the brighter side, on the continuum of sex acts, the feet being the farthest part of the body from the brain and ostensibly the mind, sometimes she imagined they weren't even her feet. The mirror aided the perception of distance. Once she put rubber bands on her ankles as an experiment, and the sensation was so distant, she could have been watching porn on the television, while someone massaged her feet with oil.

Not a bad way to score a hundred bucks.

Her feet swelled afterward, and clots ran in her family, so she decided not to use the rubber bands until the day she didn't give a damn any more. There were worse ways to go.

Over the years, Shirley turned weakness into strength. Word got out.

You want a woman good with her toes ...

But the other part she promised Lorell—ugh. A man sucking your feet was like a beady-eyed baby goat suckling your elbow. How the man—or the goat—found satisfaction eluded her.

But Lorell had his fetishes.

Feet are sweet, baby.

He preferred olive oil to canola, so she put a liter on the nightstand.

Grabbed the oil towel. Downed a stiff, stiff margarita and waited for the knock on the door.

She greeted Lorell Higgins, CPA, in her bath robe. Handed him a margarita on the house and led him by his other hand to the kitchen table. Turned the laptop computer to face him, and sitting opposite, rested her breasts on the table instead of her elbows.

"What do those numbers say to you?"

Lorell twisted his head, looked down the hallway toward her bedroom. Ran his fingers through stubby gray hair. Drew tight his lips.

"I don't appreciate you calling me at work. That was never part of the, uh, our protocol."

"Emergency. Besides, you haven't been around for a while. I wanted to do something special for you. On the house."

He smiled, crisp. Un-smiled. "Technically, it isn't on the house if you're asking me to do something in return."

"Dear. Baby Love. There you go talking the language of business. I'm talking the language of love. Carnal love."

Shirley slipped her right foot from her flip flop and walked her toes up his leg. Scooted out the chair so there was room for her knee and thigh, with her foot planted on his lap.

"I—I'm not being particular. Only saying."

"Well let me say something." She withdrew her foot, elongating the ankle and digits, keeping her leg high, so he could observe all the way to her neatly trimmed hedges. "I got something even better than olive oil for you, this time."

She stood, withdrew a twelve ounce can from the freezer. Stuck her fingers in and rubbed, then massaged the big toe on her right foot. She lifted her heel to the table top.

Lorell swallowed. Loosened his tie. "Is that bacon?"

She simpered.

He snarled. Lunged and placed her three biggest toes in his mouth, swirled the tongue—

"Nope!—not yet."

She pulled back and slipped her foot on her flip flop. Closed off her nakedness with her bathrobe.

"First things first, Lorell. What's that ledger mean?"

"Oh—that's wrong. Just wrong."

"Sooner you tell me what's on those pages, sooner these phalange-digits'll be sinning anywhere you want."

He licked his lips. Studied her face. "Isn't payment usually afterward?"

"Not when the transaction involves an alternate means of payment. Now stop wasting time. What's on that ledger?"

Lorell shook his head sideways while looking at the ledger. Spoke under his breath, "Alternate means of payment. What the hell kind of talk? Didn't come here to be spoken down to. I'm a CPA. And I can get talked down to at home. Yellow highlighter. Interesting—somebody's already been over these books. All the fishy stuff is highlighted yellow. Whoever took this image wanted to make the subterfuge easy to find. Although, for someone with my training, it leaps off the page regardless. Look at this."

He turned the computer and pointed.

"This line is yellow. I'm guessing the person with the highlighter was demarking suspected fraud. The entry doesn't make sense. Forty thousand dollars for fluorescent light bulbs. Not unless these were for a sky scraper or something—and if that was the case, they wouldn't be written in granny-hand."

"Granny hand?"

"Shaky."

"So why would a ledger have entries like that?"

He smiled, tilted his head. "Really? You don't follow?"

"Nope."

"Wait a minute." Lorell sat erect in his chair and titled back his head so his nostrils were black holes and his eyes squinty. "Whose ledger is this?"

"Nobody."

"Nobody went to a lot of trouble."

He stared.

Shirley stared back. Held her eyes open, even when they burned. At last, Lorell stood.

"Nothing I'd love more than your sweet feet, but this is my livelihood. I won't go there. So good day. And don't call my office."

Lorell turned.

Shirley let him open the front door and slip one foot out.

"My landlord. The lady who owned this place before the new prick. That's her writing. What's the big deal? What'd you find?"

"Money laundering, Shirley. You didn't know that?"

"You think I'd rub your johnson with my feet for free if I knew that?"

"Don't be vulgar."

"Well, I ain't calling you a pervert, but damn. Come on. Help me out, and I'll help you out."

Lorell pulled his foot back into the trailer and closed the door.

"I can't do anything, Shirley. I can't participate in this. Can't tell you how to make dirty money legitimate. The government will take everything I have."

"I don't want you to participate in anything. I don't even understand what this is. That's the point. I need you to tell me. So I can figure out what I'm gonna do."

"Show the police. The FBI. The Secret Service is all over money laundering. Hell, the Treasury has an office for financial crimes."

"See? I didn't know that. That's what I wanted you for.

To tell me how to handle things the right way."

Lorell rubbed his inner thigh, high. Adjusted himself.

"Come on back to the table and sit a minute, baby love."

He stepped to her and sat. Pointed. Frowned. Blinked three times, rapid.

She nudged his thigh with her big toe.

"You use entries like this to legitimize money. This is one way, at least. Say you do something illegal for a living. Like, I'm just thinking out loud, you run a brothel. You can't tell the government, hey, I made all this money. They'll know you're a criminal. They'll put you in jail and take all your money. So that's a problem ... Any time you use your money in the modern world, the government sees. Everything but cash transactions, right? You knew that?"

"Well, of course I knew that."

"Okay, so let's say you have a huge amount of money. You can't go around paying cash for everything. You can't buy a house with cash. Currency-paper-cash. You can't send it secure in the mail. You can't buy financial assets like stocks or bonds. Bottom line, you can't store wealth as cash. Just about everything you want to do with money, you need it to be digital. But the problem is, how do you convert paper to digital?"

"Bank deposit. Let them computerize it."

"Nope. You do that for sizable sums, the bank fills out a report to the feds. After a couple, they knock on your door and ask where the cash is coming from."

"I guess I don't have that problem."

"Well, someone running a brothel, as in my example, or someone selling drugs, or stolen goods, or any other illegal activity—they need to get those big dollars into the financial system without cueing Uncle Sam. He's a greedy bastard. One way is to fake the numbers of a cash business. That's what you have here."

"Forty thousand light bulbs."

"Right. They declare the money income, write off a fake business expense, pay a little token taxes and viola, the money's in the system, just like it was earned from a legal business. And, by the way, whoever ran these books didn't try very hard. It was almost like she wanted someone to catch on."

Shirley nodded slowly, little head bounces that got bigger as she connected dots between her original landlady, Betsy Peck, Clyde Munsinger, and Lester Toungate. The whole thing made sense. The Toungate Paving company rolling through and not doing shit, twice a year. The Toungate Tree Trimming. Clyde had figured it out, and after making a move on Betsy, made another on Lester.

That didn't bode well for Clyde.

Shirley grabbed the can of bacon grease and rubbed her fingers over the frozen top until enough melted to slather her feet. She put the first on the table.

"Let's satisfy that need, Lorell."

Chapter 29

Joe opened his eyes. He'd done so a hundred times—whenever the wind picked up, leaves rustled, or a new scent drifted to the back room of the cave. Between, he slept. Each time he rose to turn and curl the other direction, his back leg throbbed. At last, it almost refused to move, from stiffness.

His chest was easier to reach with his tongue. The cat's talons had opened his coat and exposed bare meat that was hot when he licked it.

At last the darkness abated and sound arrived, the rustle of squirrel on leaves. Although he'd filled his belly on man-food the night before, he felt as if he hadn't eaten in days.

Joe pressed through the back room opening into the larger cave, now bright with morning light. He stretched—but stopped when torn muscles complained. As if two legs were hobbled, he maneuvered to the edge of the cave. He approached with narrow eyes and sniffed into the breeze, detecting the far-off scent of the mountain lion from the night before. Maybe it was still there, waiting to eat its fill.

The scent of the she-coyote was closer than the lion. Fresher. She didn't have the same acidic coldness as when he found her lair.

Motion caught his eye.

A dozen yards off, a gray squirrel raced across a fallen log and bounded to a tree trunk. Behind it followed a second flash of gray. The first stopped. The second tumbled into it, knocking it from the trunk. They both flopped in the air and landed in a full sprint.

Grays.

He'd killed many over the winter. They were always an exercise in frustration. Killing them demanded infinite patience, stalking into their territory, waiting for them to play nearby—then explosive speed. As Joe lay in the outer cave, his ambition flagged. He could barely walk, let alone bound after a gray. Besides, grays were frustrating to eat. Just guts and hair.

He curled at the edge of the cave and tucked his nose into his paws. The effort of moving from the back room left him exhausted. His body seemed cold, but also hot, and his perception of the world was different than before, as if both he and the world suffered from vertigo.

Joe closed his eyes but the unsteadiness continued.

He shivered and slept.

Leaves rustled quick like feet splashing close. Joe opened his eyes and tensed for battle.

He stood—and his shredded chest pressed a whimper from his chest. The motion was more than his fevered and beaten body could endure.

Still—Joe turned the whimper into a growl.

The she-coyote leaped toward him, full speed, then cut

away before tumbling them both deep into the cave. She whirled. Bounded again, and this time, inches from Joe's face, dropped both paws to the ground before him and lunged. She danced sideways. Withdrew. Yipped.

Play?

Joe smelled her. Interesting.

Maybe another day.

Joe lay back down.

The she-coyote stood a few feet off, sniffing. After a moment she stepped to him with her head low, her forelegs extended, propelled forward with a submissive wriggling motion. Arriving at him, she sniffed his nose, and he inhaled her scent, an intoxicating femininity that triggered his lust but failed to fuel it. Joe lifted his head, licked her nose, and placed his head on his paws. He sighed.

In all the conditions he'd survived, he'd never before been existentially weak. He'd felt terror and hunger. Murder lust. Ambition. But never had he felt like a companion of the cold ground and leaves.

The she-coyote lay beside him and nudged him partly to his side. She licked the wounds on his chest. He looked at her a moment, then lowered his head to the dirt. Breathed in the scent of dried oak leaves. She stopped after a while and sniffed over his body, and again nudged him with his nose. He ignored her. She insisted. He flopped, and she now licked the sore and seeping tear caused by the other she-coyote who'd attacked his flank and partly ripped open the tendon.

He snuggled his face into the fluff of her tail but the soothing abrasiveness of her tongue and the succor of her ministrations did nothing for the vertigo and growing sickness in his stomach, the feeling his body was at war with itself.

Joe's throat rumbled. Enough.

The she-coyote lifted herself. She nosed his face, and bounded into the leaves.

Joe closed his eyes and dreamed of mountain lion.

Dead coyotes. Dead pups.
Dead Joe.

Again, the sound of leaves warned Joe awake. The sun had
moved across the sky, and now when Joe opened his eyes, the
feeling of oneness with the chilly dirt disappeared. He was
cold; his body trembled beneath his coat. The sun rays that
had warmed him were gone, and volition swelled within him.
He desired motion.

She came quickly into the entrance, and Joe perked at the
vision: she carried a limp rabbit in her jaws. She dropped it
before him, and Joe brought his nose in quick for a
ceremonial sniff and then gnashed into the hind quarter the
she-coyote had already torn open.

The meat ripped easy and still dripped with freshness.
Only moments ago the animal leaped in terror, and the flesh
still bled with vibrancy. Joe tore and swallowed. Here was
wholesome food. The flavors maddened his senses. Joe held
the corpse in his paws and pulled sinew. Spat hair. What a
game. The excitement pressed out a tiny fart. He saw one last
easily available morsel and ripped it from the carcass, then—
his belly heavy with meat—nosed the remaining rabbit aside.

The she-coyote growled low and friendly, mannerly, and
dragged the remainder to the other side of the cave. She
placed it between her paws and fed.

Joe stretched muscles that now, for their agony, felt alive.
Easing one paw before the other, he exited the cave.

The sun was low and cut through naked trees that bristled
defiant against winter. Joe lifted his leg and emptied his
bladder on a rock. As he stood, the recent meal created a
pressure in his bowels that urged a different release. He
circled the boulder and keeping nose high, cautious, he
scented the wind and found it harmless. Each step an exercise

in overcoming pain—yet feeling the better for it—Joe moved away until he was far enough, and squatted.

It was tense work, holding the position, and at its conclusion when he attempted to kick dirt and leaves behind him, he instead provoked a new suffering in his ripped rear leg. The vertigo returned. His belly was full, and he fought a gagging sensation. Stumbling and weary, Joe fought back to the cavern. He ignored the she-coyote's growly yips, and pressed into the back room. Again he curled.

After a moment the entrance blocked. In the total dark, he smelled her close, and a tingle of fear passed through him.

But the she-coyote wriggled beside him, wrapped her tail around him on one end and nestled her nose on the other, and together they slept.

Chapter 30

They got some uncanny gizmos. Technology. Only way that FBI thug tracked me with the tinfoil body hat. Got to get away from Graves' place. Altogether away—where there's so many people they can't know who is who.

I need wheels.

I'm half down the back side of Luke Graves' mountain, and with early spring the buds are green in the trees, but there's no leaf cover. I can see a mile but a mile can see me. Spot a road at the bottom, and a black pickup truck easing along, like they do in the west.

A truck would be real nice.

Downhill, my punji-stuck calf slows me. Feel the juice inside. I grab a tree and that recalls how I got snookered the first time. So I step slow and easy and take peace from the idea I'm protected above, 'cause Stinky Joe's a good pup and the Big Man wants him saved. Holed up in the mountain, I read some of Graves' Bible. God made wisdom come out the mouth of a jackass, so it ain't beyond belief he might make good come out of me.

But even thinking it, I don't feel it. Walk like I carry thirty dead men on my shoulders.

Slope levels to flat. Somewhere before me the forest road cuts the vale. I get there it might be another day before a vehicle comes along. I ready my soul to be a little more abrupt asking a lift.

Map says the next turn is a mile ahead. Then cross the bridge and grab the highway.

Tromp along. Easy to get a good lope rolling on the flat. Clothes a little loose in the posterior. Ain't but mid-morning and the air got a nip to it. Feels good. Burns like wood smoke deep in the lungs. I'll be dead someday but now I'm alive. Air's clean; sun's bright. Motion lubricates the joints.

When it's just the wilderness and your body, the mind sits separate. Regards the both.

Don't want to brood—can't really, with the sun bright.

After a mile or so I think on my pace. If I don't steal a lift from the first somebody that drives by, that's bad news for Joe. And I need a lift on the back road. Won't work to stand on Interstate 40 waving a Glock.

Come to the first turn.

March on, Baer Creighton. If you need to march all night, you will.

I think on Stinky Joe, how I always compare him to Fred. Maybe Joe compares me to all the bastards he knew first. Longer I walk, more my belly gnaws my ribs. If I was to stumble on a jug of liquor out here, that'd be a barrel a titties. And thinking on titties, as a feller is wont, I'm a mere man. Tat's got the right proportions. She looks skinny but the jugs are deceptive.

Ain't the most difficult thing in the world for a gal like that to seduce a man in his sleep.

Now that I'm in the sunshine I'll fess it straight up: I'd

enjoy waking like that every morning, if I thought my back could hold.

Make a man ask, just whose morals are in my head?

Take them back. I've no use for them.

Car!

I wave high and wide.

He doesn't slow.

All right.

Fetch Glock. Step center-road. Point. The car's nose drops. Dust at the wheels. Skids on dirt.

I make the rolly-motion. Window down.

"I need a lift."

Lotta hair inside the car. Can't see for nothing with the glass glare. Maybe there's a gun at me already.

I step to the side.

Woman. Youngish.

I lower the pistol, as all women are good, kind, and virtuous.

"Need a ride. Apologize on the gun. Just wanted your attention."

She stomps the gas. Back tires spit dirt. I swing Glock at the wheel and blast it.

"Stop the car, Miss!"

She keeps full on the gas. Both rear tires spin but the one's blown and the other ain't. This girl didn't grow up on NASCAR. She cuts the wheel hard left and hard right, each time too late, and instead of correcting she makes the cattywampus worse. Runs in the ditch and stops with a thunk.

She escaped twenty yards. I don't want her running off, so I keep the gun level at her. Walk up careful. A fair proportion of young women is plumb nuts.

"Miss, I need your wheels. I'm after my dog. Just need a little help."

I get to the window and peek inside. Put Glock down in the holster.

"So here's what we do. You got a spare tire?"

Her face is red like a monkey slapped it twice. She nods.

"Okay. See here?"

I reach to my back. Open the money bag and fetch a gold coin. Zip it closed with the same hand. Give it to her. She recoils, even seeing it sparkle. She holds it away like I give her cooties.

"That's a maple leaf. Canadian gold. It'll fetch about eight hundred bucks, last I looked. So here's the deal—"

"You're that killer—"

"Well—you see—"

"You're going to murder me—"

"No ... Well—only if—"

She holds up a small can with a nozzle. Presses it.

I back away and the spray makes me sneeze. Breeze carries off the mist. Meanwhile she puts the shifter in reverse.

I lift Glock.

"Aw shit, woman! Just keep your damn head is all. Listen. I'll swap your tire with the spare. Give you enough gold to pay the rent maybe once or twice. Get you some more hair spray, whatever that was."

"Bear repellent."

I'd laugh if she wasn't so pitiful. "I give you the money. For exchange, I get a ride to Flag. That's it. No killing, fornicating, whatever else you dreamed up. You drive off with a gold coin for your trouble."

"Oh my god, I'm gonna die! You'll kill me like the others!"

"Easy, lady. They had it coming, and so far you don't. I just need a favor. Slow down and listen."

Her head goes up and down. Pan-eyed. Mouth pouty.

"Okay. Step one. Take the keys out the ignition. Hand them over."

She does.

"Step two, pop your trunk."

"Oh God."

"Not for you. I got to get the spare."

Trunk pops.

"You got a telephone?"

Head shake.

"You ain't but twenty-five, if. You got a phone. Gimme."

She pulls a cell out her purse. Swipes it and starts pressing numbers.

I reach through the window, grab the phone out her hands. Drop it to the road and stomp with the heel. Fetch her another coin.

"I see the trouble. You got a coat or something? Grab it. Get out the vehicle. Go. Run out there in the woods where you'll feel safe, and I'll leave the car in Flagstaff for you. Sound good?"

"You're not going to kill me?"

"Godamighty woman. Just leave, right? Slide across the seat. Slip out the other side. Good to go."

"But we're in the woods."

I had an extra life, I'd kill myself. Start over.

Instead I point Glock at her head. "Get out the car. This door that door I don't care. Just get out. And walk. I don't care where you walk. Just stop talking. Make your escape. Gimme peace. Let me fix the tire."

She slides across the seat best she can with a big ass and her hands up in the air. Out the other door. Now she runs girly-girly, hands at her hips and feet skittering.

"Call the police tomorrow. They'll tell you where to find your car."

She crosses the road and heads through the trees.

Open the door, pull the brake. Fetch the jack out the trunk. Lift the car like I work at the Indy track, swap the full size for the donut spare. If there's one man needs strung up by his nuts on a cactus, it's the man who thought up the donut spare. Throw the jack in the trunk and the shot tire too, slam the lid, and done inside five minutes.

Back the car out the ditch and consult the map. Look up and, sure as hellfire, she's come back. Right there, other side the road.

"Can I have a ride?"

"What?"

"I need to go to work. I'll be late without a ride."

Last thing I need is a woman won't shut up, tangle my mind. Lure me off my plan. It's her car and technically, it's almost like I'm a thief. But the self preservation instinct is strong and I'd 'ruther set her up for failure than me.

"You promise, I give you a ride, you never tell a soul? Not a single person in the whole world?"

She nods. Vigorous. "I promise. Not a soul."

Sparks. Red. Shocks from twenty feet.

I stomp the gas.

Girl can walk.

Do those hips a favor.

Chapter 31

Shirley thought about washing her feet, but reaching them for very long hurt her hamstrings, and Lorell Higgins, CPA had been pretty thorough licking the bacon grease. If he missed any, it'd be a moisturizer.

Shirley pushed her feet into a sloppy fitting pair of wool socks and then into heavy duty slippers, designed for dual indoor/outdoor use.

She thought about what connected Clyde Munsinger, Lester Toungate, and Betsy Peck.

Betsy had been cheating the books on behalf of Lester Toungate, and hating it. Shirley had heard rumors about how Betsy's son died, and the Toungates were involved. All those years she lived like Shirley, choking on man's evil, one way or another. Finally she saw an opportunity to avenge her son's death, if only in a passive form. She hadn't taken a machete to his gonads, as Shirley would to the poor soul that ever harmed her precious son Brass.

Betsy had been more clever.

Sinister.

History said men kill with swords and women with poison. Men prefer brute strength and butchery. Women—the ability to strike from afar, over a period of time, with plausible deniability. It suited a woman's strengths. Well, Betsy chose to kill Lester Toungate with poison. She sold the trailer park to a whippersnapper bent on causing problems, and then bolted. The poison worked its magic, and the result: Lester Toungate was frantic to hunt down the information that would soon destroy his business. He needed the thumb drive.

The antidote.

And best of all: no one knew where Betsy hid.

Hats off to sister Betsy Peck.

Enter Clyde Munsinger. If the misdeeds in the ledgers were as obvious as Lorell said, then Clyde didn't buy the joint unaware. He bought two businesses at one time: a trailer resort and a money laundering service. Business? Enterprise? Fiefdom? What do you call a half-ass, skirt-the-law operation that deals in millions?

Probably just a regular old business.

Ergo—she loved that word, kept it in a mental file under Pretentious—Clyde Munsinger compiled evidence and, after getting his face half ripped off, threatened to expose Lester Toungate's misdeeds with Betsy.

For an old man like Lester, any prison time at all probably meant ending his life behind bars. No criminal wanted to go to jail. But Lester's age raised his stakes.

So Lester and El Jay shredded Shirley's place looking for the evidence.

And all of that suggested Lester already killed Clyde, and didn't find the thumb drive.

Eventually Lester would come back to her. Whether he found the dog or not, he'd return. Just to be thorough.

No.

Nah.

This is ... This is a bad movie at two a.m.

Clyde—this very minute—was in his office pulling his pud. Lester might talk with hard edges, but he was ancient.

Uh ... yeah. Ancient is when people killed even more people.

She'd settle it right now.

Dressed for April weather—colder than a reasonable person would prefer—she departed for Clyde's place. The trailer park's office was the front room of a small farm house that had been modified by adding two extra windows. So Betsy had said.

Shirley prepared to find Clyde scowling over a computer. Wouldn't even need to go inside. Just out for a stroll.

She approached. Her knees hurt. Walking ought to be outlawed. Ain't right or natural. The office was dark. Still, lots of folks save energy by leaving the lights off in the afternoon.

She'd feign a reason to stop by. Nice thing about Clyde, soon as you saw him, you thought of a reason to cuss him.

Shirley opened the screen.

The door was mostly closed, but—Shirley observed the evidence. Black boot prints up by the knob. Wood splintered where the dead bolt entered the frame; a giant piece, long and skinny, dangled on the end of two screws still in the jamb but blasted inward.

Lester Toungate likely couldn't get his foot that high, but the punk El Jay could.

Shirley's neck tingled. She turned around, slow, and took in her surroundings. Looked for parked cars that shouldn't be parked. People in windows. Cameras. She realized she had no idea what right looked like. She didn't come out often enough, this way. When she went for groceries, she exited from the back side.

She eased open the door. Bent and leaned in. The place

smelled normal, like an old office with metal file cabinets full of paper, and carpet that hadn't been replaced in thirty years. A place where someone had smoked cigarettes for dozens of years, but not in the last few months.

The thing she expected to smell—dead Clyde—she didn't.

Holding the door by the edge, Shirley stepped fully inside. She reached for the light switch, but stopped short.

Careful, in case Clyde was somewhere in the rest of the house, she moved to the side of the desk and then around behind, and stood by the chair. The desk was clean, save a few unopened letters. The computer was off. Keyboard grimy. Beside the computer, an Obama bobble head.

Shirley reached to a file cabinet and pulled the silver handle of the topmost drawer.

Locked.

Two more, also locked.

She stepped back to the door, and turned as if she'd just entered.

"CLYDE?"

She waited.

"CLY—IDE?"

She backed out of the office.

Something about Clyde ... everything about Clyde, made her skin crawl. She'd shared intimacies with him, anodyne, clinical, sex-performer intimacies, and he always emerged a riddle. Her expertise and career bonafides with men gave her the ability to intuit a man's emotional connection and manipulate it.

Always in the man's service, of course, to heighten his enjoyment.

But with Clyde, she'd always felt as if he was also a performer. Also manipulating people up and down their emotional bandwidths, not in the noble pursuit of enhancing their sexual gratification, but in the narcissistic chase to increase one of his own forms of satisfaction. After enough sex with Clyde, Shirley realized, he didn't enjoy it. He was after something else. Some other button that needed pushed.

She soaked in the office. Whatever life force had animated it ... In her heart, deep behind a black wall forbidding entrance, where intuition illuminated facts as they became apparent, Shirley knew Clyde Munsinger was dead.

She backed out, and heard footstep on gravel; light, as if kittens were at play.

She turned.

That stripper girl was out for an afternoon run. That muscular little gazelle in pink leotards and a purple running jacket. Fuzzy mittens. Loved to do laps in the trailer park.

Bitch.

Shirley waited until the girl's path on the gravel road brought her to perigee with the trailer court office.

"Hey!"

The girl jumped. Shuffled a few steps, and stopped, her face twisted with confusion.

"Hey, where the hell were you last night? I paid your damn rent!"

"What?"

"What's your name? Ulyankee."

"Ulyana."

"Okay, Ulyana. Since Clyde's been here, we've been on the same rotation. So what the hell?"

"I—"

"You know exactly what I'm saying. Don't fake that Russian *no hablo* shit."

"I paid rent with cash."

"Oh."

"What happened here?"

"Someone busted in the door."

Ulyana frowned, distant.

"What do you know about it?"

"Nothing."

"Bullshit." Shirley smiled, big. "Ulyana, love, we girls ... You know it's a different world for us, right? We have to use our heads. Tits, ass, and any other tool we find laying about. We have to work together. I know your hustle because I've played it longer than you. I know you pay rent the same as me, and last night, before Clyde came to my place he went to yours. I know he did. Just look at you. So level with me. I think something bad's happened to Clyde, and if that's the case, the people who did it to him are gonna come back for me, and when they don't find what they want, they'll wonder if Clyde gave it to some other girl. You get what I'm saying? We're in the same boat."

"Who you think you talk to? Me?" Ulyana backed away, moved her head up and down while eyeballing Shirley, toes to head and back. Smirking. "My hustle? You need protection, that's your problem."

"Who's protecting you?"

Ulyana smiled.

"Toungate?"

Ulyana said, "I don't know what you're talking about."

"Well, if it's Toungate, you better worry. Because they're the ones who just turned my place inside out. And killed Clyde. So watch your dumb ass if you think a Toungate's gonna protect you from a Toungate."

"What do you mean?"

"Clyde has dirt on them. A computer drive that has all the evidence the government would need to put the whole Toungate clan behind bars forever. They want it. They thought I had it but I don't. So they're going to start looking other places. You've been screwing Clyde. They'll come for you too."

"Oh."

"Yeah, *oh*."

"Paul. What does Paul have to do with it?"

"That's your protection? Paul Toungate?"

Ulyana nodded, less certain.

"Paul couldn't protect you from a wet paper bag if you was drowning."

Ulyana wrinkled her brow.

"It's an Americanism. You wouldn't understand. Paul's worthless."

"You know Paul?"

"Don't ask a hooker how she knows a man. He'll turn on you to suit his daddy just as fast as his daddy says so. Your only hope is to work with me. You got to tell me what you know."

"Paul was spying on Clyde last night. That's why I couldn't let Clyde in."

"What do you mean? Spying how?"

"Paul was in my trailer watching Clyde at the office, and after I paid rent with cash, Clyde went to your place. Paul watched all that."

"Inside my place?"

"No. No cameras or anything. He was just watching where Clyde was going."

"And you think that makes you safe?"

Ulyana shrugged. "Shouldn't I?"

"Not if the next time they come back I tell them I gave the computer drive to you."

"Why?"

"'Cause you're a smirky frowny Russian. Babe."

"Please—I don't want trouble."

"Well you better listen and do as I say. When I come up with a plan I'ma come get you."

"That's it? What do I do now?"

"Go to work. Take your clothes off and bend over. Same as anybody else."

Shirley considered two possible ways of carrying on the revolution started by Betsy Peck.

First, give the information to the FBI. They had forensic accountants and other geniuses who could crack the code as easily as toe-sucker Lorell Higgins, CPA. She could pack an overnight bag, grab all her cash—about thirty thousand, accumulated over the last ten years she'd been focused on retirement. She'd have to duck out of the world completely.

But then Brass, his wife Clair and daughter Vanessa would also need to hide until the FBI arrested everyone.

Who knew how much time that would take?

And Brass—man-puss that he was—would never go for it. He wanted a career as a politician. "The optics!" he'd say, as if anyone was looking save the Toungates, who'd likely want to use him as leverage to get to her.

Brass would have to fend for himself. That day would someday come, anyway. She wasn't going to live forever. But it didn't sit right with her, running off while Brass faced danger of her creation, alone. Especially since she'd raised him to cook brownies instead of shoot guns.

Last, if she did leave, where would she go?

Vegas?

That was a whole 'nother level of competition. She'd be starting without a book of clients, with nothing but discount rates and a touch of audacity in self-promotion, to get the business up and running. And she'd be putting herself on the shelf right next to those shaved clean all up and down, plastic tit teenybopper whores who, upon serious reflection, offered real value at any price.

Nah, move to Vegas, she'd be giving BJs at truck stops just to feed her ice cream habit.

Maybe Yuma, Arizona. There was a military base. Soldiers would pay to screw a wet towel.

If ...

Thinking through the problem put a fire back in her heart.

Who the hell was Lester Toungate to make her get up and leave the business she'd spent years and years, literally the sweat off her back, to build?

In a just world, Lester Toungate would be pondering where to move his business, since he just messed with Shirley Lyle.

And that brought up the second option that came readily to mind.

She could give the information to the FBI. Drive some heat on Lester, make him careful about his motions, if he knew they were surveilling him. But the coup de grace would have to come from Shirley.

And Ulyana.

Between the two of them, there wasn't a sexual angle they couldn't exploit.

Except …

Shirley knew from experience with other men, Lester had reached the age where his worm didn't fish. If it did, only with a half box of Viagra and a couple rubber bands.

She'd come at him sideways.

Besides, that punk El Jay was the one who tore her place upside down. Removed the batteries from her remote. He was young and his passions burned hot. With Ulyana's help, she'd bring down the son.

House Toungate would crash on the old man too.

Chapter 32

Lester sat on a half rotted pine log that a bear had clawed for grubs. He removed his pack to allow his shoulders a moment to work back to normal.

Nice thing about being in the woods—you're among the like-minded.

Predators.

You ever watch a video on PBS showing a big animal going after a meal—that's the way you do it. No pissing and moaning. Oh, they might parry a bit until the stronger finds his angle, but after that, pure attack. Wolves, cats, grizzly, whatever. They don't prance around. They get about the business of killing because in their estimation, killing is good. It fills their bellies. It holds their territory. Secures mates.

Killing is good for everything that matters.

It's only when you insert the modern morality that things get twisted. Hell, the Romans put their boots on the necks of entire populations. Anything with the nerve to fight back, they cut off its head. Survivors were put in chains and sold. Anybody left—they paid taxes.

In that day, followers revered the strongman. Progress came from strength.

Then along came the modern morality. Roots all the way back to Roman times. No longer did the powerful deserve adulation. Loving enemies became chic. Weakness became the currency of virtue. Kissing ass and playing meek.

The strong were still strong, and always would be. But they lost the moral high ground. Became the villain.

Nowadays power for power's sake earns condemnation. Well, screw them. Pedophiles in robes perpetrated the whole fraud.

And the only reason it worked was because all the hocus pocus, lovey-dovey horseshit was really just a masque worn by underachievers hiding their flaws.

I hide behind chastity because in truth, I'm ugly.

I'm humble—but only because I haven't done squat with my life.

Nah, the last two thousand years of so-called morality was a weak man's circle jerk, orchestrated by robed strong men a little more clever than the ones that preceded them.

Meanwhile, men with guts and ambition did what they always did. They built empires. They made weak people do their bidding. They got rich and, while their bodies were able, indulged them with any ambrosia they desired.

That's the truth of it right there. The real truth.

Lucky wove between Lester's legs, and when Lester took the dog's face in his hands and kissed his nose, Lucky lowered his hind, then rolled to his side. He lay between Lester's feet with his back to the log. Lester bent at his back as far as the muscles allowed, and on the left side if he could just bend a little more, he hoped it would finally pop, and release.

But in four years, the tightness never popped. Lester

stroked Lucky with his fingertips, barely digging into the animal's fur.

"We camp in a minute. But we need a little more distance before we give up tonight, you hear?"

Lucky flopped his tail.

Lester eased back and let the dog exist without his attention. He placed his elbows on his knees and listened to the forest. Though they walked less than a mile, the solitude muted any sound but the breeze. No machinery allowed. No industry. No products of intellect. Just things that grew slow, and if they killed, did so with teeth or talon.

Except Lester, impostor. Smuggler. Black hearted hunter.

Lester smiled.

It felt good to be the blackest hearted son of a bitch in the wood.

"That's right, dog." Lester bent one more time, scruffed Lucky's scalp at the base of his ears. "All right, time to move."

Lester stood, knelt beside Lucky, and lifted the dog's jowl with his finger. No more blood.

"Ready to get a move on?"

Lucky flopped his tail. Exhaled hard enough to move dried leaves.

Lester lifted his pack, but Lucky didn't stir.

"Let's take another minute," Lester said. He lay his pack back in the leaves.

He sat on the log again, this time a few feet from Lucky, where he could see the dog's head without having to crane his own. Lucky's eyes were closed and his breathing already relaxed enough he could be asleep.

Years. Damnable years. You don't want to stop them coming, but looking at the stack, wish you didn't have so many.

Did dogs have the intellectual horsepower to cognate on mortality? Did they see a dead animal and recognize their own bodies were pregnant with the same inertia?

For Lucky, it wouldn't be long. George Carlin famously said life is a series of dogs and Lester believed it. One after the next. Over his life he'd found a couple of his animals in a ditch, hit by a car or truck. And he saw a couple die the slow wailing death of cancer, rotted from the innards. Once the animal couldn't walk like it used to; once it started wandering, or whimpered just drinking from a water bowl... the end neared.

But did dogs know a world without them existed?

It didn't matter anyhow, to the eighty three year old drug lord who would never die. He didn't contemplate death in a personal sense.

Only asking for a friend.

"All right. Any more laying around you won't get up all night. I know you. C'mon, Lucky dog."

Lester nudged Lucky with his toe and Lucky bared fangs.

"C'mon, dog. We got work to do. Get up. Let's go."

Lester shouldered his pack, walked a few steps. Lucky raised his front half off the ground. Stood.

Lester resumed, but kept the pace slow.

After a few hundred feet Lester stopped at a stream and allowed Lucky to lap water while he turned a circle and meditated on why the hair on the back of his neck stood.

He didn't smell anything out of the ordinary—and he trusted Lucky to notice danger long before he did. Still, his senses registered something amiss. Maybe no birds whistled spring tunes. Or he smelled blood, carried on a ribbon of wind. Maybe a far off noise, audible only to the subconscious human ear.

Something amiss.

Lester thought while Lucky slapped water down his throat.

Had he chambered a round?

He broke the bolt on his .30-06 and pulled it back a half

inch. Found brass and slapped it home. He placed his hand on the hunting knife at his hip.

"You don't hear anything, huh?"

Lucky looked up.

Lester turned his head.

The feeling was uncanny. He didn't believe in the paranormal, on principal. Besides, open that box, pretty soon you'd have to ask why you didn't take the granddaddy of supernatural seriously. The book with the cross and the man healing lepers. Two thousand years of bullshit. Go down that road, there was a lot to account for. Get your ass run off a cliff with a herd of hogs.

Better to not let the mind wander too far that direction.

"Let's go, Lucky. Let's go find that mutt. Or whatever's ahead."

Lester knelt, let Lucky get a good sniff on the blue towel. "Track!"

Lucky put his nose to the air and set off faster than he moved before the break. As if before, he knew where he was going, but lacked sufficient ambition.

Now he trotted and Lester worried about the pace, what he hurried into. He let the dog lead by a couple dozen yards.

Lucky stopped and coughed. Lester arrived beside him and stooped. Reached. Lucky bounded ahead. Did the dog sense the same witching? Was he eager to render it into ordinary sights and smells.?

Nose to ground, back and forth, long bursts ahead, nose in the air, back to the ground—that dog's walnut-sized brain held more intelligence than his son Paul. Likely El Jay, too. Something beautiful to behold. Lester stopped at a birch and wrapped his hand around it. Put a little weight on that arm and lightened the load on his left leg a minute. All the tromping over rock and logs—and to be truthful, all the plain walking—taxed his muscles. One by his groin, right there— he twisted a little, and the pain was sharp, but like it needed to be, if it would ever release.

Lucky pressed on.

Lester pushed off the tree. Remembered the tragedy of Lucky's life, how he hunted fingertips and bone shards in cancer dust, because his master rewarded him with a game of tug o war. Kind of emphasized the stupidity of the whole game called existence. Animal or human.

Lester could find fault with any man he ever encountered, appraise his worth and calculate his fate. But Lucky was different.

"I'll miss you," Lester said.

He stopped at a hip-high boulder and, for a moment, lost sight of Lucky. Opening his mouth to call, he spotted him twenty yards to the left of where he saw him last. Lucky's held his nose close to the earth and his backside shook back and forth. The dog's excitement translated through distance fragmented by twigs and branches. Lester hurried.

Up there, Lucky found it.

Whatever it was.

Chapter 33

FBI shouldn't be hard to find. Shirley sat on her sofa, thinker pose.

She smelled bacon. Probably grease residue between her little toes. Her feet sweated, though she wore wool socks. They were cold.

She went to the kitchen. Opened the refrigerator and pulled out a package of bacon.

With appetite, origins didn't matter. In a good person, all desires were healthy. Pizza. Ice cream. Orgasms. Football.

Dissect a bad man and find his appetites, they're black and wormy. Even if he craves ice cream, he has a nefarious plan. He wants to let it melt so he can drown babies in it. Or kittens.

Knowing herself a good woman, she obliged her cravings.

Standing in front of a stove burner with sizzling bacon in the pan, Shirley resumed thinking about how to destroy Lester and the moron El Jay.

She couldn't walk up to the FBI and say, here's this dirt I got on a drug dealer. Goodbye.

They would ask about her identity. Not only her name. They would dig into her past. Her character. Find out her involvement. Maybe get her to say something she didn't mean to say. Send her to jail because they could.

You couldn't trust the FBI any more than you could have confidence in any other bunch of men with infinite power and money. No, if you wanted to engage them, it'd better be at a distance, with as much air space as possible.

Thought completed, the convenient thing about the FBI at the moment: Flagstaff crawled with agents. As evidence of divine intervention on behalf of the little people, they were easy to identify. They wore the same clothes and looked like city people standing in a corn field, eyes glazed and never making contact with the cornstalks.

Flagstaff was about hair, whiskers, hippies, ranchers. Denim, leather, and pastels. Guns and anti-guns. But not law-and-order, black suits and shiny shoes. White shirts. No one but federal law enforcement agents and life insurance salesmen wore white shirts.

"Damn! Double damn!"

A few months ago, in the dead of January, she opened her trailer door after a serious knock followed by a hesitant knock—almost like door-whimper. Before her stood a young FBI man, acne-scarred and short haired. Glasses that seemed to wear wing tips.

"I ain't done shit," she said.

"Uh, Miss Lyle?"

"Mizz."

"I'm sorry. Mizz Lyle?"

"Yes?"

"I'm ... Joe."

"Joe."

"Uh. Yeah. Joe Smith."

She laughed. "Yeah. I met your brother. John."

He nodded. She surmised his feeble will from his weak eye contact and down-angled head. Smart enough to hold a low opinion of himself. But he wore a black suit—the law enforcement uniform—like all the other recent invaders from the Federal Bureau of Investigation.

"You here with the FBI crew chasing that mass murderer and his dog?"

"No—I'm a ... I'm a college student."

She snorted.

"I'm sorry."

"Lord would you quit with the sorry? All right, college student Joe Smith, what do you want? Why are you here?"

"I would like to maybe, uh, engage your services?"

"What services?"

"A person I met at a breakfast house recommended your services. Tom Davis."

She squinted at him, wondering why the next governor of Arizona sent a lawman to her.

Of course, Tom Davis wasn't his real name.

She met him a few years before, when a bunch of anti-government rebels got together to drink beer and complain about taxes. She'd been in a growth stage with her business, after deciding to increase her income so she could save more for retirement. That didn't happen—but she'd started listening to men when they said things like, you oughtta go to such and such a place, lotta guys there like girls like you.

So she took his invitation and met a surly lot of bikers and assorted charlatans. Nice folk. She made a few connections and acquired a few clients—one still paid dues, regular.

Then a year ago, news broke that the governor of Arizona, Virginia Rentier, was resigning. She'd been tangled in a bunch of conspiracies, murders plots, the usual.

The funny thing: Tom Davis, the ringleader of the secessionist crew where she ate burgers and brats, was not really Tom Davis. His real name was Nat Cinder, and he was the mastermind who brought down the governor. Now half the state wanted him to run for office, and he kept putting out smoke signals to keep the rabble excited.

So what the hell was Tom Davis, aka Nat Cinder, aka future governor of Arizona, doing sending an FBI man to her doorstep?

"Get your ass in here before you freeze. Didn't they teach you to wear a coat at the FBI school?"

"I'm not—"

"Oh shush."

He entered the trailer. She closed the door behind him. Retreated to her sofa and sat. Let him stand there, nervous.

"You said Tom Davis. What'd he say to you?"

"He said you'd recognize his name, and that ought to be good enough to vouch for me."

"Even with you being in the FBI."

He turned part away from her. "You seem kind of fixed on that."

"You think?"

"Well, the FBI doesn't prosecute prostitution. Not one-by-one, as it were, per se. They only go after big fish. Big crimes. You understand, headlines."

"Uh-huh."

"That's what I read."

"So what can I do you for?"

"Isn't that my question?" He smiled.

"Two hundred."

"That much?"

"So isn't that funny? You a lawman, pretending to be a college student. Me a prostitute, pretending to be a soccer mom. We negotiated two hours of pure sexual ecstasy for a price of two hundred dollars. Is that right?"

He nodded. Took off his suit jacket.

And Shirley was reminded to add a word to her

Pretentious folder.

Per se.

The problem with having a contact in the FBI, was he didn't want to be her contact in the FBI. He'd visited at least bi-weekly for several months, but she never learned his real name.

After his first session, he always secured his appointments by telephone. She added him in her cell under the name Joe Smith #7.

She tilted the frying pan of bacon and propped the handle on a block of cutting knives, letting the grease drain to the low side of the pan. Turned off the burner and fetched her cell phone.

She dialed Joe Smith #7.

It rang and rang and rang. Shirley ended the call. Maybe he was in a wam-bam super secret FBI meeting.

She dialed again, and the line answered.

"Who is this?" A woman's voice.

"Uh. Mizz Shirley. Where's Joe?"

"Who's Joe?"

"Isn't this his phone?"

"Yeah. Joe got hisself a payphone."

Click.

Ergo ... Joe had used a pay phone along with a fake name. Not his real phone and name. Per se.

Shirley ate a piece of bacon. Burned her mouth—but it was good. Out of habit, she sat on the sofa and turned on the television. Maybe there'd be something about Clyde showing up murdered somewhere.

She endured fifteen minutes of a Jeopardy rerun, and then the news broke in.

Video played in small area on the screen, while the newsreader's pretty upper half filled the rest.

The hunt continues for a feral dog accused of murdering a Flagstaff man last night at a Hardees restaurant. In the bizarre footage now showing on your screen, captured by a security camera from an adjacent building, the man is seen carrying a chain. It's thought he was trying to somehow assist the dog, which had gotten trapped inside the cement block area containing the garbage dumpster. The dog can be seen after the assault running toward the forest on the other side of the road. If you have information about this dog—can we show the blow up image of the dog—thank you—the dog appears to be a pit bulldog or one of the fighting breeds. If you have seen this animal, or have information about its location, please call our News4 Hotline—

Shirley's mouth parted.

That Hardees was a quarter mile away.

After slashing Clyde Munsinger, the dog went on a rampage. That poor man with the chain—probably wanted to tie up the dog, to protect it, until the dog people could arrive.

Horrible.

Some of the footage showed the man on the ground, his face blurred, but with blood surrounding his head area.

Shirley closed her eyes. Her brain felt different when pregnant with a key insight.

The dog!

It was white.

It was a pit bull.

It was marked up like it had been in fights.

Shirley chewed bacon and stepped backward in a daze, considering the ramifications.

She'd given a bath to the outlaw pit bull on the run from North Carolina with a serial killer.

That was why the FBI was here. They would want to learn about the dog, right? She'd slip in the information about another man who was also looking for the dog, Lester Toungate, because he believed it carried a USB device with evidence exposing his drug money laundering activities.

"Why does he believe that?"

"Because I told him."

"What exactly are you trying to hide, Miss Lyle?"

"Mizz!"

No. You don't go direct to the FBI.

Unless ...

"Screw this."

Shirley turned on her computer. Ate more bacon. Searched for the FBI, Flagstaff.

There was none. Only the office in Phoenix. Okay, if that's the game they wanted to play. Fine. She dialed.

"You have an agent who told me his name is Joe Smith. I want to give him information. About that dog. You know. The serial killer and his dog. Well, I gave the dog a bath."

"A moment, please. Let me see if I can raise him on his cell phone."

"Who?"

"Agent Smith."

"Is that his real—uh, thank you."

The line clicked as if the call was broken. About to press END, Shirley hesitated.

Dial tone.

Ringing.

"Hello?"

"Agent Joe Smith?"

"Yes, who's this?"

"Mizz Shirley Lyle. Flagstaff."

"Oh, uhm. Has it been a month already since I helped you move? Did you still need help hanging that wall mirror?"

"What the—" Shirley swallowed. "I'm not calling about that. You guys have been hunting a serial killer from North Cackalackee all year.

"Um, yes."

"You assigned to that case?"

"Not any more. I was, uhm. I consulted on some of the technology."

"Okay. Well, I know where the dog is. The serial killer's dog."

"How?"

"I drugged him. Gave him a bath. Then he ran off. Say, where are you?"

"Phoenix."

"You seen the news?"

"What news? I mostly work with computers. I don't pay attention to—"

"Well, you can see the dog on the news too."

"What? How?"

"He killed a guy. Ate his face or something. They won't show the full video."

"What channel?"

"Four—but you can't get four from Phoenix."

"Give me a minute."

"Besides, it won't be on there right now. They switched to Jeopardy reruns."

"I'm going to the website."

Shirley stood. Walked to her window and looked outside at the trailer resort office. How much should she tell? She said too much already. She had to work it right, or risk being investigated with everyone else. Clyde's blood was probably still on her wall, in a micro sense. They could connect her to his disappearance by spraying that magic stuff from CSI.

"Holy mackerel. That guy was reaching out with the chain, maybe to put it on his neck. Did you see this?"

"Uh-huh."

"And you gave that dog a bath?"

"Uh-huh."

"I have to go."

"Wait!"

"What?"

"What are you going to do?"

"Well, that looks like the dog associated with an unsub

wanted for crimes in Arizona and North Carolina. We're going to find the dog."

"How?"

"Shirley—"

"Mizz"

"Mizz Shirley, I need to go."

"Wait! I want to tell you more!"

"What?"

"Another man is looking for that dog. He's supposed to be the biggest drug dealer in north Arizona. He'll be out there too."

"What?"

"Yes, he will. I told him the dog has information he wants. I lied because I don't want to be involved. So I thought I could give the information to you, and you could put it on the dog when you find him, and then arrest the man before he comes back here to kill me."

"Wait a minute, Shir—Mizz Shirley. What are you ... Let me digest this."

"Get your ass to my place, and I'll give you what you need."

Chapter 34

Lester stood at the center of a small arena in the middle of the woods. The ground was flat—an oval about twenty feet in diameter. Not far from a stream. A couple of boulders on the perimeter. Above, open to the sky.

Lucky shook with excitement. Nerves, maybe.

The hair on Lester's neck remained on end. It tickled. Though the temperature was chilly, after exertion, his dress had proved too heavy. The skin on his back was cold, and the muscles twitched. He became aware of himself, looking out through his eyes. Aware that the thing he called Lester, his self, was looking out through eyeballs at the woods. Almost as if the thing that was Lester was removed from the whole affair, the weird scene that had the dog freaking out, but to Lester looked like so many wind-blown leaves.

He turned, taking it all in, then again, with his gaze above, in the tree limbs. Once more, easy, looking between trunks as far as they'd let him.

If something was there, its disguise was perfect.

Lucky wagged his tail hard enough to shake his body. Lester looked to the ground where Lucky sniffed. Stooped, twisting a little to put the extra pressure on the left side of his lower back. Maybe make that joint pop.

Blood.

Enough he wouldn't have needed to bend to see it.

The leaves were smeared in reddish brown. Here and there, clumps of hair stuck to their surface. He observed scrapes made from a clawed foot, leaving parallel trenches. Lester placed his hands on the ground where they seemed to not interfere with the scene. He studied the terrain and saw what Lucky smelled and intuited.

This place had seen an epic fight. The leaves were overturned in places, wet on top. Clumps, as if sporadically tilled. Long drug claw marks, and blood sprinkled throughout, as if flung, not dripped.

Hallowed ground, where the strong battled the strong.

Lucky moved off, attracted by new smells, at the side of the arena, near tree trunks. He planted his nose in the leaves. Clawed away dirt.

Looking at Lucky from a lower angle, Lester perceived what he had missed: a trail of overturned leaves, many standing in lumps, partly on edge, that extended from the center of the bloody mess below him, into the woods. The path seemed to end near a clump of shrubs.

Only one animal that he knew of dragged away dead prey.

Mountain lion.

"Ahhh."

Commence tingling neck, all over again. Now he smelled the robustness of the earth, overwhelming like bread just pulled from the oven, but dank, not sweet.

He looked at Lucky—then to the trees, again studying a circle. Even a dog so great as the German shepherd was no match for an adult mountain lion. They liked to perch in branches and leap on deer, biting the skull base, paralyzing, and killing faster than a man with a bullet. Then they'd drag off the animal and bury it. Come back when hungry, like swinging into the drive-through at a burger joint. Meals ready and waiting.

Spend much time in the woods in Arizona, you've likely been studied by a mountain lion. They blend with just about any terrain, stay hidden and motionless, and always know more about their turf than the beast passing through. You don't sit long as an apex predator without certain traits, Lester knew.

So what had happened here?

The big cat followed the white pit bull's scent here. There'd been a hell of an altercation. Then what? Mountain lion drags food off through the trees.

The way mountain lion hunt, though, you wouldn't expect to see such a tore-up battlefield. Pit bulls had a lot of fight, sure, but not against an adult cougar. They were different classes of monster, all together.

But *if* the lion killed the dog, it was most likely right over there, under some leaves and a little dirt. If Lester had the balls to walk into a lion's fast food joint and rob it.

Lester pressed up with his arms, then helped himself erect. Now that he'd seen the trail of overturned leaves, he could spot it from standing up. Meanwhile Lucky was sniffing out another location, a couple yards off.

Lucky started digging.

Again, Lester looked to the lowest tree limbs above. He lifted his .30-06 and placed his hand on the bolt handle, but recalled he'd already double-checked it. He moved the safety to fire. Wouldn't make sense to die jiggering a switch.

He stepped to Lucky and saw the dog had exposed an animal. Certainly not a white pit bull. Lester knelt. Petted Lucky. "Let me in, boy."

He probed with his rifle barrel, then grabbed a foot and

pulled.

Coyote pup.

That enlightened things a bit. Coyote pup means coyote Ma and Pa. Mountain lion, and a pit bull that just sliced a man's face and murdered another.

No wonder he felt the goosebumps. Whatever ethereal medium connected the predators of the world, surely rippled outward from this locus. No wonder he'd felt its pull.

Now that was a mysticism worth pondering. Later.

He thought through the scene one more time. Coyotes and pit bull tangled up, most likely a territorial thing. They'd perceive each other as threats—didn't matter which was here first. Mountain lion looking for food sits out the scuffle, and when one or the other wins, comes in to bag his supper. Drags it off.

Still, that didn't say which animal was buried over there.

"I don't want to mess with your dinner, partner. But I got to know."

Maybe he'd find the pit bull, take the collar, and the whole thing would be over. Get back to rebuilding his business.

"Stick with me, here, boy."

Lester carried his rifle port arms, and looked to the trees as much as the trail on the ground. Kept Lucky at his side. If the cat made it to the dog, it would easily inflict its harm before Lester could get off a clean shot.

Careful and slow, Lester stepped to the endpoint, a clump of shrubs with the tiniest green leaf nubs poking out, with a tore up mess of dried and matted leaves below.

He knelt. Shoved a hand into the dirt.

Away, ahead, twigs snapped. Leaves danced. Brown-yellow flashed between low evergreen branches. Disappeared.

Lester shrank inside. He jerked his hand free of the dirt, then wrapped it on the rifle stock and brought the barrel level. He turned, waiting for the cougar to loose a vowel and give away his location. From the sound, it was no more than a dozen yards off, and could close the distance in seconds. It was definitely ahead of him.

Unless ...

Lester calculated. An animal has to fight for its existence, just to keep food on the table. He gets cunning. You want to let out a roar and let your dinner look the wrong way while you rush his dumb, trembling ass from the rear.

Lester turned.

Chapter 35

Some point that girl'll fetch a ride—maybe a killer will pick her up and cut her. Irony. Most likely she'll hitch a lift with a salt-of-the-earth rancher with a cell phone, and Flagstaff cops and the FBI will know where I crossed and what I'm driving.

I have a half hour, absolute tops. Goal ain't to get to Hardees where Joe defended his life. Just get away from where the feds have ten grid-square staked out with gadgets and wizardry.

I watch every car pass to see if they spot me. Hair on my arm is tall, like any second a bullet will come through the window.

Graves' mountain lair—no worry about law, government, money, food, nothing. Fella can relax deep. Now I see the difference, back living in the wild, among people.

Follow the Interstate 40 to Business 40 and grab the first big truck stop. That's where the people are, let a man blend in and wander off.

I park at the edge of the lot. Leave keys under the seat with another maple leaf. Lock the handles from the inside and walk off cool. Inside the truck stop I use the FBI man's cash to buy a Mexican poncho with all the stripes and colors, and a John Deere cap. All the beef jerky I can fit in one hand.

Why, looky-looky.

Wild Turkey.

"Take a bottle of that Turkey. Fact—two. Here, I'll put back the jerky."

"That jerky'll rot your gut."

"I know it. Yep."

He gives me back a couple ones and coins. Holds my eye too long.

He say, "I know you?"

"I look like a feller was on Dancing With the Stars, couple months back." I put on the Deere cap. "That's what most people say. Though I won't dance for nobody."

"Nah, that ain't it. You got one of those faces I guess."

"We appreciate ya."

I back out, got the willies high. Escape the Graves land just to get recognized buying Turkey.

Outside, I look back through the glass, and he's still watching.

So this is how it ends?

Nah, can't be.

Stinky Joe depending on me. Got to make speed. See if a little Turkification helps.

I crack the seal. Pull a gurgle. Choke. Gasp. Wrong pipe ... try again. Smooth. This time she goes where I want her.

Doesn't take forty seconds and the whoosh comes upon me. Use ta'could drink a half gallon and not hardly fall over. Now a three-second pull floats my valves. Yippee zippee.

Stinky Joe, I'm coming.

I set off cross the truck stop lot. Figure to cut between the big rigs' fueling station, and beyond is the mountains. 'Tween here and there is all manner of residential land, with the streets every which ways. Once I get up there, make it hard for the lawman to find me.

Slap that new Deere cap on my noggin and slip on the parka. The fella who sold them to me is the one liable to call the FBI. So he'll tell them what I got on.

Or maybe not. Could be the girl from the car that calls.

More Turkey.

Snookle. Gurgle.

Aright, here's how this rescue's gonna unfold.

God Almighty wants me to save Joe, 'cause Joe's good people. Going about said holy work, I expect protection. Hencewith and hereforth, I'll just act like I'm Baer Nobody. Hitch a ride, maybe.

Consult the map.

More Turkey.

Turns out I'm not five miles from the Hardees in question. Five miles is two pints. I drank two thirds of the first, and I'm suspicious I might need some for supper.

About face. Back inside, the same fella looks at me—but I'm protected. I fish a gold coin. Hold it so he sees it glimmer in the fluorescent light.

"This is pure one hundred percent gold, minted by the Canadians. They love maple trees. I'll trade this for six bottles of Turkey, and maybe a few dozen pieces jerky. And I need a lighter. Zippo-like. You know?"

"You'd need to go to a numismatics place or something. We use real money here."

"Real money my royal English—. Say, help a fella out. Let's make a trade."

"I don't have enough for a maple leaf."

"You know what that's worth?"

Shakes his head. "A thousand?"

"Someday soon. Right now, maybe you get eight

hundred."

"I don't know. I don't have eight hundred."

"You didn't listen. I want six bottles of Turkey and a couple packs of jerky. You got the cash for that?"

Voice behind me. "Can I see that mister? I'll maybe take that trade."

I turn. Middle age dude with hair to his ass. Braided. Got the beard. Jacket rides high over a holstered revolver. 101st Airborne on the shoulder.

I hand him the coin. He bites it. Looks at the marks. Turns it over.

"You bite it you bought it." I wink. Respect.

"Deal."

He looks to the attendant. "I'll pay for all he's asking for." Turns to me. You sure that's all you want?"

"Maybe a couple slices that pizza over there."

He nods. "The cheeseburgers ain't bad either."

I grab two. Point to the pepperoni and mushroom slices. "Mebbe five of them. Oh. I want some first aid stuff. You know. Couple items."

"Go ahead."

There's nobody else in line. I gather gauze, tape, ointment. If my leg doesn't need it Stinky Joe will, got all these assholes on him. I grab a hot pickle in a plastic pocket, and the man paying grins while I whittle the outside edge of his profit margin.

He doesn't seem to recognize me, and the other lost interest.

Last, there's little canvas satchels, like bookbags, in a wire tub. I grab a black one. Tactical.

Cash register-man scans the items, and the paying fella pays. I stow my winnings in the bookbag and keep the working-Turkey in my back pocket. Shoulder the satchel and with nary a wayward glance set off for the hills. Stop after fifteen steps. Grab two slices of pizza out the bag and start chewing.

Cross the lot. Pass rigs pumping fuel. Walk the rutted dirt where they sleep some nights. Beyond is weedy plain, then scruffy foothill—looks to last a hundred yards. Then right up the mountain. Once I get out there, I'll climb a hundred feet for elevation, consult the map and sup on jerky and Turkey.

Five miles? I'll rescue Joe inside two hours. Three, tops. Then on to Montana.

Behind me ... wheels on dirt. Got the low quiet sound, creep along fast as a man walks.

Fast as I walk.

Law?

I don't want to look. Can't!

But I got to.

Turn my head part way. Peripial vision one hundred percent. Some sort of pickup truck. Helpful knowledge. Keep walking, and try to keep the pace flat. Though under the parka my hand goes to Mister Glock.

My first drunk in months and I'm thinking like a desperado. I ain't safe to accost.

"You there!"

Huh? I know that voice—but good, or bad?

"Baer, dammit. Hold up."

"Hunh?"

I turn. Truck stops. I fetch Glock out the holster, but under the poncho.

Door opens. "You got problems, Baer; better get in the truck."

"Cinder?"

"Who else is gonna come looking for you?"

"Uh, well. Half the law enforcement."

"They'll be here shortly. You're all over the scanner. I guessed you'd set out for your dog."

I look a circle. No law, yet.

"Baer, it's me for shit's sake. Get in the truck."

Don't like the bum rush.

"Why you come?"

He approaches. I step back. Turn partways with the gunfighter stance. He stops.

"You just stole a car from a state trooper's daughter, a mile from her house, Baer. What the hell's got into you?"

"How you know?"

"I know everything. And if I figured out where you're headed, they will too. They'll be there waiting."

"Aw, piss."

"Plus they'll be all over the roads from Williams to Hardees—that is where you're going?"

Nod.

"Up to you. Damn. Thought you'd appreciate the help."

"Well, just hold up a minute. You come on a little strong is all."

"Maybe think on it in the truck, out of sight."

I got a buzz like I stuck my head in a swarm of honeybees. Just realized Ole Nat Cinder doesn't shoot sparks and his eyes is—what?

"Your eyes brown?"

"Hazel, I guess. Do they still say hazel? What the hell, Baer?"

"Well they ain't red. You got the door unlocked?"

I step-to and pull the handle. Look across the hood and see a black sedan with white plates tooling along, up by the semi trucks. Could be anything.

Pull off my pack. Grab the bottle out my back pocket. Climb inside.

Cinder engages the transmission, but doesn't move.

"You want a slug a Turkey?"

"I'm sober."

"Bully for you."

He shakes his head. Looks at me long, out the side of his eye. Cinder starts to drive, turns the wheel slow. The black sedan's moved off. He exits out the back lot and after a quarter mile turns on a residential street.

"I guess you saw your dog killed a guy?"

"Guy was gonna beat him with a chain. Them lying sonsabitches didn't show that."

"What, the news?"

"Right."

"Where you been staying, that you watch television news?"

"You didn't figure it out?"

"You with Tat?"

"I was with her. Not with her. Well. Yeah. Guess I was. Both."

"Ain't she a little young?"

"She looks fifteen but says eighteen. And I didn't do shit until she—wait a damn minute. Wasn't you pokin' Mae?"

"That's impolitic."

"What you gonna do? Dump her?"

"Hardly. I was going to wait a minute but since you bring it up, I want to ask your permission—you know. Old school. I want to marry her."

"Ha! Bullshit!"

He looks at the sky. Sees me watching. "I'm serious. I want to marry her."

"Good. But how does that fit your big plans, governor?"

"Is that a 'yes'? I have your permission?"

"Take her. Marry her."

"Good. I already did."

"What?"

"Yeah. She's pregnant and I didn't want to wait on you turning up."

"It yours?"

"Damn, Baer. You're a piece of work."

"Nah, hell. Marry her either way. Someday when you're president I'll ask a pardon."

We ride. I present big but sometimes it's just peacock feathers. Give me chance to collect my brain coherent. Can't help but smile as the news settles in. My baby got a real man, ain't a piece of shit.

"Nat Cinder, I appreciate you. I truly do. Not the ride, though that too. But you and Mae is a good thing. Good for her and I hope good for you as much. And them babies. If I die too soon, I got peace she's with you."

He looks dead ahead. Says nothing.

But his head starts bouncing small, then bigger until he nods three four times, and his cheeks pull back like a grin wants to bust his head.

"I'm pretty tickled about it," Nat says.

Chapter 36

Shirley looked out the fisheye lens of her front door. Calmed her heart. Took a deep breath. Allowed a long, measured release.

Knocking, again.

She turned away, cupped her hand at her mouth to deflect her voice farther from the door.

"Just a minute."

She waited.

Beating on the door. Plus a kick, down low, that rattled the jamb.

She twisted the knob and pulled.

El Jay strode inside. He had the walk of a newly important man, someone who thought the world wouldn't recognize his stature unless he did first. He looked at the floor, which he'd left strewn with Shirley's belongings. He nodded.

"Like what you've done with the place."

"It's over there."

From down the hall came the sound of a shower faucet and a woman's light voice, singing:

"Мишка косолапый по лесу идёт"

El Jay put up his hands. "The hell?"

Шишки собирает, песенки поет.

"Who else is here?"

"Ulyana. You know. The Russian stripper. Your brother's girl."

"In the shower?"

"Of course in the shower."

"What's she singing?"

"Hello? It's Russian."

El Jay hesitated, as if tempted to investigate.

"You want the memory stick? It's right there." She pointed.

"Yeah, yeah." He looked. "So what's the deal with you? Where was it? Why give it to us now?"

"I found it. You and Mister Toungate said you wanted it, and I don't want anything to do with anything. I just want to mind my own business."

El Jay nodded toward the hall. "So what's she doing here?"

"Oh, just a little girl play, later."

He winced.

The water-sound of the shower ended. The door opened while Ulyana finished her song; her voice drifted out clear and resonant. The Russian had pipes. Shirley hadn't known that.

El Jay raised his brows. Frowned.

In all her years hooking, Shirley had learned to recognized the signs of a man too nervous to cement the deal. His eyeballs roam nonstop. He hedges everything he says. Thinks you're a cop or a set up, one. So he tries to keep everything in play until he figures out where the danger is.

El Jay was acting like that.

"The thumb drive is right there," Shirley said. "It's in the candy dish."

El Jay kept his head pointed back the hallway. He shifted as if hit by a physical force.

Naked, Ulyana eased into the living room, walking slow, as if careful to allow each part of her that jiggled a full three seconds with each step. She stopped singing but smiled big.

White teeth. Pink nipples. Blond hair, except where she was bald.

El Jay smiled. Looked at Shirley. Then Ulyana, again.

Ulyana reached as she passed him, arm outstretched like an angel reaching toward God. Arm trailing, fingers elongated, shoulders bent to prolong their electric connection as she dragged her hand across his hip, over his mess, and forlorn, lost, bereft, away from his touch. She pouted her lips and continued through the kitchen, then the hallway toward Shirley's bedroom.

Jiggle.

Jiggle.

Jiggle.

"Hey dipshit," Shirley said.

El Jay whipped around.

She pointed a pink .38 she'd borrowed from Ulyana, her purse gun, at El Jay's head.

"Follow her down the hallway."

His jaw fell.

"You heard me. Go."

"Or what?"

"You die. Trust me. The naked girl is what you want."

Wide nostrils. Squinty eyes.

"Move, asshole. This doesn't have to be a bad thing. I'm a hooker and she's a stripper. Use your imagination."

His lips eased upward at the edges, but the calculating look still illuminated his eyes. El Jay turned.

Shirley let him stay three paces ahead so he couldn't spin

and hit the gun. As he reached the room: "Stop. Walk slow, straight in."

El Jay complied.

Shirley entered behind him. "Why should Ulyana be the only naked one? Take off your clothes."

He moved carefully, his pace indicating his displeasure; his compliance indicating his curiosity. He pulled off his jacket. Dropped it. Dragged his long undershirt over his head, revealing ripped ab muscles and chiseled pecks.

"Oh, you two'll be great for one another." Shirley said.

"Pants?"

"There's only one kind of naked."

He unfastened his belt. Unzipped. Kicked off his shoes and used one foot standing on his other pantleg to pull them down.

"You don't wear underwear?"

"Oooh," Ulyana said. "Hmm."

"So, what exactly are we doing here?"

"Get on the bed. On your back. Help him, Ulyana."

She stood behind him and pressed her body to his. Eased him toward the bed, and remaining connected to his body, climbed onto the mattress with him.

Shirley tossed handcuffs to Ulyana.

"No. I don't do bondage. Ever."

"In three seconds, you don't have a dick." Shirley pointed the .38 at his groin.

El Jay placed his hands to the metal headboard.

"Make his arms wide, Ulyana. He'll enjoy it more that way."

Ulyana cuffed El Jay at each limb. Four corners.

"El Jay. You like her, right? She could put on her clothes and leave the rest to me, but we both have a stake in this. So why don't you show him what we have in mind, Ulyana."

Ulyana climbed onto El Jay, reverse.

"There you go. Just give him ten seconds."

Ulyana performed.

"Okay. Stop. You can get off him. It's going to be a minute before he sees that again."

Ulyana rolled off El Jay and sat on the bed.

Shirley opened a drawer. "You want to help me with these?"

Shirley tossed a Homedics box the size of a tin of sardines, then another. She carried an armful to the bed beside Ulyana. When they were all free of their boxes, Shirley said, "I'm going to explain this so you can understand it. God, you're all hair and sneakers. This isn't going to work. Just a minute."

She left the room. Returned ninety-eight seconds later with a safety razor, shaving cream, electric shears and a towel. In three minutes she had him clipped close and in ten more, shaved bare, everyplace there was hair on his top half.

"Aw," Shirley said. "You two match."

"What is this?"

"So what I was going to say before. This is what we're about to do. You're going to confess all your nefarious sins. All your drug deals. Your murdering Clyde Munsinger. Your money laundering. We're going to record it all."

"I'm going to hunt down that faggot son of yours and his wife. I'm gonna—"

Shirley strode to El Jay and punched him. Her fist glanced off his face. She lost her balance and fell half on him. Elbowed his armpit climbing off. Punched him again.

"Say that one more time."

Blood ran from a cut below his eye.

"Duress."

"What?"

"Never hold up," he said. "I'm under duress."

"Two things. First, if you call that pretty girl playing with your weenie duress, you're confused. Plain and simple. But really, we're not going after you. Your confession isn't to bring you down. It's to inform on your father."

"I don't understand."

She wiped blood across his cheek, tender. "Of course not. You're an idiot. You don't have to understand, for this to work. All you have to do is know the difference between pleasure and pain. Ulyana, give me a hand."

One by one, they placed thirty electric stimulation devices on El Jay's legs, testicles, stomach, cheeks, forehead, everyplace they found skin.

"See, I looked it up on the internet. You can't really electrocute people with a car battery, like in the movies. And that's good 'cause they're heavy. But these little buggers, you turn one all the way up, you can deal with it maybe ten seconds. After that, it sucks—and not like a Russian stripper. Here, check this out."

Shirley and Ulyana began turning on the stim pads. "You feel that? Good. Okay, that's the low setting."

With all of them on, Shirley said, "You don't have a heart condition, do you?"

One by one, she and Ulyana turned each pad to its highest setting.

El Jay grinned hard, closed his eyes. Writhed. Shook. His flesh rippled without his control.

"AHHHHHH!"

Shirley began turning the pads off. Ulyana helped.

With all of them off, she said, "Okay stripper girl, show him some love."

Ulyana straddled El Jay, placed his organ in her mouth.

"Hum that tune you were singing earlier," Shirley said.

Ulyana began.

"Ten."

"Nine."

"Eight."

"Seven."

"Six."

"Five."

"Four."

"Three."

"Two."

"One."

"Stop!"

Ulyana rolled.

"So you see the game, El Jay. This is going to suck, one way or another."

Chapter 37

Cougar!

Lester jerked his rifle and fired. He yanked back the bolt, shoved it forward. The beast arced toward him. First shot missed. Lucky barked—aborted to a whine. Lester aligned the barrel and, as the mountain lion descended, squeezed the trigger. He slammed the bolt back again. The beast fell at his feet, gargling blood and wheezing. The cat writhed, rolled to its back and showed the damage. Lester hit him in the throat, but not in the center, where the spine would be severed. The animal's windpipe was blown and probably the great neck vein.

The cat would live minutes, if that.

The animal lashed with unfurled claws but not at Lester. He swiped the air, furious to have met a beast more clever and more eager to kill.

Lucky backed from the lion. Lester stepped closer. He cycled another .30-06 shell and pointed the rifle at the animal's head.

"Now take it easy, and I'll let you suffer out the end, natural."

Keeping the barrel aligned with the mountain lion's head, Lester knelt.

The cougar rested its paws on the earth. Blood flowed faster than the soil could absorb. Lester placed his hand on the beast's face and stroked his thumb with the grain. He looked into the killer's eyes, and connected.

This was the source of his earlier disquiet, all his senses pointing forward to some momentous event.

"You magnificent monster."

The lion died.

Lester held his hand to the cougar's face a long moment. Of all his killing, all the men he'd buried in the desert, or in the soft ground at the lake, there had never been one as unexpected as this, and never one to regret until now.

He stood, and then looked again, and nodded slow.

While Lucky rested, Lester retrieved two coyotes and three pups from the scene. The cat had buried each in leaves and clumps of dirt at different locations near the same shrub.

He thought on the pups. Seemed early for them, unless these were born very early in the season—which usually started about March. Coyotes wean in five weeks or so—but they leave the den as early as three weeks.

The time frame could work—it was what it was, so it kinda had to. But, in the scheme of things, the pups were too young to stray far from their den. If by some chance the pit bull survived, that den was the next place to look. Provided Lucky could sniff his way there.

Lester poked over the whole area and failed to see another burial site.

The pit bull had survived the melee. Had to have. He'd know soon enough.

Urinating on a sycamore, Lester took one last look at the mountain lion. Finished, he gave Lucky the blue towel to refresh his memory.

"All right, Lucky boy, you ready to earn your keep? Just a little bit more is all I want."

Lucky led back to the arena between the trees where the coyote battle had occurred, then swung leftward at a hard angle.

Funny—a well-trained dog wouldn't have been sidetracked by a little blood. He'd have marched right through the mess and kept after the prize. It's what made him a high dollar dog. But getting on in years, and probably aware of the lung cancer killing him, maybe Lucky just wanted to use that high powered sniffer to satisfy his own curiosity for a change.

All of life didn't use to be a morbid exercise. Not every damn minute.

They came upon a rock wall, constructed by nature of house-sized boulders extending in a roughly straight line. Not more than a dozen yards along, Lucky nosed to a recess in the rock, well-worn at the entry.

Something lived in there—it'd make sense for desperado dog to take refuge. He'd likely fit through the opening, but barely. Lucky surely couldn't.

"I hope you ain't in there."

Lucky looked up. He trotted along the wall.

"You sure?"

The dog continued, nose the air a moment, before again tracking the pit on the ground. Lester watched for snakes—it was too early, but he liked killing them. After the oddities of the last couple days, maybe a snake would be part of the party. Maybe the whole thing, starting with Clyde Munsinger's attempt on his business, and the opportunity to take out Paul, and the kids at the trail, and now the cougar ...

He'd started off thinking the blasphemy that it might be an end of life celebration, maybe deigned by the universe or the gods of Valhalla, celebrating Lester Toungate while he was alive to participate.

Maybe.

Because if ever a narrow band of time hosted an exotic mash of deadly oddities, this was the one.

Lester reached to the rock wall, stepped high over a boulder, and pressed on.

The light had fallen off since they'd left the scene with the cougar. He'd brought the bare minimum gear to enjoy a night in the wilderness. Camp wouldn't take long to set. They had time.

Lester followed Lucky, mindful that they seemed to be getting well beyond the distance from the cougar site that seemed reasonable for a coyote pup of only a few weeks to travel, even accompanied by both of its folks.

A rock rolled underfoot. Lester swung his arm for balance; banged his knee on the main crag wall. Pain shot through—but not the real kind. Just a warning shot. He stood, lifted his leg, and his knee popped. A contusion, but so what. He looked ahead.

Lucky stood broadside, pointed directly at the rock wall, wagging his tail.

"Found us a pit did you?"

Lester raised his rifle. Careful of each step, he approached.

Then stopped.

Getting right up on the den might provoke a situation. Maybe the pit comes out and tangles with Lucky—putting Lester in the position of having to shoot at the pile and hoping Lucky gets lucky and the white pit doesn't. With dark coming on, he wasn't marching back out of the woods tonight, anyway. It'd be better to camp where he could observe the scene. Then deal with the dog tomorrow. Build a fire and smoke him out.

Lester turned perpendicular to the crag and, when he'd gone twenty yards, said "Lucky, c'mere boy. Lucky dog."

He walked down a slope, crossed a creek and, thirty good paces up the other side, turned back toward the rock wall. He shifted back and forth until finding a place that allowed line of sight to the blacked entryway.

He lowered his pack, pulled a two foot section of hemp rope with a knot at each end, and offered Lucky a game of tug of war for his reward.

Lucky sat, then stretched and rolled to his side. He lay his head on the dirt and closed his eyes.

Lester strung his tarp and gathered wood. Kicked away leaves and fetched a few stones for a useless ring. Old habits. From this location he'd be able to guard that crag all night and day.

Chapter 38

Cinder says, "I want you to see something before you go chasing after that dog."

"I know they're looking for me. I'll come in from the back."

"Well, so you know what to expect."

Cinder slows the truck, cuts the wheel. Somehow the sun's already three quarters down from noon. Truck climbs a hill. Houses give way to trees, then he turns again. Puts the truck in four wheel drive and chugs up some ruts. Ain't far until we top a clear-cut dome.

"Reach in the glove box. There's a set of binoculars."

I do.

"If you stand in the truck bed, you'll see Hardees."

"We're that close?"

"About a mile off. They're looking on the other side of the road, not this way. But they could come this way too."

I climb up. Look through field glasses. There's three

police cars. Well, add two state police. Other black cars too. Whole parking lot's full. Don't know which is law and which is eating hamburgers.

"Won't be long until they get a couple helicopters, my bet," Cinder says.

He looks at his watch. "It's four p.m. The man was killed last night. What time did you see the news footage?"

"Morning. Seven maybe."

"How many police cars were there?"

"One, I think."

"So why are so many law enforcement agencies taking an interest, now?"

Shrug.

"They know you're here. You disappeared five months ago, but now your dog's been spotted. They made the connection—most likely before you even stole that girl's car."

"Borrowed. Rented. I gave her gold."

"Take some advice. That dog lasted the winter without you. He'll survive a couple days, while the heat blows over."

I climb from the bed and sit on the tailgate. Legs dangle like I'm on a bridge.

"You really—"

He reads my face.

I live all my life trying to be true to morals and true to me. Living right, not living wild. Treat men good, though they lie and cheat. Take care of my obligations. Backstop Mae and the kids since her man-choices was for shit, up until now. And mind my business. I haven't been bad. Nor good. Just trying to live, given what I know of others. But the quiet life wasn't given to me. People stuck me with a stick, and I hit them back. The noble cause I started with, an eye for an eye, led to darkness. I thought I was white-hot virtue, but winter in the cement house gave me time to think. And see.

The men I killed were evil.

But so am I.

The only thing that sits outside the human moral morass is the dog. He stays at your side. Shakes his ass. Wags his tail. Licks your face. All that human horseshit is nothing. He sits there loyal.

"Nat," I say, "Stinky Joe's out there. In the big scheme, to the stars and the mountains and the dirt, when they kill him, it won't matter. No more than when they kill me. Regular men? Their morals are corrupt. I'm not a good man, the way they measure, and I don't care. But there is one code that counts, and I don't measure against it at all, unless I save Joe."

He puts his hand on my shoulder. Little push. "Once you get Joe, then what?"

"North, I suppose."

"You want to come see Mae and the kids before you go? Won't do any harm to start after dark."

"There's a forest road out there on the map. One eighty. You know it?"

Cinder nods.

"Take me there."

Chapter 39

Time had passed. Joe couldn't measure it, but the wounds on his chest and leg had manifested a deeper vertigo, such as to overwhelm him at times, and make him vomit at the edge of the outer cave.

Then calm returned, the weariness that made him want to close his eyes, dry out and blow away. They were a shared oneness, the cave's living and dead: dust, bones, and flesh. A continuum. When his energy flagged, he sensed what would follow.

But the she-coyote's exuberance, her nursing and her play, kept him satisfied to lay and do nothing. She brought the remains of the rabbit, not so dripping with freshness, and he ate of it. Then slept.

Time passed. She carried a gopher. It tasted like rabbit and tree bark. Still, Joe fed.

At last, he woke to dim light in the main cave.

Something was different.

He placed it, the scent of man.

And dog.

Joe joined the she-coyote at the opening. She lay close to the wall, her head barely high enough to stare out.

Joe looked. The bouldered terrain sloped to a stream bed. Black cherry, oak, maple and here and there, shrub trees and evergreens. The forest was thick with life but thin enough to see through. On the other side of the creek, a man sat where the ground inclined upward, on a log before a fire.

He rubbed his hand. His forearms rested on the same weapon used by the man who reached across the plain at the beginning of winter, to crease his neck and send him sprawling.

The man leaned to the wolf-sized dog beside him and stroked his head.

The dog's eyes were closed.

The she-coyote gnarred, the noise faint in her throat. She stood, trotted along the cave wall, back and forth. Joe lifted his head. Returned it to the dirt.

The she-coyote bristled with ambition and life-lust. Joe remembered the creeping dance of stalking prey, the music of a rodent's raspy squeal. The rush of exploding over terrain as if unhinged from gravity. The young she-coyote had never learned the restraint of existence in the company of men.

She didn't know.

Joe rose, retreated from the opening, and at the back in the long deep shadow, stretched. The stiffness had eased, and though his body protested, it acquiesced. The burn-tingle of pulling sore muscles, holding them while the agony receded, lifted Joe's spirits. His belly was neither empty nor full. He was warm, and the company was fine. He could stay inside as long as the man and dog chose to lay siege.

Joe again crept to the opening, staying low. The man wore a hat. His face looked like dried leaves, and he moved like his body hurt.

Joe closed his eyes and recalled the other man, the grizzly, cheese-farting man with the gentle words and tingly belly scratches. The breeze had shifted for a moment, but when it returned the old man's scent to the cave, they smelled much alike, though this one was less pungent.

Although the man from his memory was more smooth in his motion, in the end they seemed the same. What was the difference?

The she-coyote trembled. She strode to the back of the cave, then bolted to the entrance. She nudged Joe at his shoulder. He growled.

She bounded out of the cave.

Joe shook. He watched her.

Joe whined.

Fear of the man held him. He knew the long device; he'd heard its boom and felt how it lashed out. A man with a device like that—fifty yards away—was more menacing than a lion at close proximity. Still, Joe's muscles coiled. She'd nursed and fed him. Flirted and snuggled warm with him. He tensed to spring after her.

Joe struggled to the opening and stood, chest wide and head high. To his left front, the she-coyote glided. Her body floated level and her feet blurred. She moved without bounce, and if not looking, he might not have seen her, so easy was her grace.

To his front Joe saw the old man stand from his stump. He drew the distance killer, and after a steady moment, the device blasted. A single concussion arrived, and almost simultaneously, the yip of the she-coyote.

Chapter 40

"So where were we? Ulyana, don't let him finish. Here—"
Shirley powered on the electrical stim pad wrapped around El
Jay's scrotum. "Now, long as you keep talking, Ulyana plays
with your teeny weenie. Soon as I don't like what I'm
hearing, we up the amps."

"Turn it off! I'll talk!"

"So I'm going to start with a question that'll tell me
whether you're paying attention. What's your worst crime,
ever?"

"Turn it off!"

"What's the worst thing? You sell drugs to kids? Beat
women? Molest little boys? You ever kill anybody, El Jay?"

"Agghhh. Go to hell! Agghh."

Shirley turned on another stim pad. "Ulyana, help me with
these. All of them. Set them on high. We don't have time to
play around."

They turned on each pad and pressed the up button to six,

the highest level.

"Will it kill him?" Ulyana said.

Shirley shrugged.

"Agghhhh. Arrggggg."

"Now imagine I put a sock in your mouth, and you have to do all that screaming through your nose! Answer my question! What's the worst thing you ever did?"

"Murderrrrrr! Agggh."

"Who?"

"Jesus Morales and, oh, arggh, Louie."

"Louie who?"

"I—arrggh—I—arrhhhh—don't know."

"When?"

"Three days—ahhh—ago."

"Why?"

"To steal their—arrhh—drugs. My dad's drugs."

"Why?"

"Make it stop? Uh—ah. Turn them off!"

"I said why?"

"Stake money. Own op—agghh—eration."

"Good start. You promise to keep spilling your guts when the juice is off?"

"Oh Christ! Mercy. Mercy-y-y-y."

Tears streamed from El Jay's bloodshot eyes over purple cheeks. His head jerked up and down, flopped side to side.

"We better turn them down," Ulyana said.

"Nuts! My nuts!"

Shirley turned off the scrotal unit. Then the others.

"How did you kill Jesus and Louie?"

El Jay's lungs heaved. He remained twitchy even without the juice. Muscle rolled beneath his skin.

"Ulyana, give him a little nibble. Help him think positive."

Ulyana bent over the side of the bed. Slurped.

"I'm keeping my word, El Jay. It'll be best for your nuts if you keep yours. You got your breath back? Long as you keep telling me the good news, she'll keep slobbin that nobbin. How'd you kill Jesus and Louie?"

"I shot them at the old warehouse on Macallister. They're in their car, inside the building. Probably take years to find."

"Why?"

"No one goes there but the homeless and the heroin addicts. Who are they gonna tell?"

"Excellent. This is progress. Tell me about your father's operation. Where's he buy his drugs?"

"Oh yeah, baby, like that."

"El Jay!"

"Uh—he won't let me in. I had to go around him. Please—teeth!—teeth!—it's the truth."

Shirley studied his face. Tilted her head.

"What happens when he gets his drugs?"

"We deal in meth, mostly. We have mules who pick it up from the manufacturers. Bunch of them. Small shops all over the place. You can learn to cook meth on the Internet. The carriers bring it to us. They work for us, not the cooks. We collect, then distribute to our network. That's the business, right?"

"What do you mean?"

"The drug business. We're the middle. We don't produce. We don't sell to the user. We connect them."

"Who are the producers?"

"I already said I don't know. Paul handles all that."

Ulyana pulled her mouth away from El Jay. "Where is Paul?"

El Jay looked at Shirley.

"The *lady* asked you a question."

"Pop killed him."

"What?" Ulyana said.

"Lester?" Shirley said.

"I'm pretty sure he figured out our play. Part of it. You

want to put that back in your mouth?"

"You mean you and Paul were working together?"

"Pop never wanted to expand. Never wanted to grow."

"So you two decided to steal his business? No wonder he's such a pisshead. Why not wait him out? He won't live forever."

"Nah. He'll never die. Not unless someone helps him."

Pounding on the door.

"What? Who's that?"

Shirley stuffed a sock in El Jay's mouth. "There's a blanket in the closet. Throw it on him, then wait back here."

The door thudded.

"I'm coming!"

Ulyana opened the closet. Shirley nodded at her, closed the bedroom door behind her.

Walked on her heels so her guest outside would sense her coming. She opened the door.

"Hi, Joe."

"Mizz Lyle."

"Come in. Quick."

Shirley glanced around the trailer park after letting him in.

"What's going on? You're making me nervous."

"I have all you need to take down Lester Toungate."

Shirley went to the candy dish and handed Joe a blue USB drive. "That has ledgers showing money laundering back fifteen years. All there. Every penny. I had an accountant tell me what it was."

"I drove from Phoenix. Who the hell is Lester Toungate?"

"He's only a local drug lord. I have his son, too. Another crook. A murderer."

"What murder?"

"He killed a couple of guys in his drug operation."

"When?"

"He didn't say. Yet."

"Well, I'll look at the thumb drive. If I can find anything

about the victims, we'll go from there. It might not be an FBI case."

"What do you mean? The victims are Jesus and Louie. How is killing people not a federal case?"

"All I'm saying is we'll need a lot more than what you gave me so far. Maybe surveillance, and once we build a case on one of them, maybe he'll turn on the other. These things are much more complicated than you can imagine."

Shirley grabbed Joe's arm. Dragged him through the kitchen and back the hallway. Opened her door.

"Joe Smith, FBI, meet El Jay Monroe, piece of shit drug dealer."

"Shirley! What have you done? Shirley—what is this!"

Joe turned. Saw Ulyana—draped in a blanket. No, a bathrobe that could double as a boat sail.

"Who is this?" Joe said.

"Joe, meet Ulyana."

"My pleasure." He nodded. Faced Shirley. "Please explain the handcuffs."

"Some guys like it like that. We were cuddling and tickling like teenagers, and El Jay started telling us about all his misdeeds."

"Why is there a sock in his mouth?"

"Far be it from me to question a sick man's desires."

Joe stepped to El Jay and pulled back the blanket, revealing his chest covered in red welts. The stim devices lay on the bed beside him like so many leeches, amid a sea of shorn pubic hair.

"Shirley, this is all wrong. You tortured him. Nothing he says will hold up. The court will say his confession is fruit of the poisoned tree."

"He said he killed two people. And soon as I want him to, he's going to describe how he sells drugs to kids."

"You can't! This is—oh, hell. Oh shit. I'm involved in this. Oh Lord."

"Well, he said all that, and it's up to you to figure out a way to use it to bring him down. Same as with that computer file I gave you."

"God. What's his name?"

"El Jay Monroe."

"Like the initials? L. J.? What do they stand for?"

"El Jay."

El Jay vocalized through the sock in his mouth. Joe removed it.

"Lester Junior. And these psychotic bitches tried to kill me. I had to make up stories to satisfy them. They're nuts. I'm a small busin—"

"Mister Lester Junior, I'm going to ask you not to talk any more. Your best interest. Understand?" He faced Shirley. "You hurt yourself. This is bad."

Joe withdrew his cell phone. Pressed numbers. "Yes, Nancy, this is Joe. I'm away from my computer. Need you to do a search. Lester Monroe, Junior. Any priors? Outstandings?"

He covered the receiver hole with his thumb. "You've—you realize this is criminal? He can press charges against you."

"For sex? Without money?"

"You shocked him—" Joe removed his finger. "Oh, I understand. Thank you. No, nothing else. Thank you." Joe slid his cell into his jacket pocket. "Mister Lester Junior, you are free to go."

"I want out of these handcuffs now! You bitches. Not you, officer."

"No way!" Shirley said. "He's confessed."

"It doesn't matter. In fact, if he says you tortured him—"

"It was sex. A little rough. Just sex."

"Oh, terrible. This is horrible. We can't even use him as a starting point in an investigation now. You gave the guy immunity." Joe put his hands on his hips. "You must release this man."

"No."

"But you must."

"Bullshit."

"Mister Lester Junior, consider this before answering. Would you like to press charges against Shirley Lyle?"

"Hell yeah! She fried my nuts. Take off the cuffs!"

"I can't release this man, in good conscience," Shirley said. "He paid good money and hasn't nutted yet. I've got my business reputation to consider."

"I'm not asking again."

Shirley stepped close to Joe. Leaned even closer and took his upper arm in her hand. She turned him. "Look up there to that black spot. That dot in the corner. Okay." She turned him again, now facing the opposite wall. "There's another. What do you suppose those are?"

"Ca-ca-cameras?"

"What do you think I record on those cameras?"

"Your bed?"

"Best thing for you to do is walk out of here and start working on that thumb drive. We understand each other?"

Agent Joe Smith closed his mouth.

Ulyana turned partly to her side, revealing her hand in her pocket—and the pink grip of a firearm.

Joe Smith nodded. "I appreciate the information you provided. The United States appreciates your help. The Federal—"

"Just go."

"Okay."

Shirley followed him to the front door.

Joe spoke as he exited. "You understand I can never come back here? It wasn't the service. That was always nice—"

Shirley closed the door.

She grabbed a plastic grocery store bag, then stuffed a second inside, and opened them as she strode back to her room. Two ply. She approached El Jay.

"I guess it was a mistake to bring you here and make you talk. But you threatened my baby Brass and his wife and girl. And you tore up my place."

She reached to him with the plastic bag aimed at his head. He twisted. Bucked. She slammed a fist to his balls and when he strained forward in pain, drove the side of her hand into his throat. She opened the bag and pulled it over his head. Drew it tight at his neck. She twisted the handles until the plastic sucked against El Jay's face. He bucked. Ground syllables out of his throat without the air to propel them. His thrashing motion mashed her hand to the headboard. A bruise for sure. Finally he stopped.

Shirley looked across the room to Ulyana, who looked at the upper corner of her wall.

"Oh no," Ulyana said. "You just videotaped that."

Shirley shook her head. "Nope. Look close. Those dots are magic marker. Put your clothes on. This prick won't dispose of himself."

Chapter 41

Late afternoon. Got the terrain from the topo map and a good fixing on where I'd hole up, was I a kind-hearted dog hunted by bad men. There's a draw with a crick, other side of this hill. Thing about the topo, you see the elevation lines mashed up tight, that's a rock wall. Critters hide in the crevices and holes.

Joe's a critter. Living wild all winter, I know he found some of those holes. He wouldn't survive without. That's where I head.

Cinder looked disappointed.

I hope he's good to the babies.

After my initial snurgle of the Turkey, I haven't had another drop. All I want is a belly full of water. Some of Tat's tortillas.

Hell.

Some of Tat.

I'm nothing but what I am. Too old to quit seeing beauty.

Too hunted to keep it. Too haunted to feel like I deserve it.

I'm not comfortable with people and no less without. That's why a man wants a dog. He has no power to change, and the dog doesn't even ask the question.

Move along quick. Night in Flagstaff falls like it dropped out the sky. Want to gain the upper ground before dark so I can get the lay, spot movement, lights come on while the police and FBI boys are still out. Any luck, they'll all head back to their vehicles and sleep at home in their beds. But if they camp here, I'll know where.

Come over the dome a ways to see down the slope. Move slow and careful. Step. Wait thirty. Step. Stalk like I'm in enemy territory.

Hear a rifle boom, not more than a couple hundred yards. There's no snick of the bullet in branches, no zing off rock. But I get low behind a stump just the same.

Another boom. Another, over and over. Someone empties a deer rifle.

All at once the liquor in my guts rolls. Queasy like bad meat made it too deep in the bowels to throw up. Only thing that makes sense is somebody saw Joe and either missed and kept shooting or got him and wanted to cut him to slop.

No shots the last thirty-count.

I peek over the jagged stump. No motion, no where. Look long and hard. Got chills in the back—somebody down there has a gun. Can't move in until I spot him.

But there's no motion. None.

I wait. Sometime before long, it'll be dark. Anybody down there wants to move, he'll turn on a light or start a fire. It's the way of modern man, not happy with the unseen. That's when I move.

But does Stinky Joe bleed out while I sit, too chickenshit to save him?

And what of the law enforcement? They're supposed to be everywhere. Surely some heard the noise. Surely they'll come looking.

I go down there, I'm like to shoot my way out, regardless.

Stinky Joe, hold on.

Here go.

Chapter 42

Joe snarled while the forest returned to silence.

The man rose from his seat holding the weapon that made the she-coyote yelp. Facing Joe, he strode, and the giant dog followed, and disappeared behind a boulder. The man came straight. He crossed the stream and ascended the slope toward Joe's cave.

Joe waited until he saw the man's eyes fixed on the entrance. His dog closed in.

Joe shifted backward, wormed into the back chamber, and turned to defend the entry.

The attacking dog entered. He sniffed and snorted. Outside, the old man cursed enthusiams. The dog growled, on and off, rapidly following Joe's scent. Joe stayed low but close to the opening, ready to meet teeth with teeth.

The attacker pressed inward. His size blocked most of the light, but Joe's vision already adapted to the dark his adversary just arrived to. The dog's head was large; his fangs, long. He snarled. Joe lunged, forgetting his wounds and the weakness of months of starvation. His body was fed and his muscles and brain were in accord: if the attacking dog gained entry, all would be lost.

Joe snipped—and smelled blood.

The other dog already bled.

It jerked back, hitting his head on rock. Joe snapped and sliced the dog's muzzle. The shepherd thrust inward, but the restricted opening reduced his area to move. He bounced his shoulders from the roof, and again Joe hurled himself. The other animal scraped his paw on Joe's already ripped chest and pain was sharp, then distant. The dog pushed deeper inward.

Joe stood full height. He darted in at the larger dog's neck and, as with the coyote, sank his teeth and clamped. The dog resisted, thrashed, jerked, but Joe clung with the fervor of a wronged beast given opportunity to release a life's torment.

Joe recalled nothing of his past, but suffering animated his cells. The boy with the electric, the blast of energy that left his muscles rigid and spasmodic. The bony tobacco-smelling man who threw him into a pit before other jeering men, where another dog hated him with all its life force and sought to destroy him for the men's cheers. The fat woman, the sleepy broth, and the hysterical man who bled against the wall. The man with the chain at the human food place. They harrowed seams through his mind. Sewed evil into his being. All of life was confrontation. All who crossed his path seemed to demand his destruction. All of life was death. Like cold air, Joe neither thought nor embraced it. He breathed it.

Joe squeezed his jaws with total force. The dog pulled back, but Joe wrestled him forward. Where before he wanted to repel his attacker, he now wanted to drag him inward and crush his throat, until the wheezing and whimpering stopped, until the dog oozed blood, but sound, naught.

The other pulled. Whimpered.

At last, Joe sensed the animal's fight had slipped away. Joe eased, then snapped an even deeper mouthful of neck. He jerked.

After a long moment, the dog was limp. Then it convulsed. Retreated with power Joe couldn't match. Its breath had ended, and its blood spilled unabated, but somehow the dog moved backward, out. A man grunted beyond the entry. The old man cursed with the violence of all the world's evil in one vocal blast.

The dog slid out of the opening and the old man's syllables rushed in.

I'm a murder ya!

Joe shrank back and to the side, as far from the opening as possible.

The gap flashed orange, and a blast of deafening, eye-singeing force blew through. The percussion pressed a yelp from his lungs without his permission.

Another blast followed. Joe whined. Threw himself against the wall, away from the opening, and the stinging echoes from the back. The blasts kept coming, over and over. Rock fragments zinged. His ears pounded with ringing. He tasted blood. He felt small stings on his skin, but none of the body-rolling impacts, as he had on the plain.

At last the explosions ended. The noise in his mind roared; the ringing sang high and loud. The many fragmented insults on his body morphed into the agony of his again-opened chest wound and overtaxed, half-destroyed rear tendon.

The old man's voice penetrated his ringing ears.

God I hate you.

Joe waited where even the distance-killer could not reach him.

He placed his head between his paws and watched.

Warm blood pooled below his chest.

Chapter 43

Shirley squatted, steadied herself, moved El Jay's pants to the bed. She pulled keys from his pocket and tossed them to Ulyana.

"Back his car up to the door."

Ulyana held the keys. "No."

Shirley regarded her through slitted eyes. The Russian had been helpful. Played along within the confines of her skillset. Now that their partnership was moving to a more cerebral plane, Ulyana's place was less secure. Truth was, if Shirley could have lured El Jay to bed without Ulyana, she would have. But where Shirley had rolls, Ulyana had curves.

Not all men dug rolls.

"Are you a partner, Ulyana? Or a witness I have to deal with?"

"I didn't ask for this. I was out for a run. That's all."

The cause must go on. Shirley would adopt the revolutionary mantra: any means necessary.

She'd start with inspirational logic, and if it didn't work ... cross that bridge later ...

"Your face," Ulyana said, her eye whites round. "What are you thinking?"

"You ever get fed up with the crap?" Shirley said. She stepped to and pushed Ulyana. "This is my day. I'm done. Stepping outside myself and the world around me. I don't want any of it, and by God I'm not gonna put up with it. This asshole turned my house upside down 'cause he got the power. I'm just some fat, dumb, old white girl. No pimp. No protection. No police. No body. So, all my life, assholes like this one force me to make a calculation. Do I fight for what's mine and probably lose everything? My life? Or do what I'm told? That's how they push you—until someone has enough. Well, I'm that someone. I was hoping maybe you'd be too."

Ulyana stepped wide of Shirley, kept partly turned, with her eyes locked. "You didn't tell me you'd kill him."

"We had no choice."

"Not we."

"Okay. I had no choice. He's a killer. He threatened my son. And he'd have come back for both of us. You know that."

Ulyana dipped her head. "You seem so calm."

"Me? Are you kidding? My heart's a jibber-jabber. I'm about to freak out my mind. We got a drug dealer's body on my bed. Probably pissed it too. But there was nothing else to do, and I'm just at that point. I'll take any tomorrow but the one fate has lined up. Nobody is ever gonna make me decide between my dignity and my life. I'll kill anybody that tries."

Ulyana nodded. Tiny, then bigger.

Shirley said, "Yeah?"

"Yes."

"No. I said *yeah*?"

"Yeah."

"All right. Let's deal with this prick. Besides, if the world had any justice,"— she pointed at El Jay's head, still in plastic— "this is what it would look like. That FBI man should have taken him into custody, and then they'd fry his ass. But there's no law but what we make. I'm sick of it. You wait around for other people to uphold the rules that matter, the ones that protect little people, you'll wait your whole life. They only go after the people who get in their way. No such thing as law and order, unless you make it on your own damn authority."

Ulyana stood at the door. "Where will we take him?"

"He told us. The warehouse."

Ulyana went outside to move the car. While Shirley unfastened the handcuffs from El Jay's wrists and ankles, she heard Ulyana start the engine.

She'd have to think of another way to dispose of the electric stim devices—certainly couldn't bundle them up and put them in El Jay's trunk. If law enforcement connected them to the body—if they ever found the body—it'd be easy to track down someone buying thirty E-stim devices in an afternoon, even if she'd visited six drug stores. Every one of them had ten cameras. In fact ... it'd be best if there weren't any markings on El Jay at all.

It'd be even better if El Jay didn't exist.

She looked at him. Purple welts, oval, five inches long and three wide. All over his front. Dick shriveled like a thumb after someone pulled out the bone.

Shaved.

Damn. That hair was a lot of DNA, and it would be near impossible to vacuum all of it, without missing any.

The screen door slapped closed. Ulyana was back inside the trailer.

Shirley dragged El Jay to the edge of the bed and, surprised by his relative lack of weight, threw him over her shoulder.

"You want to grab the door for me? And open the trunk

before I get there."

Ulyana raced ahead, back outside. She pressed the key fob and the trunk popped as Shirley descended her deck steps. She dropped El Jay on the spare tire and closed the lid. Wiped off where she touched the paint.

"This is his car? An Impala?"

"Shitty for a drug dealer, right?" Ulyana said. "Maybe it belongs to his father."

"Either way, precious cargo. Let me find my jacket and a couple things. I'll follow you."

"What?"

"Yeah. You got to drive."

Ulyana exhaled. Slumped.

"Viva the revolution," Shirley said.

She went inside, stripped the bed and stuffed the blankets and sheets into the pillow cases. Grabbed her coat and keys. A jug of citronella oil for the torches she never used. A lighter.

Outside, she dumped the cargo on the Impala back seat. Again, wiped off the handle.

"You know where the warehouse is?"

"No."

"Follow me. I'll go slow but you need to stay close. And if the cops pull you over, flash them your titties or something. Don't forget you got a body in the trunk."

"Uh, yeah."

"Let's go."

Shirley led through back streets. Stop signs and red lights. Easy does it. Nodding when she saw people. Smile big. Wave. Best day of her life.

Free.

She'd started a one woman revolution. No more man-shit. She felt like Che Guevara—except a woman Che. She'd butcher anybody who interfered with her vision.

Howdy, just out for a drive. Don't mind me. Or the

stripper with the corpse in her trunk.

Exhilarating.

She pulled into the warehouse parking area and cut across the lot, toward a dock with closed garage doors, where they used to load freight onto trucks. At the end, a concrete ramp led to an open bay door.

Maybe where El Jay left his murder victims?

Wouldn't it be a history—dammit!—*herstory*—worthy irony to leave him beside them?

Talk about a mindbender. What would he have done if the ghost of murder future could have shown him his own body there, just a couple days later? To be a fly on the wall ...

Shirley eased up the ramp. Turned on her headlights. As she passed into the building, it was like driving into night, close and tight. The engine rumbled loud.

The Impala's high beams glared in her mirrors as Ulyana followed.

Ahead, a parked vehicle. She studied it: the color was dark. The side window reflected jagged light—maybe it had been shattered. Nothing was moving. As she neared, the masses became blood on the windshield.

Shirley's stomach turned. Anticipating the smell of several-day old bodies, she considered stopping right here.

But the setup seemed better if the cars were side by side. More like a drug deal where, as they said on television, the shit went sideways.

As Shirley pulled forward, space seemed to close in around her. Viewed from outside, the warehouse was gigantic. Inside, with all the metal racks arranged in rows, and the claustrophobia-inducing darkness, it felt like the kind of place where zombies could climb out of the shadows.

A chill moved up her back.

Fine. It's supposed to be creepy when you kill people.

She cut the wheel a little and crept to the other vehicle.

Closer now, she saw smashed glass, two bodies, blood all

over.

Strange though, each body was in the front seat, and the side windows were shot out, not the windshield.

El Jay had an accomplice.

Paul?

Ulyana?

That was crazy.

Shirley drove around the vehicle and stopped when hers was pointed back at the entrance. Ulyana parked the Impala beside the shot-up mule car.

Shirley twisted the key to shut down the engine, but left on the lights. She stepped out. At the Impala she drew a line across her neck, and Ulyana turned off her engine.

"Come on, get out."

Ulyana removed her hands from the wheel. Placed them on her lap.

"We don't have all night."

She remained in the driver seat.

"Oh, dear. Shit. You think I'm going to leave you here? Sister? Nah, you're part of the revolution. Get out the car so we can burn it."

Ulyana turned off the Impala's engine. Cracked the door open. Shirley pulled it the rest of the way. "I have to admit, it'd be a tighter crime scene to leave you here. But you've been dealing with the same shit as I have. Sisters! You got to help me so we can get out of here."

She offered Ulyana her hand. Yanked her out of the seat and into a hug. "We got to be sisters from here out. One of us goes down, we both go down. It's you and me forever."

Ulyana seemed to stare off. Whatever. Benefit of the doubt. She was still a little in shock, perhaps. Ergo per se.

"Pop the trunk, would you?"

Ulyana leaned into the car. Shirley watched.

It would have been easy to knock her on the head. But sisters didn't clock sisters.

Until they needed to.

She moved to the back seat door, opened it, and to the trunk. As it sprung open she heard the sound of shuffling feet, far off, like sand under slippers. Bunches of them, off in the dark beyond the metal pallet racks.

"Oh no! It's the junkies. Let's go!"

She grabbed the corpse and heaved, felt a muscle in her back twitch, pull all the way to her feet. Not good.

Shirley jerked El Jay's body clear of the trunk. Shifted a few feet and dropped him to the back seat, on top of the stuffed pillow cases and torch oil. She lifted, pushed. Wrestled him to the seat.

"Why move him?" Ulyana said.

"Don't you watch TV? Better air flow."

With El Jay across the back seat, she opened the bottle of citronella and dumped it over the upholstery. She emptied the pillow cases and spread out the blankets over the front seats.

Stage set, Shirley pulled a Zippo from her pocket and turned to Ulyana.

"What the hell?"

Ulyana pointed a pistol at Shirley's face—it looked like the same one Shirley had borrowed.

"Do it," Ulyana said. "Light it."

Shirley thought fast.

Had Ulyana been El Jay's co-conspirator from the start—along with Paul?

Or was she acting now out of fear and self-preservation?

Shirley opened her heart. Dove in, reached down for the revolution to bring it up through her soul, up into the world through her mouth, released like a scream from the underbelly of the primordial soup, stinky the way sex sometimes stinks, the way men sometimes sweat and get raw, the way treachery arrives from nowhere even though it's been there all along. For that was the world. That was the rotten ugly world. Even a sister in crime would turn in a heartbeat—and a girl who'd do that wasn't a sister whether they played the same tune or not. Ulyana provoked the lust and Shirley put it down. They were farm girls working the same crop. But they were sisters no more.

"Go ahead," Shirley said. "Pull the trigger."

She stepped closer to Ulyana.

Ulyana backed a step.

"I said pull that trigger."

Nothing.

"See, I knew you were a chickenshit coward who couldn't be trusted, so I took out your bullets before I gave the gun back to you."

Shirley lurched. She swiped with her arm the way a grizzly might bat down a small tree. Caught Ulyana on the side of the head with her paw, driving her into the Impala.

The pistol fired.

Ulyana screamed. She dropped the pistol, and Shirley dove, driving her chest into the cement. She tore open her first chin, the one with bone. Grabbed the pink .38 and pointed from the ground up to Ulyana, who leaned stunned on the side of the car.

"You said you unloaded—"

"Like I had time to unload your gun!"

Shirley looked down. Growled. Life agony stirred in her lungs and came out blowing. She screamed from the vast pit of her stomach, and the sound issued like a blast from an industrial horn:

Shift, over.

She swung her pistol arm to Ulyana.

Ulyana lifted her hands. A tear pressed from her eye.

Shirley stared into her eyes. "Viva the REVOLUTION!!!"

Chapter 44

Tromp along easy like I'm looking mushrooms. Mosey.
Gander a bit. Keep headed for where the sound came from—
though with the echoes I'm not sure I got the right vector.

Wood smoke.

Ah. Light's about gone, and I want to make an
introduction before my fellow man gets skittish in the dark.
Follow my nose and the breeze, and in twenty feet I spot the
flame, not a hundred feet off. He's lower than me. There's a
rock wall. I'm on top.

How the hell I get down?

Cut left, as the slope says maybe that's the way. Move
from the fire but keep it in my sights, then hold the angle fast
in my mind when the fire disappears. Dark comes quick under
the trees. After a hundred yards or so, the rock wall is just a
nest of boulders. I circle the last and head back.

Come up on the campfire, hands out front. Old feller sit
there, face like meat left on the grill. Hands folded together,

elbows on his thighs, with a Remington behind them.

"I guess you came to see about the commotion."

"I heard it." Approach to fifteen feet, and no closer until he says.

"It was nothing."

"Did you hit it?"

"What?"

"The dog."

"It wasn't a dog. It was a mountain lion."

Got the juice on my arms, but his eyes are regular. Cold. "No shit."

"It isn't a hundred yards that way, you're inclined to see."

"He attack?"

"Come on me from behind. He made his noise up front and circled. Clever animal."

"But you was cleverer."

"Something like that."

"Well—that's a sore dick."

"What?"

"You can't beat it. Never seen a mountain lion up close."

"Tell you what, mister. I'm old enough I'll let you walk yourself." He lines his arm straight, waves it up and down. "You follow that angle. See that sycamore with the lightning-cut—right there, twenty feet. That's your angle."

"Appreciate you."

I turn and the hackles go up.

"Hey," he say. "You got a camp somewhere about here? Where's the rest of your party?"

"No party. I'm passing through, is all."

He nods. Doesn't believe me. I don't neither. He smiles. I smile. I point thataway. He nods.

The rifle on his lap already has the barrel my direction. Just a matter of him lifting straight and pulling the trigger. He can do that pretty quiet I bet, while I crunch leaves and twigs. From the black in his eye and the set of his face, and the questions, and the half lies, I get the sense this fella'd do me harm, I let him.

"I got an idea."

Drop my pack. Watch him stiffen. I hold out my hand, the stop signal. "You'll like this. You watch."

Pull out a Turkey. Crack the seal and offer.

He squints. The woods turn a darker shade of gray. "I want your opinion, before I move along, and it's only right I pay for it. You mind sharing the fire a couple minutes while we jaw this over?"

Slow, he lifts his chin.

From way off comes the sound of barking dogs—that throaty stork sound comes from a pack of beagles. Some of the most talented dogs ever sucked air. They're a considerable ways off, but dogs move fast, and this dog hunt, with Cinder's logic, is an FBI-top-ten-most-wanted hunt. Expect helicopters any minute.

Something troubled me since I spotted this old man. When I was on the hill, him down here shooting, I wasn't maybe seventy-five feet. But it sounded distant.

Maybe someone else? More deception?

At the fire I reach him the bottle and warm my hands while he sniffs it, takes a pull.

"Let's do something the old way."

He coughs the Turkey. Flashes the bottle north again for another quick sip.

"There's a white pit bull in the news. Goes by Joe. That's his name. That's my dog. I'm after him. And you was doing your level best to shoot him."

"Don't think I got him. Would he answer to you?"

"I believe."

"I wouldn't have shot, if he hadn't killed Lucky."

"That the boy at Hardees?"

Head shake. He nods ahead to a clump of fur not ten feet off. I didn't see it.

"German shepherd?"

"That dog—"

"I know. I know."

Mountain lion, Lucky, part-lies. Don't know what to make of this feller save the crackle in his voice is more sob than roar. If a man come on me finding Fred, this is what he'd have seen.

"What brought you out to look for him?"

Old man takes another pull. This one longer. Brings sleeve to mouth. "Collar." After swallowing he breathes in the alcohol air in his mouth.

"Pardon?"

"He's wearing a collar. Like a Saint Bernard. It has information."

"So … you get that collar?"

"You can have your dog. He's holed up right there."

"Where?"

"Fifteen feet. Twenty. Right ahead. See that black spot in the rock? That's a cave. You can fit in there. Your dog's in a den cut out of the back of it. He killed Lucky, trying to root him out."

I mull it ten seconds. Take five steps. Hear baying dogs, closer now. Like they come over a hill but there's another between us. Got my back to the old man. Stop. Real slow I turn.

He hasn't moved.

"You might need this."

Light beam comes out his hand. Flashlight.

I come back and grab it.

"We got a deal? Nothing funny?"

"Nothing funny."

I lower my pack to the ground.

Head for the lair.

Chapter 45

Shirley Lyle stood over Ulyana.

The stripper huddled at the front tire, crumpled, squatting with urine dripping from her pants. Her interwoven hands over her head. She sobbed.

"Couldn't shoot you, honey." Shirley said. "Couldn't do it. But you was gonna do me, so we got a real problem here."

Ulyana babbled in Russian.

"You know nobody here speaks that, right?"

Shirley wiped her bleeding chin with her sleeve. She pressed the pistol grip to her head. Too many problems to consider. Each compounding the next. Splitting off into two more, like that Disney cartoon with the brooms carrying water buckets. How could she go back to the trailer? After using a clipper on El Jay's pubes they were everywhere. She grabbed the blanket but what fell to the floor? She couldn't trust a vacuum to remove all of them.

And return to her old job? That's what the moment of

rebellion was about—saying I'm never going back, no matter the consequences.

I'll take any tomorrow but the one that's lurking.

She could no more blow a guy than walk a tightrope over Niagara Falls. Or eat one slice of pizza. It wasn't her composition any more.

And how could she go home and live a new life knowing Ulyana the Russian stripper watched her asphyxiate a drug dealer with a doubled up set of plastic grocery bags?

How could she live with a witness ... alive?

"You pulled a real stunt. Damn, girl. Now what? You want to live, you better come up with some answers. How the hell's this supposed to work?"

Ulyana stopped whimpering.

In the excitement, Shirley had lost track of the sound of shuffling shoes, far off in the racks. Feet sliding toward her.

She whirled.

A fist arced at her face. A form emerged behind it—a young man, and beside him, another. Skinny like the meth-undead but bouncing and quick—a skeleton being jerked on marionette strings.

The first punch landed. Her cheek mashed and split where his class ring drove through and shattered an upper right molar. Shirley's jaw cracked sideways.

She dropped, aware of her fall, the car, the pistol leaving her clutch, and Ulyana's white eyeballs holding hers with shock and fear.

Shirley twisted. She landed on her knee and something gave away, like bone shear. A moment later, another brain-shattering blast of pain. She flopped to her left as a booted foot flew at her mid-section. How many of them were there?

Who were they?

Junkies?

She fought the desire to curl and suffer the beating. These men would kick her to death unless she overcame them. But the feet came faster now. Two men, one at front and another at back. She heard whimpering and commanded herself to stop. But it was Ulyana.

Had to be Ulyana.

Where was the gun?

A boot came at her again. As it sank into her belly she looked upward. The man screamed sounds that seemed to never break into syllables, just shrieking man-gibberish.

Boom!

Orange flashed next to her head. Burning powder residue stung like hot sand hurled at her face. She twitched. Ulyana had the gun. Smoke wafted from the barrel. Shirley's ears rang.

The first attacker dropped.

Ulyana shifted and fired again.

Ulyana had shot both attackers. Blood spouted from the second man's neck, even as he stood there.

Ulyana would turn the gun on her, next. That's how her life would end.

So be it.

Clutching his neck, the second man collapsed.

Viva the revolution.

And if Ulyana killed her next, she'd be a little part of her revolution.

Oh well. Shirley had fought. She'd die happy.

The flesh on her chin hung where it had torn. Her knee flashed pain. Her ribs—not bad. The insulation helped.

Ulyana clawed her way up the tire and stood over Shirley. She stepped a few feet, gun in her outstretched arm, as if to dare anyone waiting at the periphery.

The shadows on her face seemed chiseled of rage, but as her angle shifted toward the Impala's headlamps, Shirley saw the truth.

Ulyana trembled, mad with fear.

"We have to ditch this joint," Shirley said.

Ulyana faced her. Lowered the pistol, aligned with Shirley's chest.

"You mind pointing that somewhere else, while you're shaking like that?"

"You were going to shoot me."

"You aimed that pistol at me, first."

"But then you didn't."

"We ain't the same. But we're in the same fix. Not just with El Jay's body. And these junkies. We're in the same fix out there, in the real world. We're tits and ass. That's all we are, unless we say different."

Ulyana's countenance twisted into a smile that squeezed out tears. She placed the pink .38 on the hood of the Impala.

"Can you give me a hand up? I think my knee's broke."

Ulyana squatted. Shirley wrapped an arm over the skinny girl's shoulder and watched as she braced against the Impala and righted herself, bearing much of Shirley's weight as well.

"Your legs are strong."

"You try hanging upside down from a chrome pole two hours a night.

"I got an idea," Shirley said. "Where did you get the gun?"

"Paul."

Shirley nodded. The motion hurt like torture on an inquisition rack, but she kept nodding.

"Perfect. Leave it."

Her weight on her strong leg, she leaned to the Impala and looked inside. Ulyana removed the plastic bags from El Jay's head and placed the pink .38 in his hand. It fell to the floor.

"Perfect," Shirley said. She spat part of her shattered tooth in her hand, placed the fragment in her pocket.

"Your blood is on the cement," Ulyana said.

"They won't ever match it to me. Goodbye Flagstaff. Know what I mean?"

Ulyana supported Shirley. They hobbled together to the

passenger side of Shirley's car, and Shirley gave Ulyana her lighter. "Roll the windows a bit and light the blanket over the seat. The oil will catch by itself."

Shirley rolled her head against the seatback. Gun in one hand, Ulyana flicked the lighter with her other and held the flame inside the car. She bent at the waist. She looked good. Movie star good.

Ulyana returned to the driver seat. The fire in the Impala burned bright.

"Let's go to a hospital," Ulyana said.

"Who has money for that?"

"Oh!" Ulyana threw open the car door and bounded to the flaming Impala. She opened the passenger door, dove into the flames, and a moment later returned to Shirley's car with a zippered money bag. She put it on Shirley's lap.

"I forgot I put that in the glove box. I found it under the seat when you told me to move the car."

Shirley felt stacks of bills through the fake leather. She pulled the zipper expecting wads of singles.

They were hundreds.

Ulyana turned the key and drove out of the warehouse.

Shirley rolled down her window and spat a mouthful of blood.

"Viva the revolution," Shirley said.

Chapter 46

Joe sensed the cabbage and cheese fart man. It wasn't his smell—not in the cave, still choking with the stink of gunpowder. It wasn't his voice. Joe's ears rang from the rifle explosions, blocking most other sounds. Somehow the timbre came through. Without hearing his voice, Joe remembered the man and sensed his nearness.

The blood pool he lay in had expanded, then stopped. Several stone fragments had sliced open skin on his back and shoulder. None penetrated.

Joe whimpered.

Concentrated.

Sounds emerged within the high pitches in his ears. Undecipherable—Joe could no more distinguish if they were from a car engine or a waterfall.

He clawed forward to the edge of the back room lair. Keeping his head low, he shuffled into the opening.

Quivering overcame him. All his muscles shook, as if

electric fear shot through his body and overwhelmed him. He couldn't imagine what further doom was outside. The noise had been like the heavens opening, and annihilation dropping out, booming with each terrifying impact. It was the sound of the great angry unknown. The ultimate enemy, with infinite hatred and cataclysmic power.

As he trembled, the garbled sounds resolved into voices, the cabbage man and the angry man.

They interacted with one another and though their voices were calm, they were taut.

A beam of light came into the cave and caught Joe in the eyes.

He growled.

"Puppydog? That you Joe? C'mere, puppydog. Oh god c'mere puppydog."

Joe bared his fangs.

Chapter 47

That's Stinky Joe!

"Oh—Joe—I can't believe it! I got you puppydog! I'll fetch you out of this place, I swear. Maybe we get some hamburgers, something? That be good?"

On hands and knees, I see him back in that cubbyhole. German shepherd couldn't wiggle through the entry. I can't either. But my head'll fit …

"Puppydog? That you Joe? C'mere, puppydog."

He comes at me all teeth and snarl!

Smell his breath and feel his teeth at the same time. He bites my cheek but backs off. I drop the flashlight but still see. Maybe he ain't full blood pit. A fight dog would still have hold. Joe scampers back and growls, but his voice turns up at the edge, high pitched. Uncertain.

Inch back a little, get hand to face and feel the cut. Puncture below the cheekbone and maybe a couple abrasions on the chin.

He don't ken it's me. Keeps on growling.

"Hey, puppydog. It's okay. I missed you like the devil. Though truth told I didn't miss the devil. He never left. But you and me was destined by fate, puppydog. Protected by the one that made you. I come through some good fortune finding you, and—yeah—see puppydog. It's all right. All good. C'mon up here and let me love on you a little. Oh! I know what I got. Just a minute."

Fetch a jerky strip. Feel along for one without the pepper all over.

"Here you go, Joe. Come grab a bite o this! Mmmm. Yummy in the tummy. C'mon puppydog. Don't nobody love you like Baer loves you."

He looks, and his ears change direction like it helps him sniff. But he won't move. Zero trust. What the hell that prick do to you? Reach far as I can but the entrance to the cubbyhole is maybe eighteen inches. Got to put my head and shoulder back in the hole.

"I do that for you, puppydog. Don't murder me."

He growls.

I spot something shiny on the rock, ahead. Shift the light full on, and rock is blistered with fresh pock marks, blast marks maybe. And the silver says it was bullets that did it.

And that's why the gunshots sounded so far away, when they were close.

"You mean he sat here and shot inside?"

Joe won't say nothing back.

"You can't hear a word?"

Joe growls, less angry.

"Mother—"

Back out the hole. "Plug your ears, Joe. One last time."

Turn off the flashlight. Stick it in my pocket.

Grab Mister Glock.

Turn around in the main cave. Slither across the ground in case that evil old masochist watches. It's dark behind me, but not full dark outside. If he's next to the fire he won't see me—eyes won't adjust.

Edge of the entry, I get my eyeballs around far enough to spot the campfire.

No old prick.

Is it me, or would a fella that means no harm stay put, while the fella set on evil would hide?

"I come out with my dog, there won't be no funny business. Right?"

"Nah, you got my word. Just bring me the information on his collar and we're quits."

There!

Not fifteen feet off, maybe forty-five degrees from the opening. Two red eyeballs.

Bring up my Glock arm and ease it out the hole, slow, so the sound is less powerful on my poor dog's ears.

Some evil is necessary, Joe.

The red eyes fade. I want them bright 'cause I can't see the Glock sights for nothing.

I'll ask him twice and piss him off.

"Didn't hear you. I come out, there won't be no funny business, right?"

"Nah, dammit! I said—"

Eyes hot red.

I pull the trigger. Glock jumps. Pull it again, again, again. Red eyeballs jerk away, disappear altogether. Hope his head did too.

My ears ring and the woods are silent. I realize what sound just ended … All them braying dogs on the trail of Stinky Joe.

They're close! Be here any minute.

I scooch back in the hole, up to the lair.

"He's dead, Joe. All that evil is gone. Now you only got the evil that loves you. C'mere puppydog. Or we got trouble coming at us."

I pitch him some jerky. He sniffs. Wriggles. I reach deeper in the hole. He lets my hand come to his face. Thumb against his cheek. Gentle strokes. We'll do it one digit at a time—so long as there's time.

"C'mere Joe. Follow me."

Joe whines.

"I get you some cheddar. I promise."

I back out the hole, and Joe twists and claws forward into the main lair. Slow and easy, I touch his shoulder, float my hand along his back. Growl changes to a whimper. Down close, I put my head on his shoulder, arm over his back to the other side of his body. Just hold on a minute. Give him some peace.

From here, the braying dogs sound like they're a hundred yards off. Maybe they found the cougar the old man shot. Something to maybe delay them.

I take the minute to love on Joe. He growls, but high and lovey-dovey.

Joe knows who I am.

Better than God or anyone else maybe.

Chapter 48

Stinky Joe smells like Ruth's hair. Perfumed. Got him in my arms up close to the nose. Smell wounds, too. An old cut seeps on his back. Plus half his rear leg is ripped. And slices on the front, like he tangled with that cat before the old liar shot it.

After I fetched him over the hill, I stopped and checked him over, made sure no wounds would kill him in minutes. Then I picked him up and kept walking, back toward the way I came, since I don't know any better. The goal isn't to get somewhere so much as get away from that lair without Joe laying any new scent. Still, a good dog'll track by ground or air, so we need distance.

I tromp like it's the marathon, and I want the medal. Punji-calf leaks right down to my boots. Pain keeps me company. But Joe growls, and I'm so tickled happy I could shit a rainbow.

Tired—though he ain't forty pound tops. Sit on a fair size

rock with Joe on my lap, lean back and rest the arms. Suck in cool night air and thank the God who protected the rescue, and gave enough moon to get me out of the woods.

But I can't carry Joe forever, and Joe's back leg won't give him a hundred yards.

Treat him to some jerky out of my pocket and chew on some of the peppered for myself. Think on it.

"I give up some pretty nice hooties for you."

Uhhh.

"Joe! You're back!"

Nothing says a man can't have a dog and boobs too.

"Well, there's rules you haven't learned. Little lady—"

Made up her own mind.

"Hunh?"

Shouldn't we keep moving?

I stand, Joe in my arms. Kiss his muzzle.

Walk.

Moon has climbed over the hill. Silver disc bright like a second sun. Flagstaff air is brittle clean at night, feels good going in the lungs when the body's working and the mind is stoked with mission.

By and by, I spot the glow of a pickup truck through the trees, see the glass reflect, and off beyond is another vehicle, can't tell the make.

Put Joe down and give him another jerky.

"I be right back. Don't move."

I don't like it…

Hunker low and grab Glock. Step by step, careful not to snap a twig. Ease along.

Hear leaves behind—it's Joe. Doesn't want left. Ahead is danger and Joe'd rather be in it than be alone, and I want to stop and loiter a minute in the grief of it, the holy ungodly evil of the created world, makes true grace suffer while evil prospers.

I touch Joe's head, gentle. Carry on.

A man sits in a truck at the edge of a clearing, next to trees. Driver window is part down. He's waiting on something.

I get a chill.

Haven't heard a baying sniffer in an hour, seems.

Dome light goes on…

Cinder!

And other people.

Butt hole puckers. Tighten on the Glock grip and hear chatter—female.

Swallow hard. This won't be easy but it needs done. Holster Glock.

Walk to the truck.

The door opens.

"Baer?"

"Mae."

Other doors. Bree, Morgan, and Joseph. Little feller looks startled by the light. They climb out. Mae hugs me. Shit, Ruth is here too. Lotta people in the king cab.

"You find him?" Cinder says.

Turn. Joe's beside me. I squat and put my arm around him. "He's been through a grinder."

"I thought that might be the case."

"Looks like you been busy."

"Your family wanted to see you off. I explained everything. You need some space between you and us. And we need the space too. This is the last time you get to call her Mae."

"Huh?"

"Yeah. I had a friend in L.A. make her some papers."

"I always wanted to be a Tricia," Mae says.

"I'm LeeAnne," Bree says.

"I'm Miley," Morgan says.

"And who's that little feller?"

"That's little Baer."

Shake my head. Let the eyes soak in water a minute. Too damn much love on the heels of evil. Christ Almighty.

"Thought you might need a way out," Cinder says, "so we brought another set of wheels."

He nods and now I see the other vehicle is a Jeep Wrangler with a Warn winch and mudders.

"That'll do, until I get pulled over."

"Well, we thought of that too, back when we did all the others. Case you ever came up for air. Here you go."

He passes an envelope.

"That's your new driver license, insurance, registration. The whole deal. You're legit."

"What's my name?"

"We had to pick something low key."

"Aw ... hell."

Mae says, "Your new name is Alden Boone."

"I knew an Alden. Was an asshole."

"Baer ..."

"Sorry." I stand. "Lemme get Joe in the Jeep."

"Hugs," Mae say. She wraps her arms tight on my shoulders and that baby belly's hard like she's due.

"I love you," Mae says.

"Love y'all."

Want to squirm, but I let her cling. The kids wrap on my legs. Little Joseph leans on the truck tire, picks his nose.

Ruth lifts him and they join the group hug. Mae cries, so the girls start. Cinder eyeballs me, like these people are my measure.

A blessing I don't deserve. But take. With enthusiasm.

"You got to go, Baer," Cinder says. He reaches. I reach. He puts the key in my hand.

"Alden," Mae says. She pulls back. Eyes shiny. Big smile.

"Got a first aid kit in the Jeep for you. All you need to fix up Joe. And a couple other surprises."

I pull away. They bunch up like for the family portrait.

Joe follows close.
I stop.
"Mae?"
"Yeah?"
"You know all those stops we made at the bank?"
"Uh-huh."
"You can have that. I don't want it."
"Visit, Alden."
"I will."
Maybe.

Chapter 49

Jeep Wrangler's the long one with four doors. Good thinking.
Lots of cargo. Black. Winch up front—never know when
you'll need to tow backwards. Extra lights on top. Big wheels
with angry treads. Cinder gave me a toy that goes through the
woods.

Open the back. Dome light.

Tat.

Marisol.

Blink.

Grin.

She climbs out.

Joe growls—easy.

"How?"

"We followed you. Hitched. Called Nat."

"Oh."

She hugs me. Bang my elbow on her Sig Sauer.

"Okay," says I. "Okay. We'll sort this out."

Chapter 50

The cabbage man was in the front and the older girl beside him. The vehicle vibrated and the noise filled his ears.

Joe slept on the back seat beside younger of the two girls. He woke to her touching his cheek, a slow caress that recalled the touch of the cabbage man. He growled and the girl stopped. But she started again, and Joe sighed.

He was again among his people.

Outlaws.

PLEASE CONSIDER REVIEWING OUTLAW STINKY JOE.

If you're like me, when you're considering buying a novel, you look to reviews to make sure you're not about to waste your money. If you enjoyed The Outlaw Stinky Joe, please consider leaving a review on Amazon. Reviews on Goodreads are also helpful. Thank you.

GRAB TWO FREE BOOKS FOR YOUR GRIT LIT LIBRARY

Building a relationship with my readers is the very best thing about writing. If you enjoyed this book and would like to know about upcoming releases of Baer Creighton, Solomon Bull, or Angus Hardgrave books, join my email list. You'll get maybe two or three emails a year. I hate spam. Won't ever do it. If you get an email from me, it'll be worth reading.

Join the email list and you'll get a free download of **SOMETIMES BONE**.

You can find the signup sheet here: http://www.claytonlindemuth.com/emaillist/

If you like to jaw with other grit lit readers, get book recommendations for awesome authors, ask me questions, or get an occasional advance review copy of a new release, then join my Facebook group, the **RED MEAT LIT STREET TEAM**. Once in the group, scroll through the recent posts, and you'll find a link to download a free copy of **STRONG AT THE BROKEN PLACES.**

You can find the join link here: https://www.facebook.com/groups/855812391254215

ALSO BY CLAYTON LINDEMUTH

Tread

With an FBI sting on his misfit secessionist group closing in, Nat Cinder blasts from Flagstaff to Phoenix on his Triumph Rocket motorcycle. Soon he stumbles onto a packet of photos showing Governor Virginia Rentier lustily paired with three high-ranking women in state government.

Though Cinder and the Governor clashed sixteen years before when his wife died in a car accident, Cinder prefers to keep his dislike of Rentier focused on her politics. He's too busy blaming himself for his wife's death, fighting his way back into his son's life, and leading a crew of beer guzzling rebels to become involved in an intrigue about the Governor's sex partners.

But when the bullets fly, Nat asks questions, and learns his sudden war with the Governor traces back sixteen years. The photos were put in his path by a provocateur who knows Nat Cinder's a rough-hewn rebel with enough weaponry cached across Arizona to start a revolution, and the secret at the bottom of his wife's death will turn him into a powder keg.

Sometimes Bone

Grace Hardgrave's daughters haven't eaten in days, and after finding no work in 1917 New York City, Grace prostitutes herself to feed her girls. Sick of degradation, she bolts for the Pennsylvania farm she fled as a young woman. The only way forward is to face the predator who made her life go wrong.

But when Grace arrives she finds the Hardgrave/McClellan feud that's been smoldering for generations is now burning hot. The seven-foot tyrant who runs the town brothels and distilleries, Jonah McClellan, found his youngest son bludgeoned to death on Hardgrave land.

But as Grace unwinds the mystery she learns everyone has a secret, an angle, and a reason to kill...

Just like her.

Grit Lit to the bone. Sometimes Bone.

Nothing Save the Bones Inside Her

In 1957 rural Pennsylvania, Angus Hardgrave works an oil rig, fights dogs, distills Walnut Whiskey... and murders wives, friends, anybody. The presence in the walnut tree on a spur called Devil's Elbow instructs Angus what to do, and following the visions has led Angus to a simple country bounty...

But Angus wants more.

Alone when her father dies, eighteen-year-old Emeline Margulies believes she hears the voice of God tell her to escape the clutches of a violent Korean War vet by marrying Angus Hardgrave--a man rumored to have pitiable luck with wives.

She finds herself trapped between a stalking rapist and a serial killer. As each decision leads her closer to destruction, Emeline must choose between following the faith that got her into trouble... Or the moxie, resolve, and evil within that promise to get her out.

Strong at the Broken Places

Nick Fister's the winningest ultra-runner ever, but he's paid a price. His daughter Tuesday took her own life. His wife is sleeping with his crew chief, Floyd. And his "greatest fan" — a former-Marine sniper — has progressed from creepy stalker to deadly menace.

Nick's chosen Death Valley's Badwater 135 as the brutal capstone to his career. When Floyd fails to show at race start, Nick begins without him — and learns shortly later Floyd was stabbed to death the night before.

Nick Fister always wins, and his relentless focus keeps him in the race. But soon the Inyo County Deputies learn about Nick's cheating wife. The troubled business partnership. The life insurance.

Did Nick murder Floyd, while queuing a psychotic sniper to take the fall?

Or is Nick Fister running for his life?

Solomon Bull

SOLOMON BULL is the son of a rebel who died in the eighties fighting for the American Indian Movement. He trains for an Arizona race called Desert Dog, designed to shred a man, while using monkeywrench tactics to unseat a corrupt senator.

Pursued by a smoking hot agent from the Treasury's Terrorism and Financial Intelligence office, a doe-like prostitute with burn marks on her back and a sick story about a demented senator, and by Cal Barrett--Desert Dog organizer and brain behind Operation Guillotine, set to decapitate the US Government--SOLOMON BULL has a difficult choice and no time to make it:

Infiltrate Cal Barrett's organization and report to the liberty-crushing Federal Government, or risk everything to embrace his dead father's revolution...

Cold Quiet Country

On his last day in power, with a blizzard threatening 18 inches of snow, Sheriff Bittersmith's is called to the scene of a crime. A farmer has been stabbed clean through the neck with a pitchfork. Two sets of tracks lead from the barn, and the dead man's frantic wife exclaims her daughter is missing. Convinced it was Gale G'Wain, the orphan who worked at the farm, Bittersmith follows the vanishing footprints into the storm.

Three miles away, Gale G'Wain is alone and close to dead. He's holed up in an empty farmhouse, half-dressed and nearly dead after falling through lake ice. Innocent, but unlikely to ever stand trial in a town as corrupt as Bittersmith, he loads his gun and prepares to defend himself against the dead man's bloodthirsty sons and the Sheriff's Department.

Set in small town Wyoming in the 70s and unfolding in a single day, Clayton Lindemuth's debut novel, Cold Quiet Country, explores small-town corruption and the lengths some people will go to exact revenge.

"Lindemuth's impressive debut...is a go-for-the-jugular country noir....Lindemuth carefully weaves characters' backstories into this thrilling narrative, and his visceral prose and unsparing tone are wonderfully reminiscent of such modern rural noir masters as Tom Franklin and Donald Ray Pollock."
Publishers Weekly Starred Review

ABOUT THE AUTHOR

Hello! I appreciate you reading my books—more than you can know. If you've read this far, you and I are fellow travelers. I suspect you sense something is not quite right with the world. It's not as good as it's supposed to be. We human beings aren't as good as our ideals. Yet, we prize and want to fight for them.

I do my absolute best to write stories that portray the human situation with brutal transparency, but also I strive to tell stories that are not as bleak as the human condition sometimes seems. There's no limit to the darkness. Light is rare. But it exists, and I hope when you complete one of my novels, you find your values validated.

I'm grateful you're out there. Thank you.

Remember, light wins in the end.